THE

FALL

OF

SUPERVILLAINY

by C. T. Phipps

MYSTIQUE PRESS

F alconcrest City.

What a shithole.

I mean, a lot of superheroes have a kind of reverent, nearly lover relationship with their hometowns, but I grew up on the streets of "The Worst City in America" and it wasn't until I was thirty that it moved up into just being one of the bottom twenty. That was a significant improvement by the way, too, thanks to me becoming one of the city's resident protectors. Props to other heroes like Gary, Mandy, and Amanda. Otherwise known as Merciless, Nighthuntress, and the second Nightwalker. I'm dating two of the three.

Don't judge.

Falconcrest City was a mixture of art deco buildings, modern skyscrapers, industrial hellscapes, and endless slums. It put the rust in Rust Belt with the bonus of being on the equivalent of a hellmouth, drawing every sort of supernatural baddy you could want to the place. The only businesses which remained in the city were arms manufacturing, a car factory that suspiciously made parts needed by billionaire superheroes for their vehicles, and three environmentally unsafe croc shoe factories.

Despite this, the city was not lacking for rich people. Quite the contrary, we had an extraordinarily large number of one-percenters in our ugly stepsister to the Cinderella City of New Amsterdam three states over. Tech bros, old money douchebags, and hedge fund managers were drawn to the city despite its nastiness, and I wondered if that was part of the hellmouth's charm. Either way, it made for a delightful target rich environment when you were a part-time supervillainess.

Foreword

Welcome, true believers, to the ninth installment of the Supervillainy Saga. I never thought we would get this far, but fan demand as well as my love of the characters have managed to keep me going. Can we make it to twelve volumes? I think we can!

It's been a long journey for Gary and company. Starting off as a geek and a fool who just so happened to be blessed with a magic cloak, he's since evolved into a geek and a fool who now knows actual magic. Well, *Dungeons & Dragons* magic, which is not copyrighted if it's 3rd Edition or 3.5. Which doesn't apply to parody anyway. Not that I've looked up these things for any reason.

Ahem.

So where is Gary going from here? Well, when last we left Gary in *The Horror of Supervillainy*, he'd successfully wrestled the Primal Orbs away from his alternate universe doppelganger and rebooted the universe. Okay, technically, our last book was *Tales of Supervillainy: Cindy's Seven*, but that was more Cindy's story than Gary's.

Still, Gary thinks he's managed to finally win big. The universe has been rebooted into a happier, nicer, and all-round friendlier place thanks to his brief assumption of absolute power. Unfortunately, Gary doesn't remember that this is exactly what his doppelganger wanted to do. While reboots are common in comic book worlds, they never quite succeed as well as the publishers intend. Be careful what you wish for indeed.

The Supervillainy Saga is a world that deals with all the classic archetypes of comic books, but also deals with the out of universe decisions as well. Comic book aging of characters, sliding time scales, and endless amounts of retcons as well as reboots. These things are normally ignored by comic book spin offs because they're (rightly) considered to be forced by editorial mandate.

However, what would it be like to live in a reality where these things were common? A place where you couldn't quite rely on reality being as immutable as you thought it was? Somewhere that feelings, ideas, the past, and people could be rewritten on a whim? What if you were a die-hard anarchist like Gary who had broken every one of his (few) rules to make your ideal setting? How would that make you feel?

Gary has managed to establish for himself quite the life. He's built himself a family, fortune, and gotten himself UNLIMITED POWER as Supreme Chancellor Palpatine would say. However, all of that is something that rests on a precarious perch. Will he be able to keep it or will his constant desire to meddle cost him everything? Especially when confronted with the fact it may or may not even be real? Food for thought.

We also have a special surprise with two bonus stories in the back that I think you'll enjoy. The first, "Dungeons and Garys" is a nice homage to not only *Dungeons & Dragons* (as well as explaining Gary's kobold minions) but also a shout-out to my friend MK Gibson and his *Villains Rule* series. The second, "Merciless vs. Hitler" is a story that is self-explanatory and ties to the main book. I also threw in what I imagined the characters would listen to, music wise, because why not?

I think this book will be one of my reader's favorites and it will upend the status quo for the Supervillainy Saga permanently.

Chapter One

It Turns Out I Screwed Up. Again.

Belinda Carlisle's "Heaven Is a Place on Earth" played as my Ultragoddess alarm clock woke me up from blissful slumber. It was 10:38, Marty McFly time, and I was still annoyed Ernest Cline had ruined my desire to replicate his room for my post-billionaire lifestyle. Still, I was a billionaire and a supervillain, so it wasn't like I had anything to complain about.

I was wearing my Merciless™ brand pajamas as I stretched my arms out and enjoyed the wonderful sunshine beaming through the windows that opened their metal shutters. Mandy, lying in bed beside me, growled and covered her face with the pillow.

Mandy Karkofsky, formerly Mandy Colton, AKA Nighthuntress AKA Calico the Vampire Cat, was a beautiful, black-haired, Eurasian woman of mixed American and Korean descent that had been raised in Londonium for her formative years. She was also a vampire. We'd fallen in love over our mutual love of metal in college and had been married before our lives had become utterly mad. She was wearing a silky, white nightgown that made her look like she'd escaped from a racially progressive Hammer Horror feature.

1

"Every goddamn day you open those curtains," Mandy muttered. "It's a wonder I haven't burst into flames."

"Sunlight doesn't actually hurt you," I replied, slipping out of the bed.

"That still doesn't mean I like it," Mandy grumbled. "I need to be dead during the day. This is why I usually sleep in the basement."

"In a coffin," I said, pulling up my holographic interface with my Swatch-style wrist computer that was just one of the many things that had hit the market under Omega Corporation's Super Technology Outreach Program. STOP was an attempt by yours truly to make sure that all the hundreds of advances in science that superheroes and villains had made over the past century reached the common man. We'd solved that global warming problem to the point global cooling was a danger (thanks to Mr. and Mrs. Chillingsworth freezing technology), made massive strides in non-lethal weapons, and finally got cybernetics to the public that didn't make people look like Nineties antiheroes.

At least since I'd recreated the world using the Primal Orbs, most of the news was good. President Anders had devoted himself to trying to get Supers to use their powers less for punching each other and more for helping their fellow man. Pardons for non-violent Supers and mooks if they helped the Great Change. Billions more for education, billions less for building giant Super-killing robots. Building back up our alliances with aliens and hidden magical kingdoms. Plus, countless programs designed to just make life better for the average Joe and Jane. It was said the scariest thing ever uttered was, "We're the government and we're here to help." Well, that was non-sarcastic these days and all it had taken was me rewriting the fabric of reality with cosmic forces beyond the comprehension of mortal man. Was it exactly anarchist to do this? No. But I wasn't sure it was a mistake either.

"Don't knock coffins until you've tried one," Mandy said, stretching her arms out forward and levitating upwards like a zombie. "Maybe you could spend some time downstairs instead?"

"You want me to go to sleep in your coffin with your corpse under me the entire day," I said, dryly. "Sounds great."

"I didn't say you'd be on top," Mandy replied, smirking with a bit of fang showing.

I smiled. "I'll pass."

"This is why Cindy should always sleep with you," Mandy said. "Dogs love sharing their owners' bed. I'm more a 'love and leave 'em' type these days."

That was an uncomfortable factoid of our semi-open relationship. Vampires weren't monogamous creatures and needed about a pint of blood per day, which unless you regenerated was impossible, and not terribly healthy even if you could. Sex and blood were intimately related to the undead so they weren't things that could happen without the other. You know, something that paranormal romance and urban fantasy had been banging our heads with since *Carmilla*. Still, I was willing to deal, and it wasn't like I hadn't created my own inappropriate relations. Cindy in point.

"Cindy is a werewolf, not a dog," I replied. "Also, a barbarian princess, lately, which I did not see coming."

[Editor: See the events of *Tales of Supervillainy: Cindy's Seven* for that!]

"Where is she, anyway?" Mandy asked, looking around with squinted eyes before I shut the curtains. "Thank you."

"Avalon," I replied. "Guinevere is teaching her sword-fighting to go along with her whole new revamp."

"Don't use that word," Mandy said. "Also, I thought Guinevere hated Cindy."

"Re-wolf," I replied, correcting myself, "and no, Guinevere hates *me*. Whenever it comes to fellow Supers of the female persuasion, she's sisterhood this, female empowerment that. Either way, she's gone for the next few weeks until we're off to the Forgotten Realms for the Great Orc Hunts."

"Forgotten Realms?" Mandy asked. "Like the Dungeons & Dragons setting?"

"Precisely!" I said. "One thing I found is that every fictional world is real somewhere in the Multiverse. Cindy, admittedly, first became interested in multiversal travel so she could sleep with an elf, but *The Legend of Zelda*'s Link and she ended poorly so she's now more into Tieflings."

"You're participating in orc hunts?" Mandy asked, not so subtly switching subjects. We had a pretty open-door policy toward monsters living in our basement these days.

"No," I corrected. "Me and Cindy are going to go kill the adventurers who are going to slaughter the orcs. Jane and some of her druid friends are going to help."

"Aren't orcs evil?" Mandy asked.

"Yeah, and?" I asked.

"Remember the tribe of kobolds you let live in the mansion basement?" Mandy asked. "They set up traps all around the bathroom. Maybe we should be more circumspect about saving monsters."

"They're political refugees from Hollow Earth. You just need to search for their traps and disarm them. You have plenty of Rogue levels," I replied. "Also, you're a vampire, you don't need to use the bathroom."

[Editor: And you can find out about that in "Dungeons and Garys" at the end of the book!]

4

Why did I have the weird feeling my life was being narrated by someone other than myself?

"Yes, I need the bathroom. I still brush my teeth." Mandy pinched the bridge of her nose, clearly not awake enough for this conversation. "I still use makeup."

"With a mirror?" I asked, cattily.

"Shut up, Gary," Mandy replied, rolling her eyes. "Anyway, do you want to do anything special for today?"

That question sent a jolt up my spine and caused my mind to frantically race. Whenever a partner asked you about a date you had no knowledge about the importance of, it was a silent challenge that I, all too often, failed miserably. Was it an anniversary? The children's birthday? Valentine's Day? Beltane? Some other more nebulous special day? It bothered me because the only special date I knew to be upcoming was Ultraday, the anniversary of Ultragod's first appearance in 1938.

"Yes, uh, doing something special for today," I replied. "The special date, that I should do something special for."

Mandy stared at me. "It's your birthday."

I blinked. "It is?"

"Yes," Mandy sighed. "Your fortieth."

I blinked and did a quick bit of calculus. "Really?"

If it sounded like I was confused by this fact, that's because I was. I'd done a lot of time travelling and reality had been rebooted a couple of times due to my efforts to fix all the problems I'd not so inadvertently contributed to.

The fact that I had two adolescent children now, for example, made me think of my life as a soap opera where newborns became adult characters seemingly overnight. Time was only slightly more bizarre on my world than your typical episode of *Doctor Who*.

Still, it had seemed like only yesterday I'd been thirty and complaining about being fired from my job as a bank teller. Now I had children that had to have been born then. I decided to mentally resolve the contradiction by not thinking about it. That worked for most of my problems.

"Wow, forty," I said. "I wonder if we're counting time in separate dimensions. Splotch got his aging adjusted multiple times by his deal with the Devil and villains called the Cosmic Editors. Can't let your swinging hero grow up and get married. No sir."

"Gary, didn't you stop aging when you became a death god or whatever the hell you are?" Mandy asked.

"Grim Reaper," I replied. "And I don't like using the G word."

"Why?" Mandy asked. "You are one. Which goes a long way to explaining how screwed up the world is now that I think about it."

"Call it the semi-faithful Jew in me," I replied, ignoring her well-deserved jibe. "It's why I refuse to work with Odin and Cu Chulainn."

Mandy rolled her eyes. "And yet you married a Wiccan."

"Well, you're a vampire now so it's all right," I said, trying to make a joke before realizing it didn't have much of a punchline.

Mandy narrowed her gaze. It was intimidating even without the fact she was a soulless creature of the night.

"Pretend I didn't say that," I said, sighing. "It's just, you know, I don't feel forty."

"You have two teenage daughters," Mandy said.

"Time travel," I said.

"You're an archmage," Mandy said. "Somehow."

"Theoretically," I said, reluctantly remembering my wizarding title as Gary the Pink.

"You helped make the world safe against evil," Mandy said. "You've accomplished things. It's okay to acknowledge getting older."

I stared at her. "Can we just pretend I'm thirty-eight forever?"

"Thirty-eight?" Mandy asked.

"Thirty-nine is a year before forty," I replied.

Mandy sighed and put her hand on my shoulder. "Sure. Let's shower. Together. In a room with no windows."

"Best idea you've said," I said. "I love you."

Mandy lowered her head and smiled. "Yeah. Sometimes I think you don't see the real me, though."

Not a good sign but I was too distracted to think much about it right now. "Every day is another tabletop gaming session and I'm power gaming my way through."

What followed was an early morning set of vampire sex that left me in dire need of fish, cookies, and orange juice. Dungeon magic also meant I had plenty of healing potions and spells to help with that as well.

Heading downstairs in my black mage robes, I saw the kobolds battling the little bio-engineered candy corn-shaped minions with spears versus swords. Stepping over them, I headed to the kitchen where Mimi and Leia were sitting and having breakfast.

Mindy "Mimi" Karkofsky was the daughter of Ultragoddess and me despite that relationship crashing and burning. She was a lovely Afro-Jewish girl with long thick curly brown hair and a large wide-brimmed hat she wore even when dressed casually. Mimi had inherited a portion of her mother and grandfather's powers that made her the strongest teenager in the world. She couldn't fly yet but could jump hella high.

Leia Wakowski Karkofsky, by contrast, was a blonde-haired young woman with my steel gray eyes. She'd inherited the

Super gene from my side of the family (despite mine being inactive) and it had given her a brain so powerful that she could read minds for miles as well as invent practically anything. She was wearing a jumpsuit smeared with grease, and a pair of welding goggles. Apparently, she'd slept in her work clothes. Leia was my daughter with Cindy and born from a liaison when I was broken from Mandy's initial death.

Serving breakfast was Case "Agent G" Gordon, who was the kind of guy who made breakfast in a business suit. Case was from another reality, the Cyberpunk World, and commuted between worlds thanks to the portal I'd set up in the library. He was a bioroid, a cyborg who had never been human, and a former assassin.

"Hello, Gary, glad to see you finally woke up," Case asked. "Will Mandy be joining us? We've got some warm blood for her. God bless the microwave and corrupt phlebotomists."

"I think she prefers it from the tap," I replied. "Do you have vampires in your world?"

"No," Case said. "Jane's world has them as an entire racial subgroup.'

"Yeah, she's got a real *True Blood* thing going on there," I replied.

Swiftly scarfing down my breakfast, I conjured up holographic feeds of the various projects I was working on for Omega Corp. Since I'd donated the corporation to my sister, it had mostly turned around its reputation as the world's most evil megacorp. Unfortunately, that left Omega Corp vulnerable to all the other unscrupulous megacorporations out there. So, I spent a lot of my time planning sabotage, thefts, and plots to make sure they stayed in line. I was still a supervillain after all, sort of.

"So, Dad, are you going to be attending the Ultraday celebration?" Leia asked.

"I don't think I'm invited," I replied, lying. I'd gotten three invitations and incinerated them all.

"All the superheroes are going to be there," Leia said, not so subtly hinting she wanted to go.

"Yeah, that's why I don't think I'm invited," I replied. "Eighties Man might be there, though."

"You're Eighties Man," Leia said.

"You can't prove that," I said, winking.

"Eighties Man is just you in Ray-Bans," Mimi said. Clearly, she was impressed with my secret-secret identity as much as her sister.

"Yes, Eighties Man, private detective and hero for hire!" I replied. "My archnemesis! He and his sidekick, Tawny Kitten! Legally distinct from Tawny Kitaen. Someday, I will get that damned hero! But until then, he can attend all the superhero meetings I'm not invited to."

"Your archnemesis is yourself?" Leia asked.

"I'd prefer not to get into that," I muttered. "Especially as a few versions of me have actually tried to kill me."

Leia didn't respond. "Sometimes, it really sucks to be a telepath and know exactly what you're thinking."

"Anyway, maybe I'll skip it this year," I replied. "Gabrielle and I might run into each other and I'm not up for that."

"Mom will be hosting it," Mimi said, immediately deflating me. "Which means if you're not going, I'm not going."

"Ah," I said, sighing.

Mimi looked away. My daughters were old enough to get to the rebellious part of being a teenager and strangely, most of that was directed at Ultragoddess. Gabrielle had effectively dropped Mimi off after her birth and left her to be raised by me as well as my associates. That was mostly retroactive history, a thing I wasn't going to even try to explain, but still informed their past.

"You should be supporting me in boycotting the celebration," Mimi said.

Leia snorted. "Gabrielle Anders is your mother, not mine. She's barely yours. Besides, it's for Grandpa Ultragod. Which yes, I know, immediately contradicts my previous statement, but I like Moses Anders. It's a celebration of his accomplishments as a superhero and the President. Besides, I'm sure Gabrielle isn't mad at you anymore, Dad."

"Gabrielle lost her powers because of me," I replied, thinking about how awkward that had made our interactions. "I'm the last person she wants to see right now. I'm sure you're both invited, though."

Gabrielle had been split into two separate beings by black ultranium, one of them being someone who cared for me and the other having all her powers. I had ended up killing the latter to save Cindy. Despite being the side that loved me, the surviving side of Gabrielle took that personally and we hadn't spoken since. Worse, she hadn't made any contact with her daughter.

"We weren't. It's a family pass so it's everyone or nothing," Mimi said, chewing on her toast. She picked up the remote for the television and turned it on, showing the preparations for Ultraday happening in Washington DC. Her mother was wearing a bulky suit of red, white, and blue armor with a cape as she held a glowing power hammer that looked straight out of *Halo*. Gabrielle was presently going by Titanium Guardian and really playing up the metal avenger angle.

The news ticker beneath her listed such happenings as floodings, mysterious illnesses spreading across the globe, and the latest celebrities suing one another. The experts suggested that there was nothing to worry about regarding the plague and I really wished I'd been paying better attention as that turned out to be important later.

10

Ultragoddess, in her armor, proceeded to do a short speech in the White House press conference room. "It is a shame that I have no children to celebrate this glorious experience with my father and mother. However, I can assure you this will be the greatest Ultraday ever."

I grimaced. "Okay, that's just dickish. Did Gabrielle absorb her evil side when she lost her powers?"

"Mom can carry a grudge," Mimi said, sighing. "She also probably thinks denying I exist keeps me safe."

"Bitch," Mandy muttered, taking the bag I'd heated for her out of the microwave.

"Only Cindy can say that word," I replied. Mandy didn't mind my extracurricular relationships any more than I minded her stream of hot and cold running concubines—vampires loved playing with their food after all—but she flat out hated Gabrielle. Possibly because we'd gotten together in college only after Gabrielle had dumped me.

"I can become a wolf too," Mandy said, her mouth covered in gore. "It's allowed. I can also become a bat and mist."

"What are you going to be doing during Ultraday?" Leia asked, looking at me. "Some great heist or nefarious ne'er-do-wellery?"

"Those aren't real words dear," I replied, having nothing planned since I'd thought I would stay home and watch the celebration. Now it sounded pathetic. "It's okay, I have a seminar on Dungeon magic to give this weekend It's going to be viewed at all the universities—assuming people at said universities watch it on my CrimeTube channel."

"The one with like sixteen subscribers?" Mimi asked. "Which given you're a supervillain should be *at least* sixteen thousand?"

"I earned every one of those!" I said. "I can't help if my reviews of *Murder She Wrote* and *Miami Vice* aren't the

11

gangbuster successes they deserve to be. They just keep asking if I actually killed President Omega or had a child with Ultragoddess."

"You did though," Case said, sitting down with his own meal that I was surprised a robot needed. It was oatmeal, eggs, and sausage. Must be for his fleshy bits.

I shrugged. "Allegedly."

Mimi glared.

"Okay, not so allegedly," I replied. "Your mother is iffy about admitting to your existence, though."

"Given the fact she just said on national television that I didn't exist, that sentence may win understatement of the year," Mimi said. "And screw her for that,"

"It's for your own safety dear," I replied. "We don't need any supervillains deciding to nuke Falconcrest City to get revenge on her via you."

Mimi just continued glaring and I admitted to myself I was kind of on her side in this.

"It's good to share Dungeon magic with the world," Leia said, thankfully changing the subject. "Many new wizards and witches exist because of it. It'll be excellent in the fight against villainy."

Dungeon magic was arguably my greatest contribution to the world and that included rebooting it after the rest of the world had gone to hell. It was exactly what it sounded like, easy-to-learn magic that functioned mostly like the system Gary Gygax and Dave Arneson had created for their tabletop roleplaying game. I would have been sued to death by its owners over it if not for the fact they'd made the rules public domain. Plus, I also possessed a literal demon for a lawyer.

"Supervillains are yesterday's news," Mimi said. "Dad killed all the worst of them. The rest are either petty celebrities, working for the government, or in newly inescapable jails. Ones Dungeon magic helps secure."

I grimaced. "Yeah, I kind of did hurt supervillainy as a whole, didn't I?"

"Isn't that a good thing?" Mimi asked. "There's no need for superheroes now if there are no villains."

Suddenly not hungry, I stood up. "Sure."

"Done already?" Case asked.

"Yes, my robot butler," I replied, feeling queasy. "I'm going to go find a dictator to rob or something. I suddenly don't feel so good."

In fact, I felt dizzy and nauseous at once. I collapsed at the foot of the breakfast table, pulling the tablecloth off as I struggled to keep standing.

Then everything went black.

I'd just had a heart attack.

Chapter Two

Dreaming of Things That No Longer Happened

Being a god, no matter how minor of one, comes with certain advantages. One of them is that I receive visions whenever I'm close to dying or I outright pass over only to snap back. Death is more a spectrum than an absolute state, it turned out. The insights I got were sometimes profound, but it wasn't exactly something I wanted to do regularly, ya know? Especially since a heart attack was a new thing for me.

Weren't gods supposed to be immune to that? Of course, I had some mixed feelings regarding my divinity. I was a monotheist but that ran into trouble with the fact that I objectively knew other gods existed. I'd met Death, Odin, Adonis, and a handful of others. It wasn't the kind of thing you could bring up with your rabbi. They were still insisting on such ridiculous things like, "Thou Shall Not Kill" after all.

"It's 'thou shall have no other gods before me.' There's considerable loophole room for other gods existing and not worshiping them. Nothing about not being a god yourself either," I muttered, getting up in a dark and empty void filled with mist like someone had turned off a fog machine. "And why is it that other dimensions always seem to have air, gravity, and pressure? There's not any source of light but I can also see? Man, Pre-Doctor Aeon physics is just junk science."

Any objections I might have had to my situation were drowned out by the sound of growling around me. Looking around, I saw *things* were emerging from the shadows. If things sounded suitably nondescript, then it was primarily due to the fact they defied description.

If I were to lend my decidedly unimaginative prose style to discussing the things, I would suggest they looked like the undead forms of aliens. Not just the pink and green skinned humanoids that passed for aliens in my part of the Alpha Quadrant either. No, these things looked like alien-aliens with lots of tentacles as well as sensory organs that couldn't even properly be called eyes.

Garrryyyyyyyy, a mental moan escaped one and washed over me like a bucket of cold water. It looked like a stack of pancakes with Venus flytrap-like stalks sticking out on the ends of its rotting tentacles.

Defiler! another thought at me with a chorus of voices. This one was nothing but a blob full of decapitated heads linked together by slime. *Blasphemer!*

"You have broken the cycle," a third said. It looked like a copyright friendly version of a beholder or at least that beholder-like thing from *Big Trouble in Little China*. Oddly, it was the most human looking thing here.

"Die!" a fourth shouted, forgoing atmosphere for directness. I appreciated that. This one was just a living shadow of something that seemed to exist in a few extra dimensions other than the traditional three.

That was when I noticed I was surrounded not just by one or two of these things but dozens that stretched on into the void and its ranks were only getting larger. They just kept appearing and slithering toward me.

Faced with what amounted to a host of damned and dirty undead cosmic horrors, I resorted to the time-honored method of blasting them with everything I had. *"Meteor Swarm! Prismatic Spray! Fireball! Lightning Bolt!"*

I drew on every one of my cheap E-Z Bake Oven Dungeon magic spells and wished not for the first time that I still had access to the Reaper's Cloak. The magic was real even if the origin was silly and tore through the first wave of my attackers with the reality that hit points were not a thing, so they tended to hit more like tank shells than punches.

It was—for the first few minutes—a quite impressive display of carnage. Chunks of tentacles, antennae, eyeballs, and slime flying everywhere. I had been, for a time, known as the Slayer of Moloch and Beelzebub. I'd destroyed Entropicus, even though I was pretty sure that bastard could never truly die. Tom Terror and President Omega had perished at my hands. However, all of that had been with either the Reaper's Cloak or Primal Orbs. Now I had to rely on my own—stolen—power and that was never going to be able to match the endless amount of sorcery I'd previously been able to call upon. Then my spells fizzled at my fingertips.

Fudge.

I wasn't even out of spells, which was a self-imposed limitation I'd given myself, not because I wanted to be more faithful to the rules of tabletop roleplaying games, but because I'd seen what omnipotence had done to Other Gary AKA Merciful. He'd become so powerful he could craft entire worlds from spells and all he needed was to murder millions of people to do it, things he'd done by using time travel and with the help of the President Omega. He was the person I feared I'd become like when I'd crafted this world and Other Earth. No, my magic had just betrayed me at a critical time, and I found myself grabbed by the legs with a whip-like ribbon appendage then raised over a monster's lamprey-like mouth.

"Okay, we'll call it a draw," I said, searching my robes for my wand and finding it absent. Of course, I didn't have any magical items here. This was a near death experience and soon to be real death vision.

"Begone! In the name of the Primals of Order and Creation, I command that! By the Rhime of Visha and the Light of Aelor!" A familiar-sounding voice spoke as glowing blasts of white-blue light shot forth before tearing into the seemingly endless hordes of abominations. "Begone, I say, by the mists of Ushami!"

The strange fog proceeded to rise and swallow up the horde around me before the whip-like appendage was severed in half, dropping me on the ground with a thud. I, of course, landed on my head because what was my life if not for a set of comic pratfalls?

"Ow! Dammit!" I said, struggling to get to my feet. "Yeah, well, I'm already dead, so what's a little concussion between friends?"

"You're not dead, Gary," the very, very familiar voice of Lancel Warren AKA the Nightwalker responded to me. "Though I note you've been closer to it in ten years of adventuring than I was in almost a century."

Lancel was dressed in a 1930s trench coat and fedora that, today, would make him look like a pick-up artist, but in his day was what dapper men of mystery wore when they weren't wearing their superhero costumes. He was a handsome, square-jawed man with black hair and piercing blue eyes. This was Lancel in his prime before age and the toll of his battles against evil had destroyed him.

"Is it ten years? Because it feels both shorter and longer," I said, stretching out my arms. "Big hug time! Come on!"

"No, Gary," Lancel said, crossing his arms. "We are not hugging."

17

I hugged him anyway. "I thought you were perma-dead! I tried to bring you back with the cosmic reboot but that didn't work!"

"I *am* permanently dead," Lancel said. "I was allowed to join the other Supreme Archmages of Earth in the Celestial House of the Magi. However, that doesn't prevent me from helping you out here on the Astral Plane against the Unborn."

"Unborn? We're not getting political again, are we?" I asked, pulling away. "Because I have *opinions* on the subject."

"Gary, stop being an idiot," Lancel said. "I know that's hard."

"I'm not an idiot," I replied. "I just play one on TV."

"Which makes your occasional moments of genius all the more surprising," Lancel said, staring at me with an even expression.

"I'll take that as a compliment," I replied.

Lancel shook his head. "That's your prerogative."

"So, what are the Unborn?" I asked. "Also, why are they jonesing to kill me?"

Lancel sighed. "They are the souls of beings that were meant to be born in the timeline but were prevented from being born by meddling with the timestream."

I grimaced. "I haven't done much of that. Lately."

Lancel raised an eyebrow. "You have done this more than any other man in the multiverse. However, the souls of such beings normally reincarnate without issue into the new timeline. The Unborn are made of the absolute worst monsters and evil doers from the timeline you erased. You unmade countless dictators, sorcerous overlords, and dark lords when you made reality brighter. Their souls refuse to be reborn as what they view as lesser beings and have mutated into the things you found here. Crawling, hungry things on the edge of reality."

"You have a gift for poetic verse." I paused, trying to cope with the fact that I was dealing with monsters who'd never existed. "So, I really benefited reality by remaking it, huh? Good to know."

"No," Lancel said, correcting me. "The kind of tampering you've done with the Primal Orbs never works. It's attempting to paper over the way reality is meant to be. There is a balance between good and evil that if you swing the pendulum one way too far, will come swinging back with equal force all at once."

"No offense, but even when I was reading *Dragonlance* as a teenager, I thought the idea of a balance between good and evil was the dumbest thing I'd ever heard," I replied. "Evil is inherently unbalanced and good, by definition, should be the ideal balance in a person. George Lucas agrees with me as Anakin was only supposed to kill the Emperor, not the Emperor and the Jedi."

"If it helps, think about it in ecological terms versus moral ones," Lancel replied, ignoring my Star Wars reference. Which should be a crime and, if I ever rebooted reality again, would be. "You have altered the equilibrium of predators and prey, which is causing unforeseen consequences."

"Like a bunch of things that look straight from a creature feature coming to kill me?" I asked.

"Yes," Lancel said. "Among other consequences. These beings crave not just your life but the lives of others you have returned—including their former victims."

"Well great," I said, sighing. "Another thing I have to deal with. Along with dying."

"That's related," Lancel said, his expression becoming even more serious. Which was like a rock becoming rockier. "You have defied your nature by rebooting reality. Broken your sacred covenant with your patron Primal."

"My what in the who now?" I asked.

"You are the Chosen of Death," Lancel said, sighing. "You brought back billions of people to life when you rebooted reality, not just on this world but other places. You brought back Ultragod, the people of Falconcrest City who died in the zombie uprising, the inhabitants of Tsavong Prime, and many other victims of evil. That has consequences, Gary."

"As mentioned, I tried to bring you back—" I replied. In the end, it hadn't worked, and I sometimes wondered if that was because I'd known that Lancel hadn't wanted to come back. I'd also failed to restore Mandy to her humanity, which was perhaps because I knew she didn't want it or at least without my asking. Maybe I'd also just forgotten in the heat of the moment since so much of my time in recent years had been spent with the vampire one.

"Which would have made the problem much, much worse," Lancel said. "As the god of death, you are meant to be infallible and hold to certain principles which you embody. Violating these results in the entire house of cards falling down."

"I saw *Dogma*," I said, annoyed at this nonsense he was spouting. "So is the fact I had a heart attack related?"

"Yes," Lancel said, "That is why you are dying. Your health is directly related to your spiritual balance."

I let that sink in. "Crap. I don't suppose there's a quick fix for this."

"Time must be set straight," Lancel said. "Cosmic forces must be realigned before they realign themselves with a lot more collateral damage. When the pendulum swings back, it will swing back in force unless you choose to make right what has been set wrong."

"That's not gonna happen," I said, simply. "So, yeah, even if I have to die over this. A lot of people are alive because of what I did. I'm...okay with that."

I was *not* okay with that, but I was putting on a brave face. Still, there wasn't really a choice if Lancel wanted me to kill a few hundred thousand to a couple of million people to save my own life. That wasn't even evil, that was just cowardly and pathetic. I might be kinda-sorta evil and sometimes pathetic, but I was never cowardly.

"I'm afraid it's not that simple," Lancel said, staring forward as if he wasn't sure what to do. It was a new and not remotely good look for him. "The consequences of this may be impossible to reverse. Even if you wanted to. If we wanted to."

"Then why are you here?" I asked, confused.

"To say goodbye," Lancel said. "To let you know you weren't alone. To know that even if there are consequences...I know you always tried to do the right thing."

"Well, that's a load of horseshit," I said, staring at Lancel. "Especially the always do the right thing part. Plus, I don't believe what you just said. The reason I became a supervillain was because I think dealing with consequences is bullshit. I'm like Captain Kirk, I don't believe in a no-win scenario."

And yes, I get that was the lesson in *Star Trek II*.

"If anyone can violate common sense and get away with no karmic backlash, it's you, Gary," Lancel said, surprising me. He put his hand on my shoulder. "Good luck, my friend. You're going to need it in the next few days."

Okay, now I was freaking out.

"What are my chances?" I asked, knowing that if Lancel was reassuring me that I was probably screwed.

"Your chances are never good, Gary," Lancel said. "You really should have died during your first mission."

"Gee, thanks," I replied. "Very comforting."

That was when I found myself unable to breathe. I choked and gagged before the entirety of the room started to spin around me. Much to my surprise, my vision started to clear, and

I saw Cindy pinching my nose and holding my mouth closed. Grabbing her hand, I pushed her off and she smiled at me.

Cindy Wakowski AKA Red Riding Hood AKA Red Cindi was a beautiful, scarlet-haired woman who had taken to wearing dragon scale armor and a wolf-skin over her body while sporting a two-handed great sword. It was quite the change from her sexy costume of the past. We were the same age but had both aged gracefully thanks to supernatural powers keeping us in our prime, or so I kept telling myself.

"See, I told you this would wake him up," Cindy said, cheerfully.

I was lying in a hospital bed in the mansion library of all places. I was in a hospital gown with an IV in my arm rather than my mage robes. Cindy was standing over me, and surrounding me were Mimi, Leia, Case, and Mandy, as well as a figure I didn't expect: the Trench Coat Magician AKA Jack Hellraiser. He had brown skin, stringy black hair, a goatee, a long trench coat, a bloody bullet hole-ridden Union Jack t-shirt, ripped jeans, tiny red demon horns, and glowing yellow eyes. A pitchfork was sheathed on his back, glowing with infernal power. The Trench Coat Magician was a rather famous figure in both magical and superhero circles.

According to the stories I'd heard, Jack was a half-human/half-devil demon who'd escaped from Hell to wage war against the infernal here on Earth. He was stronger than the average demon by far since he could maintain a presence on the physical plane by will alone, which was one of the traditional differences between a demon and a god. I didn't like him. He'd regularly called me out as a "champagne punk" and "rich sellout." Which was a fair point, but it still hurt.

"Given you're a doctor, Cindy, isn't it a pretty terrible thing to do to smother a patient?" I asked.

Cindy shrugged. "It was either this or play *Rise of the Skywalker* in the background in hopes it scared you awake."

"I prefer you smothering me," I said, pulling out my IV. "What's Jack Hellraiser doing here?"

"I'm not exactly an expert in magical maladies, Gary," Cindy said. "Also, don't you just love his new look?"

"Yeah, the MILF she-wolf called me," Jack said. "However, I had my own reasons for seeking you out, bloke."

Cindy's eye twitched at the use of the word MILF. My best friend and occasional lover was in denial over her age. Which, given we were in school together, was only a few months apart.

"Oh, and what're those?" I asked, not really wanting to deal with a problem like this right now.

"Your old chum, the President, is dying," Jack said. "He asked me to bring you to him before he passes."

"Ultragod?" I asked, staring. "Someone wants to reverse his resurrection too?"

"What now?" Jack asked, shocked.

Oh, hell no!

Chapter Three

How I Screwed Up Everything

"Ultragod can't be dying," I replied, frowning at the Trench Coat Magician. I was more concerned about Moses Anders than I was about myself.

By a long shot.

"Everyone dies, eventually," Jack said, showing a surprising lack of concern. "You, of all people, should be aware of that."

"Exactly!" I snapped, crossing my arms. "I've wasted massive amounts of magic as well as reality-bending violations of reality to bring him back."

Just saying the words caused my heart to pound and sweat to appear on my forehead. Everything in the room seemed to spin before I managed to force it away. If that was a sign, I really was cursed for trying to bring back the dead, a thing that had turned Mandy into a vampire as well as dominated so much of a career, it was one I couldn't bring myself to regret.

I knew, intellectually, that resurrection was a pox on mankind, but I'd broken my own decision to help Death become ascendant over Destruction during the Eternity Tournament. The desire to bring back his dead loved ones had driven Other Gary mad. Would it do the same to me or just kill me? I couldn't say.

24

"Why would the President want Gary's help?" Cindy asked. "No offense, he has far better heroes and villains to rely on."

Jack shrugged and lit up a cigar sized blunt. "No idea, wolf girl. I'm not exactly a friend of American imperialist demagogues either, no matter how nice they appear to be. However, he's managed to persuade me to be his messenger boy anyway. Ultragod is a lot more manipulative a sot than people give him credit for."

The smoke from his blunt—swirling with supernatural power and smells of exotic spell components—expanded far in excess than was normal for one of his. A bit of Red Dust and ecstasy too by the smell of it. Mimi, who had lungs capable of holding her breath for an hour, coughed heavily while Leia's eyes glazed over like she was viewing another dimension—which she might well be.

"Hey!" I snapped at Jack, upset at what he was blowing on us. "I hope you brought enough for everyone."

Jack laughed then breathed a massive cloud in my face. It was enough to get a stone statue high. Mind you, for me, it was about a decent Tuesday. My dealer, Nighshade, grew her weed in radioactive moon rocks.

"Ah," I said, standing up. "I guess I'd better go then."

It shouldn't have surprised me that Ultragod had used Jack Hellraiser to bring me to him. Despite his reputation as the ultimate paragon, Ultragod had a lot of connections to heroes who didn't meet his moral standards as well as villains who weren't irredeemably bad. It was part of why he'd been able to unite everyone under the banner of the Society of Superheroes.

Well, nearly everybody. There were still outliers like the Tomorrow Society who hated playing nice with any superhero group that wasn't, "Did you know Supers were persecuted? We should do something about that!" all the time. No one had told them you could hold two thoughts in your head simultaneously. Others just didn't fit into the new paradigm like the Extreme! or Bloodscream. Honestly, Jack Hellraiser was normally one of those outliers, but everyone loved Ultragod. Everyone.

"Are you sure now is a good time do this?" Cindy asked. "You've been in a coma for two days."

"Two days?" I asked, blinking. "What the hell? Why the hell did you treat me in the library then?"

That still meant a few days to Ultraday, which was a weird thing to worry about.

"You're not exactly welcome in hospitals," Cindy replied. "Even the ones we fund would drop a dime to the Foundation for World Harmony about all those agents you killed during the Dragon King heist."

I stared at Cindy. "*You* killed those agents."

"And it's very nice of you to take the rap for me," Cindy replied, cheerfully. "Remember, you're only wanted in the United States and Canada. Our lawyers will eventually sort it out. Rich people don't have consequences! Which sucks unless you're rich!"

Mandy shook her head while the kids grimaced. The only reason why Foundation agents hadn't broken down the doors to the mansion was the fact the place had a ward against it so no one looking for me would ever think to look for me here. It was a cheap way of avoiding arrest, but *Merciless' Manipulative Mark* was a 9th level spell for a reason.

"Maybe you'll get a Presidential pardon," Jack said, smirking. "Assuming Ultragod engages in that sort of cronyism."

"He does not," I said, frowning.

Moses Anders was the man I'd picked to be President of the United States because I honestly couldn't think of anyone else who deserved the job more. Maybe it was childishly naive, but I'd thought by bringing him back to life alongside his wife and putting him in the highest office in the land that he could clean up America as well as help undo the damage President Omega had done. I'd even erased President Omega's presidency from the world, papering over it and exposing him much earlier than had happened in the "original" timeline.

It hadn't quite worked out.

My "perfect" world still had a lot of simmering tensions underneath the surface and Moses had struggled through both of his terms to try to get these resolved. It turned out being the world's most powerful Super didn't give you the ability to solve racism, poverty, international conflicts, and the growing conflict between Supers as well as "normal" humans. He'd done a massive amount to solve things, but it seemed like there always were more things to do.

"If you say so," Jack replied. "You better get dressed, though, unless you want to bare your ass to the leader of what people think is the free world."

God, is this what I sound like to other people? I glared at him and raised my hands. *"Merciless' Magical Marketwear!"*

I expected to clothe myself once more in my elegant black magician's robes but instead, I found myself covered in what could only be described as Barbie pink over a white interior robe. My Reaper's Scythe, or at least the imitation I'd created of it, came with it but was sporting a pair of fuzzy dice on the end of the blade. The robes still felt as enchanted as my other attire, but something had caused them to change color and style.

"Goddammit," I muttered, realizing I'd once more become Gary the Pink.

"Uh, Gary, you want to tell us something?" Cindy said. "Because I left the island of the bisexual druids where I was learning hacking and slashing to check up on you. Seriously, they're all horny hippie chicks and bodybuilder dudes into free love. It's fantastic."

"Their sexuality doesn't matter," Mandy said, frowning. "It's a place of great spiritual reflection and purity among Arthurian pagans."

"Uh huh," Cindy said. "You're just unhappy you're not welcome there because you're an undead horror."

Mandy glared.

"Hey, vampirism is a good look for you! Eerie, dark, and pale never goes out of style!" Cindy said, raising her hands defensively. "Very Victorian."

"The Victorians thought dying of tuberculosis was sexy," Mandy said, dryly.

"Exactly," Cindy said, holding up her hands in defense. "Come on, big hug!"

"No," Mandy looked more mortified than Lancel. "Maybe it's not too early to join the International League of Sexy Female Thieves. Get myself my own place."

"That's not a thing," I paused. "I think."

"It's totally a thing," Mimi said. "They won't let me join because I'm underage."

Cindy grimaced. "They said I couldn't join because I murdered people all the time. Which is a lie. It's not *all* the time. Just most of it."

"Uh huh," Mandy said.

"Come over here. We can fit one 'get well orgy' in for Gary before he goes," Cindy said, stretching out her arms. "Mimi, Leia, go get an ice cream cone or rob the neighbors while we're screwing."

"I'm game," Jack said. "But we need to establish some basic ground rules. Especially if any of you are flammable. I've had issues during climax in that department."

"Oh really?" Cindy asked. "You should see a doctor about that. Still, I've got a few spare *rings of fire protection* around here and should be fine. Just assure me its non-transmittable with protection."

"I am immune to most human thoughts regarding sex and still want to vomit," Leia muttered.

"Excuse me, I'm going to go to Hell and punch everyone there to get that image out of my head," Mimi said. "Can you open a portal there, sis?"

"Sure!" Leia asked. "I'll get my proton pack and join you!"

I cleared my throat and looked down at my salmon-colored outfit. "Apparently, my magic is acting up. It may be related to my health issues. That and I am officially the Pink Wizard. It is a title that fills my enemies with great fear and despair."

Everyone stared at me skeptically at once.

"Presuming said enemies are Jem and the Holograms," I admitted. "And as much as I'd like to participate in a celebratory orgy, if Ultragod is dying then I should make my way to him. He's about my last ally left among superherodom."

"So, I've come all this way and you're leaving within the hour," Cindy said, crossing her arms. "Real classy, Gary."

"Believe me, it means a lot you did," I replied, walking over, and kissing her.

"Aww, doggie kisses," Jack said.

Cindy gave him the finger without breaking off her kiss. "Just promise you'll be back before Ultraday. I have my outfit all picked up. It'll be like the Met Gala for Supers across the globe."

"You're going to the Ultraday celebration?" I asked, surprised.

"Yeah, I was invited," Cindy said. "Weren't you?"

"Yes, of course," I said, annoyed I was going to have to forge the ones I burned since apparently everyone but me and Mimi were crazy about this thing.

Both Leia and Mimi stared at me in the accusing manner that only teenage girls were capable of managing.

"There won't be an Ultraday if I don't save him," I replied.

"Who says you're going to save him?" Jack asked. "That's not why I came by."

"Why else would he call me?" I asked.

Jack didn't answer. But he didn't have to. There was the possibility that Moses Anders was calling me in because I was a member of his family. If he was dying and had no hope of survival, then he would probably want to make peace with his loved ones. I shoved that out of my mind, though. I'd already wrecked the universe once to save him, Mandy, and my other loved ones—I could do it again.

"I'm going to go snack on someone," Mandy said, sighing. "Stress makes me hungry. We've got a few corporate executives left in the dungeon I've been saving."

"Just remember to release them when done," I replied.

Mandy rolled her eyes. "Don't lecture me. I'm not the one with the body count in three figures."

"You've killed ninety-seven people," I replied, not really wanting to compare body counts. "So, you almost have a body count in three figures."

"Still two figures!" Mandy said. "Wait, we're not counting the future, are we? Then it's way over three figures."

"Yeah, well, most of the people I've killed were Nazis. Both future, past, alternate reality, and present," I said, stretching my arms and readying for travel. "Let's get going, Jack."

Jack looked at me sympathetically. "You have a nice family here, Gary."

"Thanks," I replied. "It's a little *Addams Family* and a little *The Incredibles*. Mostly, it's just home."

"Yeah," Jack said, pulling out his pitchfork and aiming it before him. A blast of energy conjured up a swirling energy portal. "This will take us right to Ultragod,"

"Great," I said. "I'll be with you in just a second."

"See you on the other side." Jack walked through and vanished.

"You know he's going to betray you the moment you go through, right?" Mandy asked.

"What? No. Why?" I asked, doing a double take.

"I can smell it on him," Mandy said.

"I thought that was just a middle-aged punk from Hell," Cindy said. "Literally."

"Yeah, he's not got good things planned," Leia said. "No one disguises their thoughts with magic that heavily unless they have something to hide."

"Except for wizards," I said, inclined to give him the benefit of the doubt despite the fact I had no reason to. Well, you know, aside from the fact I didn't want any more superheroes mad at me. The Trench Coat Magician qualified as a superhero, barely.

"So, what are you going to do?" Mimi asked. "Now that you know this is a trap, I mean."

"Spring the trap," I replied, smiling.

Cindy rolled her eyes. "Stop taking advice from the Star Wars prequels, Gary. Look at how that worked out for Obi-Wan."

I waved a hand dismissively and headed toward the portal. "I've fought Entropicus, Cindy, I'm going to be able to handle a random street wizard. Guy can probably barely cast *Magic Missile*."

"He has dual infinite ammo pistols and a pitchfork," Mimi corrected. "Not that I have his poster on my wall or anything."

31

"Yeah, you've jinxed it now," Cindy muttered. "Are you sure you don't want me to go through and kill him for you?"

"I'm fine, Cindy," I said, waving my scythe at her and shaking my fuzzy dice. "It's me."

Cindy sighed. "Thank goodness you got rid of that whole resurrection ban, thing. We're totally going to have to bring you back."

That did not make me happy when I turned around and walked through the portal. Sadly, the moment I did, I saw a fist flying at me. I admit I had expected betrayal, but not for it to happen immediately. As such, I took a blow to the face and was sent flying to the ground as the portal behind me had already closed.

The two of us were in what looked like a janitor's closet, and it was large enough to hold us, shelves of equipment, and probably a hardware store or two. So more like a janitor's underground lair. The Trench Coat Magician was a dirty fighter and immediately kicked me while I was down, delivering a nasty blow to my abdomen.

"Sorry, mate," Jack said, pulling out a doll covered in a tiny little pink robe. "It's nothing personal. See you in Hell!"

The little pink doll caught fire as he held it in front of me. I felt the magic wash over and the doll's head began to melt. However, wash over me the magic did, and I felt only mild annoyance rather than horrifyingly burning to death.

"What the hell?" Jack asked, staring at me.

"I made my saving throw it seems," I said, crawling to my knees. "Either that or it only took away a few of my hit points."

"Saving throws aren't real!" Jack said, clutching his hands around two pistols that magically appeared in his hand.

"Clearly they are!" I said, shouting before jamming my scythe's pole end into his stomach. "*True Strike!*"

From there, I proceeded to start beating him over the back with my scythe like a quarterstaff. Jack tried to shoot me in the face, but it wasn't a great room for maneuvering, and I knocked both guns from his hands with a knee to his face. That was when I cast *Grease* on the ground before kicking him onto the ground.

"Will you stop using that damn big box store bargain basement black magic?" Jack said, magically conjuring his guns back into his hands then aiming them at me.

"No!" I said, lifting my palm. "*Fireball.*"

That was when I remembered some basic D&D-isms like you should never cast a Fireball spell in a confined space. The explosion of my magic washed over me and the Trench Coat Magician both. The entire room was full of fire and if not for the fact I made a point that every one of my robes was protected against fire, electricity, and cold I would have been incinerated. Funny thing, it seemed the legendary trench coat of Jack Hellraiser was also protected against my sorcery.

So, the two of us were left largely unharmed except for the soot on our faces like we were cartoon characters who survived an explosion. I'm sorry to say the fuzzy dice on my scythe did not survive the experience, though.

"That was incredibly stupid," Jack said, staring at me. He wasn't firing his pistols, though.

"Says the guy who thinks he has my number," I replied. "Believe me, I know the hour and manner of my death and you are not the guy who brings it to me."

I had no idea when or where I was going to die but the line sounded sufficiently badass that I just had to use it. I had accepted that I eventually was going to die, though. I worked for Death and had no intention of trying to cheat her of her prize. Eventually, sometime, I'd join the ranks of those who had gone before. It was only the others in my life that I hesitated to let go of and that was the cause of my current problem.

"Listen, man, I'm not trying to kill you because I want to," Jack replied. "I'm doing it because it's the only way to stop the plague."

I blinked. "What plague?"

That was when the janitor's closet filled with Foundation agents who began beating us down with truncheons.

Chapter Four

Meeting the President

It was humiliating getting the beat down by a bunch of Foundation agents. To the rest of the world, the Foundation's operatives were selected from the Special Forces and elite police units of the world. They were the best of the best and people who held the line against the supernatural, evil Supers, as well as alien invaders. To superheroes and villains, they were basically mall cops who only existed to get horrifyingly murdered to show just how dangerous something was.

Now with the threat level of these guys established as the same as your typical video game mook, you may ask why I didn't turn them to snow or seven notes of music—which is a reference to Peter S. Beagle's *The Last Unicorn*, by the way.

Seriously, my daughters have asked me to start annotating my biographies as they have no idea what half the stuff I reference is. Like, just imagine these kids—who have no idea what the Eighties were other than "A long time ago" —needed to have it explained to them when they watched *Back to the Future*. I swear, they think of the prequels as the first *Star Wars* trilogy.

Okay, wow, that was a digression even by my standards. Yes, why didn't I murder all the mall cops beating the crap out of me. First, the answer is that I generally try to avoid killing cops and government officials because they take it personally. I'm still dealing with the issues of Cindy doing it and this is my fantasy rebooted reality. Second, I tried to put them all asleep and then hold them in place with my magic only for the spells to not come to my fingertips. Yep, I was suffering ED—or eldritch dysfunction—and there was no blue pill for that. I swear, it never happened to me before. Maybe we can try again later.

"What the hell are you thinking?" Jack asked, looking at me strangely as the two of us were dragged in handcuffs down a long metal hallway by the goon squad.

"Are you reading my mind?" I asked. "Because, honestly, if this is a romantic crush thing then you could have just bought me dinner. Attacking me to get my attention is only sexy in Klingon culture."

"I'm always reading the minds of the sinful," Jack said. "It's just your thoughts sound like someone stuffed a bunch of random internet forum posts into a blender then hit puree."

"I resent that comparison," I replied. "If I was a bunch of forum posts shoved together, I'd be way more racist and sexist."

Jack sighed. "I can't believe you're a demigod. No wonder the world is so screwed up."

"I resent the term demigod. I am a full-fledged god, just the absolute lowest and tiniest breed of god you can be. Like those Chinese gods of specific roads or the patron saint of pants pockets—which I understand is a real thing," I said, slowing down our movement by not walking but forcing them to physically drag me down the hall of the underground facility we were located in.

I guessed by my surroundings that we were located at Base Alpha Zero, which was the secret headquarters of the American branch of the Foundation under Cheyenne Mountain. It was formerly the location for NORAD but was transferred to the Foundation after someone realized flying aircraft carriers were ridiculously impractical. Moving President Anders here was not a good sign, nor was the fact that a lot of the rooms we passed were covered in plastic and had some sort of medical procedures being done inside them.

A blonde, female Foundation agent beside me asked, "If I pistol whipped you, would you shut up?"

"No," I replied. "Sorry. I pay money for that treatment from women."

That was when a male agent hit me in the back of the head with his rifle butt. "Ow! Okay, I'm only giving you twenty bucks for that."

"Leave them alone," a voice spoke on the intercom. "The President's orders were quite clear that neither of them is to be harmed."

The blonde female agent looked disappointed. "Fine. Go ahead and continue your inane ramblings."

"Thank you," I responded. "Why did you try to kill me, Jack?"

"Does it matter?" Jack asked, looking bored.

"Yes, I need to establish whether this is a 'superheroes fight when they first meet before becoming good friends' or an establishment of a life-long archnemesis rivalry," I replied. "If the latter is the case, I'm going to need some credentials as well as the recommendations from two other supervillains."

"My God, you really do sound like a cartoon. I thought the other heroes were exaggerating," Jack said, shaking his head. "I needed to try to kill you to save the world."

"Is this about the time I bought a panda with Bitcoin?" I asked. "Because that's only illegal according to every government in the world and unethical according to people with basic decency."

"No!" Jack snapped. "Wait, you bought a panda?"

"He was actually an alien that needed rescuing," I replied. "Po the Panda is working as a detective in Detroit now with Detective Duck. Listen, if it's not about the panda then is this about the fact that I own my own Bitcoin? The Merciless Coin? I only set it up because I thought I got ripped off with the panda deal. Listen, Merciless Coin has a strong market value against other imaginary currencies. It's the thirty-fifth best cryptocurrency for buying drugs and NFTs."

"No! And you should feel bad," Jack said. "Hold on, are you doing NFTs too?"

"No," I replied. "I have some scruples. Also, Merciless Coin no longer qualifies as a cryptocurrency since it became the official currency of the Republic of Farnia."

"That's not a real country," Jack said.

"It is," I replied. "You can't find it on any map because the only entrance is an old British wardrobe that used to belong to CS Lewis. I can't confirm that they use Merciless Coin in said country because every time I enter, a lion attacks me, but they haven't sent any cease-and-desist orders either. As such, the exchange rate is what I say it is."

Jack facepalmed. "Are you making up all these stories? Like all the times you killed Hitler?"

"I can assure you those actually happened," I replied. "Only twenty percent of my stories are complete bullshit. The remaining eighty percent being somewhat bullshit."

"I don't want some bullshit in anything I'm eating or drinking," Jack replied, showing he was a good sport about being my straight man. It almost made up for trying to kill me. "I don't want any bullshit in what I'm hearing either."

"Good luck with that," I replied. "You mentioned a plague."

"The Nanoplague," Jack said, disgusted. "It's currently spreading throughout the world right now. It's also your fault."

I stared at him. "First of all, Nanoplague? Real original. It sounds like something made up for a bad sci-fi movie."

"It's a plague caused by nanites," Jack replied. "What else are you going to call it?"

"The Nanite Plague?" I asked. "Also, how the hell is it my fault?"

"You rewrote reality," Jack replied. "Ergo, everything that happens to the world now is your fault."

I couldn't fault that logic. I tried to anyway. "Okay, that is not how any of this works, thank you. I also need more details and why you think killing me will help."

"The Nanoplague is apparently a product of President Omega, even if he was only President for a few months," Jack replied, referring to the history I'd woven to make Ultragod president. In the new timeline, Omega had been exposed as a supervillain and an emergency election had to get rid of him before WW3 could happen. Ironically, his VP had gone on to get elected Speaker of the House.

"Omega, huh?" I said, trying to sound nonchalant. "I wonder whatever happened to him."

Jack ignored my discomfort. "It is future technology designed to attack the Super gene. It was programmed to activate after Omega has been inactive in the world for a certain amount of time, which he hasn't been because you killed him. It attacks full-fledged Supers hardest, then people with the inactive dominant Super genes from both their parents. But a plurality of people on Earth have the recessive inactive Super gene. Those people will eventually get sick and die as well."

I stared at him. "Okay, that sounds like a bunch of nonsense."

"I didn't make the science!" Jack replied, his eyes turning red for a second.

"And you're blaming me for, what, killing President Omega in the first place?" I asked.

"Yes!" Jack said.

"The ex-*Nazi* General," I replied, "who has built a genocidal plague to avenge himself?"

"Okay, you make it sound like a bad thing when you say it like that," Jack replied, looking like he was disgusted with his own words. "Listen, I didn't like the guy, but billions of lives are at stake. It's not just killing him, though. You also rebooted reality and unlike every other temporal rewrite of the universe, this one seems to have stuck. It's causing all sorts of craziness in the pattern of the universe."

Sadly, after my encounter with Lancel Warren, this one sounded more than plausible. I hadn't exactly been given an instruction manual on using the Primal orbs when I was wrestling them away from Merciful. "And you think killing me will help?"

"It might buy us time," Jack said. "Besides, you're a self-proclaimed god. You'll be fine. Go live your afterlife on Olympus, Mercilessland, or Sex Island. Wherever gods go when they die."

"First of all, Mercilessland is a theme park that I will eventually get off the ground but apparently would destroy the environment of the Hollow Earth," I replied. "Next, Sex Island is my vacation spot. It's where I hooked up with Splotch Woman and Princess Verasti of the Tsavong Empire. Still, I wouldn't want to live there. Besides, I'm reaching that point where everyone considered young and hot is looking like they're my children's age. That is a major turn off."

"I don't care," Jack said. "You're a disruption in the fabric of reality. I can see it with my infernal sight. Maybe Omega was, too, but you've thrown the timeline into chaos. You must go."

"Yeah, no," I replied. I'd just had a heart attack because I'd apparently broken some ancient mystical taboo that I hadn't even known about until now. Resurrection wasn't one of my powers, at least that I knew of, and it sure as hell probably wasn't now.

"And if millions die?" Jack asked. "Because that's how many people have already been infected."

"Why hasn't the President called a state of emergency?" I asked, returning to the Nano Plague. "How long has this been going on?"

"A lot longer than anyone expected," he replied. "As for why there's no state of emergency, it was being handled quietly to avoid a panic only to have Helios the Sun King proclaim to his Super followers that it was a plot by the government to wipe out all Supers. They started attacking all the quarantine and testing centers before burning three research centers. The evil speedster, Red Lightning, ended up spreading it globally in two hours."

"Great," I muttered. "So how many people have died so far?"

"Close to a hundred thousand," Jack said. "That's only in the past few months. It's now growing exponentially. If it's not stopped now, the numbers will be in the millions within the end of the week."

Holy crap. That would make it the single most devastating supervillain attack in history. At least on Earth.

I looked at the Foundation agents carting us around. "You guys should be wearing masks then."

"We're HRDs or human replacement droids," the blonde woman said. "No chance of infection here."

"All of the efforts of the Society of Superheroes are being put to use making sure people are put in stasis or isolated if they have the right genes," Jack said. "Which sounds way more sinister than it actually is."

"Said to the Jewish guy, yes," I replied. "How long do we have until this becomes uncontainable?"

"It's already uncontainable," Jack replied. "What we need is a miracle now. Which we also need before Ultraday."

"Which Ultragoddess is still assembling despite the fact it will be millions of people gathered together in a tiny space," I said, not following the logic of the demon.

"If a cure isn't found by Ultraday, then everyone who could be infected will be, followed by their deaths within a couple of weeks," Jack said. "Any surviving Supers will have to isolate themselves or suppress their gene. That includes both your daughters."

Like Hell that was going to happen. "And this is something that Ultragod thinks I can help fix."

"Apparently, yes," Jack replied, snorting. "As for what he wants you to help him with here, you'll have to ask him as I have no clue."

"And if I was very important to saving the world and you killed me?" I asked, wondering if Jack really was that stupid.

"I certainly would have had egg on my face," Jack replied, simply.

That was when the two of us were brought to what I was surprised to find was the center of what was clearly a massive underground hospital and research facility. There, the Secret Service, and a variety of doctors along with scientists were working around futuristic supertech. Which was legally and technically distinct from futuretech or supertech. I could see an oxygen tent where Moses Anders AKA Ultragod, the most powerful man in the universe, President of the United States, was lying in bed.

"Huh, you really did intend to take me to Ultragod," I replied.

"Yes," Jack said. "I did indeed."

"Jack! Gary! Get over here!" Moses called from his bed. "Guards, let them go."

"Gary Karkofsky is a wanted terrorist, sir," the blonde Foundation agent said, looking a bit more plastic and Barbie doll-like now that I knew she was a machine. It was in the eyes that seemed wider than normal. "We're only bringing him to you because you ordered it."

"Yeah, that was all his evil clone from an alternate dimension's future's twin," Moses said. "Release him."

"My evil clone was brainwashed, too!" I added. "By Satanic Nazis."

Jack facepalmed. "This is not a good idea, Moses. Karkofsky can't be trusted."

"I think we can deal with an underachieving criminal genius like Gary," Moses said.

"I am an incredibly achieving genius!" I snapped, walking over. "My goals are just stupid!"

To be frank, Moses Anders looked like shit. He looked like he'd aged twenty years, which was impressive since he'd looked like he was forty for over a century. His hair had gone white and there were wrinkles on his skin while his eyes still crackled with the power of the Ultra-Force. Still, my connection with Death told me he was dying, and Jack hadn't made that up.

"Are you sure, sir?" the blonde HRD agent asked again.

"The Republic of Farnia says he has diplomatic immunity," Moses replied. "Which is proof positive that you can get into the United Governments of the World if you have sufficiently deep pockets."

"Best use of Merciless Coin ever," I paused. "It turns out the United Governments of the World are incredibly easy to bribe. I'm the only nation with a satyr as my ambassador and Turkish delight as the national dish."

"You know, Gary, the CS Lewis Museum wants that wardrobe back," Moses said, pointing at me. I suspected he'd heard our conversation in the hall with his ultra-hearing. I never did understand how Moses could hear the heartbeat of a swallow ten miles away and not go insane. I guess some people really were just ultra.

"They can send a letter to my embassy AKA my spare bedroom's closet. Gizmo is currently using it to store boardgames," I replied, standing on the other side of the oxygen tent, and searching for something to say. "What happened?"

"That is a very long story," Moses said, staring at me. "I'm sorry, Gary, but I think this is the end."

Chapter Five

My Life Is Increasingly Just Live Action Gaming

Moses Anders' words were like a punch in the gut. "No, Moses, it's not the end. We'll get through this."

Moses sighed. "Maybe we will, Gary, maybe we won't. Did you really believe the Age of Superheroes would last forever?"

I was less concerned about the Age of Superheroes as a whole and Moses Anders in particular.

"You know, for a second there, I kinda did," I said, quoting the great Uma Thurman.

"Well, it's not," Moses said. "We will survive this, but I can already feel the changes in the air. It is the end of an era and you're responsible."

I paused. "I'd prefer to be remembered for something other than bringing about the end of heroism."

Moses snorted. "Heroes rise and fall, Gary. No, I mean you brought about the end of the Age of Superheroes. That's because there's not nearly the need for them anymore. There's only a fraction of supervillains out there than there used to be. It's like the Wild West. That actually only lasted a couple of decades, but it lived in our hearts for centuries."

It was times like this I remembered that Moses grew up in a time when radio plays were popular and lived through decades of Westerns. My opinion of them was mostly informed by Will

45

Smith's *Wild Wild West* and *Firefly*. It was a genre that predated me and if it came back would probably be watched more by my children.

"The plague, Moses," Jack said. "We're focused on the plague."

"The Nanoplague is a distraction," Moses surprised me by saying.

I blinked. "Someone has killed a hundred thousand people and it's a *distraction*?"

Moses nodded. "There're forces at work, maneuvering behind the scenes to seize power. Billions of dollars are being exchanged, weapons, and private meetings that I have no access to. Omega Corp, former PHANTOM sympathetic politicians, Brotherhood of Infamy cultists, and more are all seeking to enforce an agenda that I can't even guess at the likelihood. It's why I was going to announce the Superhuman Equality Act at Ultraday."

I whistled at that announcement. The Superhuman Equality Act was something that Ultragod had been campaigning for his entire career and was arguably the culmination of a hundred years of being a superhero. It outlined the rights and privileges of Supers in comparison to regular human beings as well as what regular human beings could expect in terms of protections as well as guarantees of privacy (against, you know, telepathy or whatever). It was something I probably would have instituted during my rewrite if I'd believed it was possible. You could only rewrite powers within your limits of belief, I supposed. I guess its passing was something that Ultragod had begged, borrowed, and stolen to get every vote possible for. Even so, it was a miracle he'd accomplished it and I understood why he didn't want to delay it.

"You think these people want to stop it?" I asked, wondering who he thought was part of this hypothetical conspiracy.

"I think they want to stop *you*," Moses said. "There's a surprising amount of chatter among the remains of PHANTOM, SKULL, and several other terrorist organizations. That is why I sent Jack to get you. You are somehow at the center of it."

"How flattering," I muttered. "A bunch of racists and domestic terrorists are fanboying. At least I'm glad I envisioned a world where they're an annoyance rather than a massive threat."

"Famous last words," Jack muttered.

"You rebooted the world, Gary," Moses said. "I've done that a few times myself and it always results in inconsistencies. People come back with different personalities, histories are altered, and time no longer flows in a straight line. Did you know I used to have a brother named Aaron?"

"No, I did not," I said, blinking.

"Well, I don't anymore," Moses said. "He disappeared along with Ultra-Gorilla and the League of Ultra-Cousins. French Ultragod is particularly missed. He was basically me with a mustache."

"I'm sure someone will eventually bring them back," I said, thinking of the decidedly not funny fact that Mandy used to have a daughter and still remembered her from her time travel. Yet, in the rebooted timeline, there was no sign of her having been ever born. That filled me with a kind of existential terror, and I prayed to God, Death, and Paladine of Krynn that it was Merciful rather than me who'd erased her with an errant thought.

Moses frowned. "Except, when you rebooted the universe, you'd already helped Death win rulership over the current age in the Eternity Tournament. Which, if I recall, means she cancelled resurrections. I even got to go off with my wife to a better afterlife."

"But you *came back*," I replied. It was difficult thinking about the events surrounding the tournament without a tinge of bitterness. I'd been forced to let go of Lancel, Moses, and Mandy's human soul. The fact I'd encountered all three (or at least versions of them) since then didn't change my feelings at the time.

Moses blinked. "Because you brought my wife back too. Polly's presently in a medically induced coma down the hall. You also brought back all the people who died in the Falconcrest City zombie apocalypse and who died under President Omega's reign of terror. About, oh, thirty to forty million people."

Lancel suggested I'd also brought back people on other worlds too. I wasn't sure how that worked. Maybe as some kind of domino effect. By saving certain heroes, they were able to save planets in other star systems.

I sucked in my breath. "Yeah, I tried to make the world a better place."

"You succeeded," Moses said, ignoring that I'd done it with reality alteration rather than any real social reforms. "About eighty percent of superheroes have retired due to lack of emergencies. Almost all violent supervillains have either been locked up, depowered, or killed."

"Except for Merciless and his family," Jack said.

"Except for them, yes," Moses said, not even bothering to argue.

I stared at him. "That actually terrifies me."

I'd been aware of how much the world had changed but it was starting to be clear that there were domino effects from the changes that I'd instituted which I hadn't accounted for. Had a year, or however long this age of peace had existed, really caused most superheroes to think it was time to quit? Should I have left a few Leatherfaces and Saurons around to keep everyone in tip top shape? I hadn't wanted to put superheroes out of business after all.

"It *should* terrify you," Jack said, showing just how much he despised me with a single look (hint: it was a lot). "You can't unbalance the universe like this and not have it come back, pissed off and wanting payback."

"So, I've heard," I said, thinking of my encounter earlier today with Lancel. I should have told Moses about it, but I chickened out. He was the one man in the world since my father and Lancel's deaths that I feared disappointing.

"I think you're the keystone, Gary," Moses said. "Your life force, your godhood, your whatever is what is keeping these changes in place. I think those people are all protected by your survival."

"Apparently not very well," I said, noticing that Ultragod and his wife were apparently dying here.

"If you're killed, Gary, then it's possible all the changes might snap back," Jack said.

"Which is better than the world as it was?" I asked, wondering if Jack had really thought through trying to kill me.

"It might also have gotten rid of the plague," Jack said.

"Might?" I asked. "You're going to kill me on might?"

"I trust my gut," Jack said, shrugging.

"I have a *Power Word Kill* I'm going to shove up your ass," I said, ready to kill the guy again. "That or a *Web* spell down your throat."

"Sounds kinky," Jack said, smirking.

It was hard to dislike Jack. A pity he'd decided my death was the key to saving the world.

"So, just so we're clear," I said, taking a deep breath. "There's something cosmically wrong with the universe and I'm somehow central to all of this."

"It's your story," Jack said, surprising me with his meta-ness. "But yes. There's someone with an awareness of the way the world should be who is willing to kill everyone to strike at you."

"Also, almost all the world's heroes are retired," I said. "Which I think they should be unretired for."

"No," Moses said, surprising me. "This has to be kept a secret. The rest of the world is doing its best to keep a wrap on both my condition and the Nanoplague's spread. It won't hold long but it only has to hold until you find a cure."

"That is an awfully large amount of faith for you to put in me given I am not someone to put faith in," I replied, clutching my scythe shaft tightly, and no, that wasn't a euphemism.

"I have even more faith in you than that because you have to do it before Ultraday," Moses said, surprising me.

I was starting to get a headache and I wasn't sure if it was because I was having another heart attack or because our situation was so badly screwed. "What do I need to do?"

"What you do best, Gary," Moses said, simply.

"Make sarcastic quips?" I asked.

"No, Gary," Moses said.

"Reference *Star Wars* and *Dungeons & Dragons*?" I asked. "Because I'm very good at both."

"No," Moses said, annoyed.

"Bat way above my league when it comes to romance and casual hookups?" I asked. "Which I should probably not mention because one of those women is your daughter."

"Supervillainy," Moses said, sighing. "I need you to be a supervillain."

"Good, because I don't think your daughter will be forgiving me anytime soon," I replied.

"Gabrielle just needs time," Moses said. "Also, her powers back. Oh, and a situation where her parents aren't dying in a manner vaguely related to you."

I grimaced. Ouch. Yeah, maybe I needed to focus on that.

"Yeah, that. Okay, what supervillainy do you need done, precisely?"

"I need you to rob another planet of its crown jewels," Moses said.

I blinked. "Yeah, that's pretty supervillain-like. Which planet and what royal family or are we going to find out the Windsors really are lizard people? Because David Icke blames the Jews for the alien shapeshifters and that is absolutely wrong. I know the actual shapeshifting lizard people and they're not kosher."

"The Tsavong Empire capital world and the White Witch Queen," Moses explained.

"Oh, super," I said, grimacing. "You couldn't send me somewhere easy? Like Entropicus' palace on Abaddon?"

The Tsavong were one of the closest alien races to Earth, being a shapeshifting race of conquering aliens who hadn't evolved much from Ancient Roman times. Gladiators, conquest, and slavery, but with the added benefit of starships. They also had an immortal sorceress as their queen, so they weren't reforming any time soon. Princess Vashi had told me all about it while she was impersonating Splotch Woman. She'd had a whole invasion planned, which I'd thwarted by convincing her to just hang out on Sex Island instead. It had been Dino Island before the tourist board had rebranded the place. Can't say it didn't work.

"I'd send you there if they had what we need," Moses said.

"Which is?" I asked.

51

"It's the remnants of the Crown of the Gods," Moses said. "I wore in World War Two when trying to bring an end to the conflict once Hitler was resurrected. All the gods of Earth created it to stop the Great Beasts that had been foreseen. It provides omnipotence when fully powered but was damaged beyond repair during the battle at Castle Lupindorf. It can still serve as a powerful amplifier to arcane and divine magic, though."

I knew this story due to an exceptionally bizarre chapter of my life, even by my standards, where I'd helped an alternate Moses Anders resist the allure of the Crown of the Gods [Editor: See "Merciless vs. Hitler"!—last time, I swear]. Alternate Moses had been ready to rewrite all of reality to be a nicer, happier, and less racist place. I'd stopped him because it was going to be an illusion and now I had just proven myself to be an enormous hypocrite.

I'd changed the world to stop Merciful from doing the same, but I hadn't had the strength to just leave well enough alone. Maybe this was my punishment. No, that was stupid. I would fix this, and we would all move on with our lives.

"And I'm guessing this lady won't voluntarily part with it," I said, suddenly realizing why Moses was hiring a thief for this than a bunch of superheroes.

"No," Moses said. "The White Witch Queen would rather exterminate her entire race than part with the crown."

"Does she have an actual name? The White Witch Queen is a mouthful," I replied, finishing my drink.

"Valdira Rama Thotep the Fifteenth," Moses said.

I blinked. "Right, so the White Witch Queen. I go there, grab the crown and you have something to enhance any spell you might make to cure this plague."

Easier said than done, obviously.

"Get it done before Ultraday," Moses said. "I'm pretty sure I can hang on until then."

I frowned. "You better. The kids would miss their granddad."

"I'm glad I got a chance to know them," Moses said, having always treated Leia as equally his granddaughter as Mimi. "Now I need you and Jack to start working on this."

"I'm not inclined to work with the guy who just tried to sacrifice me," I replied. "I mean, it's not an unreasonable request."

"He won't do it again," Moses said.

"Yeah, I really will," Jack said.

"No, you won't," Moses said, his voice firm and his gaze penetrating.

Jack sighed. "Fine, I'll do this for you but only because I owe you for all the saving of the world you've done. After this, we're even."

Moses chuckled and frowned. "I believe in you. You'll pull this off."

"That's your problem, Ultragod," I said, referring to him by his title rather than name. "You believe in people way too much."

Jack and I left Moses' side after that, the two of us accompanied by Foundation agents before we were escorted to an empty break room. The absence of the Secret Service was notable, and I had to wonder if they were being kept from the President's condition, or if there was something else.

"You know I could have gotten you if we hadn't been interrupted," Jack said, the two of us now alone.

"Not on your best day, Jack," I replied.

"It's not about my best day," Jack replied. "It's about yours. Your powers are fluctuating. I can feel it from here. One second, you're going to be at full power and the next you'll be as helpless as any other mortal."

"I'm not exactly helpless without my powers," I said.

"And what would you do if you didn't have any powers?" Jack said, his grip tightening around his kukri.

I pulled out my Desert Eagle automatic that I had hidden in the back of all my robes. "Semi-automagic. That was the original title of the Dresden Files before Jim Butcher changed it."

Jack smirked. "Well, at least you won't be completely useless in fixing your mistakes."

I didn't put away the gun. "I think I'll go my own way. I won't be needing you on this trip."

Despite the fact I'd just been in a weeklong coma and was as confused as anyone about what was really going on, I was anxious to get started. Moses had been like a second father to me and while it hadn't worked out between me and his daughter, I would do just about anything to save him. Everyone else wasn't so much secondary, there were about forty million people in danger here, but they were less "real." Moses was the face of this struggle for me, and I wasn't about to abandon him or his wife. I would do this, with or without Jack.

"Do you trust that you can open the portals necessary?" Jack asked. "It'd be fine by me if you ended up in Hell or worse, Raven's Roost."

"Raven's Roost is Falconcrest City's ugly stepsister," I said. "It's where they send the people who lower the tenor of our art deco hellhole. The only place with a more corrupt police force and higher wealth disparity, pre-Merciless reforms. The Mordor to our Gondor. The Shellbyville to our Springfield. The Valley to our Los Angeles. I need to get on fixing that place."

"Because it's up to you to fix the world," Jack said, testing me.

"Uh, yeah, duh," I replied. "Supervillain,"

Jack smirked and gestured, conjuring another portal. "I won't kill you, Merciless. As much as I'd like to and believe it might save a lot of people, I made a promise to Ultragod. A wizard's promise is the only thing that can be relied on. Still, I think this scavenger hunt is going to fail and we're going to have to come up with a new plan before Ultraday. Otherwise, we'll be living in *Black Death 2: Vengeance of the Plague.*"

I thought about how everything that had happened since I'd picked up the Reaper's Cloak all those years ago: time travel, zombie apocalypses, Mandy's death, Mandy's resurrection, Mandy's possession, my daughters, *Mortal Kombat*-esque tournaments, Hollow Earth adventures, alternate realities, crazy redneck alien sheriffs, and evil doppelgangers.

It had been a wild and insane ride, but most of it had been driven to try to repair the damage I'd caused by taking the cloak in place of Mandy. I'd tried to fix all my mistakes, but it just seemed to be wallpapering over the cracks in the wall. I needed to make a last-ditch effort to bail out this sinking ship and if I failed then none of it had been worth it. I should have stayed locked up on the moon after I killed the Extreme.

"I don't disagree, Jack," I said, staring at the portal. "You have my permission to sacrifice me because I'm not going to let this world that I've created fall apart either. No matter the cost."

I was surprised that I meant it, too.

Chapter Six

Preparing the Heist

Heading back to the mansion, I didn't exactly get the response I was hoping for from my family on my new super-duper important mission from the government.

"Let me understand this," Cindy said. "You wake up, ditch us, visit the President, and are now going to steal the crown jewels of an alien space empire to stop a plague. Somehow."

All of us were gathered in the library and I couldn't help but get an Agatha Christie/Clue vibe to the whole thing. Well, if Agatha Christie/Clue starred a supervillain family consisting of myself, Mandy, Cindy, Mimi, Leia, and our special guest star. I missed Diabloman at times like this and the fact he was married to my sister, Kerri, should have meant he was back in our lives.

Instead, Cindy and Mandy, both had made it clear they wanted nothing to do with our former associate and he'd kept his distance. Cindy hated Diabloman for betraying me and held a grudge longer than I did, while Mandy blamed him for letting Spellbinder drive around her body for years. Which, fair enough, was kind of dickish of him. If I'd learned to forgive and forget, though, why couldn't anyone else?

"You forgot the Trench Coat Magician trying to kill me," I pointed to Jack, not intending to forgive and forget what he did. "Because he did. So don't like him."

Jack frowned at me. "I said I wasn't going to do it again. By which I mean that I almost certainly will. Sorry, not sorry."

I glared at him. "You're not helping, Jack."

Mind you, I'd already asked Mandy to pickpocket his pistols and replace them with identical replicas I'd conjured.

"Well don't," Cindy said, glaring at him. "Or I will inflict unforgettable suffering on you."

"I've been in Hell, luv," Jack said.

"I also have the world's best lawyers," Cindy said. "Imagine being tied up in decades of legal work, hearings, court trials, and appeals. The Society of Superheroes covers most legal fees but you're not exactly on their A-roster. I bet I can get them to cut you loose."

Jack smirked and pulled out a cigarette. "You're a ruthless one, aren't you?"

I removed the cigarette from his hands. "No smoking while children are present."

"Where?" Leia asked, looking over her shoulder.

Mimi snorted.

"You have no idea," Cindy said in a tone that was distinctly flirtatious. It made me wonder if she was going to let him off the hook for trying to kill me because he was hot.

Which, fair enough.

"Is this like that time you made us watch *Night Court* to learn about the American legal system?" Leia asked. "I wasn't even born when that show was reruns."

"Watch it have a reboot while this is being adapted to be a biography," Cindy said, snorting.

"It's still the most realistic of all legal dramas," I replied, "And that's what DVDs are for, dear."

"What's a DVD?" Leia asked.

"It's like a streaming service that only contains three or four episodes," Cindy explained.

57

"That's terrible!" Leia said, horrified.

"On the plus side, it doesn't disappear when the rights shift to another company," Mandy chimed in.

"Oh, so it's like an NFT for movies," Leia said.

"Oh, you poor, sweet summer child," I said, saddened that I had failed her education so thoroughly.

"I'd say it's the opposite of an NFT because it isn't dependent on the whim of a server and has inherent value," Mandy said.

"Thank you, Mandy," I said. "If I could conjure a rainbow, I'd say 'The More You Know'."

Only of which half my readers would get as well.

Jack crossed his arms and rolled his eyes. "We already did an NFT joke."

"It deserves two," I replied, dismissing him with a wave.

"Okay, why are you helping the President?" Mimi asked, surprising me with her reticence. "You're an anarchist."

"One, he's your grandfather, and two, anarchy is complicated," I replied.

"Not really, you're just an enormous hypocrite," Jack muttered.

"You're working for him too," I replied. "Also, I'm way more punk than you."

"I'm sorry, the huge mansion says otherwise," Jack said. "Also, the hedge fund."

"Hey, my dad killed the President!" Mimi said. "The bad one! Who may or may not have ever been president in this timeline. Wait, was he, Leia?"

Before I'd rebooted reality—which was a statement by itself—the Earth's default reality had been constantly shifting due to manipulation by time-travelers. Presidents changed, pop culture altered, and people popped into existence or were erased at the drop of a hat. A lot of it had been due to the actions of President Omega, a time-traveling dickhead from the future who had gotten sick of his utopian future before deciding to wreck it with supertech from his century.

Basically, he was Biff from *Back the Future Part II* except instead of *Gray's Sports Almanac*, he had universal fabricators and a wallet-sized computer with all human knowledge. The rebooted reality had undone most of his changes, but a lot of people had a weird sense of déjà vu and inaccurate memories that explained the Mandela Effect.

The Mandela Effect being where you remembered something wrong about reality like Nelson Mandela dying in prison or the *Bernstein Bears* books rather than *Berenstain Bears* books. Yes, it was me altering reality and not you just having a bad memory. Which, as we know, was always the more likely option. In this case, no one was quite sure if President Omega was the impeached former President or not, not least his army of fascist anti-Super followers.

"It's complicated," Leia said, checking a strange homemade device. "Time is less linear than you might believe."

"And President Omega was a dirtbag even by politician standards," Cindy said. "Did you kill him for good or is he back?"

"I have no idea," I said. "I'm not sure you can kill a living temporal paradox."

It was one of my great fears that President Omega would someday return. While Merciful was my archenemy—it was hard to beat yourself for that—I had to say Charles Omega was probably the man I hated most out of all my foes. Not only was he a literal Nazi, but he was just such a *pointless* asshole, a guy who got up in the morning and fired rockets at people or ruined their credit rating just to ruin lives. I'd done a lot of bad things in my life but the sheer senseless malice of it all pissed me the hell off. I killed people, yeah, but only fascists and guys who annoyed me. Completely different.

"You can't mess with time," Jack said, a long, red, clubbed demon's tail unfurling out from the back of his pants. "There's no way to reverse the evils that men do. You can only go forward and not backward. What you did destabilized all of the world's magic and reality."

"Still a better anarchist than you!" I snapped, coming up with the lamest come back since, "No, you!"

"That's not a defense!" Jack said.

"Who said I needed a defense?" I asked, shrugging. "I came, I saw, I did."

"I thought we agreed you'd not use your college motto in front of the girls," Mandy said, sighing.

"I never used that motto in college," I said, turning to her. "Because if you're smart, you keep your mouth shut. You keep your head down and watch out for weaknesses in your peers. Ones you can exploit. No, wait, that was high school. Also, I suspect the kids know about...it."

"It?" Mimi asked.

"They're acting like we don't know what sex is," Leia said.

Mimi stared. "Cindy was a prostitute when she was our age."

"Okay!" I said, clapping my hands. "It's time for me to go! I wish you all the best and know your hearts go with me."

"So, you want us to come with you?" Cindy asked, ignoring the comment about her early years. "I should point out that I already did the world's greatest heist in *Cindy's Seven*? Movie rights not optioned."

"Didn't that end up horribly?" Mandy asked. "You know, what with my being there and seeing it end horribly?"

"The real treasure was the friends we made along the way," Cindy said. "Also, the few million dollar antiques we retrieved.

I just need to figure out what happened to the authentic dragonlance we acquired. I had a buyer in Dubai who was willing to pay me the cost of a small island for it."

"Oh, I gave it to Margaret Weis," I said, pausing. "Probably should have asked you before I did that."

Cindy twitched. Her eyes flashed yellow, and her fingernails turned into talons. Her body visibly shook with rage.

"Are you okay?" I asked.

"I think she's turning into a werewolf but is so angry that she can't pull it off," Leia said, lifting her scanner. "Wow, I've never seen these readings before."

"It's okay," I said, lifting my hands. "I'll go back in time and steal it from myself."

Cindy spoke an unintelligible series of barks and growls.

I proceeded then to pull a dragonlance out of my robes. "No, I'm just kidding. I instead paid for her lawsuit against Hasbro. I was just off polishing the shaft."

"Goddess, Gary," Mandy said. "Really?"

"That wasn't a euphemism!" I said. "Not everything I say is a double entendre!"

"Precious!" Cindy said, grabbing the dragonlance and hugging it. "I was wrong to want to sell you. I promise I'll just steal all the money I was going to sell you for. I love you more than my children!"

"Cindy—" I started to speak.

"It's okay, Dad," Leia said. "Let her have this."

Cindy hugged it more. "You didn't answer my question, Gary. I want to help you with this. Oh, and I was lying, Leia and Mimi. You know I love you every bit as much as the dragonlance. I mean, it's not autographed. Oh wait, I see Gary got it autographed! I now love it slightly more than my children!"

Mandy swiped the weapon from Cindy.

"Aww!" Cindy said. "Come on! If we got Margaret Weis to autograph my children, I'd love them just as much."

"Seriously, Dad, I'm not sure about you going alone to the Tsavong capital world of Tsavong Planet," Mimi said. "You could use some backup. I mean, backup that isn't trying to kill you."

"Really, that's what it's called?" I asked. "No points for originality I guess."

"Also, the Trench Coat Magician is kind of lame as a superhero," Leia added. "I mean, he's only loved by old British comic book writers and fans of *Assassins Creed: Black Flag*."

"That's a joke that's going to age well," Jack muttered.

"There's more going on than the plague," I said, pausing. "During my heart attack, I had a mystical encounter with Lancel Warren. Also, a huge bunch of aberrations from the Far Realm, which aren't just a bunch of D&D knock offs of Lovecraft's writings anymore. It turns out that Jack Hellraiser was right—"

"Wow, that's a sentence I never thought I'd hear from you," Jack said, pausing. "Or anyone, actually."

"Whatever the case, reality has been knocked off kilter by the reboot," I said, feeling somewhat but not all that guilty about doing it. "I don't know if it's related to this Nanoplague business, but it sure as hell can't be helping. You guys need to be ready to do something if the Crown of the Gods doesn't fix everything."

Leia stared up at me. "You are actually terrified of us getting killed and are just trying to shuffle us away."

"That too," I said, acknowledging my telepathic daughter. "I do know that you and Mimi become the guardians of the timestream or something, though, so I do have that going for me."

I didn't normally condescend to my family of absolute badasses, but I was honestly terrified by Lancel's warning. I'd tried to fix everything, and it had apparently backfired. If Greek mythology taught me anything, it was that these sorts of things tended to backfire spectacularly. Worse, they tended to reflect back onto your loved ones, too.

"We're only time cops, not time lords," Leia said, before pausing. "Mostly because I haven't figured out how to build a TARDIS. Yet."

"It's also weird how we didn't do anything about President Omega," Mimi said. "It seems like our future selves that work with the Time Cops would want to, I dunno, deal with the world's worst time criminal. I mean, worse than Dad."

"I'm fine coming in second for exploiting time travel for personal gain and fun," I replied. "By the way, trying to save the Romanovs? Bad idea. No cute Don Bluth movies here. It turns out that family is antisemitic."

"Who possibly could have known that, except anyone with any grasp of history," Mandy muttered, rolling her eyes. She'd never approved of my misuse of the Nightwalker's time machine, even when I took her on a trip to meet a young Keanu Reeves.

"Maybe President Omega was necessary for our birth, and we couldn't interfere with his time manipulation because it was necessary to guarantee our existence," Mimi said, ignoring my statement. "Then his time crimes might actually lead to the formation of a time police."

"Ooo," Leia said. "Then it'd be a predestination paradox."

"No time travel speculation!" Cindy said, Mandy's hand on her head and keeping her away from the dragonlance.

"Seriously, is this cursed or something?" Mandy asked.

"It's just her fantasy addiction mixed with low blood sugar," I replied. "She'll be fine if you wave the future copies of

George R.R. Martin books at her and give her a live rabbit to eat."

"This family is so goddamned weird," Jack muttered. "And my father was Satan."

"We'll keep an eye out for massive destabilization in the space-time continuum, Dad," Mimi said. "You just stay alive."

"It's what I'm best at," I said, giving my children a hug.

"I'm upset you're not taking me on the heist," Cindy said, finally giving up on the dragonlance. "However, I'm going to pretend you think it's because I'd betray you to steal the Crown of the Gods and proceed to restructure the universe in my image instead of yours. Which is a sign of villainous respect and not icky worrying over my safety."

"Yes, that's it exactly," I replied. "I fear you overthrowing me and becoming the new Dark Lord."

"In your place, I'd set myself up as a queen, as beautiful and terrible as the dawn," Cindy said, "Yada-yada-yada."

"You'd be the only queen I know with fleas," Leia muttered.

"That happened once and don't mock your horrifically incompetent and nurturing mother," Cindy said.

"It's hard, Mom," Leia said.

"I know, dear, I know," Cindy said. "Have fun storming the alien castle, dear."

"Jane is the deer," I replied. "I'm more the archmage!"

I could see Jack grit his teeth at that description. It was the same look I'd seen on a lot of other magic-users—the older non-Dungeon magic using kind—toward me. As much as Jack Hellraiser was a rules-breaking rogue, he was apparently still conservative enough to hate that I'd opened the floodgates of sorcery to the common man. Though, in his case, I suspected it was less classicism and more, "I liked X band before they were cool and became sellouts." I'd ruined sorcery for even the street mage set.

"Good luck," Mandy said.

With that, Jack performed his *portal* spell again and conjured yet another one in the middle of my library.

"Seriously, how many times did you memorize that spell today?" I asked him.

Jack glared. "You realize that's not how magic works, right?"

"Mine does!" I said, cheerfully. "Also, a good ten million other users of Dungeon magic."

"Yeah, that," Jack muttered, walking through the portal.

"You know he's going to try to kill you again, right?" Cindy said, holding the dragonlance again, before sighing and giving it to our daughters as a sign of her love.

"I prefer *Critical Role*'s Exandria," Mimi said.

"I play *Shadow Run*," Leia said.

Cindy hissed and grabbed it back. "You have no appreciation for the classics."

"It's okay," I said, raising my hands. "Superheroes always fight it out when they first meet. It's like when Ultragod and the Nightwalker first met. Ultragod beat the Nightwalker then the Nightwalker rallied around to beat Ultragod. It's a way of establishing a warrior's bond before they team up against some other, actual villain."

"Uh huh," Cindy said. "Sometimes I think you seriously overestimate the goodness of superheroes, Gary."

I shrugged and walked through the portal, only to be pistol-whipped in the face by Jack.

Goddammit.

Chapter Seven

Where I Cheat by the Rules of First-Person Narration

The crack of the pistol butt against my jawline was far from the hardest I'd ever been hit, but certainly took the wind out of me, particularly since Jack Hellraiser had superhuman strength. If not for the protection magic woven into my cloak, I probably would have suffered a broken jaw. Either way, I did hit the ground with a thud and the portal closed behind me.

We were in a shining metal hall of the kind you might see in the Death Star, though smoother and more alien. The place had a distinctly antiseptic scent to it, and I could tell the air tasted different with none of Earth's pollution but several chemicals that I didn't quite recognize. The Tsavong, at least according to their Superpedia page, breathed nitrogen so they had an oxygen and nitrogen mix that was breathable by humans.

Jack Hellraiser was standing over me with both of his pistols drawn and his trench coat flowing in a nonexistent wind. There was an expression of resolve on his face that told me he'd made his decision to take me out but that he wasn't happy about it. Which I couldn't have cared less about. It didn't matter if Jack felt bad about his betrayal, he was still frigging betraying me.

"Dammit, Cindy is never going to let me live this down," I muttered, sitting on the ground.

"Nothing has changed, Merciless," Jack said, coldly. "You're still a disruption in the fabric of reality and it's only getting worse."

"Hold on," I said, lifting my hand. "I have to say the line."

"The what?" Jack asked, stupidly not using his guns to kill me then and there. I suspected one of my powers had to be distracting people with nonsense.

"Curse your sudden but inevitable betrayal!" I said.

Jack stared. "*Firefly* went off the air in 2002, Gary. Also, it wasn't that good of a show to begin with. It's a kinda Confederate apologetic and there're no Asians in a future supposedly settled by the UK and Chinese."

"You lying liar who lies!" I snapped. "Also, you're wrong about killing me. And kind of right about *Firefly*, but I still love it."

"It may be the only way to save the world," Jack said, clearly not wanting to kill me, but not having been convinced not to. "Killing you, not loving *Firefly*."

"And what if I'm the only person who can fix it?" I said, standing up. "Did you ever think of that? Merciful was the one who was using the Primal Orbs and I don't think anyone else has a speed dial to Primals. Have you thought about that? What if the only person who can make all this right is the person who did it?"

Jack didn't immediately respond. "That's a chance I'm willing to take."

I narrowed my eyes. "Are you even the one taking the chance?"

"What?" Jack asked.

"Jack Hellraiser, occult detective, isn't exactly the A-List when it comes to supernatural guardianship of the universe," I said, crossing my arms. "The whole saving the world and saving reality thing has never been your scene. You're a guy who is infamous for running con games on Tiamat-Abaddon, the Lesser Kings of Hell, and the occasional archangel. If I really was a big disruption to reality, where the hell are the big guns? Isis the Invincible, Merlyn, the Great Ghost, or even Guinevere? Hell, the frigging Nightwalker. He's dead but that's never stopped him before. There's also the one on Earth-B."

"Lancel Warren visited you," Jack said. "A new Supreme Archmage hasn't been appointed yet since his death. It means the wisest man in the world decided this was a problem."

"You should work on that," I said. "I'd put my hat in the ring, but I'd be an absolute trash fire as the defender of reality. Personally, I think Amanda Douglas should be the next Supreme Archmage. But Lancel Warren *talked* with me. He didn't attack me. He set out to warn me. So, you're doing this on your own."

The fact the two of us were hashing it out in the middle of what I presumed to be an alien hallway only added to the bizarreness of everything going on. At any point, a bunch of Tsavong shapeshifters might come upon us and trigger a massive fight. Which, you know, was better than being killed, but I was pretty sure I could handle the Trench Coat Magician. Another thing he wasn't very good at was ambushes as he should have just opened his portal open into a sun or the Mariana Trench.

"You're right," Jack said, pointing his guns at me. "Prepare to die!"

He fired both guns and they shot out water that bounced against my face.

Jack blinked. "Okay, both of these guns are metal pistols identical in weight and density to my normal ones."

"I may have paid my vampire wife to replace them with exact replicas I constructed in our short time after your first betrayal," I replied.

Jack stared at me. "Bullshit."

I raised my hands in surrender. "No, I actually established it earlier for my readers."

"What the hell is wrong with you?" Jack asked.

"The possibilities are endless," I admitted. "But what kind of fool would I be to trust you after betraying me?"

"You've trusted people who have betrayed you multiple times," Jack replied. "Diabloman, Spellbinder, Ultragoddess—"

"Yes, but you're no Diabloman or a hot lady, so screw you," I replied. I was also at the limit of my patience with this guy. Bringing up Spellbinder was the last straw. She was someone I didn't trust for obvious reasons. "By the *Azure Bands of Zuk'teran!*"

From my fingertips shot forth a glowing rainbow of blue bands that wrapped around Jack like a ribbon on a gift and tied him up while suppressing his magic. It was the most powerful spell I'd memorized and had been something I'd been hoping to use upon the White Lich Queen. Now I was down a ninth-level spell and couldn't trust my only ally here. Fun fact: Zuk'Teran was my homebrewed Archmage GMPC for when I was Gamemastering at Falconcrest University.

A smart man would have immediately used a *Teleportation* spell to get back to Earth but, unfortunately, that magic didn't function like it did in *Dungeons & Dragons*. There, all you had to do was know your destination to travel. Here, it turned out you had to know your destination as well as your starting point. Which seems like obvious geometry, but I hadn't bothered to consult a star chart before coming here.

I knew enough about "real" wizardry that magicians like Jack Hellraiser got around this by making pacts with cosmic entities like the Great Beasts, gods of multiple star systems, Star Trek's Q (or something effectively indistinguishable), and so on to do the calculations for them. Unfortunately, I didn't have any such entities that I had made such a pact with, so Jack was my only option to get out of here.

Jack grumbled and struggled with his bonds that prevented him from calling upon his powers. "So, what now?"

I cast an *Invisibility 10ft Radius* spell over us, and a *Silence* spell based on a bubble effect that was focused on the user. If all of that sounded Greek to you and you aren't a Greek (or geek in this case), understand that I'd paid a lot of money to the mathmagicians among Dungeon magic users to work out the basics for how my spell list functioned. I may have been the creator for an entirely new yet derivative form of altering reality, but I still had to have subcontractors working out the petty details.

"Now, we finish the mission," I replied. "Somehow."

"Are you serious?" Jack asked, looking back at me.

"Yep," I said. "Get up."

The *Azure Bands of Zuk'teran* lifted Jack up and started marching him in front of me as the bands linked back to my fingertips.

"You'd be safer killing me," Jack replied.

"That's not my style," I said.

"You've killed more people than cholera," Jack snapped, ceasing his resistance once he realized it was futile.

"Only if we count Nazi-Earth and I swear I thought the big red button disarmed the nuclear weapons," I replied. "Also, all of the humans left were brainwashed Barbie and Ken clones. Seriously, they didn't have genitalia."

"You've also killed superheroes," Jack said.

"Only the Extreme!" I replied, growling. "People who won't stay dead for that matter, even when I have outlawed resurrection via cosmic fiat!"

"They're clones of the originals," Jack said. "It only matters if you believe in the soul."

"You mean that thing I can manipulate as a necromancer?" I asked. "The thing that has been scientifically proven to exist over and over again? That soul?"

"Pfft, science," Jack said.

I rolled my eyes. "Keep walking, Trench Coat Flasher. We're bound to run into some Tsavong at some point."

"That we haven't is disturbing," Jack muttered. "It's possible they're all at the Great Ceremony."

"The Great Ceremony?" I asked.

"Did you do any research on the Tsavong?" Jack asked.

"In the few minutes I've had between you trying to kill me?" I asked. "No! Also, the Tsavong aren't my favorite historical comics to read about the Society of Superheroes. I think the space opera stuff produced by Amazing! comics is kind of lame and prefer the gritty, street level stuff."

Jack rolled his eyes. "Gods above and below, I'm dealing with a child."

"I know your real name is Jacob Kowalski, Jack Hellraiser, so let's not throw stones in glass houses," I replied.

"The Great Ceremony is when the White Witch Queen uses her powers to drain voluntary and not-so-voluntary sacrifices from the Tsavong populace. She attempts to use it to repair the Crown of Gods in hopes of ascending to become ruler of the universe," Jack explained. "Millions die every year with no result."

"Because the crown can't be fixed," I said. "Ultragod said so."

71

Jack stared forward and shook his head. "Ultragod, the Nightwalker, and Guinevere aren't always right, Gary. You've been at this a few years but not as long as I have. A lot of heroes have put their trust in the Big Three, believing them to be infallible. It makes the moments when they screw up all the worse because you don't see them coming."

I had no response to that. "Right, well, let's just be quiet until we find the throne room."

An hour later, we were still walking. The *Invisibility 10ft Radius* and *Silence* spells had long since stopped working, but we hadn't encountered anyone. It was getting to the point of ridiculous and my feet were aching like crazy. The *Azure Bands of Zuk'teran* were still binding Jack, though.

"Seriously, there's gotta be a map or something," I muttered. "I wasn't this lost when I visited Disney World for the first time, and I was six."

"Maybe we should make small talk," Jack muttered.

"Why, so you can figure out my emotional weaknesses and a way to use them against me?" I asked.

"Yes," Jack said.

"Alright," I said. "You start us off."

"What would you do if you weren't a supervillain, Gary?" Jack asked. We were about to head into some sort of coliseum, and I heard cheering in the distance. It was as good a place to go as anywhere since the closest thing to life we'd encountered were cleaning droids and a giant robot death machine that completely ignored us.

"Are you asking me what I would have done if I never became a supervillain or are you asking me what I would do if I suddenly stopped now?" I asked in return.

"Does it matter?" Jack asked.

I looked at him sideways. "In the context that if I hadn't become a supervillain, Mandy and I both would have probably died in the zombie apocalypse that destroyed Falconcrest City. Then I would have definitely died when President Omega launched the Exterminators to kill all people with the Super gene. Which I have, just one of the inactive ones. It gives me another reason to want to cure the Nanoplague, because I'm probably infected now. Which either is Ultragod being a devious mastermind or all of us being idiots there."

I really hoped I hadn't infected my daughters.

"Fair enough," Jack replied. "So, the latter."

"I forgot the question," I said, thinking about all the Super gene nonsense I'd been mentally going over.

"What you'd do if you weren't a superhero," Jack explained.

"Supervillain," I corrected him.

"I know you're Eighties Man," Jack said. "You need more spells than the basic glasses one to be unrecognizable. At least with fellow magicians."

"I tried being a movie director once," I admitted, ignoring his statement.

"You did?" Jack asked.

"I mean, it was really just an extensive money laundering scheme from stealing a bunch of gold from the Elemental Plane of Minerals. I got a bunch of tax breaks from the Australian government."

"Uh huh," Jack said.

"They closed that loophole, but I got to do the *Supervillainy Saga*, *Cindy does Falconcrest*, and *Night of the Bilbys* I through V."

"Wait, Cindy did porn?" Jack asked, all too intrigued. I couldn't help but wonder why because it wasn't exactly hard to find naked pictures of Cindy on the internet. Hell, it wasn't that hard to find naked ones of me.

"Softcore only. Weirdly, *Cindy Does Falconcrest* was the title she chose for her biography," I replied.

Jack shook his head. "No, that's still tied to crime. I mean if you really didn't want to be a supervillain."

"I'd want to run a women's pro-golf league," I replied.

Jack stared at me. "What?"

"Clearly, you haven't seen Cindy in a short plaid dress," I replied.

"Sorry, just having difficulty with imagining you in the country club set," Jack said.

"Clearly you missed the point of the movie *Caddyshack*," I replied. "Which is that golf is awesome, just the rich assholes who play it suck. Mandy used to love it."

"Used to?" I asked.

"She's a vampire," I said. "Night games are apparently not the same. Plus, you know, super strength kind of ruins it."

"Cindy has super strength," Jack said.

"I know, but she doesn't mind cheating," I replied. "She's also banned from women's professional tennis for this exact reason. A loss to tennis skirts as a whole."

"I'm sensing a fetish here," Jack replied.

"I have no idea what you mean," I lied. "Besides, we all have our fetishes. Mandy is into blood, girl metal, and blood. Cindy is into long phallic objects that kill dragons. Also, me."

"Your wife really likes *Dragonlance*," Jack said, making conversation that I was certain was designed to lure guards here. Thankfully, there was no sign of those.

"Cindy isn't my wife," I said, knowing she'd never accept even if I offered. "And yes, she does. From the time she was fourteen to the present, she's been constantly updating her *Erotic Adventures of Tika the Barmaid* fanfiction. She only stopped last year."

"Because she grew out of it?" Jack asked, clearly not understanding the fanfic writer's mind.

"No, because Ransom House paid her a fortune to change the names and remake it about how Razor Mason, billionaire not wizard, gets Tina the Barmaid into BDSM. The movie is already in production."

"Uh huh," Jack said, wondering if I was taking the piss or not. Which I was not.

"She would be very honored if Margaret Weis or Tracy Hickman sued over that," I replied. "Personally, I've always been intrigued by other dragon possibilities. Particularly involving shapeshifting. I've already wiped aliens, vampires, and werewolves off my bucket list."

That was when we came to a massive set of doors marked with the symbol of a skull with a crown. They were almost a hundred feet tall and clearly meant for someone more important than us.

So, I was a bit unsettled when they opened at our approach and a fanfare was played to announce our arrival.

Chapter Eight

The Sexy Giantess Tries to Kill Us

The massive doors opened to a Roman-style gladiator arena or, perhaps, I should say Geonosian. You know, those bug guys from *Attack of the Clones*. Yes, I'm quoting the prequels a lot lately.

Either way, we were in a big alien coliseum with row after row of Tsavong as well as other species sitting in the bleachers. A huge holographic display was showing images of what I presumed to be recent battles to the death between the Tsavong and animals, superpowered aliens, and even the occasional robot.

It occurs to me I should probably describe the Tsavong's biology since readers in other universes may not be familiar with them. In their natural form, they're a sexless, orange humanoid, reptilian race covered in smooth scales. As smooth as a Ken Doll, as the Metatron would put it. Mind you, they're reptiles, so it's not like their females would have breasts anyway. It means, yes, when I talk about dating a Princess, she was mostly putting it on for my benefit. Most Tsavong are happily neither and both sexes with no nods to traditional ideas of gender.

The White Witch Queen did not subscribe to this school of thought. She was very recognizably female and had adopted a form that embodied a lot of ideas about that status from Earth as well as other planets. She was about twelve-feet-tall, possessed of long white hair unlike most of her otherwise bald race, and shapeshifted to a more aesthetically pleasing to humans' form. Picture a giant orange Monica Bellucci in revealing robes if that doesn't pander to too many fetishes.

Or, hell, if it does.

I don't kink shame.

Resting on the top of the White Witch Queen's head was the damaged Crown of the Gods that looked like it was made of black iron and encrusted with black gemstones that previously glowed with the power of all my universe's pantheons. A couple of the gemstones flickered with light, which was a bad sign since when fully powered, the Crown of the Gods allowed its wearer the power to rewrite reality as effectively as the Primal Orbs. How it had gotten into the hands of the one reptile woman with boobs was anyone's guess, but not pertinent at this time.

"You know what I'm thinking?" I asked Jack.

"What mountains we can climb?" Jack asked, looking up at the White Witch Queen.

I blinked. "Okay, *now* I'm thinking that, but I would need a lot of drinks first. Even if the no touching wands rule wouldn't come into play with her between us."

"I'm just saying there's plenty of room," Jack said.

Dammit, I was going to hate having to kill him. I really hoped I could figure out a way not to. "No, Jack, I was wondering why every alien race seems to have gladiator arenas. This is the kind of Vance Turbo Golden Age of Sci-Fi stuff that people with faster-than-light travel should have evolved past."

"That assumes that technological progress equals social progress," Jack said, lazily ignoring the fact we were obviously the main attraction here. "Not every culture can be like the ones in *Star Trek*."

"I dunno, have you ever noticed *Star Trek* is actually kind of terrifying as a setting?" I asked. "Except for the Federation, every other planet is a military dictatorship, ruled by a computer, or the playthings of cosmic gods."

"SILENCE!" The White Witch Queen shouted, her voice booming throughout the arena.

"Do you think she can hear us?" I asked.

"I SAID SILENCE!" The White Queen summoned a fireball in the palm of her hand like the Wicked Witch of the West and hurled it at my head.

I ducked under the flame, and it sailed over, exploding behind me with a deafening boom. If not for the magical protections woven into my cloak, I also would have been doused in fire too.

"YOU, MERCILESS, HAVE BEEN CHARGED WITH DISRUPTING THE NATURE OF THE SPACE-TIME-MAGIC CONTINUUM!" The White Witch Queen said. "YOU MUST DIE IN ORDER TO SET RIGHT THE BALANCE!"

"I totally agree!" Jack shouted up at her.

"THEN I WILL EXTERMINATE THE EARTH AND ALL OF ITS PIDDLING MORTALS!" The White Witch Queen shouted.

"Crap," Jack said, looking down.

"Mmm hmm," I muttered. "Turns out the slaving sorceress is a bad guy."

"DO YOU HAVE ANYTHING IN YOUR DEFENSE?" The White Witch Queen asked.

"I haven't hurt anybody!" I snapped back. "I was trying to make reality better!"

"THE UNBORN HAVE FLOCKED TO MAGIC USERS LIKE A STAR MOTH TO FLAME," The White Witch Queen shouted. "OUR WORLD HAS BEEN ASSAULTED THOUSANDS OF TIMES SINCE THE TRANSFORMATION OF REALITY! THEY DRAG OUR KIND FROM THIS DIMENSION TO THE EVERLASTING DARKNESS! ONLY TWO IN EIGHT SURVIVE!"

I blinked, staring at the White Witch Queen. "Well, shit."

"Told you," Jack muttered. "I mean, yes, in the previous universe, everyone on this planet was dead due to it being eaten by Pyronnicus the Living Sun, but that doesn't absolve you from the fact everyone here is dying due to something caused by you."

I stared at him. "Oh, screw you!"

Seriously, this was not the time.

"YOU MUST DIE, CHOSEN OF DEATH, TO EMPOWER MY CROWN AND AT LAST GIVE ME THE POWER TO REWRITE REALITY AS I SEE FIT!" The White Witch Queen said.

"Okay, her solution to rewriting reality screwing up the fundamental laws of the universe is to rewrite reality some more." Jack looked up at the White Witch Queen. "Lady, that won't fix anything!"

"I'd say the definition of insanity is doing the same thing over and over again expecting something a different result, but as a self-professed nutjob, I find that labels are uncreative," I replied. "Can we have a truce for five minutes, Jack?"

"I promise by the Dark Lords of Hell not to kill you until we've beaten this crazy woman," Jack said, sighing. "At least if you take this seriously."

"I make no promises," I said, dissolving the *Azure Bands of Zuk'teran* and freeing Jack.

"CHOOSE HOW YOU WILL DIE!" The White Witch Queen shouted.

"Snu-Snu!" I shouted.

"Old age!" Jack said, simultaneously before looking at me. "Dammit, I should have chosen yours."

"You snu-snu you lose." I shrugged. "I had the same feelings here as I did when I first saw that giant lady from *Resident Evil: Village*."

I hadn't always been a hedonistic supervillain but after Mandy's death until her mental resurrection, I'd been in a dark place struggling to find a way to fill the void. Then the discovery she was possessed by Spellbinder had done an additional number to my brain. Vampire Mandy and I had been struggling to make common cause ever since. Ironically, the times we most felt alive when we were partying together like it was 1635 AD and we were both evil aristocrats. She'd been the one to introduce me to Dino Island.

"YOU SHALL DIE AT THE HANDS OF THE UNBORN!" The White Witch Queen shouted, raising up her hands to the cheering of the crowds.

"Man, why bother giving us a choice if you're not going to abide by it," I said, shaking my head. "This reminds me of when Cindy and I were banned from ComicCon. I told her, her drow cosplay was just deep purple makeup. I mean sure it was also lingerie and there were kids present but—"

Jack shook his head. "Please kill me now."

"GRANTED!" The White Witch Queen shouted.

That was when the gates around the area began to open up and I felt the nauseating presence of unnatural creatures that were antithetical to the nature of reality. They were the same ones I'd encountered during my heart attack and made me feel like I wanted to pass out then and there.

I couldn't help but think about what Lancel had told me, that I had defied my nature as the Chosen of Death, which had stuck at my very core. I was supposed to be the lowest god on the totem pole of divinity but a god I was, and this was like Zeus being against lightning or a horny bastard. Poseidon making deserts. Odin being a peacemaker.

Maybe the only way to fix things was either for me to die or to fix the balance between life and death. Which, in simple terms, meant either everyone I'd resurrected would have to die again or at least an equivalent number would have to. But if we were reduced to operating from *Final Destination* rules then the Great Author of the Universe had officially run out of ideas.

As before, the things that came slithering toward us looked like someone had gotten creative with their *Call of Cthulhu* or *Dungeons & Dragons' Far Realms* fan art. About the only thing I was grateful for regarding them was that they didn't seem to be interested in the *other* kind of art I'd seen with tentacle monsters.

"A reminder that this is all your fault," Jack said, starting to cast some spell that only required finger gestures.

"It's okay, I can handle these things," I replied. "Dungeon magic is the Open Game License solution to all your murdering needs."

"You know Wizards of the Coast tried to revoke that, right?" Jack replied, conjuring a wall of fire between us.

"No!" I said, genuinely horrified. "Is that legal?"

"They will make it legal," Jack said.

God, two prequel references in the span of a few minutes. Things had gotten bad. Of course, it was only Defcon 1 level if I started referring to the sequels. Like, Kylo Ren would have been a really good villain if they'd focused on the fact he was a school shooting-Alt Right-incel rather than try to make the guy redeemable.

Oh shit.

"*Fireball!*" I shouted, sending one over the wall of flames into the oncoming monster horde.

"It's no use!" Jack shouted. "The Unborn are truly immortal! They're mistakes woven into the fabric of creation! They'll just heal anything we throw at them!"

That was when a thing that looked like a combination of an illithid and a drider, a driderthid if you will, burst through the flame wall and howled at me. I cast a *Prismatic Spray* at it, causing it to explode into a thousand pieces that disintegrated into nothingness.

Jack stared at the sight while the crowd gasped. It was like Eighties Hulk Hogan or Rick Flair being beaten by a jobber. Oh, Merciful Moses, I'd been reduced to pro-wrestling metaphors.

"It looks like I'm the solution to immortality!" I said, proudly. "Mortality!"

Weirdly, killing the driderthid caused the pain building up in my chest to recede slightly. Maybe it was a coincidence or maybe my theory about equivalent exchange was correct. I'd brought back millions, possibly billions of people from the dead by remaking the universe to be a slightly kinder place. Now the receipt had come, and I'd forgotten my credit card.

However, by killing these immortals, normally unkillable— if that wasn't redundant—abominations, I could make it up to Death. My version of washing dishes to pay off the tab. Okay, I'd lost the metaphor there somewhere.

"They're breaking through!" Jack said, calling upon demons and gods I didn't recognize the names of to shoot beams of eldritch forces at the enemy. He also conjured hellfire with his pitchfork and blasted the attacking monsters. True to form, the monsters healed up almost instantly, but it kept them distracted enough for me to start raining down my own spells.

The mood of the crowd changed as they saw Unborn after Unborn annihilated by our sorcery. I didn't know what exactly had happened here on Tsavong Prime but if they had been persecuted by these creatures and couldn't kill them, only capture them, seeing them get their ass kicked was something that had to be pleasing. They were starting to cheer us on and that was visibly pissing off the White Witch Queen but there was something about her expression that told me she wasn't nearly as upset as she should be. Don't ask me why. It was just supervillain's intuition.

"Yes, we're doing it!" Jack shouted, weakening the Unborn enough for me to finish them off with my magic.

"And you jinxed it," I said, firing a single blast of magical force from a finger gun that blew off the last head of a hundred headed hydra-like thing. Now it just looked annoyed, headless but annoyed. It was also just one of a dozen other creatures still coming at us. "Yeah, I'm out."

"Wait, what?" Jack asked.

"I used up most of my spells fighting these things in my coma!" I snapped, falling back behind Jack. I checked my extra-dimensional pockets for some of the magic items I'd had my Dungeon magic practitioners make for me online, only to note I'd expended their content too. Apparently, three *wands of fireballs* weren't enough. "I have to rememorize everything now!"

"Are you serious!?" Jack asked, staring at me.

"I'm a wizard not a sorcerer!" I shouted. "There are rules!"

"From a goddamn board game made in the Eighties by ripping off Moorcock, Tolkien, and Jack Vance!" Jack said, showing a suspicious knowledge of *Dungeons & Dragons'* origins. "Gary Gygax is not a god!"

I stared at him. "The punk thing is just a facade, isn't it? You are a closet geek!"

"Memorize the god damned spells or we are going to die!" Jack shouted.

"Fine!" I said, pulling out a spiral notebook from my extra-dimensional pockets and started reading. "You're lucky I cheated and only need to read the names of the spells!"

"You forgot the names of the spells? How does that make sense?" Jack shouted, using his pitchfork like a flame thrower to hold back the Unborn but not doing a very good job of it.

"Magic!" I replied. "Also, don't you have magic pistols?"

"You stole mine!" Jack shouted before being grabbed by one of the horrific creatures that had more mouths than I could count.

"*MERCILESS' METEOR MADNESS!*" I shouted, calling upon another Ninth level spell that I'd memorized.

It was like *Meteor Swarm* but *more*. Doubly so since we were in space (and don't try to argue that the Earth is in space too). The sky cracked open and glowing flaming balls of fire rained down, slamming into the hordes of monsters throughout the area. It also was meant to hit the White Witch Queen as well, but she had a force field around herself.

Either way, the arena was now full of many charred and burned-out monsters that had previously been the stuff of nightmares. There had been some innocent casualties as well in the stands—assuming you considered aliens who loved watching innocent people die in an arena innocent—but there wasn't much I could do about that now.

Jack was lying on the ground, his clothes burned off and his trench coat in tatters. His half-demon heritage had protected him from most of the damage, but he still looked like he'd taken a severe beating. His pitchfork, at least, was unharmed.

"I hate you, Gary," Jack muttered as he tried to crawl to his feet.

"Yeah, I get that," I muttered, looking up at the White Witch Queen.

"I can't wait for Hasbro to sue you," Jack said, standing up.

"Parody is legally protected," I replied. "I'm in the clear with all use of D&D trademarks."

"That is not how copyright law works!" Jack shouted.

I was feeling strong, stronger than I'd probably felt at any point in my life save maybe when I'd fought Entropicus with all my friends' powers or seizing the power Merciful had accumulated through multiple planetary genocides. All the Unborn's final deaths had filled me with their divine energy and started healing spiritual wounds I hadn't even known I'd been suffering.

I could sense my followers clearer, ranging from the kobold tribe living in a twenty-level dungeon in my basement, an online fan club of teenage girls who worshiped me because I was hot, a group of middle-aged housewives for the same reason, and a group of roleplaying game occultists who thought I'd grant them magical powers (and I had!). I decided to look those guys up for a game if I made it through this.

That was when I heard the White Witch Queen laughing triumphantly. "Yes, the sacrifice is ready!"

Ah, damnit.

Chapter Nine

I Really Should Have Seen This Coming

"Gary, what have you done?" Jack asked, looking at me in horror.

"Who knows!" I said, throwing my hands up in the air. "It could be anything with me."

Which was probably the most honest I'd ever been in my life.

The White Witch Queen cackled like a, well, a witch as she raised her hands into the air. "The Crown of the Gods was damaged beyond repair, or so they thought, but still remains a powerful focus! But the true power to it can be restored with blood magic and the eldritch energies of the Unborn! The sacrifice of a tainted god, an oath breaker to his divine nature, will repair the crown and give me the ability to recreate this world as I see fit!"

"I think reality has had quite enough of that, thank you!" I shouted.

I admit, I'd screwed the pooch this time around. This was clearly a trap and I'd walked right into it. I was so used to dealing with overconfident dumbass villains—and sometimes heroes—who underestimated me that I'd completely missed the possibility that an intergalactic space witch might have enough respect for me to use me as part of her evil plan.

Live and learn.

"Jack, we have to—" I started to say only to blasted in the back by raw black magic.

Honestly, what I knew about real sorcery could be fit between the pages of a Simon *Necronomicon* (if you don't get that joke, look it up online). However, I was pretty sure that if I'd been a normal human being, that blast would have obliterated me outright. Whether it was because Dungeon magic granted its users hit points, the fact I was now more godlike than I'd ever been outside of my fight with Entropicus, or some other factor—it only hurt like hell. Either way, Jack was trying to kill me again. He wasn't holding back either as I perhaps stupidly had hoped he would after getting to know me. When did I become a frigging optimist?

"Son of a bitch," I muttered, falling on the ground. "Are we still doing this?"

"Sorry, Gary," Jack said, summoning a glowing ball of fire. "Except, I'm not sorry at all."

"*She's* the enemy!" I shouted, conjuring a *Globe of Invulnerability* that absorbed the blast completely.

The Tsavong crowd's mood was incredibly fickle as they immediately got into the two champions fighting it out between them. I had to admit, were I into blood sports, I would have admitted they were getting their money's worth. I couldn't see a way out of this without killing Jack and I wasn't one hundred percent sure I could do that. Jack was another opponent who didn't underestimate me, and I had a feeling he would be going all out to take me down. It made me wonder if he'd been holding back against the Unborn in hopes that I would exhaust myself. If so, he would regret letting me re-memorize my spells.

That was when he easily tore away my defensive spell with a wave of his hand. "This is bigger than her, Gary! You're a threat to everything there is!"

"Yes! Yes!" The White Witch Queen said, watching us. Honestly, it was clear she was getting aroused by this and that was… distracting. Seriously, I'm not into macrophilia normally, but I was getting some weird feelings here. My kinks were tame really and aside from my weird desire to sex up a dragon, I didn't have many I'd be ashamed to admit in public.

"Don't make me destroy you!" I said, not feeling at all confident as I dispelled the next curse that shot a horrifying black ribbon at me made of anti-matter.

"Your Dungeon magic is a joke, Gary!" Jack said, continuing to invoke the power of demons, angels, and pagan gods regardless of their contradictory nature. The benefits of being a polytheist I suppose. "You should have taken that *Mystery Science Theater 3000 job* and left supervillainy forever!"

"Felicia Day complained!" I said, teleporting out of the way with a *Blink* spell before the ground dissolved a foot deep around me. "She, totally erroneously, believed I was a guy who sent her a bunch of weird e-mails a decade ago. That was Cindy, dammit!"

"Choose your next words carefully, Merciless," Jack said, levitating into the air in what was an innate ability for superhero sorcerers. Which annoyed me. "They're probably going to be your last. *By the Power of the Hoary Hosts of Hagramor, I banish this foul denizen to the blackest pits of Hell!*"

"Whore-y hosts? That's a real spell?" I asked, briefly imagining a bunch of demon prostitutes dragging me off to Hell. Which, okay, if you were going to specifically kill me was probably the way to do it.

I could feel the magical change to the air, though, and knew that Jack wasn't joking. He'd also come up with a clever solution to the fact that killing me would empower the White Witch Queen, which was do a spell that would carry me off to a dimension of eternal torment. Given I'd personally killed off a few Archdemons and irritated the Queen of Hell, Tiamat, by asking if she had a five headed dragon form, that was probably a good place to send me if you never wanted to see me again.

"Hoar is a type of frost, dipshit!" Jack said. "*Begone!*"

Unfortunately, flippancy wasn't going to save me. Which was a shame since flippancy was the thing I did best. The floor opened beneath me as I saw the flames of Hell burst up along with various nasty looking hands and leathery wings spread forth. The damned were always eager to escape—can't imagine why—and seemed especially hungry for me.

Jack's spell didn't just end with the opening of the portal beneath me, though. Either he didn't realize magic was incredibly screwed up in this area due to all of the Unborn or because he'd messed up the spell itself. Either way, the portal to Hell that I fled from by levitating upward and turning insubstantial was far from the only rift that was occurring. Instead, there were tears starting to appear everywhere around us.

Not all of them were to Hell—which was a rare sentence— but tore holes in space time to the Alchemical Plane of Fire, Platonic Realm of Forms, other alien worlds, and deep space among other locations. If that sounded cool, note that a lot of those were innately hostile to living things and a few of the rifts opened in the bleachers. Screams of horror and terror filled the air as the crowds were subject to even more horrifying death. I wasn't a big fan of the Tsavong, but Jack had crossed a line here. Which, weirdly, offended me more than his trying to kill me.

"Why won't you die!" Jack shouted, intensifying the magic that was tearing reality apart around us. The Hell portal grew around me as I felt it trying to pull me in like with an explosive decompression-like effect.

"*Dimension Door,*" I whispered, causing two portals to appear in the area, one directly in front of me and one directly behind Jack. Then I pointed my finger behind his head and shouted, "*Power Word Kill!*"

I honestly expected it to backfire on me or bounce off. Instead, no, the spell went cleanly through whatever defenses the Trench Coat Magician had and sent him spiraling down into his own Hell portal. The demons tore his body to pieces and then dragged them down, no longer ascending to try to grab me. I could see his brains splattered down on the ground from where the grizzly destruction of his skull had occurred. His pitchfork lay untouched, glowing with hellish power.

Shit.

If you remembered the Rules of Supervillainy, the actual rules rather than the title of my biography's first volume, you'd know the first one is never to kill a superhero. I'd killed superheroes before in members of the Extreme!, but they were heroes in name only and worked for the fascist President Omega. The Trench Coat Magician was another matter entirely and I felt like it was a ridiculous waste for him to die.

"I made up all that bonding stuff I told you!" I shouted at his corpse, picking up his pitchfork. I felt disgusted with myself. It was a rare feeling for me after killing someone. "I hate golf and the only movies I've ever made for my private use only! I've only ever wanted to be a supervillain! Oh, and Cindy never did porn! She only does tasteful erotic movies!"

It didn't make me feel better. Worse, looking among the scattered remains of the dead hero's brain matter was electrical circuits and wires that I recognized from a late-night special on *Dateline*. It was mind-control hardware from PHANTOM. The kind that required grabbing someone and subjecting them to a six-hour surgery because otherwise mind-control was inconsistent at best.

It not only told me the Trench Coat Magician hadn't been acting of his own free will—meaning I'd killed an innocent man, something that had only happened like, ten times in my career—but that PHANTOM or some remnant of it was still around despite the fact I'd literally wrote them out of reality. Which meant the Nazis were back.

Double shit.

"Hahahaha," the voice of the White Witch Queen said, dripping with contempt. "It seems even your own allies are willing to turn against you Merciless, Failure God and Fallen Chosen One of Death."

I stared up at her, noticing the arena was now mostly empty as either the attendees had fled or had been killed. Which wasn't my fault, by the way. The Hell portal was still open, and I fired a *Delayed Blast Fireball* into it, giving me a second to escape to another part of the arena.

"You don't know me, Lady," I said, worrying about being alone in opposing Hot Lady Sauron here.

"On the contrary," the White Witch Queen said. "I know you well, Merciless. The Chosen of Death who rewrote the universe to be a pale, pathetic, pleasant version of itself. You lacked the imagination to either make it a paradise or a hell that you ruled openly. You are infamous throughout the dimensions as the one who cast down Entropicus, slew the Great Beast Zul-Barbas, and are destined to inherit the title of Earth's Supreme Archmage."

Oh crap, someone else who thought I was way more competent than I am. "Lady, you've got me all wrong. You know the old TV show *Get Smart*? The spy parody from the Sixties that starred Inspector Gadget's voice actor? I'm basically the supervillain version of that. Bumbling dude who somehow is in charge despite his hotter female coworkers being far more competent. Specifically, ones who are inexplicably attracted to him. I can't explain it."

"I will drink the marrow from your bones," the White Witch Queen hissed. She lifted her hands in the air and green energy began to gather around them. "If your own partner was unable to be the one to slay you, God of Death and Rebellion, I shall happily do the deed myself. Tonight, Gary the Pink shall die!"

Every time someone brought up that title, I died a little inside. "Can we talk about that name? Is there a place I can appeal it? Some sort of wizard's council? If I'm Death's champion, Gary the Black is an obvious pick. Hell, I'm even open for Gary the Many-Colored. I played Joseph once in my high school version of the *Technicolor Dreamcoat*. Plus, I'd like to show my LGBTAS+ allyship. You know, Lesbian, Gay, Bisexual, Trans, Asexual, and Supers Plus."

"Die!" the White Witch Queen shouted, throwing the green ball on the ground where I stood.

I normally had some sort of response to this situation. I would cast a spell or whip out some sort of magical item to help myself. Unfortunately, I'd exhausted all of those, too, in my attempts to kill off all of the Unborn. Three wands definitely weren't enough when dealing with hordes of aberrations.

It had to happen eventually, but I was going to get written into the *Book of the Dead*—legally distinct from *The Book of Midnight*—permanently and this was about as good a place for it to happen as any. Dying at the hands of an all-powerful alien archmage at least wasn't how I expected to die (and if you want to know that, it's in bed with either Mandy or Cindy when they lose control—you love a vampire or werewolf then you take your chances).

Holding up the late Trench Coat Magician's pitchfork, I prepared for my end in eldritch fire only to feel the weapon absorb all of the energy aimed at me before shaking with the newly acquired power within. Turning it around, I aimed it at the White Witch Queen and released its collected force. The explosion shot forth from its throbbing shaft and splashed all over her.

Which is totally not how I should have phrased that.

Yes, it seemed Jack Hellraiser's pitchfork was designed for the purposes of not only channeling magic but redirecting it as well. It transformed in my hand, shifting and changing from a trident—I somehow got the sense that it was very firmly a trident and not a pitchfork—into a sword that could best be described as, "someone forged this after watching a lot of anime while listening to a bunch of power metal."

It was wholly impractical looking for a sword, with a serrated blade, spikes sticking out of the hilt, a glowing purple gemstone, and proportions way too large for a single-handed blade. Nevertheless, I felt it channel the unholy energies around me and cause my body to shake with power. I decided, in a moment of Gary-oscity—dictionary defined as "the state of being or related to being like Gary"—to name it the Merciless Sword.

Yeah, real original, I know.

The rest of the arena was still falling apart, though, with the dimensional rifts starting to interact with one another in a way that couldn't be good. Green lightning crackled between them, and monsters began pouring out of every side. I could hear alarms throughout the abandoned city outside as starships started to take off from the planet.

I had no idea if we had an Alderaan situation brewing here, but I wouldn't have been surprised, and I needed to focus on figuring out a way to prevent that from happening. The Tsavong might be an interstellar race of conquering slavers and fascists, but they didn't deserve...okay, I lost my train of thought somewhere. What was I saying? Oh yeah, there were probably kids here and I didn't want to blow up the planet because the next generation was probably going to be less of a bunch of assholes.

"Hahahahaha," a soft female voice spoke, distracting me from my moment of triumph.

"What in the world?" I asked, looking up to where I'd reflected the White Witch Queen's magic back at her.

Standing there, not remotely obliterated, was the White Witch Queen. Except her orange skin was mummified against her flesh and her long white hair was stringy as well as hanging from her. Her eyes had rotted away, only to be replaced with glowing white braziers of Unborn magic. Her zombie-like form made her formerly tight cleavage-displaying outfit hang off her like a loose shroud.

"I see," I muttered. "So, it's not the White Witch Queen. It's the White *Lich* Queen."

The mad alien despot fingered a bit of her hair and twirled it around her forefinger. "Do not like my true form, Merciless? You found me beautiful once."

In the words of Ashley "Ash" Williams, Patron Saint of Monster Slayers from the *Evil Dead* movies, I said, "Lady, you got real ugly."

I had questions about Princess Vashti's claims about being her daughter now and wondered if I'd been catfished. Which, I suppose, was better than the alternative.

The White Lich Queen didn't seem to find that amusing as she put her hands on her hips. "I have seen your future, Merciless. Do you know what the stars have portended for you?"

I started looking for a way out of this situation because I didn't exactly have time to start reading my spell book again and had used up my most powerful spell that I'd rememorized to take down Jack. I had only a couple of second-level spells left and none of them were combat focused.

"Cloudy with a chance of rain?" I asked. "I'm not really into the whole astrology thing, Lady. I figure all of those cosmic alignment charts got thrown out of whack when we started the debate over whether Pluto was a planet."

At this point, I decided I'd failed in my mission here and needed to make a rare retreat. Maybe if I'd had the real Reaper's Cloak or the scythe, I'd stand a chance, but I didn't. There was a reason that *Dungeons & Dragons* wizards fought with parties rather than alone.

"Failure," the White Lich Queen said, sneering with her desiccated lips. "Both personally and professionally.

"Your reconstruction of the universe is falling apart and all those you sought to bring back from the dead are doomed to die once more, in worse agony than before. You betrayed Death by trying to restore Ultragod and the other fallen heroes. You betrayed your spouse by forcing her into being the undead horror that she secretly loathes being. You betrayed the mothers of your children by constantly forcing them to be second best to a dead woman."

I paused, stopping my search for an exit. "Okay, this is getting a little personal. Do you read my blog? Where the hell are you getting all this?"

The White Lich Queen chuckled as the skies turned green and I started to see buildings in the backdrop of the arena's skyline collapse. Tsavong Prime was starting to collapse. Worse, their Empress didn't give a shit about it. She was entirely focused on me. "I have made a study of you and your career, Merciless. I even sent my agents to acquire books of your hedge wizardry. It took me a few weeks to master them."

Oh crap.

"You did?" I asked.

"Allow me to demonstrate,' the White Lich Queen said, pointing down at me. "*Time Stop*."

Dammit.

Chapter Ten

Hard Truths

Time Stop was, in my humble opinion, the most ridiculously overpowered spell in all of Dungeon magic and that included *Wish*. It was a bit like super-speed, which in real life was pretty much the reason that the Society of Superheroes never actually lost a fight when the Bronze Medalist or the events in which his family participated. People thought Ultragod was overpowered? Pfft. There's literally nothing that tops the ability to take multiple actions per turn, except maybe magic.

Because magic had *Time Stop*.

It was a self-explanatory spell. The caster causes time to stop around themselves and everyone around them is frozen, but they remain able to do whatever the hell they want. Stab someone in the eye, loot their pockets, draw erotic art, or whatever.

I'd considered banning *Time Stop* from the spells available to mere mortals via Dungeon magic, much like *Wish*, but I'd been convinced by Leia that time manipulation was the innate right of wannabe chronomancers like herself. Given I was now frozen in place with the Merciless Sword in my hands—but fully aware—it was probably going to go down as my final mistake in a career full of them.

Interestingly, you would have thought I wouldn't be aware while stopped. It would, from my perspective, just go from the moment I was frozen until when the spell ended. That wasn't the case and it made me wonder if the magic was more a form of paralysis. I never actually bothered to learn the physics behind how Dungeon magic worked and that was probably another thing that my scientist daughters would have been infuriated by.

Then again, my consciousness wasn't the only thing unaffected by the *Time Stop* magic that had frozen pieces of debris in the air, my physical body, and the last few fleeing citizens trying to get out of the arena. No, I saw the rifts around me were continuing to grow and throw more strange energy into the air. The White Lich Queen merrily strolled down the steps that led from her balcony to my side, passing by a few terrified frozen Praetorian Guards that she pushed aside like so much rubbish.

"Do you know what I will do once I have absorbed your energy, Gary?" the White Lich Queen said. "I am going to reboot the world exactly as you did, but I will not be limited by your lack of imagination. I am going to end humanity. It will never have existed, along with so many of your histories and conflicts. They will be not even a foot note. But I will make sure that their spirits are reincarnated in other species. I will inflict unimaginable humiliations upon your mates, your children, and your allies. They will be slaves subject to degradations from which they will beg for death, and tortures that would break the mind of the strongest warrior. You, however, Gary will be unchanged? Stripped of your magic and the honors of Death—something I think you've already done to yourself—I will force you to *watch*. Watch as the universe you created to be your utopia becomes a hell for every sentient being in the cosmos."

Unfortunately, for her, the White Lich Queen hadn't studied the rules of Dungeon magic very clearly. There was one big difference between it and the kind in the rulebooks: *talking wasn't a free action.* Feeling the spell collapse and the energy enter the Merciless Sword, I proceeded to blast her with hellfire in the face. It distracted her only for a second before I shouted, *"Web!"*

The White Lich Queen screamed as the flames died on her body, but her eyes and mouth were covered in a thick viscous substance that I had shot forth. Okay, seriously, I wasn't doing this deliberately. It would only hold her for a second as I cast my last spell, *"Merciless Hand of Grabbing!"*

A long, glowing, day-glow green hand emerged from my fingertips, not particularly large or strong but capable of getting the job done. Okay, maybe I *was* doing this deliberately. The enchantment grabbed the Crown of the Gods off of the White Lich Queen before pulling it back to my hands. I felt it burn against my skin as the divine energy I'd stolen from the Unborn was now flowing between us.

"Imbecile! You have no magic worth speaking of to enhance!" The White Lich Queen shouted once she pulled the webbing from her face.

I briefly wondered if I could just destroy her outright with a wave of my hand like I'd done to Dracula. Unfortunately, just thinking about that gave me a firm NO from somewhere beyond my consciousness. I'd offended Death, just like Lancel Warren had said, and she'd stripped me of powers I hadn't even known I'd lost. Once I'd been trusted with the power to send the undead and wayward ghosts (who were just the dead) on to their final resting place. I'd been so caught up in my false paradise that I'd ignored that I'd royally screwed the pooch with my cosmic patron. Great. Another thing I had to make right if I survived this.

"I have a different idea," I said, figuring that if I was supposed to be sacrificed to give her the energy to repair it, there was another option.

I put the crown on my head. An unending series of possibilities filled my imagination as I saw the Multiverse stretch before me. I saw Case's cyberpunk dystopia, Jane's vampire and werewolf filled planet, John Henry Booth's hellish wasteland ruled by the Great Old Ones, and a world where politicians were honest. Okay, I was making that last one up. However, I saw how the future and past interacted as well as how these worlds interacted with my own. Case's world would eventually be discovered by aliens and become a *Star Trek*-esque utopia before falling apart to become the reality Cassius Mass, space pirate, lived in.

That world's humans would eventually master science to ascend to become Vorlon-and-Q-like beings before creating their own fantastic planets with everything from elves to magic. Which seemed like a step backward to be honest, even if I did like fantasy series that did that sort of thing like *Dragon Riders of Pern* or *Shannara*. Either way, the cosmos was mine to rewrite and make mine as I willed.

Again.

My world? Like a magic eight ball, I couldn't see past the inky blackness of the immediate future and got the message, "Vision fuzzy. Try again later." Hopefully, that wasn't a sign my world didn't have one.

The White Lich Queen had enough of a face left to look terrified. "Shit."

I smiled, staring at her. "Do not mess with the Master of the Universe."

I punched her in the face and her body shattered into uncountable sparkles of light, her spirit moving on to her Soul Jar that I planned to destroy just in case. Because, really, it turned out liches were an actual thing, and you couldn't leave these things alone.

That was when the world exploded.

Well, sort of.

I may be exaggerating for dramatic effect. More precisely, the rifts around me started to merge and multiply exponentially. The effect was enough to start tearing the planet apart. If I'd more experience with the Crown of the Gods, I might have figured out a way to save it, but the tiny remnant of the planet's population was already disappearing into the craters emerging throughout the world. Volcanoes were exploding and the odds of anything surviving past this point were approximately jack and shit.

There was also an incredibly selfish motivation lumped in with the sheer practicality of realizing Tsavong Prime was a lost cause: I needed to save the Crown of the Gods power to save the Earth. Yeah, yeah, *Star Trek* and other sci-fi says I shouldn't love my home planet above any other world in the cosmos since we were all equally important. Yeah, well *Star Trek* can suck it. My Earth came first because that's where my family was, goddammit.

Still, I had no idea how to teleport across the cosmos either, and I wasn't sure if it was as easy as clicking my heels three times to come back to Kansas. The Crown of the Gods showed me I could do anything, but it didn't come with an instruction manual and my last attempt to rewrite reality had apparently backfired horribly.

So, instead, I jumped into one of the rifts. "Geronimo!"

That was when the world exploded behind me.

For real this time.

And I should point out that as the second planet I may have accidentally destroyed, there was a lot of blame to go around. This wasn't something I was planning on making a habit of.

Nazi-Earth shouldn't really count as a planet anyway, it was more of an eyesore. I also fully attribute this to being the White Lich Queen's fault and if anyone asks you at the Intergalactic Court, that's my story and I'm sticking to it. Assuming I managed to survive long enough to be brought to trial for geocide. Is that what you call blowing up a planet? I didn't look it up on the Superpedia.

I probably should have checked to see where the portal I'd jumped through led, for example. Because it dumped me in the middle of the sky, several thousand feet in the air, spiraling down toward a frozen mountainside below.

"Dammit!" I shouted, trying to figure out if I'd memorized *Feather Fall* before I hit the ground and realizing even if I did, it would end before I came anywhere near the ground. If Gary Gygax had been running this as a tabletop game, his official Word of God ruling as Dungeonmaster would be, 'Time to roll up a new character, chief.'

Well screw that.

I'd put in forty years into developing Gary Karkofsky AKA Merciless: The Supervillain without Mercy™, give or take a couple of reboots, and I wasn't about to throw him away. Sheathing the Merciless Sword in the extradimensional folds of my costume, I waited for some genius idea to pop into my head as I sped toward the ground at an increasingly high rate of speed.

None came.

My cloak's levitation powers, a pale imitation of the ones I'd gotten from the real Reaper's Cloak, weren't doing great. I didn't have a fly spell and attempts to get my spell book out resulted in it flying from my hands into the air. Yeah, that was going to look good on the video played at my funeral.

Crap.

Oh yeah, I had the frigging Crown of the Gods on my head and knew how to wield phenomenal cosmic power, but figuring out how to use it to save my life from splattering against the ground like a bug against a windshield was apparently beyond my efforts. The second time in as many minutes I'd tried to use it but found my ignorance of magic as well as my powers stifling an attempt to do good. I debated what my last words would be, closed my eyes, and ended up muttering, "I only have one regret." Which just caught a bunch of snow and ice in my throat that caused me to choke.

What was my one regret? Was it rebooting reality and utterly screwing up the universe? No. No it was not. Getting myself captured and missing the first five years of Leia's life because I was trapped in a weird supernatural prison by Merciful? Not that either. The entire emotional and mental disaster of Spellbinder possessing Mandy's body and turning Diabloman against me?

No. Though that was related.

It was getting Mandy killed and resurrecting her as a monster she hated. It was only in my final moments I really acknowledged how monumentally selfish and self-destructive that had been for me. How much Mandy—the vampire she'd become at least—put on a brave face, and pretended to enjoy the life I'd condemned her to. I should have been there for her more and accepted who she was, undead abomination and serial killer of evil doers that she was. Let her know that I accepted her for the monster she was. Okay, probably not in those words.

It would have been a depressing but appropriate note to go out on, but as you're only about halfway through the latest volume of my biography, I think you can probably guess there's slightly more story to come. There's probably a book where the protagonist is killed in the middle of it before the story switches narrators, but we have a word for that kind of avant garde twist: crap writing.

So, seconds before I became nothing more than road pizza, I found gravity cease to exist around me. A glowing Glinda the Good Witch-esque ball of light appeared around me, keeping me from dying horribly. It made me wonder whether I'd been rescued by Ultragod again since I'd once been captured in one of these, or even Gabrielle but it didn't have the same beautiful golden light. Instead, it was a dark shadowy, well, translucent black. You know, like when you put a black t-shirt up against your face and can see past it if you try hard enough? No? Just me? Okay then.

"Hello?" I asked, wondering who my rescuer was and wondering if I'd gone from the frying pan into the fire. I immediately dismissed that thought since a *planet exploding* was pretty much my definition of the hottest fire possible. Even when I blew up Nazi-Earth, I'd gone back in time to fix it and ended up killing my first Hitler. Yeah, that was how it got started. In the revised timeline, the planet ended up inhabited by a bunch of hippies who had a United World of Democratic Countries by 1977. Then it got blown up by Entropicus during a big crisis event but that wasn't my fault.

Nothing was my fault.

The credo of the supervillain.

If you repeated it often enough, you sometimes even believed it.

"Hello, Mr. Karkofsky," a deep baritone voice spoke, with a slight English accent.

The shadow bubble disappeared around me and I fell about ten feet, landing in a pile of snow and rolling down on the ground. I was at the foot of a mountaintop's highest peak with a fantastic view of, well, more snow-covered mountains. It made me start to want to hum the *Skyrim* theme. Either that or conjure a pair of skis.

I searched for the source of the voice and felt the man's presence before I saw him. It was like being washed over with cold water, which wasn't a great thing in the middle of a snowy mountain. Yeah, it was damn cold, and I didn't even have any 1st level spells left to warm me.

Turning around, I saw a six-foot-six faceless figure in a hooded black robe. He looked a great deal like Peter Jackson's Ringwraiths or Dementors, but on steroids. He had a professional wrestler's build and was wearing frost-covered armor underneath it. His presence was more singularly intimidating than just about anyone I'd met other than perhaps a handful of people, Entropicus and Ultragod among them.

I also sensed the spark of the divine. Monotheist as I might be, I'd met a few gods and gods among gods in my time: Death, Odin, Adonis, and the Great Beast Zul-Barbas. They all shared a similar energy that was hard to put into words, but you knew it when you felt it. It was the biggest proof that god wasn't just something people called you but a separate race of beings like *homo sapiens* versus Neanderthals or DMV attendants. I used to have the tiniest whiff of it and since killing the Unborn and wearing the Crown of Gods, I had a lot more of it.

Oh, and behind the guy was a dragon. It wasn't the largest dragon I'd ever seen, which is a rare statement unless you lived in Westeros or Krynn, but about the size of an elephant, not including tail or neck length. It possessed a brilliant blue set of scales and a sleek feminine style, which was weird to say about a dragon, but I called 'em like I saw 'em.

I'd always loved dragons, which was an odd thing to bring up. But it was one of my weirdest hangups since I felt guilty about it. I'd met two dragons in my lifetime, one the shapeshifted cultist who killed my wife and the second being the Dragon King. Both had been evil creatures that had inflicted misery on my family—but I still loved the beings. Maybe it was the dinosaur-loving kid inside me.

"Hi," I said, realizing that both were waiting for my response. "I am Gary Karkofsky, the Pink Wizard! I mean, Merciless: The Supervillain without Mercy! I make the people fall down! Do you speak English? Hebrew? I can even mangle some Klingon. Seriously, when I had the Reapers' Cloak, I spoke all languages. Wait, you introduced yourself in English. I feel like an idiot."

Okay, not my best introduction. The thing was I actually did have a *Comprehend Languages* spell woven into my current cloak, but my brain was a bit flustered from getting my ass kicked ten ways from Sunday.

"You feeling like an idiot is probably your natural state, Gary," the dragon said in a soft female voice incongruous with being a thirteen-thousand-pound reptile with wings. Or were dragons birds? Was it a *Jurassic Park* thing? If so, why didn't dragons have feathers? I would question that they probably should as flying creatures, but the fact was that I'd met three now and all three of them had been completely lacking in plumage. They also had very bat-like wings despite the fact that bats were mammals.

Focus, Gary!

"Yeah, probably," I admitted. "So, uh, who are you two, Ms. Dragon and Mr. Nazgul?"

The Ringwraith-looking fellow said, "My name is Jacob Riverson, Gary. This is my companion, Ketra. I am the King Below and a Wraith Knight. The Dark Lord of my world and a lord of evil as well as cold. I'm here on behalf of Death."

Well, that was a helluva introduction. "What does she want?"

"She wants me to teach you how to be a god."

Chapter Eleven

God Lessons from A Legally Distinct Sauron Substitute

"Teach me how to be a god?" I asked Jacob, which was an odd name for a Ringwraith. Sorry, Wraith Knight. "Sorry, I'm already in enough trouble with my rabbi."

Jacob sighed, which was impressive for a man with seemingly no physical body under that hood and armor. "Gary, this will go far easier if you just shut up and listen."

"Why would I want it to be easier?" I asked, looking at the dragon to avoid meeting the gaze of someone with no eyes.

"I feel I have gained vast insight into your soul," Jacob muttered, grumbling. "But to start with, the Crown of the Gods is resting on your head and causing you to disintegrate."

"Ha!" I said, mocking him. "I don't know what you're—"

That was when I noticed my skin was flaking off. The energy from the Crown of Gods was interacting with the Unborn's stolen power. My veins were turning a bright green and I could see arcs of electricity swirling around me. I didn't feel bad—quite the opposite really. I suspected that was a very bad sign. I supposed this must have been what Gollum had been feeling as he turned from a hobbit into a cannibalistic cave monster.

"Well shit," I muttered. "What happens if I don't take it off?"

"You will become as the White Witch Queen," Jacob said. "A being who cannot die but cannot truly live either."

I stabbed the Merciless Sword in the ground and removed the Crown of the Gods. "I'd rather be dead-dead."

Undeath was something that I held an instinctual revulsion for, not simply because just about everyone did outside of young adult novels. To be caught between the worlds was to divorce you from all the wonders of life and give you only a pale shadow of its joys in return. You could only experience an echo of what you enjoyed before your death. I knew because, well, I'd experienced a hint of it with every undead I'd destroyed or fed upon. It was something that Mandy had once alluded to. She could never stop loving me, but it would always be second to her true need of blood.

"And yet you forced the state of undeath on your wife," Ketra the dragon said, seemingly reading my mind.

Ouch. Low blow there. "She adjusted."

"Did she?" Ketra asked. "Or did she simply learn—in between her time being possessed by Spellbinder and in the future—to playact the role of a living woman? Someone happy and content being your consort while hungering for the blood of the living?"

"This is way too personal a conversation to be having with two complete strangers and since I'd avoided having anything similar with the people I loved, I'm going to make like a tree and get out of here," I said, having no idea how to do that. I just needed to find where my spell book papers had flown off to, find a *Teleport without Error* spell, and get myself back home to cure the Nanoplague.

Moses wouldn't be happy with me blowing up the Tsavong homeworld, but the benefit of employing a supervillain was plausible deniability. I suspected he was more likely to be upset over Jack Hellraiser's death. That was harder to pin on the White Witch Queen since my capacity to lie to the world's greatest superhero was between zero and minus infinity.

"Good luck with that," Jacob said.

"Toodles, Lord Soth," I said, remembering I had an all-powerful artifact that could take me anywhere I wanted. I tried to figure out how the Crown of the Gods could be used to transport me across time and space. Instead, it filled my mind with countless realities, and I couldn't sort through them all to where I wanted to go. Dammit.

"Don't," Jacob said, pointing at me.

"Don't what?" I asked.

"Don't make *Monty Python and the Holy Grail* jokes," Jacob said.

I blinked then raised my pointer finger in the air. "You have *Monty Python and the Holy Grail* jokes on Fantasy World?"

"The World Between," Jacob said, "And yes, our archives are quite extensive. This is one of those post-apocalypse far future fantasy worlds. Death explained your entire history to me in a twelve-hour dream that also included relevant pop culture references. I admit, I was expecting a bit different from meeting the most powerful god in the multiverse."

Okay, that was more meta than I was expecting, but at least it gave me a sense of what I was dealing with here.

"The World Between?" I asked, skeptically.

"Yeah, that's what our world is called," Jacob said. "It's between the World Above, Heaven for lack of a better point of reference, and the World Below, which is the Underworld."

"You could say it's a *Middle Earth*," I replied, smirking. I didn't know why I was joking around as much as I was. Maybe it was because I was honestly unnerved by this guy and not just because he was the first undead horror I'd encountered that I didn't feel any compulsion to send on its way. No, instead, he felt like he was a part of the universe and every bit as important to its function as gravity. It sounded weird when put into words but *felt* accurate.

Jacob felt his face, which was impressive since he was an insubstantial ghost. "I can see this is going to take a while."

"Are you really going to waste time on this guy, Jacob?" Ketra asked.

"I'm afraid so," Jacob said. "Mr. Karkofsky is a constant of his universe and important to its stability but he's now dealing with forces far beyond his ability to deal with them. Clever tricks and luck will not avail him anymore. He must be trained."

"I'm eighteenth level," I said, dryly. "I think I can handle myself."

"Ah, yes, *Dungeons & Dragons*," Jacob said. "I've been informed about that too."

I blinked. "Death staging an intervention for me is really weirding me out. However, if she wanted me trained, why not come herself?"

"She has an affection for people like you," Jacob said. "But you broke her heart with your betrayal."

"There's no one like me," I said, puffing up my chest. I was ignoring the betrayal comment right now.

Jacob's expression, well, I had no idea for obvious reasons but somehow projected annoyance.

"What's your level? I doubt there's anything you can teach me I haven't already used Dungeon magic to give myself."

"In your fictional game world rules?" Jacob asked. "That in no way reflect reality? The ones that you are using your divine power to inflict on the rest of your world?"

"Ah ha!" I said, pointing at his chest. "That's where you are incorrect! I have a magic spell that allows me to know what anyone's level is! It approximates the capacities of even non-gamers. It's one of the few spells I have left!"

"We don't have time for—" Jacob started to say.

"*Know Level!*" I shouted, throwing my hands into the air.

Jacob sighed. "Fine."

I stared at him. The information on display was like the Matrix code for what he could do. "You son of a bitch. Sixty-seventh level? What is this *World of Warcraft* bullshit? Oh God, you're a raid boss, aren't you? Unfair!"

"Are we sure he's not insane?" Ketra asked.

"Death didn't tell me he wasn't insane," Jacob said, perhaps admitting something a lot of people had been hesitant to point out. "Gary, you're a mediocre wizard and everything you've got is stolen, given to you, or taken from magical items."

"I'd argue mediocre is being generous," I said, showing a rare moment of honesty. "People spend decades learning sorcery-sorcery and even then, it doesn't always pan out. You must sell your soul to demons, swear yourself to gods—which amounts to the same thing depending on the religion—possess the right bloodline, or have a focusing object. That's why Dungeon magic exists. It's the great equalizer of sorcery."

"In the same way that handing a loaded gun to a child is, I suspect," Jacob said, causing me to look at it in an entirely new way.

"You have guns here too?" I asked, trying to deflect the conversation.

"Yes, Gary," Jacob replied. "It's just we also have magic swords and arrows that can blow up castles."

"Cindy would love this place," I said, pausing to consider events. I was intrigued by the prospect of learning from Jacob but had a mission to complete. "Well, Cindy would love it if you have any parts that are warmer. However, I need to get this crown back to Earth. I don't have time to go to magical trade school."

"In addition to being a mediocre wizard, Gary, you have been blessed with godhood by Death," Jacob said. "A reward for winning the Eternity Tournament. You will never age, and you can share your power with your followers as well as work miracles to answer their prayers. To answer the question of 'what is the purpose of life.' That is your burden now."

Death had bestowed this all without a by-your-leave. I'd been happy serving as the occasional psychopomp for wayward ghosts and pulling off a variety of heists with my ever-increasing family. I had my problems—Spellbinder impersonating my wife for one—but they'd been miniscule compared to the ones I'd had after getting divinity. It turned out when you accepted the job of being Chosen of a Primal, though, you eventually had to pay the bill. It's just paying the bill was what most wizards, particularly evil ones, had no intention of paying. They saw godhood the Greek way, all perks and no responsibilities.

"I never asked for that," I replied, dryly. "I don't want it."

Ketra chuckled, causing a bit of flame to shoot out of her mouth. "Jon Snow reference! I get that one."

"Okay, now you're telling me you have HBO here?" I asked, confused. "Also, that was unintentional for once. I dropped off Westeros after the last season. Cindy is back into it due to *House of the Dragon* but I dunno. Once burned, twice shy. I still can't get into any of the new *Star Wars* series after the train wreck that was the last sequel."

"People need gods, Gary," Jacob said. "Whether they call them such or not. They need someone to embody the goods as well as the bads. Whether they are called heroes, villains, ideals, or ideas. It is as important as breathing."

"Don't let Richard Dawkins hear you say that," I said, pausing. "Fun fact: he married one of the Companions from classic *Doctor Who*."

"You are meant to usher the Age of Heroes to its end," Jacob explained. "I have been witness to that sort of thing myself. For the world to move on, it needs to be allowed to die just like a person does."

"I don't want the Age of Heroes to die!" I snapped. "You just said people need heroes!"

"And they need new ones," Jacob said, sighing. "That is why Death turned her face from you and this world is suffering so badly. You won the Eternity Tournament and Death became the Primal in ascendant. An end to the resurrections and a chance for the victories of the good over the evil, yes, indeed, the evil over the good too, to have meaning. You then used Merciful, the insane twisted parody of yourself, to undo that change, and brought back trillions. A thing only you could have done."

"It made the world better!" I shouted, tossing the crown on the ground, and pulling the Merciless Sword out.

Jacob stretched out his hand like Darth Vader and the Crown of the Gods shot into his hands with telekinesis.

"Well, crap," I muttered. "I really fell for that."

"The world is dying, Gary," Jacob said. "The first victims will be the people you saved but then your sin will compound and trillions more will perish. Destroying the Unborn helps right some of the wrongs, but a sacrifice needs to be made to right the balance. Let me help."

I had no response for that. Because I knew it was true.

Jacob put the Crown of the Gods on his head.

"No, don't put the crown on!" I said, watching Jacob do just that.

113

The Crown of the Gods glowed, and I shielded my face from what I expected to be either Jacob exploding or the world becoming a nightmarish hellscape under his control. Instead, the glow faded, and nothing appeared different.

"Okay, done," Jacob said, removing the crown and handing it back over.

I stared before taking it. "What?"

"I've corrected the flaw in your universe," Jacob said. "The remaining Unborn have all been rewoven into the space-time continuum and their existence erased. The fracturing nature of the space time continuum has been healed and is now stronger than ever. I also fixed that Nanoplague business that was already infecting most of your planet's population. I didn't return any of those you resurrected to the death, but they are no longer protected by your magic. Besides, ninety-seven percent of them, if the Crown's divinations were accurate, had already died again. In simple terms, crisis averted. The universe is no longer falling apart."

I opened my mouth. "It can't be that easy."

"Believe me it wasn't," Jacob replied. "It probably wouldn't have worked if you hadn't just blown up a planet as a sacrifice."

"It wasn't a sac…" I trailed off and coughed before stabbing the Merciless Sword back in the ground. "Yeah, let's just keep that between us, shall we?"

"Sure," Jacob said.

It occurred to me Tsavong Prime had only been restored from Pyronnicus destroying it because of an off-hand desire to try to undo the damage to so much of the world by supervillains, monsters, and corrupted superheroes. I'd tried to rewind the clock on President Omega, Merciful, and Entropicus' evils but hadn't even really been thinking about some distant space empire when I'd rebooted the universe.

I'd just gone, "Make everything better and nicer! The heroes win! The bad guys lose! Except when the bad guys were cool!" It had been a profoundly selfish wish and rather than everything becoming better like Link using the Triforce in *The Legend of Zelda: A Link to the Past*, it had just ended up like all the other Legend of Zeldas where Ganon ends up coming back then screwing everyone over a few generations later. Which, honestly, really would have encouraged me to leave Hyrule as your typical Medieval peasant.

I'd brought back billions of Tsavong with a wish and all that had happened was they'd died a year later at the hands of monsters in an even more monstrous way. What did this mean for the others? For the people of Falconcrest City? For Ultragod? Hell, for Mandy, the first person I'd brought back with black magic? I didn't know.

I stared at him then slumped my shoulders. "Ninety-seven percent, huh? So, it was all for nothing?"

"Well, not that remaining three percent," Jacob replied. "You tried to alter the nature of time and space but in the end were only able to spackle it over."

"Spackle over?" I asked. "Just how modern is this world?"

"Yes, because masonry is something so distinctly modern," Ketra muttered. "Also, we're a world settled by space travelers."

"Ah, so it's like Pern," I paused and waited for a reaction. Neither said anything. "Oh, so you get HBO here but not Anne McCaffrey?"

"Sure, Gary," Ketra said.

"Your dragon is really sarcastic," I replied, feeling defeated but also calmer. "I'm starting to like her."

"She wasn't always a dragon," Jacob said.

Ketra proceeded to shapeshift before my eyes, like a pair of images slowly morphing into one another with exceptionally good CGI. I'd gotten used to the sight with Cindy and her werewolf transformations, but it was still something that tickled my mortal capacity for awe.

The raven-haired woman who stood before me was wearing blue dragon scale armor, had a curly Eighties hair style that reminded me of Pat Benatar, and a pair of dragon wings sticking out of her back like a succubus. She had a bit of a Larry Elmore's fantasy art vibe. Which, yes, meant that I was standing before a hot dragon.

"Nice to meet you," I asked. "How did becoming a dragon work out for you?"

"Quite well, thank you," Ketra replied. "However, everyone looks crunchy now."

"Ah," I replied. I looked down at the crown in my hands. "How did you pull this off and I couldn't?"

"Sixty-seventh level," Jacob said, adapting to my style of humor way too well. It was one of the things annoying me about him. He seemed utterly unphased by all my jokes and disrespect. That had been my primary tool against superheroes and villains alike, but it seemed like I'd finally overplayed my hand. No one considered me a fool anymore, justified or not, and that meant I couldn't take people off guard. I needed to come up with new tricks if I was going to survive the next few months. I had the sneaking suspicion my utopia, rescued by Jacob or not, wasn't going to last.

"Funny," I replied, taking a deep breath, and gathering my thoughts. The crown felt weak in my hands, and I suspected most of its power had been expended. Still, it was an object of immense arcane might and I needed to figure out what to do with it.

Jacob sighed. "Or, if you want to put it in non-game terms, I actually have studied how magic works and understand its fundamental principles. I'm not half-assing it based on natural talent and stolen sorcery."

"But I'm so good at both!" I whined, half joking before sighing. "Ugh. I really screwed the pooch here, didn't I?"

"Eww," Ketra said.

"It's a metaphor!" I snapped. "Seriously though, I can't stay here, Jacob. I've got to get back to my family and tell Ultragod about PHANTOM. Even if you've cured the plague, there's clearly a lot going on out here."

"Six months will pass here to every hour of your time," Jacob said. "That's also, coincidentally, when the next alignment of our dimensions will occur."

I stared at him. "You and Death have every angle covered, don't you?"

Jacob nodded. It was the only facial gesture he could manage. "Unless you improve into someone who can use their abilities effectively, divine or magical, then you stand no chance of surviving the storms ahead. Worse, neither do those you care about. Like it or not, you are a god."

"What does that even mean?" I asked, throwing my hands up in the air.

"It means that you have a responsibility to those who follow you," Jacob said. "A duty to answer their prayers. Even if it is just with cold comfort. To be a god is to become an embodiment of a concept and to provide an example to others of both good as well as bad behavior. They are the way the minds of sapient beings sort through the immensity of infinity."

I paused. "No wonder I hate the idea."

Chapter Twelve

Training Montage Set to *Rocky IV*'s "Hearts on Fire"

The next few months were the toughest of my life, and I'd spent time in both a brainwashing prison and Falconcrest City High School. Jacob Riverson was a punishing instructor and, for some reason, seemed to think running me ragged while teaching me how to sword fight was the best way to teach me about magic.

In fact, as I got myself blasted down a snowy mountain top for the fiftieth time that day, I had the revelation as to Jacob's teaching strategy: he was going to beat the crap out of me until I was willing to listen to his deranged magical physics lessons without any backtalk. Well, the joke was on him, I could give backtalk even when frozen and exhausted.

"There are eight spheres of magic, Gary, which are born from a connection to the Primals. There is Black Magic born from Death, White Magic born from Life, Red Magic born from Chaos, Blue Magic from Order, Green Magic from Creation, Yellow Magic from Destruction, Orange for Fate, and Violet for Destiny," Jacob said, holding out a glowing blue sword that he called *Chill's Fury*. Because apparently, we were in a heavy metal album.

I stared at him, climbing to my feet and my breath visible. I was covered in bruises that covered bruises. "Okay, first of all, I'm pretty sure that's just *Magic: The Gathering's* rules for how sorcery works. Second, I feel bad for Fate and Destiny. Orange and Violet just don't seem like proper mystic colors."

"As the Chosen of Death, all Dungeon magic is black magic. While you changed the rules of magic in your world, without knowing how regular magic worked, you also are the catalyst for those who wield sorcery in your name," Jacob replied, ignoring my quips. Which probably made him the only guy I would be completely unable to distract in a fight. His level of patience was beyond belief—which I supposed made sense since he was an undead wizard king. Tolkien had his be thousands of years old.

"So, the Moral Majority was right? *Dungeons & Dragons* really is a gateway to the Devil?" I asked. I was a little surprised at the revelation I was the source of Dungeon magic, if Jacob was right at least. It meant all my practitioners were my clerics. Jane Doe would *hate* that.

"You're a god, Gary, not a demon. Which is a fine distinction but a distinction, nonetheless. Infernal magic is not related to the eight, it is a corruption of the existing magic of the spheres," Jacob said, giving an unpleasant look at the Merciless Sword that had been knocked out of my hands.

Three months wasn't enough to become a competent wizard, but Jacob's boot camp was enough that I was no longer completely ignorant of how magic worked. Give me a couple of decades and I might have been able to not embarrass myself at the next MagiCon. Unfortunately, I didn't have a couple of decades. I didn't even want to spend the next few *days* training. I wanted to get back to my family. Jacob had reassured me no time at all was passing back on Earth and I'd be back for Ultraday, it was passing for me. Being separated from the

119

people you cared about had the uncomfortable consequence of forcing you to think about all the things you could have or should have done.

"Thanks," I muttered, about ready to collapse. "Great worldbuilding exposition. Really brings the setting to life."

"You need to balance the other seven spheres with yours," Jacob replied. "Otherwise, the Universal Pattern will be disrupted."

"Okay, now we're ripping off *The Wheel of Time*," I said.

"But the benefit of your connection to Death is your Dungeon magic is not limited to the system you have created to channel it," Jacob said. "It is merely a gateway to a higher level of consciousness and power."

"Sort of like pot?" I asked.

"Congratulations, Gary," Jacob said.

"On what?" I asked, slumping my shoulders.

"You are starting to annoy me," Jacob admitted.

"*Starting* to annoy you?" I asked, stunned. "I used up all of my best material in the first month!"

"Get better material," Jacob responded. "React."

"What?" I asked.

That was when Jacob fired a ball of glowing blue fire at me before I barely managed to get up a shield spell in time to block it, sending me once more to the ground. That shield, what Jacob called a barrier, had taken everything out of me. I wasn't sure if I'd gotten a concussion out of it.

Jacob sighed. "You're still too slow."

I stared up at the sky, muttering a line from "99 Luftballons". "It's all over and I'm standing pretty, in this dust that was a city."

"Yeah, I think we're done for today," Jacob muttered.

"Thank God," I said, staring upward. "I think I see the great cosmic turtle the world rests on. It's fighting a clown-spider."

Jacob walked over and helped me up with one hand. "You should have used the sword or turned insubstantial."

"I used to be a lot better at this. Back when I had the Reaper's Cloak," I muttered, standing up. "However, I no longer have that."

"You still need to appease Death," Jacob said.

"How?" I asked.

"Figure it out," Jacob replied, grumpily.

Real helpful there, Jacob. "Also, I thought you hated infernal magic. Why encourage me to use the sword?"

I waved the Merciless Sword around a bit before sheathing it in a scabbard Jacob had made for me. He was apparently a super magical blacksmith. It turned into a bracelet on my wrist. Not my usual fashion but you can't have everything.

"It is the Sword of Samael, used during the Rebellion," Jacob said. "It was created by your god's servants and thus is a weapon of good rather than evil. It just was tainted during his fall and fell into the hands of Jack Hellraiser later. Only a pure soul would be able to channel its true power and bestow the power of an archangel upon its wielder."

"Not really my mythology," I replied, shrugging. "Same street, different houses. By the way, how do you know all this? Death?"

"I've been watching you for a long time, Gary," Jacob said. "Ever since Death came to me."

"Hopefully not in the shower," I replied.

Jacob shook his head. "You have struggled to keep that which you cannot. You refuse to end relationships. You refuse to let the dead go. You refuse to accept what cannot be changed."

"Yeah, that's why I'm a supervillain," I said, correcting him. "Heroes are defenders of the status quo."

121

Sure, I was going back and forth on being a hero or villain. Some backsliding was to be expected when making a major life change.

"Or is that simply what you tell yourself because you want to avoid the responsibility of being a hero?" Jacob asked. "As long as you're a villain, you don't have to carry the burden of having to use your powers for good. Except, you haven't been using your powers for evil especially either."

"Ultragoddess would disagree," I said, wondering if I could use the Crown of the Gods to restore her powers.

"I believe you are a supervillain because you desired to have few expectations to live up to," Jacob replied. "Your brother died a meaningless death and you wanted to honor him by becoming a better criminal. However, you are not someone who wishes to be a criminal. You wish to change the world for the better but feel that would be a betrayal of him. You also feel crushed by the weight of sacrifice that heroes like Ultragod are expected to give to prop up a corrupt society. A hero, in your mind, should not be a defender of the establishment but an opponent of evil. To burn down a crumbling society so that a new vibrant one can be built."

I narrowed my eyes and pointed at his chest. "You're not my therapist, chief. You're my magic instructor. If you want to instruct me in the ways of the Force, go right ahead. However, you're not my Obi-Wan."

"Then who is?" Jacob asked. "I know, too, what it is like to want to save your world and be treated as a monster. To have also done things that were unforgivable in the name of the greater good. I, too, have loved people I could not let go of and destroyed relationships by being unable to choose one to care for."

I started to walk away. "You don't know me, Jacob. Do you know what happened the one time I tried to be a superhero?"

"Probably," Jacob replied.

"My hometown was overrun by zombies," I said, stopping in mid-step. "The Reapers' Cloaks had caused the dead to rise, and an evil cult was taking advantage of it. A hundred thousand people died. Maybe I was responsible, maybe I wasn't. But that's not what broke me. It was when I tried to fix everything and save everyone that I made the worst mistake I ever made."

I hadn't spoken about this in years. I'd altered reality, sought forbidden magics, and done God knows how much else to paper over it. It was the nasty evil heart of everything I hated about myself and what could never be undone.

"Which mistake?" Jacob asked, knowing damn well what I was referring to.

"I got my wife killed," I said, staring forward at nothing in particular because I was trapped in the moment that I'd lost Mandy. "That's what superheroism does. It gets the people you loved murdered. Better to be the bad guy."

"Is this why you delude yourself to the nature of your bride?" Jacob asked. "Her misery? Because otherwise you could never forgive yourself?"

He was referring to Mandy.

"Some crimes can't be forgiven," I said. "They just have to be endured."

Jacob's response surprised me. "That, Gary Karkofsky, I know more about than you could possibly imagine."

I responded in a calm and mature manner by flipping him the bird with both hands. From there, I proceeded to march over to the temple. Well, "temple" was a stretch. It was more like the building that Jacob had either conjured or taken over that we just so happened to be squatting in during my Dagobah training.

The building was vaguely Asian in style—I couldn't tell you what country or even if that mattered in Not-Middle Earth, sorry—with a dojo and hot springs in the back. There was enough room for three people, and I spent most of my non-training time either sleeping or meditating. To tell the truth, I had no idea if I was meditating since as far as I could tell, that was just closing your eyes and thinking hard about something. If that was the case, I had been lied to by *Star Wars* about it being a deep spiritual experience.

Either way, I undressed and slowly slid into the pools of warm water that were the only respite from the blistering cold on the rest of the mountain. The pools in the back were one of the two things that made the daily battering tolerable. The other one arrived a few minutes later, undressing as well before sliding in. The dragon woman was in her human form again, wings still sticking out of the back as she sat across from me in the warm bubbling water. Ketra's human form had a lot of scars and signs of battle, including burns, which I had to wonder about. Apparently, shapeshifting didn't cure any of that. She was also elfblooded, which was a fancy way of saying half-elf. Though they called them Sidhe around here. S-I-D-H-E not S-H-E for clarifications sake to my audiobook listeners.

"You look like shit," Ketra said in her typical friendly fashion.

"Thanks," I replied. "I feel like it too."

"I don't know what Jacob is trying to accomplish with you," Ketra said. "You're never going to be a decent wizard."

"Sometimes the abuse is for its own sake," I said, staring over at her. "What are you doing up here anyway?"

I knew it was Jacob's job to put me through my training montage and, in the words of *Mulan*, make a man out of me. I wasn't so sure about Ketra's part in all this, though. She scouted the terrain, sometimes spoke with Jacob, and flew around the mountain a lot. Like most dragons, Ketra knew magic as well, but I wasn't learning anything from her on that end.

"Watching over Jacob," Ketra said. "I had a family once too, Gary. Now it's gone. He's all that's left."

"The undead wizard king is your only family?" I asked, not having pried too much into her life.

"You have a problem with that?" Ketra asked, defensively.

I hadn't been able to learn much of Jacob and Ketra's history while staying with them, even with all the training as well as other activities I got up to. Near as I could tell, Jacob was the Big Bad god of evil on this world, but that was because he'd inherited the role. He wasn't a bad guy and the forces of quote-unquote good were assholes. However, it wasn't quite a reversal of "Elves Good, Orcs Bad" either. It was more that the planet was a lot more complex than your typical *Dungeons & Dragons* campaign. More like, "Elves racist, Orcs assholes, cyclical generations of war with humans caught between."

"Not in the slightest," I said, looking at Ketra and sighing.

You might be wondering if mine and Ketra's relationship was sexual in nature. In which case, get your mind out of the gutter and yes, obviously. It was going to be six months on a deserted island—or isolated mountain peak in this case—and the only other prospect was an undead ghost king. Ketra seemed about as enthusiastic, saying, "Shut up, do exactly what I say when I say it, and we should be fine."

To which I'd replied, "Cindy?"

Either way, one more item off the bucket list and it wasn't like Ketra wasn't a decent sort or uninterested. I didn't have many standards, but I always had to be friends with my lovers. Which put me one over Cindy—and man was she going to be jealous. Still, my mind wasn't with Ketra when I was with her. Instead, I was wondering about what Jacob had said about

Mandy and how I'd failed her. Not just the living Mandy but the unliving one.

"Gary?" Ketra asked, splashing over at me. "You're zoning out again."

"Yeah," I said, taking a deep breath. "Was thinking about sex and family."

"Hopefully not at the same time," Ketra said.

I rolled my eyes. "I left myself wide open for that one."

"You did," Ketra replied.

"I need to get out of here." I sighed. "I need to find out what they're up to."

Ketra blinked. "We might be able to help one another there."

I paused, staring. "How?"

"Would you be willing betray Jacob?" Ketra asked, hesitatingly.

"Yes," I replied, instantly.

Chapter Thirteen

The Party Does Not Meet at an Inn

Ketra and I didn't speak much more about the whole issue of betraying Jacob until about three days later when the Dark Lord of Dark Lordliness was called away. I had no idea what for—he wasn't exactly keeping me in his confidence—but it gave us some time alone. Honestly, this was the shittiest fantasy world I'd ever been to. I hadn't gotten to explore anything other than the top of the Misty Mountains Cold (or whatever the hell they were called) and that was a bit like going to Disneyworld and staying in the parking lot.

Instead, Ketra transformed into her dragon form and gave me a look. "We will only have a day, Gary, so get on my back."

"Errr," I paused, staring at her. "Do we have to do it this way?"

"What?" Ketra asked, looking confused.

"This is going to sound weird..." I trailed off.

"No kidding," Ketra said. "Everything that comes out of your mouth sounds weird, Gary. On my world, you would have been locked away as a mad man while people wrote down your ramblings as possible prophetic visions."

I blinked. "Ah, we have internet commentators filling that role on my world."

"See?" Ketra suggested, as a perfect example of my insane speech. Which, fair enough, point to her.

"I'm not comfortable riding on your back," I finally admitted my discomfort.

"You're afraid of falling off?" Ketra asked, confused.

"No," I said. "Well, yes, but no. It's just, uh, well, we've had sex. Riding you after that makes it weird."

Ketra's big reptilian eyes blinked. Somehow, she'd managed to emote very humanlike surprise. "Oh, for fuck's sake. *Really?*"

"It does!" I shouted.

"The fact I'm a dragon should make it weird!" Ketra snapped.

"I don't make the rules!" I said. "Imagine the business cards! They could say Gary the Pink, Merciless: The Supervillain without Mercy, Superhero Private Eye, Dragon Rider (teehee)!"

"You're the one who added the teehee," Ketra said, her voice low and grumbling now. Which I felt was more appropriate to her body that was the size of a small house.

"It's implied!" I replied.

"You can add necrophiliac for screwing a vampire," Ketra said.

I paused. "Technically, I can add furry due to Cindy's werewolf status. Oh shit. Outside of anime and YA fandom, no one is ever going to take me seriously again."

"Get on my goddamn back," Ketra said, again paraphrasing Cindy.

"First, I want to know what we're going after," I replied. "Also, how it's betraying Jacob. I'm happy he's taking time apprenticing me in the ways of sorcery and it hasn't led to turning me into a bird or fish like *The Sword in the Stone*. However, I kind of feel like I'm missing out on the whole magical student experience too. Not Hogwarts. That ship has sailed. However, maybe there was a GED or college level set of courses I could take. Magical community college. It's how I got my PI's license."

"We're breaking into the Unspeakable Vault," Ketra said, sighing.

"What's in there?" I asked, knowing what was coming next.

"We don't speak of it," Ketra said.

I closed my eyes. "Yep. Saw that one coming."

Ketra paused. "What might be in it is one of the Primal Orbs."

"Oh, goddamn those things," I muttered. "I have had *enough* of them."

"It contains either the Orb of Destiny or the Orb of Fate," Ketra explained. "Either of which has the power to put you back in touch with your family. Probably transport you across reality back to them as well."

"I'm kind of unclear about the difference between those two," I admitted, pondering what she was saying. "Fate and Destiny have always been synonyms as far as I've been concerned."

"Destiny is your best self, Fate is your worst," Ketra said. "How you live your life is an eternal struggle between those extremes."

"Ah," I replied. "Glad to know that."

"How do you not know this?" Ketra asked.

"I'm catching up on a lot of magical stuff, okay!" I replied.

"The man who rewrote the laws of magic on his world never bothered to get any lessons on how to do any of it," Ketra said, shaking her head.

"*Rush* drummer Neal Peart once spent months mastering how to do a specific bit from a *Genesis* song he liked. Later, he was informed by the band's sound engineer that they'd recorded that bit with the tape slowed down," I replied, spreading my hands out. "All of my achievements are due to ignorance of them being impossible."

"Is that supposed to be impressive or horrifying?" Ketra asked.

I paused. "You know, I'm not sure. What are you getting out of this?"

"Excuse me?" she asked.

"What's your stake in this?" I asked. "I like Jacob just fine despite the fact he's a rip off the Lich King Arthas—*World of Warcraft* never had a better villain—but he's family to you. Why do this?"

"I, too, want to reunite with my family," Ketra said. "But I made Jacob promise that I should not. Promises are binding in my world."

"Ah," I said. "It'd be useless for me to ask for more clarification, wouldn't it?"

"Yes," Ketra said.

"Good," I said, before walking up and climbing on her back. "Would you be offended if I started singing the theme song to *The NeverEnding Story* while I ride you?"

"Yes," Ketra said. "I have no idea what that is, but yes."

"Too bad," I said, feeling the weirdly soft scales pulsate with her breathing beneath me. "Turn around! Look at what you seeee—"

Ketra responded by taking flight, causing me to grab desperately ahold of her armored plates while being blasted with the icy winds of the mountaintop. It occurred to me that I would have benefited from a pair of goggles, a helmet, or even a barrier spell. Unfortunately, I couldn't open my mouth without getting pelted with more wind as well as ice. So, instead, I just buried my head into her scales and missed ninety percent of the whole miraculous dragon riding experience.

The flight, such as it might be called, took about two hours and was as miserable an experience as you could imagine. I would have thrown up twice, but the turbulence meant every time I was about to, I ended up having it forced back into my stomach.

Yeah, fantasy art was never going to be the same for me.

Either way, the two of us settled down in what was best described as steampunk fantasy ruins. Some real *Final Fantasy* shit with massive pipes, discarded electrical plants, Gothic cathedrals, miniature castles, and crumbling wooden buildings. It was a bizarre juxtaposition of styles and didn't make any more sense when we landed in what appeared to be a city park now covered in permafrost.

Once grounded, I slid off Ketra's form, slammed into a mound of snow and proceeded to finally lose my lunch. After the heaving stopped, I conjured a bottle of blue fluid with the *Merciless' Magic Mouthwash* spell.

"How was your trip?" Ketra asked, restoring herself to winged human form. She was once more in her blue dragonscale armor and armed with a sword at her side.

"Like flying a World War 1 biplane," I said, taking a deep breath before gargling. "Which is to say, it sucked. Where the hell are we?"

"Everfrost," Ketra said, as if that explained it.

"It looks like Victorian London had a baby with Bara Dur," I replied.

"It was the former capital of the King Below and his armies," Ketra said. "Once the center of all that was evil and industrial in our world."

"Seriously, the Tolkien estate is going to have words with you guys," I replied.

"In the end, time and war drove it to ruin," Ketra said. "Jacob walks the ruins from time to time while pondering what fortunes led him to here and whether they could have gone differently if he'd been a slightly different man."

That was a familiar story. "You should never ponder how things might have been. Because you can't ever be other than who you are or who you were. Only you might be."

Mandy had told me that when she was still alive, whole, and human. It had been about her lost chance at being a Foundation agent. In the end, she had died as something far greater, a superhero. It had been advice that would have saved her life had she followed it.

It's advice I'd never taken.

"You are more alike than you realize," Ketra said, frowning.

"More like opposites," I replied. "I never wanted to be responsible for the world. I suspect it's all Jacob ever wanted to be. Unfortunately, if this World Between is one of three, then it was three worlds too much for any man to carry."

"Yes," Ketra said. "In any case, the entrance to the World Below is beneath us."

"We're going to Hell?" I asked. "I should note that I'm not exactly popular there."

"It is a literal world below," Ketra said. "More like a cavern. It is there the Tower of Everfrost has been laid low, carrying the spirits of enemies long dead as well as secrets that Jacob wants to keep buried."

"Sounds super easy!" I said, realizing why she'd chosen me for this.

"You are a thief, are you not?" Ketra asked.

"More like a mage that steals," I said. "I don't think I have any rogue levels."

Ketra replied by lifting her sword into the air. It shot forth an enormous blast of fire that exploded in the air like a particularly effective fireworks display.

"Do I want to know?" I asked.

"A signal to the rest of our party," Ketra said. "I believe we will need help in our attempt to break open the vault. Also, the chances of the hordes of undead in the city awakening to devour us are fairly minimal."

"Having experienced a horde of undead trying to devour me, I'd rather that not be minimized as a risk," I replied.

Much to my surprise, a trio of individuals jogged out of a grove of trees to greet us. Apparently, they'd been in hiding, which wasn't a good sign. There was a long black-haired man covered in tribal markings and wearing black studded leather armor while sporting what I swore was a Medieval version of an electric guitar. There was a balding dwarf who was wearing a cassock and a large Bishop's hat, but had a drum set attached to his front. The man had white face paint on, as well as several diabolical markings I vaguely recognized. Finally, there was a five-foot-two female elf—sorry, Sidhe—who carried a bow but no quiver, while wearing bright green flower-encrusted clothes. She had a long multi-colored cloak that changed its mixture every few seconds. A crown of stag horns was resting on her forehead, also with flowers.

"They look like a power metal band," I replied, thinking of *Spinal Tap* for some reason.

"We are indeed a band of mercenaries," Ketra said. "They aren't from this world, though."

"Where are they from then?" I asked.

"A world of complete losers and wannabe warriors," Ketra said. "You know, yours."

"Ah," I said.

The black-haired man spoke. "I am Ser Matthew the Bold, the leader of the band and Skald of Ages. With mine electrified lute, I am capable of sending forth powerful magical wails that lay waste to mine enemies."

"No one else talks like that on our world, by the way," Ketra said.

"I noticed," I said.

"This is our drummer," Matthew said. "Brother Stephen the Lucky. He is a Priest of the Fool King."

"The Fool King?" I asked.

"I had a vision of a god falling from the sky who bestowed vast power to those who did not deserve it, and humiliated the powerful," Brother Stephen said. "He also is a god who attracts women far out of his league."

I paused and wondered if he was referring to me. Nah. "Uh huh."

"Brother Stephen is our third priest," Matthew said. "The previous one choked on vomit while the first exploded for no apparent reason."

"It wasn't his own vomit either," Brother Stephen said.

I looked over my shoulder to see if God was punking me. "Okay, I was joking about the *Spinal Tap* thing."

"I am Trace'e Gunther, Sorceress of the Fifth Order!" Trace'e raised her hands in the air. "I defend the woodlands and animals in the name of all that is elfish. But you know, in a cool and not hippie-esque way."

"I shouldn't get attached to these people, should I?" I asked.

"Probably best not to befriend any of these guys," Ketra replied. "I mostly hired them as trap fodder."

"You wound me, milady," Matthew said, putting his hand over his heart.

"Only if I miss," Ketra said. "Where's the other one?"

A large half-orc, or at least something vaguely hulking, came out of the bushes with a suit of full plate armor the bottom of which he was reaffixing. Were there half-orcs on my world? I dunno, maybe it was cosmetic.

"Sorry, nature called!" the half-orc said. "Man, they don't tell you about the dangers of bean meat on adventures, do they?"

"This is Ser Stephen Ott the Black Knight AKA Other Steve," Matthew replied. "Other Steve is a knight of the Dread Order of Fear, worshiper of the Dark Lord, and Wrath of the Black Sun. He draws his power from dark and nebulous forces while existing to spread misery across the land."

"Sup!" Other Steve said, waving. "I also sell imaginarium paintings. They're paintings that don't exist outside of the artist's minds, but you can buy them and trade them, on the off chance that he actually paints one later."

"So, NFTs." I stared at them and then back at Ketra. "Seriously, am I being punked?"

"They work cheap," Ketra replied. "Gentlemen—"

"Ahem," Trace'e cleared her throat.

"And the self-proclaimed elf," Ketra added. "Who is a woman."

"Thank you!" Trace'e said.

"This is Gary Karkofsky," Ketra continued, "AKA Merciless: The Wizard without Mercy."

I accepted the localization given we were dealing with foreign markets here. Besides, wizard was probably analogous to supervillain given most people blessed with godlike power tended to abuse it horribly—me included.

"He's a demigod," Ketra said.

"Minor god," I corrected. "I got my full god certificate a long time ago."

"You're a demigod if you don't have an avatar or domain," Ketra said, surprisingly arguing the point. "Either way, he can make things explode and that's all we need to finish this heist. Are there any questions?"

Other Steve raised his hand. "I question bringing on a new party member at this juncture. Coming in this late, he shouldn't get a full share of the treasure involved. At the very least, I feel I should prepare a proper contract that illustrates what expectations and—"

"Steve, I will slap the shit out of you if you don't shut up," Ketra said.

Other Steve made a pair of finger guns. "Right."

"Is the Dread Order of Fear a legal firm?" I asked.

"Yes," Ketra said, surprising me. "In lots of parts of the world, knights don't actually get on horses and do fighting. Their titles symbolize their place in the Imperial Bureaucracy."

"That is both historically accurate and gravely disappointing," I replied.

"I should clarify I can kill people!" Other Steve said. "I am a trained soldier of the Imperial Army and I also play handball on weekends."

"You couldn't recruit a fellow elf, preferably a female one?" Trace'e asked Ketra. "I'm not saying you had to be prejudiced, but I think elvish solidarity among women is an important aspect of opposing the patriarchy."

"You're not an elf," Ketra said. "You had your ears flesh crafted that way and it pisses off the actual people with Sidhe blood, myself included and I *hate* elves."

"Thank you, I am one sixty-fourth Sidhe high lord," Trace'e said, sniffing the air. "At least that was what FairyGeneology.com said. I feel like I might be more Sidhe than you. I, after all, have embraced the ancient heritage of our people that was destroyed by contact with the humans."

"Why are we taking this loser on?" Brother Steve leaned in and whispered to Matthew, except it was so loud everyone could hear it. "By which I mean the new wizard. How lame do you have to be to pretend to be Merciless? I mean, Merciless is like a B-tier hero at best."

"Villain," I corrected.

"He's only a C-tier villain," Brother Steve said. "No offense."

If he survived this, I'd kill him.

"Obviously, they're fucking," Matt replied, strumming his electric lute. "Ketra and the Gary imposter, I mean."

"Ah," Brother Steve said. "Questgiver's girlfriend. That's why he's here."

Ketra sighed. "I'd be upset but I just hired you as cannon fodder from another dimension so I'm letting this one slide."

"Somehow I thought the World Between would be more…serious," I replied.

"It usually is," Ketra said, waving for everyone to follow. "Come on, let's get going. The undead are on the march."

That was when I heard the telltale sound of the damned moaning by the thousands.

Chapter Fourteen

An Old-Fashioned Dungeon Crawl

"Well, that's not good," I said, feeling the unpleasant feeling of a massive number of undead coming this way. Though strangely, I was feeling a little bit of my old psychopomp desire to destroy them all again.

I had completely shut Death out of my life by the reboot, which I think she took as me cheating on her or oath breaking or Red Wedding or something. Either way, she had stripped me of my powers that I hadn't even known I'd had but left me as a quasi-god. However, all the deaths that had happened seemed to be making her less angry with me. Particularly those of the Unborn and kinda-sorta accidentally blowing up the Tsavong homeworld.

Whoops.

Listen, if you want to hook up with your ex again, there's some basic advice to do it. None of which remotely replies here. However, the short version is that appearing contrite (even if you're not) combined with small acts of kindness will probably make them willing to give it another shot. Or just random sex until they find someone better. No, I'm not speaking from experience. I'm speaking of another guy.

Uh, Dave.

Yes, Dave.

Dave…Jarbofsky?

Okay, I'm speaking of me. That was the mother of digressions, wasn't it? Either way, I was okay with throwing down with a horde of the undead. If that sounded stupid and insane, then you should know by now that's just how I did things. Wait.

"Quick, we need to open the entrance to the World Below," Ketra said, looking down at the ground.

"It's been sealed for an age," Matthew said. "The King Below did it to entrap the Mad One."

"Only a god can open it," Ketra said. "Thankfully, we have one."

Other Steve rolled his eyes as the half-orc puffed up his chest. "Gods are nothing more than metaphorical parental figures to the placate the superstitious masses."

Brother Steve rolled his eyes as if this was a very familiar argument.

"Aren't you a paladin?" Trace'e asked, annoyed.

"Anti-paladin," Other Steve replied. "Also, since I don't believe in the gods, I see no reason not to exploit the beliefs in them for my own ends."

"You have a future in politics," I replied pulling out the Merciless Sword. The magical item morphed and twisted into a quarterstaff in my arms. The morphic nature of the object was something I was getting accustomed to.

Outside of the park, I could see the undead horde gathering. There were zombies, skeletons, wights, ghosts, wraiths, and a hundred other varieties of dead things. There was even a penanggalan, which is a woman's head that can detach from her body. Those were rare. No vampires or liches, though. Those were boss monsters and you only faced those at the end of the level. Hopefully.

139

Anyway, I had no idea how to break the magic spell on the ground that Jacob had laid to prevent anyone from going down to the World Below. I'd trained my mystical senses to be other than completely useless, but I wasn't exactly 20/20 in them yet. More like if I squinted hard, I could see the picture in the magic eye display.

"Now would be a good time to reveal yourself, mighty Fool King," Brother Steve said. "Reveal your glory for all to see."

"Please, there are ladies present," Matthew paused. "Well, Lady Trace'e and Ketra. Which is close enough for government work."

Ketra glared at him.

"Though this be our last hour against impossible odds," Trace'e started a speech, "I want you to know that I have never spent time in a nobler set of company. Not even the Earthmother could give me a more—"

"Please, just shut up," Ketra said, looking like she was getting a migraine. "Let Gary concentrate."

"Dammit," I muttered, slamming down the quarterstaff's end onto the ground. "*Open Sesame!*"

The ground cracked and thundered before a large hole opened just in front of us. The hole had a set of ornate stairs leading down it and I couldn't help but be reminded of the original 8-bit The Legend of Zelda.

"Time to move," Ketra said, gesturing for the others to follow. "But—"

"But we haven't even searched for traps!" I said, pausing. "I feel like we need a dedicated rogue for this party versus a spoony bard!"

Matthew snorted and ran down the stairs past me. "You can stay up here and get eaten like suckers! The destiny of the greatest skald in the world is far...AHHHHHHHHHH!"

Matthew's scream died off with a sickening death rattle.

I blinked. "Well, that didn't take long."

The three remaining members of Ketra's recruited mercenaries exchanged glances which told me they were now reconsidering their escape through the stairway below. Given it apparently led to this reality's version of Hell, they probably should have had that thought earlier.

"I was going to say time to move but be cautious," Ketra said. "Gary, please cast a spell to detect traps."

"Okay, but that's cheating," I replied, casting *Find/Detect Traps*. It caused a large glow to appear down below.

Behind us, the horde was less than a hundred yards away and a few of the more physically adept undead were now running toward us. While I was still willing to throw down with the horrors, I could tell the rest of my group wasn't—well, maybe Ketra—and it was best that we entered the dungeon.

The others followed me, Ketra taking up second position and the others following in the rear side-by-side. No sooner had their heads passed ground level did the entrance to the World Below seal over, plunging us into darkness.

"Thankfully, I have infravision!" Steve said, cheerfully. "The benefit of being a dwarf!"

"I, too, have infravision!" Other Steve said.

"As do I! The benefit of being an elf!" Trace'e called, right before the sound of a five-foot-two woman falling down a flight of stairs. "OW! DAMMIT! OW! DAMMIT! OW!"

Ketra spoke several words in a language I didn't recognize, and the darkness dissipated with the creation of a glowing miniature sun, roughly the size of a bowling ball, which took flight above our heads. We were in a long ornate stone hallway at the foot of the stairs, murals on the wall depicting the creation of the Three Worlds by three gods. One good, one bad, and one balanced between them.

Typical fantasy stuff.

Halfway through the hallway were the unfortunate remains of Matthew the Skald. He had been impaled in a dozen places by spears that had shot through from the floor and ceiling. I was genuinely impressed he'd managed to get a scream out before he'd died, to be honest.

Other Steve removed his helmet and put it over his heart. "He was taken from us far too soon. I call dibs on whatever is in his pockets."

"The hell you do," Brother Steve said, offended. "Matthew and I were like brothers. So, anything he owns is mine."

"Huh, so this is what being part of a heist crew is like," I muttered. "This is why I never joined the Nefarious Nine."

Ketra reached over to a hidden compartment in the wall murals and pulled a lever that resulted in the spears retracting, causing Matthew's body to fall with a sickening thump. "Having known Matthew for a minute, I can tell you there's nothing worth robbing on his corpse. I suggest that the best thing you could draw from his corpse is to watch your step."

"We're not amateurs!" Other Steve said, snorting.

"You're professional tomb robbers?" I asked, dryly.

"That's right!" Brother Steve replied.

I rolled my eyes. "Let me try something."

"Go right ahead, Merciless," Ketra replied.

I pulled out a piece of white chalk and started drawing on the ground. It was a more complicated spell than I was used to, but I'd learned a few things from Jacob during my time with him. Muttering a variety of words that I barely managed to avoid jumbling, a large figure made of rock emerged from the stones and formed into a sexless stone figure.

An earth elemental.

The physics of summoning was something I'd never given much thought to but apparently it was kidnapping beings from other planes then magically enslaving them. So, every time your *Final Fantasy* character brought forth Bahamut or Tiamat, they were screwing over some random people in another dimension. I only engaged in it here because, well, earth elementals were all assholes. Seriously, I was surprised by this fact myself, but every one of them was a complete jackass.

"Orders?" the creature asked.

"Walk ahead," I said.

The stone man walked forward and what followed was it being blasted with electricity, freezing cold, fireballs, and a pit trap that it crawled out of. None of these seemed to cause it the slightest bit of distress, but alerted us to each individual trap that my magic might have detected but didn't disable. Either way, it cleared the way down the hallway and substantially increased the expected lifespan of our little party.

"It's not exactly the *Tomb of Horrors* but we're definitely above the *Keep on the Borderlands*," I said. "Jacob isn't screwing around in his dungeon design."

"In the old days, many travelers sought to bring back their dead loved ones," Ketra said. "Others sought the power of the World Below to gain revenge on their enemies or vast wealth through dark pacts."

I paused, keeping an eye out as I took the lead. "Yeah, I don't know anything about that."

Ketra rolled her eyes. "Either way, Jacob thought turning the passage to Everfrost into a death trap would discourage both."

"Did it?" I asked.

"No," Ketra said. "The only reason we haven't encountered the bodies of hundreds of young fools is because the slimes, oozes, and giant amoebas devour them."

"They also clean the human waste," Brother Steve said. "You may notice there aren't any chamber pots around here."

"Eww," Trace'e said.

143

"Not much of an actual nature girl, are you?" Brother Steve asked.

Trace'e glared.

"As fascinating as I'm finding this insight into dungeon ecology, I went before I left," I replied. "Also, I think we're here."

The end of the hall, which had a door my earth elemental had knocked down, opened to a sight that ranked up there with the more impressive ones I'd seen during my career as a supervillain. It was a vast, icy cavern and by vast, I meant several kilometers long and a kilometer deep with stalactites and stalagmites the size of buildings.

The chill in the air was immense with icebergs interspersing themselves between the enormous stone formations, all of them as large as the rocky protuberances. Their contents were as notable as their size, showing elaborate spikey buildings as well as mansions like the ones we'd left above. People were also frozen inside the ice, their auras still living as far as I could tell with my mystic senses—imprisoned and tortured at once.

At the heart of the enormous chamber, I saw what I assumed to be the Tower of Everfrost, which was a tower the same way that Buckingham Palace was a house. It started at the bottom of the cavern and reached the very top. There was a palpable aura of evil to the place that seemed to contrast directly to Jacob, who was dark but not repellent. I knew evil and for many, it was just a word for circumstance, greed, or revenge. For me, it was a word for a lot of the assholes I dealt with and also now this place. It was also our destination.

A long bridge lead from our position about halfway up, towering over most buildings and covered in slippery ice. There was no sign of my earth elemental.

"This would have made a great album cover," I said, nodding my head in approval. "Maybe I could do a crossover with Blind Guardian or Rhapsody of Fire."

"An entire city of the damned to loot," Brother Steve said, his eyes flashing with greed. "Now if I only had an icepick."

"Our focus should be the Unspeakable Vault," Ketra said, continuing her annoyance at the group.

Brother Steve chuckled and stepped out onto the bridge. "There's no reason we can't do bo...AH!"

A shadowy giant eagle thing with glowing red eyes descended from the sky and scooped up Brother Steve in its claws before pulling him back up to the cavern's heights where I saw there were hundreds, if not thousands, of the creatures.

"Oh yeah," Ketra said. "I should have probably mentioned the shadow vrocks. They drain the heat out of every living thing they encounter."

"We have to rescue him!" Trace'e called up, conjuring a druid's staff.

That was when frozen chunks of Brother Steve rained down, tinkling against the bridge, and falling into the chasm below.

"Yeah, I don't think that's happening," I replied, dryly.

Other Steve—who was just Steve now—nodded. "He has gone to a better place. Which is what I would say if I believed in an afterlife."

"We're in the World Below!" Trace'e pointed out. "This *is* the afterlife!"

"Are we?" Other Steve asked. "Or is just an illusion created by incredibly advanced aliens to enact their fantasies? What if we're all just phantasms created for the amusement of beings infinitely more powerful than ourselves?"

I had to wonder what his words sounded like without my translator magic because I was pretty sure that couldn't be accurate. "Listen, Elon Orc, we don't need a Simulation Hypothesis right now."

"Orc is an ethnic slur," Other Steve said. "The proper term is Formor."

I stared. "Really? Oh wow. I feel really racist."

"It's really not," Trace'e said. "My parents threw orc around every day and had bigger things to worry about than what the humans called us."

I gave her a sideways glance. "Funny, you don't look orcish."

"Don't let her fool you, she's a London orc through and through," Other Steve said.

"I'm not!" Trace'e panicked. "I'm a pure-blooded Sidhe and you can't prove otherwise!"

I had so many questions.

Ketra looked like she wanted to push both off the side of the bridge into the chasm below.

"There's nothing worse than a self-hating Formor," Other Steve said. "In any case, do we have any protection against the shadow vrocks?"

"Speed," Ketra said. "Everyone get ready to ride."

Chapter Fifteen

A New Party Member Joins!

K etra's plan was insane.
I liked it!

Ketra assumed her draconic form and all three of us piled onto her back, this time with no objections from any of us. The vrocks ended up descending upon us almost immediately. Ketra held them back with a blast of lightning that caused several of the creatures to disintegrate back into the nightmarish ectoplasm they were born from.

Seriously, ectoplasm isn't remotely as cool as they depict it in *Ghostbusters*. It's basically liquid evil. I mean, it looks cool, don't get me wrong. Whenever someone is throwing shadow stuff in a movie or fantasy novel, they're usually throwing ectoplasm. It's the raw stuff of the Underworld and comes in immaterial, semi material, and tears through steel like it was tissue paper. The shadow vrocks were made of the latter.

"I hope you know what you're doing!" I shouted.

"Not a bit!" Ketra said, taking flight across the frozen city before us.

"That's my job!" I shouted back.

The plan—if you can call it a plan—was just to fly as fast as humanly (dragonly?) possible across the cavern while the shadow vrocks nipped at our heels. I would have preferred something a bit more cautious—and this was me talking—but I certainly couldn't argue with the results.

"Shoot them!" Ketra called out as our enemies descended from all directions.

Actually, prepared for combat today and rested, I hurled fireballs and lightning at the attacking shadow monsters. The magic tore into their bodies, sending them back into their base otherworldly matter.

"I can't! I'm holding on!" Trace'e shouted, clinging for dear life to one of Ketra's wings.

"Coward!" Other Steve shouted, conjuring a demonic great sword and going after a shadow vrock, slashing it across the chest.

As if the universe was punishing his hubris, one of the vrocks struck him across the face and caused him to fly off the side. That would have been a perfectly justified ending to the lawyer blackguard if not for the fact I grabbed him with a *glowing hand*, then pulled him back.

"You're welcome!" I shouted, ducking another shadow vrock's attack before swatting it away with the shapeshifted Merciless Staff.

"Fine! I'll cast something!" Trace'e said, closing her eyes and lifting her hands in the air before muttering something in very badly pronounced elvish.

Much to my surprise, a glowing nimbus of sunlight appeared around Ketra's form and incinerated a half-dozen vrocks that had started to claw at Ketra. It also drove the remaining hordes of demonic creatures backward. We were about halfway across the city, and I didn't hesitate to release a half-dozen more spells off to destroy more of the monsters surrounding us.

Equally surprising to Trace's magic being useful was the fact that my own spellcasting was far easier in terms of channeling the energies. As much as I'd "cheated" to make it easier than in the books, it was now possible to combine tactics, channeling, and invocation into one easy trio of actions. The link between "real" magic and Dungeon magic had blurred rather than one replacing the other.

I wasn't sure if Jacob had taught me much about being a god, other than vague platitudes about great power equaling great something or other, but at least I hadn't entirely wasted my time here. There was an old saying that a complete amateur was more dangerous to a seasoned swordsman than a fellow veteran, and I was proof of that concept. Unfortunately, I could no longer rely on raw power and dumb luck if I was going to survive.

But why do you need skill to survive? I could almost imagine Cloak's voice speaking to me. *You've made a paradise, haven't you? One where superheroes and villains don't have to fight in the street every week.*

It wasn't Cloak's actual voice, or Lancel Warren in this case, as it wouldn't have the mocking tone I was imagining above.

There will always be more fights, I said, not quite convincing myself.

You were supposed to usher the Age of Heroes to its death, the false Cloak taunted me. *If not the paradise you created, then what does that mean?*

I don't know, I said, suddenly afraid. That was when I realized I wasn't just imagining the voice. It was coming from this place, and I remembered we were in Hell, or at least some place that was immediately adjacent.

I may not have been the most informed occultist out there, but I'd had enough encounters with the Underworld to know Hell wasn't fire pokers up the ass or burning forever. It could be, mind you, but that was mostly because one hundred percent of Hell's inhabitants were assholes to one another. The more insidious and horrifying nature of Hell was the fact it was a place that caused you to torture *yourself*.

Imagine a lifetime of regrets, imposter syndrome, and insecurities before having all of those turned against you. I found that infinitely worse than actual torture-torture. Ironically, it meant that the purest of evils were incapable of experiencing the worst Hell had to offer. Those with no guilt or shame were incapable of even knowing they were being tortured by Hell. Because they couldn't dream of Heaven, they didn't know what they were missing. They made up most demons and were incapable of growth or self-reflection.

Yeah, it sounds stupid but that's cosmic philosophy for you.

Which one was I? The Good who had done Evil, the Bad who had failed to be better, or the Evil who was in denial? At least I wasn't the Ugly. I was *People Magazine's* Sexiest Male Supervillain last year. Don't bring up the fact that I literally rewrote reality as an asterisk to that—I was a runner up in the original timeline. Either way, I was almost overwhelmed by the guilt of all my failures.

"Gary, more fireballs!" Ketra shouted and shook me out of my crushing depression.

"Fireballs, ahoy!" I shouted, blasting an entire flock of the creatures with the largest one I'd ever summoned.

"We're almost there!" Trace'e called out.

"Almost is not there!" Other Steve cried out, swinging his great sword around repeatedly like an orcish Kurgan.

"Keep tight!" Ketra shouted.

I grabbed tight to one of her loose scales and buried my fingers between the spaces, which was oddly slimy, and sucked in my breath. The other passengers did the same and we were aimed directly at the Tower of Everfrost. Specifically, a very large, cathedral-like, stained glass window on its side.

"This is gonna suck," I muttered.

Ketra breathed out her lightning once more and shattered the window of the tower before we broke plenty more of it when she passed through its remains. The shadow vrocks pursuing us broke off before entering the Tower of Everfrost as if it would be entering a fire.

That was not a good sign.

Either way, Ketra's gigantic dragon body entered the interior chamber that seemed to be some sort of demented chapel to the King Below. It reminded me a bit of a *Castlevania* level because it was unnecessarily huge, had free floating candles, and there was art depicting either Jacob or someone equally faceless conquering the world. I didn't get to pay much attention to events, though, because Ketra's massive frame crashed against the ground, destroying multiple pews as well as depositing us right in front of a stone altar surrounded by statues.

"Ow," Ketra muttered, clearly having broken multiple bones. She was handling it like a champ, though.

"Heal, friend dragon!" Trace'e said, her hand glowing as she waved it over the injuries she spotted.

"Yeah, we haven't gotten the treasure yet!" Other Steve said.

"Shut up, Steve," I muttered, sliding off Ketra and debating whether I could do anything to help.

One of the things that Jacob had taught me was to try to divorce my brain from the D&Disms that underpinned Dungeon magic. But also to respect them. Basically, I was the one who put the rules in place, so they didn't need to be in place but because I'd put them in place, I had to understand them because the rules shaped the magic.

Which, blah-blah-blah magic.

Blah-blah-blah, the Force.

151

After that, I'd tuned out and started humming the disco version of the *Star Wars* theme.

Either way, there wasn't much I could do and simply kept my hand on Ketra as she was patched up as much as possible. Once that was done, she transformed back into her human form and began casting her own healing spells on herself.

Which, good for her.

Obviously not needed, I decided to check out the altar and found the four statues around it were dressed in clothes. Hats, coats, pants, and shirts while only the flesh and hair were transformed into stone. It didn't take a genius to figure out they'd been people who were turned to stone.

"Well, they're dead," I muttered. One of the things I'd learned about magic was that a lot of the things we learned from cartoons were false. A person turned to stone was as dead as a human being turned to ashes.

Except, when I patted one of them on the arm, I felt warmth as well as a pulse.

What the hell?

"Stone stasis," Ketra explained to my confusion. "It's a common tool of the magically created monsters that Jacob put to guard the Tower of Everfrost. They freeze people in place but keep them alive and preserved until the monster can use its saliva to restore them. You know, for eating."

I stared at Ketra. "You know, I'm starting to think Jacob has a bit of a dark side to him."

"Jacob Riverson. The God of Evil? That Jacob?" Trace'e pointed out.

"Yes," I replied, ignoring her sarcasm. "Seriously, Jacob has an inner mad architect here. He and Acherak should compare notes."

"Gary—" Ketra started to say.

"Acherak is the villain from *Tomb of Horrors*. Except, he's a demilich, not a lich. However, a demilich is a super-lich rather than a lich because they've mostly transcended the physical plane," I replied. "Which is just stupid naming as far as—"

"Gary!" Ketra interrupted. "Can you help them?"

I blinked; the thought hadn't even occurred to me. Probably because I was an asshole. "I think I have a *Stone to Flesh* scroll. I never bothered to learn the spell because, well, it just turns a statue into a dead body. Man, there was egg on a lot of faces when people thought it would work like the ones in the book."

Yeah, okay, maybe introducing Dungeon magic to *everyone* hadn't been a completely great idea. I'd put a warning on the books, though. Who could have realized that people would often ignore them and assume it would do what they thought it should do rather than what was written? Oh, right, anyone who knew anything about people.

"Uh huh," Ketra said. "Just do it."

"I only have one, though," I replied.

"Choose but choose wisely," Trace'e said. "For, okay, I forget the rest of the saying. Something-something will give you life. Oh, forget it."

I wondered if they had internet streaming on this world. "I'll pick one and maybe we can find if any of these guys know what we're facing here."

"Obviously not well," Other Steve grunted before sniffing the air. "What kind of scummy graverobbers actually try to rob Hell? Despicable."

I ignored Other Steve's obvious sarcasm and tried to pick who I'd turn back. Maybe I could help the others later, but I was more interested in the now. Who was the leader? Who might know the most? What might they know? In the end, some details jumped out at me about this group: not the least that they were from my world.

You might think that was a premature decision, but I learned this by checking their wallets, which were in their decidedly non-petrified pockets, and noted that most of them were from Atlas City, Florida. They were also part of the American Dungeon Magic Association, Tabletop, and LARPers League—which already made me feel bad about their deaths.

In the end, I chose the last of them by their armor. They were an androgynous-looking man dressed in a specially formed practical suit of reinforced carbon-fired plate that was designed for maximum mobility. But it was the insignia that cinched it for me. They had put the original Ultragod symbol, the one from the 1940s, with the UG in a star on it. Call it a little weird but everyone else's heraldry was skulls or dragons as well as an ad for an internet stamp service. At least no one had Shoot-Em-Up's logo of a Klan hood with two crossed Confederate pistols. One guy had worn a t-shirt of that while in line to get my autograph at ComicCon.

No, he wasn't dead.

My kids were there.

Either way, I pulled out the scroll and read over it for a few minutes before stuffing it back in my bag. I'd left a spell slot open for just this sort of occasion. Don't argue with me about this not being how scrolls or spells work. Screw the rules, I make them.

"Okay," I said, clearing my throat and raising my hands in the air, wiggling my fingers. "Let me remember the spell incantation: *Stone to Flesh!*"

Ketra rolled her eyes.

The others looked enraptured as Disney pixie-dust twirled out of my fingertips and twirled around one of the statues. The stone slowly crumbled away from their face, and they fell to the ground, seemingly stunned by their return to living flesh.

"Double EXP bonus for style!" I shouted, holding my hands in the air.

"Shh!" Ketra loudly made the noise with a finger across her mouth, defeating the purpose of a shh, looking annoyed. "You don't know what you're going to attract."

"Monsters, I'd wager," I replied, less than serious about our circumstances. After all, we'd already lost two of our party on this ordeal. "But this group might prove to be more helpful to me than any contents of an Unspeakable Vault."

Jacob had told me it was six months to an hour between this dimension and his. Which was possible. I didn't know much about planar physics and parallel realities, but that sort of thing happened. People spent months in fairyland only to come back and find only hours had passed or the reverse. Nazi Puncher, always a favorite, had missed the entire latter half of the twentieth century by stopping in Valhalla to beat up the Norse Gods' Germanic imposters created by Loki. Man, that guy had needed some therapy.

But what if Jacob had been lying? What if our worlds were closer together and I'd abandoned my family for months? What if it was possible to return to them right now? Both answers offered troublesome possibilities. While I'd rather the second be true, I didn't want the first to be true solely for the ramifications. I'd come to like Jacob and was hoping my Obi-Wan wasn't my Svengali. Look it up if you don't get the reference.

"Gary Karkofsky?" the freed adventurer said, further confirming they came from my world. They had a light Londonium accent, which basically was Royal Pronunciation English but from a weird steampunk country ruled by supervillains.

I looked down. "Yeah, so I'm told."

"Hi," the man said. "I'm...Larry."

"Larry what?" I asked, having already stolen their wallet and found out their name. It had been alongside a Trans Alliance membership card and a Foundation junior agent card. They were about twenty, which made the latter questionable but not impossible. Their hair was stark white, which I took to be dyed, and mixed European and Asian ancestry.

"Larry...Karkofsky," Larry said, lowering his voice. He sounded embarrassed. I couldn't imagine why.

"Wow, you are a superfan," I replied, basking in their adulation. Okay, yes, the fact they had my last name may have had a bit more to do with my freeing them from being turned to stone than the fact they had an Ultragod symbol on their armor. I just didn't want you to feel I was shallow. I mean, I am, but I'm not totally shallow. Like ninety percent tops.

Larry looked embarrassed. "I wasn't exactly going to go by my old family name. They weren't terribly understanding."

"Ah," I replied. "Changing the subject now. So, you're what, like a knight of something?"

"Paladin," Larry said, embarrassed. "It turns out you can be one with Dungeon magic if you make the proper oaths and hold to a Lawful Good code."

"I'm so sorry," I replied. "I'll patch that out when I update Dungeon magic again in a month. Why are you on Fantasy Planet?"

"The World Between," Ketra corrected, apparently listening in with the others.

"Whatever," I replied.

"I'm kind of looking for you," Larry said, once more making me think they were a superfan. "I hired on with this group of adventurers because an omen spell told me you were going to be here in a few months. I think you can help me find my birth mother."

Find his birth mother? Named after me? Ah crap.

I sucked in my breath. "Oh wow. Again? Listen, I apologize for missing your first twenty years. I'm quite careful about this—"

"Not you," Larry said, pausing. "Albeit I can understand why you would make that mistake. As far as I know, you aren't my father."

"But the name..." I trailed off.

Larry frowned. "Actually, I chose Larry Karkofsky because there was a poster of you in the government office where I legally changed my name. The eighty-year-old lady behind the counter was a fan. Not enough Jewish supervillains in her opinion. It worked out well, though, because you turned out to be handing out free magic and that saved a lot on polymorphing myself. Plus, hey, I got superpowers in the process too."

"Oh, thank God," I replied. "No offense. Any future children I have, I want to be there for. I missed the early childhoods of my kids due to cosmic retcons. Who is your mother and why you do you think I know her?"

This wasn't the place to be having this conversation but, and this will shock you, I was easily distracted.

Larry looked abashed. "Well, you married her. So, I figured you knew where she got off to."

"Wait." I stopped all movement and stared. "What?"

"Her name was Mandy Colton."

Chapter Sixteen

An Utterly Ridiculous Monster

"Well, fuck," I said.

"You're married?" Ketra asked. The subject never having come up because, well, Mandy considered us to be divorced or at least "until death due we part" and I wasn't sure she was Mandy by the strictest definition.

"Sort of," I replied.

"Sort of?" Larry asked, looking up.

"Yeah, I'm sorry but your mother is dead," I said, doing my best Clegg Lars impression.

A look of horror passed across Larry's face. "I see. I'd known you were no longer together, but I guess I hoped —"

"Sort of," I interrupted. Okay, I was handling this terribly. "I should have led with that."

"*Sort of?*" Larry asked, his voice now having a bit of an edge to it.

I hadn't exactly been keeping a secret identity, what with living in Lancel Warren's mansion and buying up Omega Corp with all the stolen money I'd gotten from my various capers. However, Mandy had done her best to go off the radar. People knew about Nighthuntress and Calico the Vampire Thief but didn't realize they were my wife that had disappeared off the face of the Earth. Indeed, some people speculated I'd killed her

158

since apparently supervillain also meant misogynist in some people's mind. Jerks.

"I know I'm giving you emotional whiplash here," I replied, raising my hands in surrender. "However, your mother is a vampire now."

"Oh my God!" Larry said, horrified.

"Well, she's really mellowed out," I said, pausing. "There was a whole period where she was a soulless killing machine and then possessed by the ghost of Spellbinder. But she spent a bunch of time in the post-apocalypse future it seems, and now is either back to her old self or doing a long con on me. Which I can't discount because I know her soul has gone off to Wiccan Heaven or whatever they believe in. I probably should have paid more attention to her explaining her religion or at least Ultra-Searched it online."

Larry stared in horror. "What the hell?"

"But she is going to be ecstatic to meet you!" I said, realizing how horribly I'd botched this.

Was I responsible for this? One of the few tensions in my marriage with Living Mandy (God, how I hated drawing a distinction) had been the fact I'd always wanted kids while she...didn't. Kind of the thing you should really confirm before you jump into marriage as well as something you can't really compromise on. Later, I'd found out the reason wasn't just because children were body-deforming parasites that sucked up all your time and energy. Sorry, Leia, Mimi, I'm just quoting Cindy.

No, Mandy's reason for not wanting kids was the fact she'd had one before. She'd been a teen mom and not the glamorous kind they exploited on reality TV to horrifying effect. Mandy had gotten pregnant while her father was working as a spy out of Londonium's American embassy, and he took her child within minutes of the birth. Mandy may not have been ready to be a mom—she said as much—but it had been a traumatizing experience all round. Then it had gotten weird. Weirder.

Teenage pregnancy, parental disapproval, closed adoptions, and so on were all mundane traumas. Things you could find in your typical Madonna song. However, later I'd learned that Mandy's child had been retconned from reality by the Primal Destruction. Destruction was an enormous man-child who resembled Comic Book Guy from *The Simpsons* and hated the idea of superheroes growing old, getting married, or having kids. He just wanted one more day (forever) of pretending they were perpetually swinging singles.

It had been one of the reasons why Mandy's soul had moved on and she'd given me the encouragement to defeat Entropicus as well as to end Destruction's reign across the Multiverse. Which, if that sounds like a load of continuity and exposition, sorry, we're on the ninth volume of my biography if we count Cindy's book.

"So, I'm never going to meet my mother," Larry said, sadly.

"Don't be prejudiced," I said, trying to find a positive spin on the possibility of a demon walking around in his mother's corpse. One that had her personality, memories, and possibly a fragment of her soul if I believed the vampire involved. "She's really nice once you get to know her."

"Gary, we need to move," Ketra stood up and dusted herself off. "We need to get to the Unspeakable Vault before the monsters return."

"Oh yeah," I asked, turning back to Larry. "Can you fill us in on how you and your friends became lawn ornaments?"

"They're not my friends," Larry surprised me by addressing that part first. "The Florida Freebooters are just a group I was traveling with. They weren't exactly interested in using their powers to help other people, only enrich themselves."

"And what's wrong with that?" Other Steve asked. It made me wonder if Other Steve's group was another LARP hero group that Jacob and Ketra had brought to this world. If so, that opened a lot of questions. Had I created a tourist industry of nerds invading Fantasy World?

"Everything," Larry said.

I was inclined to agree with Other Steve but wasn't about to correct Larry. I was already starting to mentally refer to Larry as Paladin in my head. No, no, that wasn't enough for someone who was using my last name. No, mentally, Larry was now Ultra-Paladin™! I'd be sure to trademark it when I got back home. I was sure the Anders family and their army of lawyers would have no problem with that whatsoever.

"You didn't answer the question, kid," I said, immediately regretting being condescending.

"I don't know what killed us," Larry said, sighing. "It happened so fast. We were arguing about looting the church—"

"I don't think it qualifies as a church if it's not Christian," I pointed out. "Which this place is manifestly not. So, it's more like a temple. Which also offends me."

That was one of the things I had most against being treated as a god or worshiped as one. Fame was something I'd never wanted, let alone becoming some sort of idol for people to venerate. Indeed, I'd become a supervillain precisely because I didn't want to be any kind of role model. The fact Jacob had a whole planet of people worshiping him made me uncomfortable. Except, he was the God of Evil. Which meant, was I any different?

Crap.

"Either way, welcome to our group," I replied.

"If he's getting an extra part of the treasure, I'd like to vote on it," Other Steve said. "I don't think he's qualified."

"We're only releasing one of them, right?" Trace'e said. "I mean, saving everyone is heroic and all, but we can do that after we divide the treasure, right?"

"Honestly, I feel we should charge them for their medical care," Other Steve said.

I surveyed the other members of my party. "You know, I never thought about the similarity between adventurers and a gang of supervillains before. However, right now, I wish Diabloman was here to smack the hell out of you. Except Ketra."

"Hey!" Trace'e said.

"Sorry, but you're an elf and thus inherently awful," I replied.

"Thank you! I love having my elvish identity reaffirmed," Trace'e said, smiling broadly. "None of you can understand what it's like to be taken as someone other than who you are."

"Can I punch her?" Larry asked. "Hard?"

"Speaking as the only dragon in the group," Ketra said. "Shut the hell up, all of you. There's something nearby."

"Something?" I asked, ignoring the request to be shut up.

That was when I heard a massive thumping noise reminiscent of the T-Rex in the original *Jurassic Park*. Looking down at the ground, I saw some melted ice had formed into puddles and was vibrating with the movement.

Oh hell.

"I do recall we felt something like this," Larry said, looking around furtively. "Also, an absolutely horrifying noise."

"Great," I muttered. "Well, we're in Hell and in an evil god's castle. So, we should expect monsters. I wonder what sort of nightmarish abomination—"

That was when a huge animal noise reverberated throughout the cathedral interior. It was also a very familiar sounding animal noise, turned up like it was on loudspeakers. "COCKADOODLE DOO!"

I blinked. "You have got to be shitting me."

"Oh no," Trace'e said, looking terrified. "A cockatrice."

"Hehe, she said cock," Other Steve muttered, proving he was twelve years old at heart. Either that or a forty-year-old online multiplayer gamer.

"A cockatrice?" I asked, trying to remember my *Monstrous Manual* or at least those early *Final Fantasy* games when every monster wasn't a hot anime bunny girl or genie. "Aren't those little rooster sized monsters that can turn you to stone?"

"The ones in our world are a bit larger, Gary," Ketra said, gesturing to the nearest exit. "Let's get the hell out of here."

I didn't get a chance to move as the THING arrived. Yes, "thing" was all in caps because I had no idea how else to describe it. Well, yes, I did, I could describe it as a dinosaur-sized rooster with glowing red eyes. The creature moved through one of the doorways in the back of the cathedral and raised its head like it was surveying a barnyard. The creature only had feathers around its neck as the rest of its body was covered in thick-ass scales.

"Okay, I have no idea how to react to this," I replied, staring at the sight.

The rooster's eyes then shot terrifying energy beams that tore up the ground where they stuck heading toward us. Ketra tackled me out of the way, her speed enhanced by her human-sized wings, and Larry managed to conjure a glowing energy shield that was larger than his entire body. Which was impressive Dungeon magic for a paladin. Their spell slot list was crap.

Trace'e managed to escape the death ray eyes of the cockatrice (a rare sentence if I ever said one) by turning into a sparrow. Unfortunately, Other Steve charged with his sword drawn instead. Unfortunately, because this was a world without saving throws, he was immediately petrified by the creature.

"Quick, Gary!" Trace'e called out. "Turn him back into flesh so we can fight it!"

"I only had the one scroll," I shouted back. "You have to wait for me to rememorize my spells."

"Rememorize...what is that nonsense!?" Trace'e called back, turning back into her elf form before hiding behind a statue of Jacob. An actual statue-statue since it was about twenty-feet tall and built into the side of the wall. I also didn't think Ringwraiths—sorry *Wraith Knights*—could be petrified.

I got that reaction a lot, even when I 'fudged' the rules like re-memorizing spells without bothering to take a six-hour rest like I did back at the Tsavong homeworld. Yeah-yeah, I cheated. The Dungeon Master—who is me—didn't call me out so it's all fair.

"Long story!" I shouted, throwing lightning bolts at the cockatrice that shrugged them off like rain drops. Damnit! Who knew these things were so tough! Oh, right, Larry's group probably did now.

"Turn into a dragon!" Trace'e called, still flying away.

Ketra conjured a shield around herself and me, blocking another blast of the cockatrice's petrifying gaze. "Making myself a bigger target right now is not going to help things!"

"To think, Other Steve gave his life for you!" Trace'e shouted, turning back into a normal person.

I was ninety-nine percent sure that there was no religious or moral doctrine that would accept what Other Steve did as sacrificing himself. I was honestly planning on ribbing the guy about getting killed by a giant chicken when I managed to fix him. That, of course, made me feel terrible when the cockatrice—which I'd mentally named Elvis for reasons that will be inexplicable to sane minds—smashed Other Steve with its beak then started drooling on the remains before scooping them up in a gory display of magical violence.

"Well, shit," I muttered. "Time to pull off another miracle. Or at least come up with a plan of some sort."

"For Ultragod and the cause of justice!" Larry shouted, lifting his sword and a glowing aura appeared around him before he charged at Elvis.

Elvis turned his head toward Larry and another blast of glowing energy shot from his eyes. Not sure what else to do, I reacted in the only way I could.

"*Fly!*" I shouted, regretting that I didn't say, "Fly, you fools!"

The magic poured from my fingertips and sent Larry flying. Larry didn't react as if I was desperately trying to keep my dead wife's son from horrific demise but as if I'd come up with an incredibly daring plan involving him.

Ultra-Paladin, as I was going to have to convince Larry to let me rename him, did a somersault in the air and proceeded to jab his glowing sword right between the eyes of the cockatrice. The creature continued blasting its eye beams in every direction, letting forth rooster cries that sounded like they'd been blasted through a loudspeaker.

Ketra took advantage of the momentary distraction to conjure a bow made of light that reminded me of the one from the old *Dungeons & Dragons* cartoon. Well, you know, aside from the hundred other things that reminded me of that around here. She rapidly fired two shots of glowing arrows that pierced the cockatrice's eyes, blinding it as well as ending the threat of its petrifying gaze.

Larry drove his sword deeper into the skull of the creature and caused it to fall over, landing with a thud on his former adventuring party as well as a half-dozen pews. All of them crumbled beneath the cockatrice's weight, scattering debris throughout the area. It also sealed the ending of our fine feathered friend.

I stared at the shattered stone statues, the corpse of the cockatrice, then up to Larry.

"Well, they're dead. Hey, Larry, are you alive?"

"Yes!" Larry shouted back. "Barely."

"Yay! We won!" Trace'e shouted, throwing her hands up in the air and stepping out from behind Jacob's statue.

"You didn't do anything!" Ketra said.

"I cheered on morale!" Trace'e said. "Also, I'm not critiquing you for violating the balance! That animal was an important part of the natural order!"

"It was a magically created monster living in a castle *in Hell*! It has no place in the natural order!" Ketra shouted at the top of her lungs. The words echoed through the cathedral interior and spread throughout the castle.

That was when I heard a large series of growls, howls, and noises that were every bit as monstrous as the cockatrice's own. Except there were dozens of them now coming from multiple directions. Ketra had just announced our presence to every other horrifying abomination in the Tower of Everfrost.

Ketra paused. "Okay, that one was on me."

Trace'e shook her head. "I am very disappointed in you, Ms. Ketra. First you bring your boyfriend on the quest and next you announce us all to the monsters inside. I hope you're happy."

"He is not my boyfriend," Ketra snapped. "He is a friend who I have sex with! We also temporarily live together. Which is completely different!"

Larry got up off the ground. "Don't you already have a girlfriend?"

"What happens on Fantasy World stays on Fantasy World, Larry," I replied. "I don't begrudge Cindy's relationship with

166

the guy who looks like Bradley Cooper at the local hospital, she doesn't begrudge me."

"Really, Bradley Cooper?" Larry asked, revealing where he landed on the preference spectrum.

"Actually, it's more like the entire medical staff and that's just Thursdays, but the supervillain lifestyle is one of sex, drugs, and rock and roll. Except for me, it'd be more sex, gaming, and rock and roll."

"You mean superhero," Larry said, sounding all too innocent in that moment. "I thought you reformed. You and Red Riding Hood saved the world a couple of times."

I burst out laughing at the idea of our reformation. "My bad. Yes. Of course."

Seconds later, we were running away from a pair of twenty-foot-tall iron golems that smashed through the walls.

And a giant fiery red bull.

Oh, and a winged ice demon that otherwise looked like a Balrog.

Yeah.

This was going to suck.

Chapter Seventeen

Speaking of the Unspeakable Vault

W ell, we managed to survive.
　　Barely.

The three of us remaining from our original adventuring party plus our newest member ducked in and out of the surrounding rooms to avoid the horde of indestructible monsters hunting us down like animals. Unfortunately, we couldn't hide and every time we entered a new room, it meant we'd often encounter new monsters that forced us out of one of the other doors that were inevitably present. Sometimes we looped around and doubled back in hopes of getting the creatures to fight one another or fooling them for a time.

It got very *Scooby Doo*.

In the end, exhausted as we were, we managed to make it over the Bridge of Totally-Not Khazad Doom without having to sacrifice the party wizard until we arrived through a tight crevice in what seemed to be natural cave formations covered in ice. This opened up to a three-story stone temple that resembled a human skull. Its mouth had a missing tooth that formed a passageway and its eyes contained burning witchfire braziers. It was the kind of place where Skeletor would build his den. There was a light "bug zapper"-esque hum coming from the passageway inside the skull and the entrance was completely opaque.

Outside, I could hear the monsters screaming in frustration with some sounding suspiciously like Godzilla and a few saying things like, "I am Synistar! I hunger! Run! Run! Run!"

Yep, I was pretty sure Jacob had either been to Earth or had been watching the place for a very long time.

"Well, that was a less than heroic series of encounters," Larry muttered.

"Any fight you can run away from is still a victory," I replied.

"I'm pretty sure that's not how the saying goes," Larry said.

I gave a dismissive wave. "This place is a bigger meatgrinder than *Dragon's Lair*. The original one from the Eighties that didn't have any button prompts."

"Is it really appropriate to discuss video games when some of our companions are dead?" Larry asked.

"Yes," I replied, crossing my arms.

Larry waited for more. Seeing he wasn't getting any, shrugged. "Okay then."

"This is it," Ketra said, taking a few breaths.

"What?" I asked.

"This is the Vault of the Unspeakable," Ketra said, pointing to the giant skull. "No one who has entered has ever survived."

"You might have mentioned that," I replied.

Trace'e looked at the vault with naked hunger in her eyes.

"It's why it's unspeakable," Ketra said. "It's managed to keep its secrets for centuries as a result. The only reason I know it contains the Primal Orb and what I'm after is because Jacob told me. It was a slip up as he said that even he can't remove what is placed there."

"Seems rather stupid," I replied. "Why put anything in the vault at all then?"

"I gather there is a way to open it, but it requires another god to do it," Ketra said. "Hence, you."

"Oh joy!" I replied, feeling used. "The real reason I'm here."

Ketra rolled her eyes. "Yes, Gary, the reason I invited you is because I thought you might be able to contribute."

"What is it you're after anyway?" I asked, guessing I probably should have asked earlier.

Ketra sighed. "Eggs."

I blinked. "Eggs."

"Specifically, my eggs," Ketra said.

I opened my mouth, closed it, then turned to one side. "I have *questions*."

Ketra sighed, looking annoyed and back at the way we'd come. A giant three-headed dog was pawing at the crack we'd slipped through. "I wasn't always a dragon. I used to be a normal human woman before I made the transformation."

"And this resulted in you...laying eggs," Larry said.

Ketra glared at him with such an intensity, I suspected he would catch fire. "Dragons can procreate once every century. You lay four eggs and then a male comes along and fertilizes them."

"Yuck," Trace'e said, nervously looking over her shoulder at the vault.

"Yes, a lot less fun than the other kind of mating," I said, shrugging.

"That's why dragons shapeshift," Trace'e replied. "Much easier to get yourself off with those human or elf bodies."

I stared at her. "That puts an entirely new spin on dragons demanding maiden sacrifices."

"Why, what did you think they were for?" Trace'e asked.

I stared at her. "I have no response to that."

"Also, dragon males aren't needed to fertilize the eggs," Ketra said. "Any sapient male can do it. It's where half-dragons come from."

Both Larry and I stared at her.

"What?" Ketra asked.

"Lady, I come from a world where a radioactive scorpion can give you superpowers and what you said makes no goddamn sense," I replied. "How? What?"

"I'd rather not discuss it," Ketra said, sighing. "Either way, I asked Jacob to put the dragon eggs away in the vault after my last breeding cycle. I'd lost a lot of friends and family, so I wasn't eager to consider raising any new spawn. However, time passes—"

"Really? This is about having kids?" Trace'e asked. "What kind of adventurer are you?"

"Trace'e, come over here so I can elf-slap the shit out of you," Ketra said, raising the palm of her hands.

"There's no need for violence," Trace'e said, before reaching into her robes and pulling out a revolver. "Except there is!"

I did a double take. "Is that a *gun*?"

"Back off, chumps!" Trace'e said, her voice shifting from her normal one to one that was distinctly London in origin. "This is a stick up!"

"What the hell is going on?" I asked, not necessarily afraid so much as, well, confused.

"She's holding us at gun point," Larry said, sounding about as impressed as I was.

Which was not at all.

"But why?" I asked.

Trace'e sneered. "I am actually a member of the Assassins Guild of Falconcrest City!"

"You...are?" I asked, wondering when and where that had happened. Was there a tourism industry of Fantasy World that

I didn't know about? If that was true, I should have been getting a cut of this.

Ketra shrugged. "And?"

"And this was all an elaborate trap to get the Primal Orb within!" Trace'e cackled. Literally cackled.

"So, you're not an elf?" I asked, confused.

"We knew that!" Ketra said.

"I am an elf in spirit!" Trace'e snapped. "People should understand that."

"It doesn't apply with races!" Larry shouted, now pissed off.

I didn't blame him.

Trace'e sneered. "You used to be someone, Merciless, but your recent failures have proven you're unworthy of anything but scorn!"

"Oh, I proved that way before now," I muttered, wondering what recent failures she could be referring to. It wasn't like I was lacking in them, but they were mostly things nobody else knew about. "Wait, does that mean you *weren't* born an orc?"

Trace'e responded by firing the gun near my ear, causing a massive ringing.

"Mother pus bucket!" I said, feeling the side of my head. "Does no one know how much that hurts?"

"I do! That's why I did it!" Trace'e sneered, moving toward the humming doorway in the giant skull. "Now prepare for the ascension of the Druidess!"

Trace'e then jumped through the door.

There was a crackling hissing noise.

Then nothing.

"She's dead, isn't she?" Larry asked.

"Yep," I said. "Doorway of Oblivion, aka a Sphere of Annihilation. You put it on a doorway or down a shaft and there will always be hordes of dumbasses who jump through. Smog the Dragon King—or Queen as it turned out—loved it."

"Damn," Larry said.

Ketra walked up to the vault. "Well, I didn't expect the team to make it through. However, we did, and now it's time to figure out a way in."

"Figure a way in?" I asked.

Ketra gave me a sideways look. "Yeah, why do you think you're here? Only a god can enter, and you qualify—technically."

"Yes, technically," I muttered, wondering if I should try and use the Crown of the Gods again before realizing that was undoubtedly going to backfire on me.

"What are you looking for?" Larry asked. "No offense, I was here for you."

"Fortune and glory, kid," I said.

"Does everything you say have to be a movie quote?" Larry asked.

"No, sometimes it's video games," I replied, examining the scene before me. "In any case, I'm trying to get home. I don't suppose you know what's been going on there?"

Larry shook his head. "I left almost a year ago and have been planeswalking ever since. I visited a world where Cthulhu had destroyed everything, a planet where monsters were open and legal, and a couple of cyberpunk worlds that may be this one in the distant past."

"Sounds like you had a pretty interesting set of adventures," I replied.

"What about you?" Larry asked.

"I was unable to stop the Tsavong Queen from blowing up her own planet," I said, coughing. "Yes, deeply traumatizing. She also killed the Trench Coat Magician!"

"Oh no!" Larry said, appalled. "He's one of my favorite superheroes."

"Yeah, but a terrible anarchist. Probably one of those *communist* ones," I muttered, doing my best impression of a gatekeeping philosophy student.

"Versus free market?" Larry asked, confused.

I pointed at him. "You shut up!"

Ketra sighed. "Can we get our focus back on the Unspeakable Vault?"

"I'm ready to open it!" I lied, raising my hands. "Prepare to be astounded by the godlike power of the all-powerful Merciless: The Supervillain without Mercy™!"

"You have no idea how to open it, do you?" Ketra asked.

"Silence!" I said, pulling out the Merciless Staff that turned into the Merciless Sword again. I proceeded to walk up to the door and poke it.

"Seriously?" Larry asked. "You're going to destroy your magic sword here?"

"It's not my magic sword!" I said, cheerfully. "It's like Wallstreet, it's always best to play with other people's money!"

The second the tip of the Merciless Sword touched the end of the door of oblivion, there was an explosion of magical light as positive charges hit negative, or whatever the mystical equivalent was. I was thrown back thirty feet and hit the ground with a thud. Thankfully, I didn't hit my head, or I probably would have cracked my head clean open. Instead, I just felt like I'd stuck a fork in a wall socket before being hit by a truck.

"*Lay on Hands!*" Larry said, putting his hands over me. The paladin's hands glowed and most of the pain subsided.

"Really? You don't touch me to do that?" I asked, raising an eyebrow.

"LARP rules," Larry said.

174

"Ah," I replied, sitting up to look at the doorway that no longer was an opaque black. Much to my surprise, my plan had worked, and the skull was slowly opening its mouth to reveal a passageway illuminated by blue witchfire torches.

"And now One-Eyed Willy's treasure will be ours!" I said, shaking a fist.

"*The Goonies*, really?" Larry asked.

"What's wrong with the *Goonies*?" I asked, getting up.

Larry shrugged. "Just thinking it's a little weird for a middle-aged man to be quoting a kids movie from the Eighties."

"Clearly you don't know me at all, Ultra-Paladin," I said, slowly climbing to my feet. Much to my surprise the Merciless Sword showed no damage from its use. A blessing after all the disaster dominoes we'd had fall over on us.

"It's time to collect our reward," Ketra said, walking past me. "I owe you, Merciless. Let's not make this a habit, though."

Larry watched her leave. "Warm personality, that one. Are you sure you're together?"

"It's more a 'two ships passing in the night' thing," I replied, pausing. "Well, two ships anchored beside one another over a few months period. If I didn't sleep with the women who verbally abuse me, I'd be down to like two."

Larry stared at me.

"It's the fault of all the anime I watched growing up," I replied, following Ketra. "I have a kink, what can I say?"

The interior of the Unspeakable Vault was half-museum and half-hoarder's lair. There were beautiful magical items, stacks of old books, taxidermy animals, and a few relics that seemed to date back to Earth's history. Venus De Milo was here, the statue not the superheroine, and so was a Statue of Liberty miniature. Oh, and what looked like an old Mortal Kombat arcade cabinet. I saw no sign of Ketra's eggs, but maybe they were in a box somewhere.

"Well, this is weird," I muttered, surveying the place. "Are you sure this isn't just Jacob's basement?"

"I have what I came for, Merciless," Ketra said, confusing me. "The question is whether or not what you want is here."

"You don't know for sure?" I asked.

Ketra shrugged. "Would you have come if I'd admitted it wasn't?"

"Yeah," I replied. "I like doing favors for my friends."

Ketra blinked. "Alright then. I'm sorry."

That was when Larry called over. "Hey, Gary, there's something you should see."

"What's that?" I asked, walking over.

There, nestled on a stack of what seemed to be Fantasy World newspapers reporting on elvish royal weddings, was a large pulsating orange ball of unearthly energy. It was the Orb of Fate. The Orb of the worst that could happen to someone or the worst person they could become.

Damn.

Not the orb I wanted.

Larry reached to touch it.

"No!" I shouted, touching the orb instead.

Shit.

Everything went orange.

Chapter Eighteen

There Is No Fate but What We Something-Something

I woke up on top of a rooftop in Falconcrest City. Touching the Fate Orb had transported me here, presumably. Maybe it was one of those vision quest things that happened every now and then when you were a super person. We were big on symbolism and personal growth stories. Too bad I never learned from mine.

However, it wasn't Falconcrest City-Falconcrest City. At least the Falconcrest City of today. Instead, it was the Falconcrest City of about thirty years ago. The city didn't have any of its new towers, low-income housing built in the last few years, or a skyline visible through the horrific smog that choked the lungs just to breathe it. It was the Falconcrest City of my childhood when the Nightwalker had been unable to do anything other than stem the bleeding of a city suffering from a thousand wounds.

To be fair, Lancel Warren had been undermined by the people he trusted the most. The police, media, and industry in the city had all been under the control of the Brotherhood of Infamy. They had been eager to bring about the end of the Age of Superheroes and happy to line their pockets by leaving everyone else in abject misery.

That had been a long time ago. The city had been ravaged by a zombie plague, the death of its champion, and more. Things had gotten better but the reasons hadn't been especially great. I'd killed most of the worst supervillains—the Brotherhood of Infamy—and pumped a few billion of their stolen fortunes back into the city. Ironically, though, it had been my evil authoritarian doppelganger who had fixed the place. He'd inspired everyone with his lies and put away the dangerous while liberating the oppressed.

It attacked everything I believed in, that people just needed to be shown the way and not crushed under the oppression of someone making all their decisions for them. However, that had been exactly what I'd done to the entirety of the world, rewriting it to my pleasure. I tried not to think about the similarities. Between us.

And whether it was worth it.

To simply ditch the benefits of "free will" and just stack it all up like Legos into the shape I wanted it to be. Because, honestly, no one cared how the world got to be a nice place for everyone. They didn't want to be the one who made all the decisions. But if that meant what I thought it meant, if it really was just about the ends justifying the means, then both superheroes and supervillains had it wrong. Evil was just a matter of perspective.

"Wow, that got dark," I muttered aloud, standing up. I wasn't dressed in my Merciless robes; I was just in a hoodie and jeans.

"Yes, it did, didn't it?" a voice spoke behind me.

I really hoped it was going to be Lancel Warren behind me but knew it wasn't. Still, I admitted I wasn't expecting the sight of the white ski-mask-wearing guy in all-white paramilitary gear with a noose around his neck, carrying an M16. His Nineties antihero Klansman look was made more ridiculous by adding a cape that looked like a bath towel. It was Theodore Whitman AKA Shoot-Em-Up.

"Didn't I kill you?" I asked, happy to do it again. I tried to conjure a fireball, but it didn't appear in my hands. "*FIREBALL! LIGHTNING BOLT! CLOUDKILL!*"

Nada.

Of course.

"Your magic comes from your divinity and altering of your reality with the Primal Orbs, Merciless," Shoot-Em-Up said. "It doesn't work here. Mind you, now that you've bathed in the light of another Primal Orb, you're severed from it forever."

I stared at my fingertips. "Yeah, well, I didn't need Dungeon magic anyway. Magic users are always lame in superhero stories anyway. It's so incredibly undetailed that the only person who really makes a proper magic system is Brandon Sanderson and I only liked *The Reckoners* trilogy."

"You know they're going to die, right?" Shoot-Em-Up asked.

I paused. "You'll have to be more specific."

"Everyone," Shoot-Em-Up said, staring at me. "Everyone you love. Everyone you hate. Everyone. You can't save them."

"Are you sure you're Shoot-Em-Up and not Edgelord?" I asked. "Because Edgelord sounds like that. He is the Lord. The Lord of the Edge."

I didn't think this was the real Shoot-Em-Up. I wasn't kidding when I said I'd already killed him. He had been my first kill: with a plain old gun I'd shot him when I was fourteen. I'd wanted to avenge my brother's death and quench the anger by killing the person who'd ruined my father and mother's life. My life. Kerri had gotten over it easily enough, she could just talk to Keith's ghost. But the killing had just made the pain worse, deeper.

All the killing did.

"You know Mandy never came back, right?" Shoot-Em-Up said, conjuring an image of my wife drinking blood from an abusive spouse. It floated above his head.

"You're not telling me anything I didn't know," I asked. "She died because of me."

"No," Shoot-Em-Up said, conjuring images of the rest of my family. Mimi. Cindy. Leia. Lisa. Kerri. "Mandy died because she decided to be a hero."

The image above our heads became the dragon killing Mandy. I didn't even remember its name, had blotted out most of the memory. However, she'd been fighting as Nighthuntress and without powers. It had gotten her killed.

Everything that followed had just been an attempt to try to make up for that. The use of the *Book of Midnight*, getting Merciful to resurrect her (only to have her possessed by Spellbinder), and then trying to accept her as an undead predator.

Shoot-Em-Up conjured another image, this time of Mandy writing a letter at her desk by her coffin. She was using a pen, which I just found archaic.

"Let me add some sound effects," Shoot-Em-Up said.

DEAR GARY, Mandy started narrating her own letter. YOU HAVE NO IDEA HOW HARD IT IS TO WRITE THIS LETTER.

"Ah crap," I said, knowing where this was going.

IT IS HARD BEING THE SHADOW OF SOMEONE YOU NEVER KNEW BUT WERE MADE IN THE IMAGE OF. I FEEL EVERYTHING MANDY FELT BUT ONLY AS A PALE ECHO. I AM A VIOLENT, EVIL CREATURE. TIME HAS ALLOWED ME TO CONTROL THE HUNGER. BUT EVEN THE SHADOW OF BEING THE REAL MANDY IS MORE HAPPINESS THAN I EVER EXPERIENCE FROM ANYTHING OTHER THAN THE BLOOD.

"Okay, gross metaphor but she's a vampire," I said, making a joke with absolutely no mirth in my voice.

I CAN'T CONTINUE PRETENDING TO BE HER, THOUGH, BECAUSE I AM A THREAT TO EVERYONE YOU LOVE. ALL I SENSE WHEN I AM AROUND THEM IS FOOD AND ONLY THE SHADOW OF THE LOVE I FELT WHILE ALIVE KEEPS ME FROM GOING AFTER THEM. WORSE, I AM HOLDING YOU BACK. I SEE HOW HAPPY YOU ARE WITH CINDY AND YOUR CHILDREN—

"You can stop now," I said, dryly. "I have an idea where this is going. Probably since I woke up and she said we needed to talk."

"No, I think we'll continue," Shoot-Em-Up said.

"She needs to know about her son," I replied, looking at him. "Maybe that will jog her memory. It doesn't matter if she loves me."

Those were the hardest words I'd ever said in my life.

"Your Mandy is dead," Shoot-Em-Up said, aiming his M16 at me. "You want to know what I really think, Merciless? I find it interesting that you had ultimate power in your hands. The ability to rewrite reality as you saw fit and all you did was make it a slightly less shitty version of your world. Your sheer lack of imagination disgusts me. You didn't even have the decency to make yourself ruler of the world. You just put Ultragod in charge of the planet and hoped he would solve it for you. He won't live either."

An image of a nuclear bomb going off and consuming Ultragod along with hundreds of other heroes as well as thousands of bystanders appeared above his head.

"Don't..." I trailed off.

"Do you want to know how Jane Doe dies? As an old woman trying to defend her grandchildren from a lynch mob of bigots? G? He lives long past any person who cares about whether he lives or dies in a dimension that is always threatening to fall apart from internal strife, when he just wanted to live in yours where good is cherished and evil is punished. Cindy? She dies with blood on her teeth and a curse on her tongue, wishing she had more time," Shoot-Em Up ticked down the people I cared about one after the others. I saw the images of how they would all die. "Your children."

I charged him, dodged out of the way of the gun firing over my shoulder and deafening me, before delivering a spin kick to his jaw. Shoot-Em-Up went flying across the roof and I grabbed the gun he'd dropped before aiming it at his head.

"Huh," Shoot-Em-Up said. "I am surprised you could do that."

"So am I," I said, wondering where that Matrix move came from and deciding I didn't care. "Goodbye, Ted. It's been a pleasure killing you again."

Shoot-Em-Up removed his mask to reveal my face beneath. "Hi, Gary."

"Please tell me there's not a universe where I'm a Klansman," I said, not pulling the trigger. "Because I'm not into the self-hating Jew thing. Wait, are you Merciful? Because, seriously, I hate the fact he's my archnemesis. The whole idea of being my own worst enemy is so cliche."

"I'm your Fate, Gary," Shoot-Em-Up Gary said. "The absolute worst version of you that you can be."

"No shit," I said, staring at him. "I'm not a fascist, though."

"You're an anti-hero, though," Shoot-Em-Up Gary said. "You've killed hundreds of supervillains and plenty of more Nazis."

"Nazis don't count!" I snapped.

"And it worked," Shoot-Em-Up said. "You did the dirty work necessary to fix your world. Killed the people like Shoot-Em-Up, Tom Terror, Psychoslinger, and President Omega. In the original reality, before you altered it, that was how things were meant to go. Not *Merciless'* reality but *your* reality. The Age of Heroes ends because the Age of Villains ends. You win. The bad guys are gone. The good guys get to have their happily ever after. The story ends."

"No," I said, lowering the gun. "That's not how it's supposed to be. That's Shoot-Em-Up's logic."

"Maybe the problem was just Shoot-Em-Up was a racist piece of shit rather than some understanding people needing to be put down," Shoot-Em-Up Gary said.

"Yeah, maybe," I said, shooting him in the face. I'll spare you the description, but it was exactly what you'd expect the results to be.

It didn't make me feel any better.

"Not your own worst enemy, huh?" Jacob's voice spoke behind me.

"Seriously, how does everyone get behind me without me noticing?" I asked.

"Magic," Jacob replied.

I turned around and saw the Wraith Knight standing there with the Primal Orb of Fate glowing in one shadowy hand. He closed his hand and it vanished before he crossed his arms.

"This was all a test," I muttered, realizing I'd completely missed the forest for the trees.

"Yes," Jacob replied, dryly.

"And I failed," I replied.

"Miserably," Jacob said. "I wanted to see if you had it in you to stay the course and see through your training."

"But Han and Leia will die if I don't!" I said, trying to make a joke.

Jacob didn't respond.

"Right, probably not a good time for movie references," I said, ashamed of myself. "So, Ketra wasn't actually after her eggs?"

"She does want to have children but her way of doing that is more traditional," Jacob said, his voice heavy with irony. "You might want to check back in a couple of years."

I grimaced, unsure how to react to that. "Oh wow, I am so glad I am rich."

Seriously, this would be hard to explain to the others. I'd promised I wasn't going to be a rap-star type of supervillain and yet here we were.

"She has her own hoard," Jacob said. "I doubt she wants child support."

Wow, they had child support in Fantasy World? Huh.

"I'm no deadbeat dad," I said, pausing. "Wait, will they be born mammals or reptiles? Or archosaurs? People always forget about the archosaurs."

"I'm fairly sure dragons do lay eggs so I wouldn't know the mechanics of it or even if it is possible," Jacob said. "But I sincerely doubt it."

"That's evil. It's like something my sister would do," I said. "What about Larry? Is he real or part of the test?"

"Larry is real," Jacob said, keeping his gaze level. I think. "I brought him to this dimension to give you a sense of how your actions have been affecting everyone. You need to be able to understand the broader consequences of the power that comes with being a god."

"I'm not a god," I said, shaking away the idea. "I'm just a supervillain."

"You can be both," Jacob said. "I know something of being hero, villain, and both. God and Devil as one. The superheroes of your time are the latest incarnations of the mythology that humans need to comprehend the broader concepts of good, evil, and everything in-between. They tell these stories to their children not to let them know that monsters are real, children already know that. They tell these stories to their children so that they know monsters can be beaten."

"We have a very similar quote on my world," I replied. "And which am I? Hero or villain?"

"Yes," Jacob replied.

I sighed, defeated. "Maybe Shoot-Em-Up me was right. No, wait, that can't be right. Shoot-Em-Up me is an asshole."

"Fighting evil does not make you evil in itself," Jacob replied. "It is fighting evil without mercy or compassion. Theodore Whitman, the Extreme!, and other individuals from your world have been lost to the rage inside them. There have been Garys of other worlds that have been destroyed by the hatred in their hearts. You are not one of them."

"Not yet," I said, sadly. "So, what happens now that I've screwed up?"

"You go back home," Jacob said, simply.

I understood that and nodded. "Sorry. You wasted a lot of time trying to whip me into shape."

"It was not time wasted," Jacob said. "You have cleansed your mind of all the garbage you had before and now can learn to be a proper wizard. It will simply require you to do a lot of self-study first."

He pulled out a massive thick hardback tome that he dumped in my hands. It simply read *MAGIC FOR DUMMIES* on its cover. Which wasn't the first sign that Jacob had a sense of humor but was the best one so far.

"If this book costs a thousand dollars, you've successfully recreated my college experience," I replied.

Jacob then removed his cloak, which surprised me as I expected to see some horrific bony ghost underneath but instead saw a very bulky South Asian-looking dude with hints of other ancestry. He also had long black hair and a beard like an Indian Aragorn.

"Huh," I said, staring. "Not what I expected you to look like."

"How did you expect me to look like?" Jacob asked.

"I plead the Fifth," I replied. "Also, the internet would hate this revelation."

Jacob offered the cloak. "Take this."

I felt the material of a Reaper's Cloak for the first time in a long time. "I can't take this."

"Do it," Jacob said. "You'll need it for the times ahead."

"*What* times ahead?" I asked.

It was too late, though, as I found my surroundings disintegrating before I fell into a deep dark void.

Again.

Chapter Nineteen

There's No Place Like Home

I was back!

It was a disorientating sensation moving from the Orb of Fate's vision quest world—have I mentioned I hate vision quests? Because I *hate* vision quests—to the physical reality of my home in Falconcrest City. I was inside the library, and nothing seemed to have changed from where the Trench Coat Magician and I had gone off to visit Ultragod. It was disorientating after so long away and I briefly checked myself to see if I was all there.

I was now wearing the Reaper's Cloak that Jacob had given me, which felt familiar and empowering in a way that I hadn't felt since Lancel Warren had ascended to a higher plane of existence. Briefly, I wondered if Jacob would start talking to me, but there was silence. Status quo seemed to be good but not so much that he would be there to continue holding my hand like Obi-Wan Kenobi or Yoda.

I checked my extradimensional pockets too and noted that Jacob's *Magic for Dummies* was still there. There was also the Merciless Sword now the size of a dagger and in my regular pocket. I could feel its power radiating outward, though. I took a second to conjure a ball of fire in my hands without Dungeon magic, check, then a ball of ice, double-check. I briefly turned insubstantial like a Ringwraith and turned back. Check-check-check.

I had to admit that I'd missed my old powers and, while I fully intended to relearn things like how to create dimensional portals as well as heal the dying, this was a pretty good compensation package. I also had three months of training in fighting and thinking tactically, which I now realized was Jacob's primary purpose in teaching me. It hadn't been learning to use Dungeon magic or regular magic specifically, but giving me a foundation to think about using it better. To understand the philosophy behind sorcery and godhood.

Well, the joke was on him! I hadn't learned a goddamn thing! I was going to go back to being a selfish asshat who abused his power in every which way possible!

Loser!

That was when I saw the Crown of the Gods. The dark crown glowing with an unholy energy that made me want to reach over to it and place it on my head. I thought about Shoot-Em-Up Gary's words and that I could have used my powers to make the world genuinely better. Had I learned nothing? What if I could fix things slightly further? Resurrection for good guys and not bad guys. Mandy, returned to true humanity, able to be with me the way we were meant to be. Hell, why not just bring back Keith while I was at it? Why not?

My journey felt like a dream now. It was like that movie Jane told me about where a person got dumped into an alternate reality full of talking animals and weirdness before finally getting back to their family. What was the name? Oh right, *Spider-Man: Into the Spider-Verse*. Honestly, it just seemed like a Splotch family rip off.

"Maybe it wouldn't hurt to retcon the universe just a little bit more..." I trailed off and reached down to the Crown.

"Mr. Karkofsky?" A voice spoke from beside me, for once, but no less surprising.

"Ah!" I said, jumping and bolting to one side. "Goddammit, do I just have no situational awareness? Dammit!"

Much to my surprise, Larry Karkofsky was standing there in his armor. There was a little trans flag emblazoned on it and some Pride stickers which hadn't been there before. Which were weird additions for Jacob to add, but it *was* June. Still, I was grateful to see Ultra-Paladin since he'd prevented me from making a really bad mistake. For now. I shut the pockets of my cloak and put the Crown of the Gods from my mind.

"How did we get here?" Larry asked.

"Our comic writer changed," I explained. "He's aborted the whole Fantasy World arc and is retconning a bunch of stuff. Expect to get back to some old girlfriends, all progress in your life to vanish, and a bunch of references to the period of time your comic was published when the writer was a child."

Larry stared. "What? Also, I'm gay so it would be boyfriends."

"Right," I said, grasping Larry by the shoulders. "Welcome, Larry, to Stately Warren Manor. I want to welcome you into the family and let you know I'm adopting you—"

"What?" Larry repeated.

"As my archnemesis," I explained. "We have an existing family connection, a sort of Pagan Min-Ajay Ghale *Far Cry 4* thing going. You are the son of my wife AKA what is called a stepson. It's perfect for creating cheap heat between us. I'll ask you to rule the world with me and you'll say no. But I'll escape when you defeat me—"

"I don't want to be your archnemesis, Gary," Larry said.

"That's a very hurtful thing to say," I said, staring at him. "A lot of people would be flattered to be my archnemesis."

"Given the fact I renamed myself after you, I think my fandom should be obvious," Larry said, as if explaining himself to a small child. "It's more the fact you mostly fight Nazis, Gary. It's not a good look to be your archnemesis. You've never actually been much of a villain."

I gasped in horror. "I know I tried briefly to reform but that was never going to stick."

"Note I said never," Larry said, sighing. "You're about as much a villain as Indiana Jones."

"I'm a killer and a thief!"

"So was Indiana Jones," Larry pointed out. "Mind you, he has a PHD, so he has that on you too."

"Actually, I do too," I pointed out.

Larry blinked. "Really?"

"Yeah, I got an honorary doctorate in Criminology from the University of Londonium College for Supervillains," I said, not pointing out that I only got that after I'd rewritten the world to my pleasure. Which I thought was a pretty good thesis. "Technically, that makes me Doctor Merciless, but Cindy threw a fit when I tried to officially change my codename. Apparently, she thinks the only person who should be referred to as doctor in the house is the person who did the homework. She finished last in her class but that's still better than ninety-nine-point-nine percent of people. Cindy was also juggling three supervillain hench jobs at the time to pay her student loans."

"You know Ultragod cancelled all of those," Larry said.

"AND FUCK HIM FOR IT!" Cindy shouted from down the hall. "Everyone should be poor and miserable and need to commit crimes to pay them off like I did!"

Larry looked up. "How did she—"

"Werewolf hearing," I said. "Apparently, I haven't been gone long enough for her to notice my absence. At least not long enough to care."

"How long would that be?" Larry asked.

"About two years," I guessed. "Anyway, I think we should go talk to the others."

Larry sucked in his breath and nodded. "I look forward to finally meeting my mom. I was never able to find her before because of Colt Colson hiding her identity from me. You know he died last year?"

I didn't respond because, well, I'd been there and saw him die with my own eyes. Agent of The Foundation and war hero or not, he'd been a real asshole. "So I heard. Did he raise you?"

"No, he had me with another family," Larry said. "He did show up on occasion, though. Oddly, he was the most supportive of my transition but said it would hurt my chances of being a Foundation agent."

"So, you became a superhero on your own," I said, my mouth dry. It was the same as Mandy's story.

"Yeah, or so I'm trying to be," Larry said, looking around. "So, where is Mandy?"

I was about to explain the Orb of Fate had given me a vision of her writing me a 'Dear John' letter and I wasn't sure if she was still here when two unexpected people entered my room: Diabloman and my sister Kerri.

Shit.

Diabloman was my first new supervillain friend when I'd set on my quest to become Merciless: The Supervillain without Mercy™. Cindy didn't count because we'd known each other since childhood. For a while, he'd been my best friend as well as mentor. Then he'd made an understandable but awful choice to keep his sister Spellbinder's secret that she was impersonating my dead wife, Mandy.

Man, it seems insane even now to mention it. Spellbinder wanted to live again and Merciful had given her the opportunity to do so. I'd accepted it because I'd run into slammed door after slammed door of Mandy's soullessness being unfixable. I'd taken Spellbinder's actions when they were revealed—rape by deception legally—poorly. And by poorly, I mean I banished her soul to Hell. I let her out, at least I think I did, and then I rewrote the universe. Diabloman hated me when the universe had been rewritten.

Now he was my brother-in-law.

Everything I'd rewritten hadn't been consciously done. I didn't think, "Hey, why don't I brainwash my divorced former best friend into forgiving me and my unmarried sister into getting hitched?" But that was what I did. I'd walked in and found they'd been married for a couple of years and Diabloman didn't have any memory of his sister being resurrected or damned. He was just standing there, happy as a six-foot-eight professional wrestler in a devil mask can be.

My sister Kerri had hair as white as mine, large almost anime-esque eyes, and a Christina Ricci facial structure. She was a tiny thing, about five-foot-three, which was normal height for a woman but made her stand out like Natalie Portman among the frequently six-feet-and-over superhero set. Were it not something I'd bleach my brain over, I'd wonder how Diabloman and she were intimate.

Strangely, my sister wasn't followed by her usual trail of ghosts. That was her superpower, by the way, she could summon and speak with the dead. Technically, she could control them, but she'd never do that as she had the personality of a fluffy kitten crossed with a puppy. Pitten. She was wearing a black business suit dress with hose and carrying a large black purse.

"Hi, Gary!" Kerri said, cheerfully. Which was her default state. If she had a tail, it would be constantly wagging.

"Good afternoon, Gary, I see you have prepared for Ultraday," Diabloman said, gruff but happy. "You have your old costume back."

"Something similar," I said.

"This is Larry," I said, gesturing to, well, Larry.

Larry had an expression of extreme pain on his face as he was standing in front of one of the most infamous supervillains on Earth. "Larry, Larry Karkofsky."

Kerri narrowed her eyes. "Gary, is this another one of your kids from the future!"

"No!" I snapped.

"I'm not," Larry said, raising his hands defensively. "Wait, what do you mean *another*?"

"You'll have to meet my kids," I said, registering what they said. "Ah, so it is Ultraday. Splendid. Just in time to fix everything. Again."

Kerri and Diabloman looked at me strangely.

"Gary, were you mystically transported to another universe where you've been gone for months?" Kerri asked.

I blinked. "How did you know?"

"Well, there's an ancient blue dragon on the front lawn telling people she's here for you to fertilize her eggs. Which apparently is done without body touching and I don't want to know any more. I assume it's like turtles, though, and you just sort of spawn over them."

I looked out the window at Ketra. She was resting lazily in dragon form on the front lawn as the kobolds gave her scales a buff and wash. Apparently, she'd been there a while. "Funny story about that—"

"Clearly, you are unfamiliar with the concept of not wanting to know more. I'll get some Kleenex and lotion."

"Kerri—" I asked, hoping to die in that moment.

193

"We used to share a bedroom when you were fourteen," Kerri said, reminding me why sisters were of the Devil. "Believe me, I didn't want to know about a lot of that stuff. But yeah, I did. Even when you changed the sheets every day when you thought I wasn't looking."

"Please kill me now," I muttered, facepalming.

"You did have separate beds, right?" Larry asked.

"Oh yes," Kerri said. "Across the room and everything. Except for the ghost of the murdered teenager who haunted the house. I didn't tell Gary about her because *they* shared a bed."

"I am not siring any dragon kids," I said, making a firm decision not to proceed with this. "I'm sorry. It was meant to be more of an off-world romance. Sort of like Gabrielle's space husband or Mandy's relationship with Alucard."

"From *Castlevania* or *Vampire Hunter D*?" Larry asked.

"Yes," I replied. "I need to let Ketra know."

"Well don't worry about it," Kerri said. "I just found out you'd had an affair and she'd come to Earth to raise her kids. Plus, I know how super sensitive you are about kids due to your deep-seated family issues. I made it all up to amuse myself."

I stared at her, remembering my words to Jacob. "You are pure evil!"

"Yes, I am your sister," Kerri said, smiling. "Ketra is just staying in our dungeon until she can get her own place."

Diabloman chuckled.

"Never have I been gladder to be asexual," Leia said, walking in with Mimi. Both were wearing extremely fashionable, custom-tailored dresses with accessorized purses. Both enchanted, I know, to be bags of holding.

"Can you erase the memory of this conversation from my mind?" Mimi asked. "I never wanted to know this much about our dad or aunt."

"See, you're giving me permission but later when I bring it up, you'll be pissed," Leia said. "Like when I erased what happened to all those dead cats."

"What?" Mimi asked, doing a double take.

"See!" Leia said.

"Gizmo," I said, using my daughter's codename. "Have you been raising dead animals again?"

"It's not resurrection if they're zombies!" Leia said. "I'm exploring the limits of this whole stupid 'no resurrection' rule!"

Mimi stared in horror. "Is that what happened to my pet koala!?"

"Those are illegal to have anyway!" Leia said.

I took a deep breath. "Leia...I am so very proud of you."

"Gary!" Kerri said.

"You are showing some true initiative in mad science," I said, clasping my hands. "Even though it is literally my job to destroy all undead."

"Except Mandy," Leia said.

"Yes, except her," I replied.

"And Ghost Detective," Mimi added.

"Him too," I said, remembering the hero who consisted of a trench coat and deerstalker "Plus any other undead I spare because I'm a massive hypocrite. Like that time that I ended up crossing over with the *Casper* cartoon and decided not to send him to Hell because he died really young."

Diabloman didn't show any reaction to my mention of Hell or consigning people there.

Good.

"Hi, Mimi," Larry said, waving to Mimi.

"Hi, Larry," Mimi said, waving.

I did a double take. "Wait, you two know each other?"

"Yeah, we're Ultrabook friends," Mimi said. "He's Mandy's son. Hey, bad news, she's stepped out to go find herself. Like outside of the state. Probably."

"What?" Larry asked.

I took a deep breath. "We'll find her for you, Larry."

I wasn't sure about finding her for me. My feelings for Mandy dwarfed those for any other woman, which was unfair to Cindy, my best friend, and Gabrielle, who I only seemed to hurt (and vice versa). However, I'd not only gotten Mandy killed, but my efforts to restore her had caused her immeasurable pain. I also was still only halfway there for considering Vamp Mandy to be her own person separate from the woman she was.

There were also questions that still needed to be answered. After Spellbinder's soul had been banished from her, I'd half expected Mandy to return to being feral. Except, she hadn't. Maybe she'd been playacting to a role, but the previous Mandy had been a violent killing machine only interested in blood. The new one claimed she'd learned to control herself in the future fighting President Omega, but aside from appealing to my love of the idea of dating a vampire Sarah Connor, I had no way of verifying that. There was always that doubt in my mind that she was telling the truth and things had just magically worked themselves out without me. Maybe that had been what had driven her away.

Or maybe I just was pathologically unwilling to let go.

"Merciless?" Diabloman asked, snapping his fingers in front of my eyes.

"What? Hmm?" I asked, blinking.

"You zoned out again," Mimi said. "Probably due to brooding about Mandy. You do that a lot."

"I do not!" I said, lying my ass off.

"Telepath," Leia said, tapping her head. "I know when you're lying, Dad."

"Is it child abuse to consider locking you in a death trap?" I asked.

"Then Mom is guilty every day," Leia said. "Which is sadly less of a defense than I'd hope."

I paused. "Yeah, I've decided to go to the Ultraday celebration, kids."

I knew what to do with the Crown of the Gods now.

I was going to give it to Ultragod.

Let him fix the world.

Chapter Twenty

A Grim Sense of Foreboding

"Wait, you actually thought I wanted you to be the father of my children?" Ketra asked, walking beside me in our group. She was in human form with a halter top and pants that made think she'd gotten to my Earth well before I had and adapted to the fashion.

We were headed down the halls of Warren Manor and it still struck me as bizarre how big this place was. Even turned into a refuge for interdimensionally displaced *Dungeons & Dragons* monsters, it was shocking.

"Well, yes," I muttered.

"For the love of the gods, why?" Ketra asked, confused.

"That is a very good question," I said, embarrassed. Okay, good one, Jacob. I underestimated your sense of humor.

"Yes, Dad, because we would LOVE a bunch of half-archosaur siblings," Mimi said.

"Don't be racist, sis," Leia said, typing away at her infopad.

"It's not racist," Mimi said, defending herself. "Racist would imply systemic power imbalances baked into the structure of society. Its *prejudice*, which is completely different."

"Both are bad," Larry said.

"Yes, but I'm Team Snow not Team Daenerys," Mimi said, reaffirming the source of her bias was Season Eight. "When can we take HBO hostage and force them to remake the series?"

"I like *House of the Dragon* but it's way too time-skippy," Larry muttered.

"Do you have any idea what they're talking about?" Diabloman asked Kerri.

"No," Kerri said. "Teenagers speak a different language."

"Si," Diabloman said, reminding me he had a daughter of his own.

"I'm not a teenager," Larry said, sighing.

The group turned and entered a room I was sure I'd never been in before, where Cindy was being attended to by a staff of what appeared to be about fourteen specialists. They were adjusting her dress, makeup, nails, and social media feed. I was fairly sure the cost of it would bankrupt some movie budgets.

"Uh, hi, Cindy," I said, looking at this. "What are you doing?"

"Prepping for Ultraday, dipshit!" Cindy said, looking like a princess as she insulted me.

"It's not the Infamy Gala," I said, referring to the Atlas City event.

"You know that's controlled by the Brotherhood of Infamy," Diabloman said.

"Wait, seriously?" I asked, stunned.

Diabloman somehow showed confusion through his mask. "Yes. You only wiped out the Falconcrest City branch."

"Huh," I muttered. "I'm just saying there's more to life than being beautiful, Cindy."

"And you know who says that, Gary? Ugly people," Cindy said, wrinkling her nose. "No one must think I'm a day over twenty-eight."

"You're thirty-nine," I pointed out, "And only for a month more."

Cindy's teeth turned into rows of steak knives, and she growled, slobbering as she spoke, "You shut your goddamn mouth and you never open it again!"

Her makeup girl frowned and slapped her, causing Cindy to revert to normal. "Do not make me do your lipstick again."

Cindy whimpered and obeyed, lowering her head. Then she seemed to notice the rest of the group. "Gary, why are a winged Pat Benatar and a Kurt Cobain lookalike here?"

Ketra waved. "I'm Ketra, I had a bunch of meaningless sex with your husband."

"Not my husband. More like a live-in partner in crime until I can find someone better," Cindy corrected, only slightly hurting with her words. "Alternative response: not exactly a short line, sis. Since his wife died, Gary discovered that being famous completely overrides his obnoxious personality when getting hookups. Really, do not run a blacklight in this mansion."

Mimi looked ready to vomit. Leia looked like she was desensitized to the horrors of human sexuality. Kerri, however, just grinned as the fact that anything that embarrassed me was a source of personal amusement. Which fair, was what sisters were obligated to feel.

"Hey!" I snapped, appalled. "I am not just a walking hormone!"

Everyone looked at me, including Cindy's makeup staff.

"Family members are not allowed to make those jokes," I said.

Kerri, Mimi, and Leia looked away. Apparently, my female blood relatives really did think it was their right to do so.

"Nice to meet you," Cindy said, with faux sincerity. "Who's the kid?"

"Not a kid," Larry said.

"This is ULTRA-PALADIN!" I said, introducing Larry by the new codename on which I hadn't let him have any input. "Sacred defender of the Mystical Fire, Defender of the Defenseless, Helper of the Helpless, and newly trademarked hero of the Omega Corporation superhero division!"

Larry blinked. "What now? Can he do that?"

"Oh yes!" Kerri said. "He totally dumped like a billion dollars in Omega Corp stock on me and forced me to be the CEO of the company despite my complete lack of any formal training. Well, I was a secretary at a factory for a while. They made aglets."

"Surprisingly, that worked out really well," I said. "Even before I rebooted the universe."

"Yeah, it turns out the entire system is rigged to make sure it's nearly impossible for the rich to lose money," Kerri said, clapping her hands. "Even if you really screw up, the government just bails you out."

"Enough social commentary," Cindy said. "You think you've had a bad day? I've been on the phone with your niece the entire time."

"Why, what happened to Lisa?" I asked, wondering about Keith's daughter. She'd moved out when she'd joined the Texas Guardians. Unfortunately, she'd been kicked out when I'd done a celebratory assault on their headquarters. You know, just to help her settle in. That had gone over like a ton of bricks.

Worse, the entire incident had pushed her into radicalizing and becoming a member of the Tomorrow Society. As I'd mentioned, I wasn't exactly fond of those guys even though I considered myself a Super ally due to having a family full of them. Unfortunately, they were a little too militant, and this was me talking. I might have been more sympathetic if not for the fact they had tried to get Mimi and Leia to run away from home and live with them on Super Island where they were forming their own nation. It reminded me of my cousin that decided to move to Israel and join a kibbutz. I hoped Lisa was alright.

Cindy, unfortunately, confirmed she was not. "Her phone got hacked and video of her with her boyfriend, the Backwoodsman, got leaked."

"Merciful Moses," I muttered, shocked and appalled. "I should talk to her. Backwoodsman? Really? The guy is *Canadian*."

Kerri swatted me on the shoulder.

"Old too!" I snapped, rubbing my shoulder. "Seriously, I thought she was his teen sidekick."

"She's twenty-two," Kerri said.

"Like I said, teen," I replied, feeling less old now that I'd hit forty than everyone else was now unreasonably young.

"I doubt she wants to talk to her uncle about her sex tape, Gary," Cindy said, rolling her eyes.

I paused before grimacing. "Yeah, in retrospect, that's obvious."

"Mind you, she didn't appreciate my advice to monetize it and get herself an OnlySupers account," Cindy said, ruining any sympathy she might have accrued. "Mine accounts for twenty percent of my revenue stream and I own oil wells in war torn regions that the Society of Superheroes hasn't gotten to patrolling."

"You should really sell those," I said, disgusted.

"That's what you said about the sweat shops!" Cindy snapped.

"Yes!" I spoke.

"They make sweatpants in those!" Cindy said, ripping off *Glass Onion*. "Red Riding Hood brand sweatpants made with real sweat!"

Larry cleared his throat. "My name is Larry Karkofsky. I understand you know my mother."

Cindy narrowed her eyes. "Gary, is he another kid of yours from the future?"

"Man, if I had a nickel for every time that happened, I'd have two nickels," I said, realizing I had the perfect set up for a *Phineas and Ferb* reference. "Which isn't a lot, but I do find it weird that it's happened twice."

"Plagiarizing cartoons isn't cool, Dad," Mimi said, looking up at me.

"You try and come up with as many zingers as I have to!" I said to my daughter.

"So, you're Mandy's kid, huh?" Cindy asked.

I looked around. "Did everyone know about this except me?"

"I mean, Mandy didn't know," Cindy said, "until today at least. I mean it's probably not the only reason she's packed up and gone to brood on a rooftop somewhere. There's also Gary. I mean, he's probably eighty percent of what's wrong in her life."

Larry stared.

"Thanks, Cindy," I said, crossing my arms. "Really."

"Superheroes love being miserable," Cindy said as one of her hench-staff brought her a juice box. She slurped it without taking it into her hand. "So, really, Gary, you're like the perfect boyfriend. It's just she has to share you and she hates sharing even her lipstick."

"Cindy—" I started to say.

"So, we just need to go to alternate Earths, kidnap your alternates, and blow those Earth's up," Cindy said.

"Cindy!" I snapped.

"It's the perfect plan!" Cindy exclaimed. "I mean, unless destroying your home Earth's results in you becoming a fascist world-dominating despot like Merciful. Who, I admit, was just like you until his Earth was destroyed, so maybe the plan needs work."

"So, she didn't want to meet me," Larry said, taking a deep breath. "I'm sorry to bother you guys."

"Seriously, just blame Gary," Cindy said. "It's what I do all the time."

I put my hand on his shoulder. "Mandy looked for you, mourned you, and struggled with your loss her entire life. I'm sure she is just scared."

"Or, you know, a soulless undead abomination," Cindy said. "Which she also is. So, where the hell have you been, Gary? Ultragod has called like four times, and you've only been gone a couple of days."

I coughed. "Speaking of which, is there like a horrifying plague that's killed millions?"

I didn't quite know how to ask about that without sounding like a madman. Thankfully, I was already considered legally insane in thirty-eight states, including Michigan, so I was well off the hook here.

"Oh, the Nanoplague?" Kerri asked. "Yeah, everyone had that for like an hour. Then suddenly everyone got better. Presumably, some superhero solved it."

I blinked and breathed out a sigh of relief. "That's good."

"It's a shame," Cindy said. "Leia could have come up with a treatment and sold it for millions. If she didn't actually cure-cure it. If you know what I mean."

"I really don't," I said, turning to Leia. "Was your mother always this evil?"

"I think she's gotten worse since the dragon heist," Leia explained. "That's made her think she can be an antihero too."

"Since Guinevere is training me as a superhero, which means I'm good and I can do anything I want," Cindy said, proudly. She then started singing in the key of Disney's *Frozen*. "No right, no wrong, no rules for me. I'm free! Let morality go! Let morality go! The perfect Cindy is here!"

Rather than touch that with a ten-foot pole, I decided to answer Cindy's question. "I was in another dimension, going through a training montage. I befriended a Ringwraith. Rode a dragon."

"Hey!" Ketra said.

"You heard it that way," I said. "Failed my Jedi training because too much anger was within me. Oh, and I met Larry."

"Hey, again," Larry said, still looking devastated. "I guess I should be going, now. Nice to meet you all."

"No, no, no," I said, waving my hand to him. "Come with us to the Ultraday celebration. I'll introduce you to the President."

"Yes, make your first impression as a superhero by showing up with a supervillain who has killed a thousand people," Cindy said.

"Nine hundred and eighty-nine!" I snapped, pausing. "If we're counting only humans from this dimension."

Mimi looked up at me. "*How?*"

"Don't ask questions you don't want answers to, dear," I replied. "Also, I had nothing to do with the death of the Trench Coat Magician. He is living on a farm upstate. He lent me his sword. No, wait, it's not his sword. It's a replica. With the exact same powers. Which he got me. Because it's cool looking."

"I had one, but I couldn't lift it," Cindy said. "Also, Jack Hellraiser is a demon."

"Yeah, and?" I said, confused.

Cindy stared at me. "Demons are immortal. If you killed him, he comes back."

I blinked. "Oh, thank Death! I was not looking forward to explaining why Jack Hellraiser was on a farm…upstate."

Diabloman sighed. "*Madre de Diablo*. Gary, what did I teach you about killing superheroes?"

"Don't?" I asked.

"Yes," Diabloman said.

"Well, I didn't, so ha!" I said, pausing. "Nine hundred and eighty-eight!"

"You still stole his father's sword," Ketra said.

"Oh yeah," I said, looking down at my knife. "I should probably return that to him. How do you summon a demon?"

If that seemed overly forgiving of Jack Hellraiser after his multiple attempts to kill me, take note that these sorts of fights were just part and parcel about the superhero versus supervillain dichotomy. Hell, superheroes fought each other all the time. In this case, it seemed to have been the result of mind control too. Which was like the ultimate "Get out of Jail Free" card. It was also PHANTOM tech, which was kinda important given than PHANTOM was supposed to have been completely wiped out in my revised world. I should probably tell someone about that.

Everyone was looking at me, though.

Including the beauticians.

"What?" I asked.

"You don't know how to summon a demon, Dad?" Mimi asked.

"You do?" I asked, confused.

"Yeah!" Mimi said. "It is like the most basic spell. That's why demons can make so many deals. Aren't you supposed to be a wizard? This is like Harry Potter entry level stuff!"

"I hate that franchise," Larry muttered as only someone who really loved something until it became terrible can. That was the *Star Wars* sequels' voice.

"Seriously, it's very easy," Diabloman said. "My sister and I were summoning demons by the time we could walk."

"Well, you and your sister were born to a Satanic cult as children of one of the Great Beasts so I'm not sure that's a good endorsement," I said, before thinking. Which was basically my entire life in one sentence. The speaking before thinking part, not the part about being born in a Satanic cult. No, I was born to an insurance claims adjuster and a schoolteacher.

Everyone continued staring.

I pulled out Jacob's *Magic for Dummies* and started flipping through it. "Fine, I'll summon him. Anything anyone else want to dump on me while I'm already suffering grievous emotional heartbreak from being abandoned by my one true love?"

Ketra blinked, shocked. "I'm sorry, Gary, I had no idea—"

"Not you!" I said.

"You have a lot of one true loves, Dad," Leia pointed out. "Just saying."

Mimi looked guilty. "About things that would tick you off—"

I stared at her. "What are you hiding?"

Mimi sighed. "Now may not be the best time but I'm kind of   dating...a   Splotch."
I gasped in horror. "No! Which one?"

"The black and Puerto Rican one?" Mimi asked, looking down. "Marco Montoya AKA Toner."

He was the teenage Splotch and probably going to inherit the mantle of his uncle and grandfather. I knew because I'd got on well with the Splotches, even inviting one to live in Falconcrest City so he could nemesis his crush on Nikki Tesla. Which was totally different from stalking or so I told my therapist.

"Age-appropriate no less!" I said, staring. "I am very disappointed in you, young lady. Please tell me you met while he was trying to stop you from doing a heist."

"No," Mimi said. "It was at a protest for Supers' rights."

"I don't even know you," I said, shaking my head. Looking down, the alien language of the book became English. Another function of the Reaper's Cloak. "Oh, here's how to summon a demon. Huh, that is easy. Wow, why did I make Dungeon magic in the first place?"

"You cheated when using it," Cindy said, finishing her preparations. She looked like she was trying to split the difference between fashionable and lewd like, well, most starlets at the Infamy Gala. She pulled it off, though. "You need somatic, verbal, and material components. None of which you use. You need to rest six hours between re-memorizing spells—"

I glared at her.

"All I'm saying is that'd never fly at my table," Cindy said, crossing her arms. "You might as well have just had Epic levels and all eighteens in your stats for the fact you're gaming the system!"

I turned around and walked past Diabloman and Kerri to go summon a demon.

Chapter Twenty-One

Demon Summoning Is Supposed to Be Easy

It shouldn't have surprised me that Stately Warren Manor had a dedicated demon summoning room. Lancel Warren was once the most powerful wizard in the world and defender of it against all things creepy and kooky, mysterious, as well as spooky. Altogether ookie. However, I hadn't exactly gone out of my way to learn magic the traditional way, if the entire rest of the past relative few months wasn't enough of a lesson.

The room was basically a big chamber full of bookshelves, material components, as well as a big area to sit down in for summoning. Lancel had a stack of yoga mats that were each covered with a different variety of summoning sigil. It was kind of hilarious that he just switched them out whenever he was going to a different type of demon. The candles were from Bed Bath & Beyond, which either meant the candles didn't matter or that the now-deceased store had been a center of evil sorcery. I knew which I believed, and it wasn't the first one.

I was presently sitting, lotus style, with the *Magic for Dummies* book across my legs. I'd gone with the simplest of the ceremonial summoning mats and lit about a dozen candles like a birthday cake. Finding the right chant was something I was presently debating since the words mattered less than the intent. This was perhaps my biggest issue with learning sorcery since focusing on any one thing was a struggle for my ADHD brain.

We still had about four hours until the Ultraday ceremony, but that wasn't a lot of time when it came to magical rituals. So, I ended up spending two and a half hours studying the *Magic for Dummies* book, making post-it notes, and watching a few CrimeTube videos on demon summoning while the others got increasingly annoyed.

"You know, Dad, we can do the ritual for you," Mimi said, standing over me with Diabloman by her side.

Kerri and Cindy were at the door, the others having all gone on to do their own things. Ketra was already setting herself up in one of the levels of our kobold-dug dungeon, Leia was preparing for Ultraday in her own mech-suit sort of fashion, and Larry seemed to think demon summoning was something he couldn't ethically be part of. Personally, I imagined he was snooping around his mom's room and that wasn't exactly ethical itself, but I understood why he might be doing it.

"No, no," I responded to Mimi a little too late. "I've got this."

"That's what you said about assembling the IKEA furniture," Cindy said. "Somehow it ended up possessed and trying to eat us."

"Deathbed: The Bed that Eats," Kerri said. "It was very naughty for a ghost. Not at all like the King."

"How is he, anyway?" I asked, distracted.

"Oh, he went back down to Graceland," Kerri said. "Because, you know."

I didn't know, but I suspected it was another unfortunate reminder that life was still going on in my increasingly less-utopian world. That was another reason I hadn't summoned Jack Hellraiser yet, not because I couldn't—I figured out how to do it within five minutes—but because I wasn't sure I wanted to know just how badly things had gone off the rails.

I wanted to think I was utterly unlike Merciful who, at last count had: killed Ultragod, started WW3, allied with a frigging Nazi in President Omega—even if he intended to betray him—abused his robot kids, locked me up with Mandy in a 1950s simulation, put Spellbinder in Mandy's body, and used Gabrielle as a giant battery to get humanity off fossil fuels for a few years. In short, a real dickhead. However, he'd done it because his universe had been destroyed and he'd been driven insane by it. I considered him to be nothing like me, but Cindy had seen him as basically me after Mandy's death but times a few million.

I hadn't seen Merciful lately, but he was out there, lurking, somewhere, I was sure. He couldn't go back to his home planet of Earth-B even though it was circling in the exact opposite position of our Earth from the Sun. You could even book a shuttle there if you wanted to visit a world where people still went to the malt shop and used words like swell.

However, I was starting to understand the allure of absolute control that had driven him mad. He'd been an even more powerful wizard than the Nightwalker and it had made him think he could fix everything. Once you believed that, it didn't matter who you hurt because you could always fix that too, right? I suddenly could see the road and how he'd gone down it. I didn't like that feeling at all.

"Fuck it," I muttered, closing the book in front of me. "IN THE NAME OF GARY KARKOFSKY, MERCILESS: GOD WITHOUT MERCY, GOD OF SEX, GAMING, AND ROCK AND ROLL. I SUMMON JACK HELLRAISER."

I then threw up the horns.

With both hands.

Diabloman stared at me. "You invoked *yourself* to do magic?"

"The book says I can," I said, lying.

"It does not!" Diabloman said.

Mimi facepalmed. "Dad, that is not how magic works, and you are just embarrassing...and he's here."

Mimi trailed off because the air was now full of sulfur and brimstone-smelling smoke. In the middle of said smoke was a very different looking Jack Hellraiser. He was about four hundred pounds larger and a foot taller with all of it being red demonic muscles stuffed in a trench coat. A Ramones shirt replaced his bullet-ridden Union Jack. His jeans were torn from the amount of demon stuffed into them. Jack also had cloven hooves instead of shoes. Still the same hair, face, and goatee, though. It was his demon form, obviously, but Jack looked significantly less likely to kill me. At least in the context that he wasn't trying in that moment. Indeed, he seemed almost relaxed. Which wasn't the attitude I expected from him given that I had sent him to Hell and stolen his trident.

His voice had also dropped an octave and become a lot gravellier. "Sex, gaming and rock and roll?"

"I gotta be me," I explained. "Sorry about killing you."

Jack gave a dismissive wave. "It's okay, I've been killed a few times already. I just have to wait in Hell until I reincorporate or one of my girlfriends summons me."

"How long does that usually take?" Mimi asked.

Jack looked down. "Depends on how boring their husbands are being."

"Hello, Jack," Diabloman said.

"Speaking of people who killed me," Jack said, frowning. "You know, Gary, more people would trust you if you weren't hanging around the genocidal hero-killer."

"Everyone trusts me," I said, offended. "I'm the most trustworthy supervillain of them all."

"That may be accurate," Cindy said, standing in the doorway with my sister. "Which is just sad."

"No, *Ultragod* trusts you," Jack said, dryly. "Which is inexplicable to the vast majority of us, especially since him trusting you is why you were able to kill him."

I shook my head. "Listen, I don't...wait, you remember that?"

"You talk about it *all the time*," Jack said. "Did you not think the Society of Superheroes wouldn't figure out you rebooted the universe? It took us some time to put it all together, but word has spread around."

"No!" I said, too hastily. "I mean, I didn't reboot the universe! How silly!"

Diabloman, Mimi, and Jack all stared at me.

"I admit, we expected a bit more from you," Diabloman said. "You effectively took over the world but it feels pretty much the same."

"We're all very proud of you," Cindy said, sounding extremely sarcastic. "Even if it is all kind of an American middle-class liberal world takeover. Throw in some giant statues of yourself for Moses' sake. When other villains take over the world for a few hours to a week, they at least make an impression. Make everyone slightly less hot than you and me. I mean, Sovi-Ape turning the world into communist apes wasn't great, but at least it was memorable."

"Sovi-Ape is forbidden from coming into my house," I said. "My Polish grandparents would never forgive me."

"It's true," Kerri said. "Their ghosts wouldn't."

"Uh, yeah, so Jack," I said, unsure how to continue this conversation as the revelation of what I'd done was not one I'd prepared for. Especially since it had the potential of exposing what I'd done to Diabloman. "You were brainwashed?"

"Yes," Jack said, taking a deep breath and breathing out fire. "PHANTOM is back."

I stared at him, confused. "How?"

"What? You thought you got rid of all the fascists in the world?" Jack asked.

"Yes!" I snapped.

"Well, you didn't," Jack said, sneering. "As long as the exploitative capitalist system —"

I cleared my throat. "Listen, let's stick with the fascists who have jet packs and laboratories where they make zombies. PHANTOM. The mooks of evil doers for generations."

PHANTOM had been founded by General Omega, Tom Terror, Nazi Ape, and Baroness Blight after Ultragod had taken down Hitler during what should have been the early part of America's involvement in the war. The Fascist Four had run the Nazi war machine during the final days of the war and had franchised out with alien super-science, unemployed Imperial Japanese ninjas, as well as demonic magic of a kind that Jack Hellraiser probably considered cultural appropriation.

An entire cottage industry of super-spies had been created to fight during PHANTOM's heyday in the Sixties and more than a few wars had been fought against their puppet governments. My dad had been a Vietnam II veteran, for example, and that had been awkward with the fighting alongside the very people Nixon had been bombing earlier that year. That, of course, had been before Nixon had been found out to have been replaced by his extradimensional doppelganger, Scaremonger.

Anyway, time had worn-down PHANTOM with Sovi-Ape killing Nazi Ape. Baroness Blight had eventually turned to corporate mad science and ended up dying at the hands of a bunch of environmentally friendly teens in the Nineties. Tom Terror had met his end at my hands. And General Omega? Well, General Omega had gotten elected President of the United States under a fake name and started WW3 before I'd reversed that. He'd been disincorporated but not killed, so I figured his power base was gone since I'd taken over Omega Corp and de-Nazified it. Mission Accomplished.

Why did that feel like an ominous choice of words?

"Someone started rebuilding it awhile back," Jack said. "You may have gotten rid of the organization on this world, but the underlying causes are still there, and this isn't just me being my usual anarchist self. People still hate Supers. People still hate that the pretty bird doesn't want to sleep with them. People still hate that *those* people get a vote. He started recruiting and once he had a base, he started the usual cloning and building up his doomsday machines."

"Who?" I asked, staring.

"I dunno," Jack said, admittedly. "However, he's probably the person aware of the Nanoplague's coming and may have been the person to release it. I got jumped outside my flat and when I woke up, someone had been operating on my brain with a mixture of science and sorcery. It had me doing things I'd never do before."

"Like trying to kill me?" I asked.

"Like working for the American President," Jack said, shaking his head. "Ugh. Why, Moses? Now you're just like the rest of them. The Presidency only exists to protect the billionaires!"

Did I really sound like this to other people? Instead of critiquing him, I snapped my fingers. "Rebel-rebel, I need you to focus."

"I'm probably not the only superhero he's compromised," Jack said. "Maybe there's something a lot more sinister going

C. T. Phipps

on with all the retirements happening. Plus, I'm pretty sure they've been making their own baddies in other timelines and worlds, circumventing all you've been doing here."

I blinked at him. "You're saying the Nazis are *commuting* to this world?"

"Yeah," Jack said, shaking his head. "I might not remember much but I overheard a few things during the brainwashing sessions. There's apparently a PHANTOM interdimensional council formed of Nazis afraid that this reality has been conducting raids on their worlds, assassinating their Hitlers, and forcing them underground years earlier."

I looked over my shoulder, not exactly guiltily, but embarrassed. "Huh, that sounds ridiculous. I wonder what dashingly handsome sex machine might have done that."

Mimi facepalmed. "Oh, Dad."

"I make no apologies for Hitler murder," I said, dryly. "We need to warn Ultragod."

"Assuming he hasn't been compromised too," Jack said.

"If he has, we would have noticed it," I replied. "The President is under a microscope twenty-four seven. Also, if PHANTOM is back then they almost certainly will strike at Ultraday. The Superhuman Equality Act—"

"Which is stupid," Cindy said. "I learned to believe in superhuman supremacy as soon as I became one."

I ignored Cindy, which was rapidly becoming my go-to move during political discussions. "—is going to be announced. That will be the perfect target for them."

"He's not my President," Jack said. "But I'll spread the word."

"Good," I muttered. "Now, we just need to find any other possible clues to what PHANTOM is up to."

"Oh, that reminds me," Kerri said. "The Terror Twins—they're Tom Terror's incestuous aristocrat children—took over Omega Corp. They did that hostile takeover thing."

I stared at her. "You didn't think that was worth mentioning?"

"I didn't want to bring down the mood," Kerri said.

"We're still rich, right?" Cindy asked.

"Oh yes!" Kerri said. "I wanted to use the money from the buyout to build a spook sanctuary for dead children of foreign wars, but apparently Gary's lawyers prevent me from doing that."

"But we're still rich, right?" Cindy asked again.

I felt a headache coming on, which was a testament to how patient I'd become. After all, half of the stuff being talked about would have caused me to go on a killing spree just a few years ago. I didn't want to mention, though, all of this was fixable. I just had to get the Crown of the Gods to Ultragod's hands. Which was ironic because I'd possessed it once before and tried to keep Ultragod from using it [see "Merciless vs. Hitler" short story! – The Editor]. We could fix all of this with a snap.

"Oh, that reminds me," I said, taking out the Sword (presently Dagger) of Samael. "This belongs to you."

"Keep it," Jack said, surprising me. "Dad has like a million of those and I'm working on my magic guitar."

He conjured a glowing ax that became another kind of ax that he started playing. I shrugged and put away the dagger. "If you say so."

Diabloman looked down at me. "May I have a moment alone with Merciless?"

The others exchanged glances but shrugged and went into the hall, leaving me with the man who used to be my best friend. The exception was Jack Hellraiser, who disappeared in a cloud of sulfur that caused me to cough. It made sense that he didn't care about getting his pitchfork back if he could teleport on his own. Also, I had the sneaking suspicion this gift was probably going to backfire on me in the future. I wondered if he'd stuck a bunch of Greek soldiers in it or rigged it to explode.

"I'm having a really bad day, D," I said, sighing. "I haven't even had a chance to deal with the Mandy situation."

Diabloman shut the door to the demon-summoning room and locked it before turning around. "I know what you did to my sister."

Well, crap.

Chapter Twenty-Two

Diabloman and I Hash It Out

"**O**h, you do, do you?" I asked. I decided at that moment to play dumb. It probably wouldn't work but there was a small possibility that he didn't know exactly what had happened with his sister.

"Si," Diabloman said, his tone making it clear he knew exactly what had happened between us.

"Look over there!" I said, pointing behind Diabloman.

Diabloman didn't look.

I crossed my arms. "Now, wouldn't you have felt silly if there was actually something behind you. I think this is a very good example of why you should trust your partners in crime at least until the money is being counted."

"Yes, trust," Diabloman said, sounding not so much trembling with fury as I would have been had someone consigned Kerri to Hell, but tired. Resigned. That would have been reassuring if not for the fact I'd seen Diabloman take that resigned tone when he broke people in half.

It wasn't like I was afraid of Diabloman. I mean, I probably should have been, but I was pretty sure I could take him. His magical tattoos gave him super-strength, super-speed, invulnerability to magic, and the ability to summon demons, which he never had in the entire time I'd known him. That was combined with being a master martial artist. Diabloman practiced "The Art of the Masked Warrior", which was basically professional wrestling except it could kill you. Diabloman knew lots of magic, too, ranging from Mexican folk magic to outright infernalism. He was also a genius and master strategist that had led a few supervillain team-ups. Plus, he'd destroyed the universe.

Okay, maybe I couldn't take him. Indeed, I'd never seen Diabloman at full strength. When I'd met him, he'd been beaten down emotionally as well as physically. The dark magic running through his ink had ravaged his insides as well as the guilt from killing his sister. He'd gone cold turkey from evil sorcery and that had bought him a few years. When he'd discovered Mandy was really Maria, he'd also been overjoyed—never mind what I'd felt on the subject. When I'd banished her, he'd sworn revenge and we'd just sort of waited for the other to make the first move.

And he never had.

Nor had I.

Which seemed to be what was happening here as neither Diabloman nor I spoke.

For a full minute.

I finally coughed in my fist, breaking the silence. "Yeah, so I banished her to Hell after she assaulted me. I let her soul loose. Then I screwed with your mind when I retconned the universe. That wasn't consciously, though. You want to throw down, I'm prepared, but I'm not going to apologize. I'm still furious. I don't care that she was a hero. The only thing I care about is that it hurt you, but not enough that I wouldn't do it again. No one would even be questioning this if the sexes were reversed."

"Maria apologizes," Diabloman said, shocking me from the fight I was expecting to have.

I blinked. "What?"

"You retconned me into a marriage with your sister, a woman with the explicit ability to *talk to the dead*," Diabloman spoke, enunciating the last words as if he were talking to a very stupid child. "Did it not occur to you that the first person I would attempt to conduct a seance with would be my lost sibling?"

I took a deep breath and stood up from where I'd been sitting on the ground. I was a tall guy for your average nerd, more Ryan Reynolds than Michael Cera. However, Diabloman still towered over me. "I think your mistake clearly is assuming any sentence that involves me and thinking has any relevance."

"This is no time for jokes, Gary," Diabloman said.

"I have yet to ever encounter such a situation," I said. "Even at my dad's funeral, I made balloon animals. Kerri agreed that he would have wanted it that way."

Diabloman sighed. "Maria told us everything. About the reboot of the world, about how she agreed to Merciful's deal in order to live again, as well as how she genuinely fell for you while wearing Mandy's form."

I struggled to maintain my composure. The fact that I was trying, I think, said a lot about how well I was taking this. "Yeah, boo-hoo. She felt terrible about lying to me about my wife coming back from the dead. About using me."

Diabloman didn't react, instead just continued. "She also said that what you did was justified and that it helped cleanse her of the darkness within. It was the punishment she needed to ascend to the heavens after her crimes."

"Good for her," I said, balling my fists. I didn't want to start a fight, but this was a subject that could only end in tears.

"Yes," Diabloman said, looking down. "I, too, would like to apologize."

That took the wind out of my sails, and I found myself unclenching my fists. "You didn't do anything wrong by coming after me. No matter how much I hate…how much I'm angry at your sister. No matter that I can't forgive her, I don't blame you. Family is family."

"Many people claim to be family and that everything they do is for them but only terrorize the people that are closest to them," Diabloman said, sighing. He reached up to his mask. "I am unworthy of this."

"No," I said, holding up my hands. A luchador's mask was one of the most important things in their strange little tradition. Once removed, they could never be restored. "Don't."

"As you wish," Diabloman said, sighing. "This mask is a heavy burden, Gary. You have no idea. Many times, I no longer know if there is a man underneath it. Who is Jose Gonzales? Does he even still exist?"

I had literally forgotten that was his civilian identity. I wasn't about to mention that, though. "There's no difference between Gary Karkofsky and Merciless."

"I know," Diabloman said. "Which makes me worry for you, old friend."

"Are we?" I asked.

"*Que*?" Diabloman asked.

"Friends?" I asked, taking a deep breath. "There are some wounds too deep to ever heal. Some things that can't ever be forgiven."

"I thought you might be my way to redemption, Gary," Diabloman admitted. "You were so full of life, hope, and willingness to view us, the supervillains, with the eyes of a child."

"I did a lot of stupid things in my early career," I said. "I even teamed up with Tom Terror to break out of the moon's prison."

"Yeah, that was really strange given he was a general of the Third Reich," Diabloman said.

"I thought that was his evil(er) ancestor!" I cried. "I didn't know he was the same as the Nazi one! I thought he was Tom Terror the Third, not the First. I mean, you don't hold a person's ancestors against them."

"No, they were all the same person. Tom Terror pretended he was his Argentinian descendant by removing his brain and putting it into a cloned body with a full head of blond hair. Claiming that he wasn't the original Nazi Tom Terror was all a PR stunt," Diabloman said. "That was when he was dating the Ultragoddess made of putty. It was around the first death of Ultragod."

I clutched my head, trying to keep all this straight. If all of that sounded ridiculous, imagine trying to keep it all straight during your day-to-day interactions. Splotch had once tried to explain the Clone Crisis to me, and I ended up thinking he should have just gone on a killing spree. The Nineties were a weird time, man.

"I know that *now*," I said, pausing. I had a lot of emotions, and I was struggling with sorting through them. "I want to forgive you, D. I really do. It's just that I'm still carrying a lot of anger around. Letting Mandy die was the worst mistake of my life. So was turning her into a vampire, but I can't regret doing that either. Because I can't let go of her or what I feel for her. My guilt, love, and mistakes are all the same thing with her."

It was a surprisingly nuanced description for how I felt. I just wish I could have told it to Mandy, vampire or not, and let her know how sorry I was. I also needed to act less like I wanted to act for once and how she would have wanted me to act. Well, OG Mandy would have wanted me to become a full superhero and that wasn't going to happen, but I could act better.

"Now you know how I feel about Maria," Diabloman said. "It was not that I killed her and her lover, the Guitarist. It was the fact that I corrupted her. She did not just die but remained

223

trapped between worlds and able to see life as it should have been. In the end, the desire to experience a life she never got to enjoy drove her mad."

I had no response for that. "I forgive you, D. I am not so nice a guy as to forgive her, but I'm willing to let it rest. I can reserve most of my anger for Merciful. Who, I think we can agree, is a real dickhead."

"I admit, you do have issues," Diabloman said. "Evil future selves are a common event, but he is a particularly pernicious one."

"Ooo, good word choice," I said. "But he actually isn't my evil future self. He's the Gary Karkofsky from the universe you destroyed. That drove him crazy, and he really-really hates me for leading the life he was supposed to lead."

Diabloman stared at me.

"What?" I asked.

Diabloman facepalmed. "Everything is my fault."

I patted him on the shoulder. "I can assure you that Cindy will find some way that this is *my* fault."

Diabloman sucked in his breath through his mask then looked up. "I do not believe it can ever be like it was, Gary. You have shown me your dark side and it is every bit as terrible as the one that I have seen in myself. But you have done things for me that I could never repay and taken an enormous burden off my soul."

"Yeah, I wasted a fricking wish on redeeming you spiritually," I muttered, remembering what I'd used my unlimited all-powerful wish for winning the Eternity Tournament on. I'd gotten godhood as a consolation prize. "Err, no offense. Just saying, 'hey, Gary, why not wish your wife back' was right there."

Diabloman laughed. It was the bitter chuckle of a shared grief. "Thank you, anyway. Let us try and work together to rebuild our friendship for Kerri's sake."

"You two are actually together?" I asked, unsure about how to approach that. "I mean, knowing that you were retconned into a marriage by my subconscious or whatever?"

"Your sister and I have bonded greatly," Diabloman said, surprising me. "I never thought I would find love again after my wife, Rosa, left me. She never forgave me for the fact that our daughter, Lucia, became a superhero as well."

I didn't want to comment on the fact Lucia AKA Diabolique wasn't exactly a superhero but every bit the antihero that people sometimes accused me of being. She tended to bounce between the Extreme!, Texas Guardians, and Tomorrow Society. Last I checked, she and Lisa were considering forming their own spin-off team. I really hoped that Lucia wasn't involved in the whole Wildebeest thing since I heard he'd dated her as well. Which is just not appropriate behavior for a hundred-year-old cyborg werewolf. No, I don't know why he's called Wildebeest if he's a cyborg werewolf.

"Kerri is basically the nicest, sweetest person in the world," I said, sighing. "She's someone who hates when we clear spiderwebs and thinks black cats are the cutest. Kerri missed her calling as the star of a Tim Burton movie."

Diabloman then hugged me, which was a bit like a bear grabbing me. "We are now family, and you are my brother. I promise, though I may someday kill you, you will not be harmed by anyone else if I can prevent it."

I gave Diabloman a gentle—not quite sarcastic—pat on the back. "There, there."

"If our first child is a boy, I will name him Gary," Diabloman said. "If the child is a girl, I will name her Garina."

"Please don't," I said, turning insubstantial to get out of his hug. "In any case, we have a celebration to get to and Nazis to warn people of."

"Si," Diabloman said. "Let us be heroes."

I grimaced at his description. "I hate that word."

"You are capable of great deeds, Gary, terrible but great," Diabloman said.

"That breaks Rule #183 of the Rules of Supervillainy," I explained. "No more quoting Harry Potter."

Diabloman looked away. "Putting you in charge of those was a grave error."

"Yeah, they're like the Ferengi Rules of Acquisition or Evil Overlord's list now," I replied. "We just keep adding to them."

"You hate the Evil Overlord's list," Diabloman said.

"I really do," I admitted. "If I followed all of those rules, I might as well not be an Evil Overlord at all. They take all the fun out of being a supervillain. I mean, why capture someone to put them in an easily escapable death trap if you aren't going to gloat?"

I walked past Diabloman and felt a great weight lifted off of my shoulders. It wasn't like we'd repaired our relationship. As D said, it was probably impossible. However, we'd made a lot of progress in bridging the gap between us. Perhaps someday we'd be able to be friends again. If not, well, it seemed he and Kerri were happy.

Maybe I hadn't been a complete screw up here.

Famous last words.

Kerri, Cindy, Mimi, Larry, and Leia were waiting outside for me. Ketra was a newcomer to this world and had no reason to care about this. Personally, as pleasant as my drill sergeant had been while we'd been on Fantasy World, I hoped she would find a cave or bank to hide out in soon. Mandy, of course, wasn't present, and I was still too petrified of finding the letter downstairs to go investigate.

"Are you coming, Kerri?" I asked.

"No, I hate crowds." Kerri shook her head, shuddering. "I also doubt Diabloman would be any more welcome than you would be as Merciless."

"Well, I have to be there for the President," I said, pausing, "But I have a way to get around the Secret Service."

I didn't know much non-Dungeon magic, but I'd learned one or two actual spell-spells both from Jacob as well as the Dark Witch. Spreading out my hands, I conjured a pair of sunglasses and put them on my face. The result was my Reaper's Cloak transformed into a pink shirt and leisure suit as a boom box appeared on my shoulders. The machine started playing the theme to *Beverly Hills Cop*. A little Don Johnson stubble appeared on my chin as well.

"Gasp! Eighties Man!" Kerri said, clapping her hands together. "King of the Retro! Man, who wants his MTV! Guy who is clearly not my brother!"

Mimi looked over at Leia. "Just so we're clear, she actually does know that Dad is Eighties Man, right?"

"Gasp!" Cindy said, presumably faking shock. "You're Eighties Man!?"

Leia shrugged. "You never know with these guys."

Chapter Twenty-Three

Ultraday! Nothing Could Go Wrong!

Cindy, Leia, Mimi, Kerri, Diabloman, Larry all stood there waiting for me to create the portal to the Ultraday celebration. While Diabloman and Kerri weren't coming, they were there to see us off. Larry looked uncomfortable and I knew I should probably speak with him about what was going on, but I was just glad he was coming. In a weird way, he was the biggest connection I had right now to the original Mandy—and someone I was determined to reunite with the shadow of his mother. Incredible disaster as that might turn out to be.

I put down the Boom Box of Destiny, presently playing Kenny Loggins' "Nobody's Fool" (The theme from *Caddyshack II* for those not up on their soundtrack trivia) and pulled out the Sword of Samael in its knife form. The knife transformed into a sword, and I heft it up to try to cut a hole in reality.

"Gary, are you sure it's wise to use the Devil's sword?" Kerri asked, watching from the sidelines.

"It's okay," I said. "Jewish people don't believe in the Devil!"

"Just demons," Leia said, wearing a pleasant summer dress with a minimum of attention paid to makeup and fashion. It was, all in all, a fantastic contribution to her normal fashion sense. She was also playing around on her infopad, which was hardly a rare occurrence for her.

"What are you doing?" Mimi asked.

"Day trading," Leia said. "I'm using Dad's golden parachute and buy out money to build a corporation devoted to mad science."

Cindy gave me a sideways look. "See, this is why I don't let her touch my side of the fortune."

"Hey Dad, you own Trans-Bavaria now," Mimi said, looking over her sister's shoulder.

Cindy's face drooped. "I always wanted my own country!"

"Stop financing war crimes!" Leia said, frowning. "Then maybe I'll buy you your own country."

"Oh, everything finances war crimes!" Cindy said, defensively. "Where do you think sneakers come from!"

"Yeah, my vote of no confidence as CEO was due to my decision to have our cybernetic war panda division in China only use ethically sourced volunteer pandas," Kerri said, pressing the tips of her forefingers together guiltily. "Ooo, man, were those guys mad."

"Cybernetic war pandas are big business," Diabloman said, nodding. "It's the merchandising."

"Now I feel guilty about my Pandamon cards growing up," Larry muttered.

"Ooo, we should compare decks," Mimi said, cheerfully. "Sadly, Leia mathematically sorts hers in the most crushing combinations and it just takes all the fun out of it."

"Winning is fun," Leia said, not taking her gaze from her infopad. "Dad, do you want the city of Raven's Roost?"

"No one wants Raven's Roost," I replied, clumsily raising the sword over my head.

"I do!" Cindy said. "We can crowdfund a massive campaign to move everyone there somewhere decent and keep most of the money!"

"Never change, guys," I said, swinging the Sword of Samael like the Reaper's Scythe. I hoped the two magical artifacts worked the same way.

I was pleased to say the sword sliced through space/time just as easily and created a portal to the Stephen Soldiers Memorial national park near Washington DC. It said something that the government hadn't bothered to do anything to honor the tried-and-true WW2 hero known as the Prismatic Commando (former AmeriCommando) until after his death. Then again, Stephen Soldiers hadn't been the sort of guy who cared about statues or honors. Indeed, he probably would have said to make any park named in his esteem into something honoring the common soldiers who'd dedicated their lives to preserving freedom.

"I bought all your holdings, Mom," Leia said. "You're fired."

Cindy's omega phone pinged, and she pulled it out of her $15,000 purse before checking it. "So, you did."

"I'm sorry, Mom," Mimi said. "Except not really. You're kind of terrible."

"It's fine," Cindy said. "I'll just go back to scamming suckers by saying Ultragod stole the election."

Everyone turned to look at her. "Wait, that's you behind all those ads?"

"What?" Cindy asked. "You'd rather the money go to someone who actually believes it?"

I stared. "Cindy, you may actually just be too evil for me."

Cindy shrugged. "I'll just pretend to be redeemed for a few months and get with a superhero. Then everyone will forgive me for all the crimes and give me a pardon. It's a common tactic. Certainly, it worked for you and Ultragoddess."

Sometimes there were no words. "Let's get going, guys."

The others were already in a heated argument, though.

Cindy sighed. "Fine, I'll donate the money to charity, but I'm not giving up my co-ownership of the National Weapons Association Network. That's the only channel that shows my reality show."

I shook my head, picked up my boom box, and walked through the portal, finding myself on the edge of the crowd gathered for the President's speech. It was smaller than expected because most of the people who wanted to attend were outside of the park, kept away by Foundation agents as well as the Washington D.C. police force.

Most of the crowd were a collection of VIPs ranging from reporters to politicians to a sea of retired heroes. Many of them were wearing their uniforms, some no longer quite fitting right, while others were showing their civilian attire as if a badge of honor.

"Dammit!" Cindy said, stepping through the portal. "Costume was an option! I'm way overdressed for this."

"It's also in the middle of a park," I pointed out. "Not the place for high heels." Cindy lifted her hand and showed off a diamond studded ring that included some stones stolen from the Dragon King's horde. She proceeded to lift a few inches off the ground. "*Ring of Levitation.* Massed produced by Bad Wolf Industries in conjunction with Hasbro. The first sign your whole Dungeon magic fiasco wasn't a complete disaster."

"I may be starting over on that," I murmured, not wanting to get into the fact Jacob may have removed all the Dungeon magic I'd known to let me start over without the baggage. "Get back to basics. A clean fresh start."

"You should rename all of the spells, copyright it, and charge everyone every time they use it," Cindy said. "At the very least, make a monthly service."

"Not everything is about money," I said, getting an odd sense of déjà vu.

"You know who says that, Gary?" Cindy said, increasing said sense.

"Poor people," I interrupted. "I get it. Actually, I think rich people say it much more often."

"It looks like it's going to rain," Leia said, walking through the portal with Mimi and Larry as it closed behind them. She was looking at the sky and, indeed, gray clouds were forming above us. "You'd think they could get some weather control for this public announcement."

"Or set it at the Four Seasons," Cindy muttered. "You might as well set this at a lawn and gardening store."

I turned my head back to my children, only to do a doubletake as they were now dressed in thick galoshes, plastic rain yellow raincoats, and yellow hats. They also had translucent umbrellas in their hands.

"How?" I started to ask before thinking better. My children were second and fourth generation Supers. They followed cartoon logic even more than I did. Besides, any question I had could probably just be answered with "magic" or "science".

"Ugh," Cindy said. "I'm going to get wet and not in the good way."

"You can always do the dog fur shake," Leia suggested.

"Ha-ha," Cindy said. "Not in this jewelry. It's like throwing away money."

Leia handed her mother her umbrella before pulling out an identical one from her pocket that could not fit one. Yeah, we were dealing with extradimensional super-science or sorcery here.

Cindy took it and looked at Larry. "So, you're Mandy's bastard, huh?"

"Yeah," Larry said, looking uncomfortable.

"Nice to meet you," Cindy said. "I just want you to know I hate Joan Rowling too."

"Uh, thanks," Larry said, offput as only someone approached out of the blue about their identity by a stranger can be. "Can we just be friends by never speaking again?"

"Sounds good," Cindy said, making finger guns. "If you ever want to market the Ultra-Paladin brand, well, talk to my daughter. She owns my company now."

Larry smirked, clearly assuming she was joking, and Leia hadn't literally made a few billion dollars in the past hour. "I actually haven't settled on a name. It seems disrespectful to try to take part of another superhero's name without their permission."

"Otherwise, you end up in a lawsuit like that poor Pakistani girl, Prism Girl," I replied. "You know, with Colonel Prism."

"That was Colonel Prism's lawyers, and you know it!" Leia snapped, uncharacteristically intense. "Prism Girl is awesome and the best superhero to come out in the past twenty years!"

"What are you, in her fan club?" Cindy said.

Leia stared. "I hosted Prism Con in our backyard last month."

"Oh," Cindy said. "I thought it was an invasion by a gang of Rainbow Brite cosplayers. Either that or a Pride Day thing."

"In any case, Ultragod has spent his entire life trying to be a symbol to inspire others," I said. "He absolutely wouldn't object to you using the Ultragod brand to save the innocent, protect the helpless, and so on."

"Yeah, but his lawyers would kill your entire family and eat them," Cindy said. "Which, wait, your family is Mandy and the Coltons, who are all a bunch of evil superspies."

"Morally ambiguous superspies," Larry corrected. "Also, a family of Londonium dentists raised me."

"What happened to them?" I asked.

"They got killed by a giant robot," Larry said.

"Shit, I'm sorry," I said.

Larry shrugged. "It's like the third most common way to die on the island after car wrecks and heart disease. I just don't want to get in any trouble with the Anders family."

"Which is why you've named yourself after the only guy who has killed Ultragod and Ultragoddess," Cindy said.

"Wait, what?" Larry asked.

"I didn't kill Ultragod!" I snapped, panicked. "That was Merciful pretending to be me! Also, ix-nay on mentioning killing the President-ay at his celebration-ay."

"You've also killed the President," Cindy said. "Admittedly, not this President."

"I'm pretty sure I didn't kill-kill Charles Omega," I muttered. "Much to my disappointment."

Larry looked ready to run for his life and I didn't blame him.

Thankfully, Mimi came to save the day and grabbed him by the armor by putting her hand on him. Which if that doesn't make sense, Ultragod and Ultragoddess don't have super-strength and invulnerability so much as a form of hard light telekinesis that permeates their body. They're tough as well, but it's useful for things like picking up crashing planes or lifting buildings since they don't fall apart due to physics.

"Hold up. My granddad gave me the legally trademarked and copyrighted name Ultragirl last year. I don't want it. I'm doing my own thing. But I'm allowed to pass on one variant to a sidekick or recruit to the Ultra-Family. So, yes, you can be Ultra-Paladin," Mimi said, making the papal finger gesture. "I dub thee and knight thee in the name of the House of Anders. Blah-blah-blah."

"Wait, your granddad?" Larry did a double take. "You mean the rumors about Gary and Ultragoddess are true? I always thought they were just—"

A few months ago, the Daily Surveyor, which was the news agency people turned to when the Omega News Network (now independent) wasn't extreme enough, did an exposé about the idea of Ultragoddess and I being together. Ultragoddess had rather brusquely dismissed the very idea. We were already broken up over the whole, "my killing her evil side that cost her the powers she'd had for decades", but it had really hurt. I mean calling me a criminal psychopath? That's fine. Saying I was a creepy weirdo? That was just uncalled for. Oddly, I'd started getting more fan mail from Super women afterward.

"Malicious slander?" Cindy asked.

"No, Cindy," I said, annoyed. "It's libel when you print it."

"You stole that," Cindy said.

Larry looked conflicted about all these revelations. "Wow, everyone really is related in superherodom."

"Listen, let's just go find Ultragod and I'll give him his magical artifact," I said, not mentioning it would make him the most powerful being in the Multiverse. "Then Leia can get back to her day trading."

"Oh, I stopped day trading when I collapsed the Londonium economy. Err, sorry, Larry," Leia said, looking up. "Sadly, Gizmo Industries is stuck at being a Fortune 500 and 1 company. A shame, but I figured I didn't want to start any wars on Ultraday."

"Well, there's always tomorrow," I said, more than slightly terrified of my daughter.

"We may have to blow up a server farm in Alabama after the announcement," Leia said, her eyes darting back and forth. "You know, for reasons other than covering up mass wire fraud and insider trading. For some other reason that's completely different."

"I have guys, don't worry," I replied, patting my daughter on the head. "But yes, please pay attention to Ultragod's speech, Leia. This will be a historic day."

"I predict there's an eighty percent chance of supervillains attacking," Leia said, shrugging. "I intend to spend the entire time commenting on internet forums about your biographies. There's some heavy discussion since they went on sale this week."

"I'm sure—" I started to speak.

"They think you've dramatically overpowered your character and are sick of the love triangles," Mimi spoke up, holding her own infopad.

"People love the love triangles!" I said, appalled. "That's like how soap operas survive for eighty years!"

"People hate the love triangles," Mimi said. "They like Mandy, Gabrielle, *and* Cindy but are just sick of the drama."

"Cindy also shouldn't get a sequel, novel" Leia said, showing me the posts. "They find her whiny."

"Hey!" Cindy said.

"Top picks from the polls are thirty percent Mandy, twenty percent Gabrielle, ten percent Splotch, six percent Death, and two percent Cindy," Mimi said. "There's also one write-in vote from another dimension that thinks you should hook up with someone named Kitty Pryde. Which was posted by Weredeer2000 and no points for who that is."

"What's the remaining thirty-two percent?" I asked.

"They think you should hook up with Other Gary," Mimi said. "It's the fifty-third most popular fanfic pairing on WeirdPad."

"I hate the internet," I muttered.

"Why only two percent?" Cindy asked. "It's because they think I can do better, isn't it?"

"Don't ask, Cindy," I said, looking over at her. "In that way lies madness."

"They think you're a rip off of a previous supervillain called HarleQueen," Leia said, reading from a sheet. "Apparently, she was a Golden Age supervillainess. She has a sexy granddaughter younger than you are, too."

Cindy blinked. "How many forum users are on this superhero board?"

"It's a major site so like eight million," Leia said.

"Get me their names," Cindy said. "They must all die."

"Mom—" Leia said.

"All of them!" Cindy said.

"Doesn't she not age as a werewolf?" Larry asked.

"Shh," Mimi said, putting her forefinger to her lips. "It's more fun if you never remind her of this fact."

"The same for your father," a familiar female voice spoke nearby. Thankfully, she wasn't behind me, and I saw her arriving.

It was Gabrielle in a suit of Ultranian armor and she was accompanied by the new Prismatic Commando (formerly the new AmeriCommando), Sam Eagles.

I gave us a fifty percent shot of not being arrested.

Chapter Twenty-Four

There're No Easy Answers

So, hands up, people, does anyone have a relationship that is a raging dumpster fire? One in which you still cared about the other person but just couldn't make work? Wow. That is a lot of hands. My divine awareness has never been more pitiable. Or I'm just guessing for a funny joke. Either way, "raging dumpster fire with superpowers" is roughly the best way to describe my relationship with Gabrielle Anders AKA Ultragoddess AKA Revolutionary Girl AKA Titanium Guardian.

We'd started dating in college, unaware of each other's pasts, and I proposed to her. Unfortunately, I had just been kidnapped by The Cackler for the same reason any supervillain kidnaps a love interest: to be a dick. Gabrielle overreacted to my nearly being killed and erased my memory. There were some studies that indicated faulty use of Ultra-Hypnosis could cause long-term emotional instability but since I was fine, I didn't pay them much mind.

I'd eventually gotten my memory back and we'd given it another shot. Something that had happened after both Mandy had died and Maria was walking around in her undead corpse. Oh, and Cindy had given birth to Leia before leaving her for my sister to raise. If that sounded inappropriate, well, no shit,

Sherlock. It was incredibly inappropriate. Gabrielle and I had gotten engaged, she'd gotten pregnant with Mimi, and reality had been rebooted.

Things had come to a skidding halt when Gabrielle had been split into two beings, Good and Jerk, and I'd killed the Jerk side of her. As I mentioned before in this volume of my biography, it had cost Ultragoddess her powers and that wasn't something most relationships could survive. We'd barely spoken since she'd called off the engagement and there were rumors that she was involved with Samuel Eagles AKA the AmeriCommando Part Deux (now Prismatic Commando Part Deux). I hoped they were true because Gabrielle deserved to be with someone who made her happy and because I had an infinite number of Muppet jokes to make about his name.

Titanium Guardian, as she was currently going by, wore a gold and white suit of armor that was emblazoned with the Ultragod family symbol. Which was a U in a star. I didn't know why she didn't just go by Ultragoddess, but I suppose powers and branding were intrinsically tied. While no longer the most powerful girl in the universe, the alien battle suit still allowed her to throw down with everyone from the Behemoth to small armies. Supposedly she'd been sighted in Syria, the Russian Border, and Trans-Bavaria despite the illegality of superheroes helping in wartime according to the United Government's Treaty on Superhuman Affairs.

Prismatic Commando II was wearing a suit of alien space armor that bore a distinct red, white, and blue color. There were some questions as to whether Sam the Eagle here deserved to be the new Prismatic Commando. He was getting pushback for taking the codename of his mentor—and possible illegitimate father—from both sides of the aisle. Some people didn't think he was worthy of the title and others didn't think he had anything to prove. My opinion? I didn't care in the slightest.

"Hello, Gary," Gabrielle said, a hint of sadness in her voice.

"Who's Gary?" I asked, looking around as if Merciless was hiding somewhere. "There is only Marty McAwesome, the Embodiment of a Bygone Era."

"Gizmo actually installed perception filters in our armor so we can see through disguise magic," Gabrielle said, referring to Leia by her codename.

"Leia!" I said, looking down at my daughter. "I am very disappointed in you. Helping the heroes!"

"Sorry!" Leia said. "I swear, it was only for the money!"

"Hello, Mimi," Gabrielle said, looking down at her daughter.

"Fuck off, Mom," Mimi said, flipping her mother off and not even looking her in the eye. She just sort of looked to the side and sneered.

Yeah, relations between mother and daughter weren't exactly great. I had no desire for my daughter to take sides between Gabrielle and me. Hell, I wasn't of the mind that there was a conflict between us. Unfortunately, Mimi had decided there very much was a war going on and had decisively come down on #TeamGary. While I also wanted to heal the rift between them, I did have to admit that I saw where Mimi was coming from, and this wasn't about me. Gabrielle had been almost completely absent from her life. How absent? Mimi considered Cindy to be more of a mother to her than Gabrielle, God help her.

"You're coming of age, Mimi," Gabrielle said, as if Mimi didn't realize it. "You need to prepare for your powers to reach their full potential."

"I don't want my powers to reach full potential!" Mimi said. "I want to steal monuments and leave educational clues! You can't do that with omnipotent power!"

"Edutainment really warped your little mind, didn't it, Mimi," I muttered. Who knew that was the bad influence parents really had to watch out for? It also explained her disturbing interest in acapella.

"I blame bad parenting instead," Gabrielle said, shaking her head at the two sisters.

"Well, then you don't have any blame," Cindy said. "You were never there."

Gabrielle glared at Cindy. Her expression could easily be read as, "Don't you hate it when the worst person you know makes a valid point?"

Leia reached over and gave her sister an over the shoulder hug. "I don't want you to be super-strong and powerful either! I'm a mad scientist! You're an Ultra! We're half-siblings! It's like tailor made for us to become archenemies!"

"You need to go to Ultraworld," Gabrielle said, trying to stay on topic. Which was a bit like herding rabid grizzly bears. "There, the Ultranians can train you in the proper use of your powers and how to save lives."

"I've been to Ultraworld, Mom!" Mimi said, scowling. She was referring to one of the rare times Gabrielle had asked to spend any time with her and it had involved a "working vacation" with her child in the one place where it wouldn't impact Ultragoddess' reputation. "It's full of people dressed like they're in Flash Gordon and speak in Shakespearian English despite the fact they're all aliens. Their king can't talk and is always getting overthrown by his brother who he keeps reinstating as chancellor. Even though his brother is named Evillo! It's a silly place."

"Like Camelot!" I said.

Literally, only Sam the Eagle chuckled.

"You're all uncultured heathens," I replied. "Really, Larry, you too?"

"Monty Python was a bit before my time," Larry said.

"Nonsense!" I said. "We'll have a movie marathon when we get back."

"This is Larry Karkofsky AKA Ultra-Paladin," Cindy said. "He's Mandy's son."

"Hey," Larry said, waving uncomfortably.

"So, as a half-vampire, do you hunt other vampires?" Cindy asked Larry. "Because I think that's Mandy's thing."

"It's also Bloodscream's, but Mandy does it better," Gabrielle deadpanned.

"I'm not a half-vampire," Larry said.

"Wow, your dad was also a vampire?" Cindy asked, completely missing the point. "How are you not exploding in the sun?"

"Don't try to figure it out," Leia cautioned Larry. "She's looking forward to my becoming a werewolf even though she was turned into one by Dad's evil doppelganger."

"Good doppelganger," I said. "He's just a genocidal fascist while I'm a kind-hearted revolutionary. No, don't try and unpack that."

"So, Mimi, want to chip in and buy Dad a dictionary for his fortieth birthday?" Leia asked. "I have a couple of billion dollars to spare. I'm not counting the Merciless Coin that is really just there for money laundering."

"I know, forty and dating a twenty-eight-year-old," Cindy said, flipping her styled red hair. "It's so Hollywood."

Cindy was obviously saying I was forty and she was twenty-eight. Which was, let's say, particularly ridiculous with Gabrielle. Not because Cindy intended to fool her but because Gabrielle was every bit as snarky as Cindy.

"Really?" Gabrielle asked, looking straight at Cindy. "Who is he dating?"

Cindy glared at Gabrielle. "Do not toy with me, Tin Can Girl. I have a magic sword that can pry you open like cat food. Which would be a better metaphor if it was dog food but the only dogs who eat canned food are spoiled little bitches. Which I am not. Usually."

Larry coughed into his fist. "It's very nice to meet you. Your daughter is a wonderful person."

"You seem like a nice guy, Larry," Gabrielle said. "It's good to meet you. Fair warning, the Secret Service will kill you if you ever share that Mimi is my daughter."

"They really will," Sam the Eagle said. "It's for her daughter's protection."

"Really?" Mimi asked. "Because given my father, the women he lives with that I kind of think of my other mothers, the literal army of goblins—"

"Kobolds," I said.

"It seems like I'm pretty secure as is," Mimi said. "So, I can't help but think it's because you're actually ashamed of me."

Oh Moses, this was somehow going to get even more awkward. "Hey, great news, PHANTOM IS COMING!!"

Everyone looked at me.

"Wow, I am never living that down," I said, sighing. "I mean, they're coming and it's good because we can kill them! Because they've returned and it would be good to get rid of them! They have mind-control! Alternate realities are involved! Badness! It's crossover time!"

Neither Gabrielle nor Sam the Eagle responded to the news. They were just staring forward.

"Those are not the faces of people surprised by this news," I replied.

"How can you tell, one of them is wearing a steel mask to disguise their emotions and the other is AmeriCommando," Cindy said.

"Prismatic Commando," Sam corrected. "Two-point-oh."

"Sure, man," Cindy said. "My joke was a bait and switch. You know one to deliberately to insult Ultragoddess, sorry, Titanium Guardian, by implying she's got a steel face. You agree your mother is terrible, right, Mimi?"

I was going to have to have a talk with Cindy. Apparently, she didn't hold any of my reservations against playing the kids against Gabrielle.

"She's trying to turn *me* into Ultragoddess," Mimi muttered.

"Is that so bad?" Gabrielle asked.

"Yes!" Mimi said.

"We'd spend so much more time together!" Gabrielle said.

"Too late!" Mimi said. "Alternative response: *that's* the problem!"

I put two fingers in my mouth and blew a whistle. "Back to the PHANTOM matters. You guys know there's a possible attack coming?"

"Yes, Gary," Gabrielle said, rolling her eyes. "The government is not completely useless."

I burst out laughing at that. It took a second to calm down. "Oh, wait, you're serious."

"I think someone else should have rebooted the world, Dad," Leia said, looking up at me. "Just saying."

"There's always someone plotting a terrorist attack," Sam the Eagle said. "Particularly at an event like this. We were more concerned about the Nanoplague. If it came out that millions were dead because of that, it might—"

"Make the government look bad?" I asked, sarcastically. "Yeah, it just might."

"I assume we have you to thank for stopping it?" Gabrielle asked, showing no emotion.

"Yes," I replied. "And any planets that were destroyed along the way were the fault of the Trench Coat Magician."

"Pardon?" Gabrielle asked, confused.

"I mean *Mystery Science Theater 3000*'s Mike Nelson," I replied, switching gears. I'd forgotten I didn't hate Jack Hellraiser. "A few extra planets destroyed won't hurt his reputation."

Gabrielle shook her head. "Thank you, Gary. The world appreciates your efforts."

I sincerely doubted that. As much as I was a capable super criminal, I had only barely managed to stay out of prison and was still considered a menace to society despite all the good I had done for the universe. The only reason I hadn't been forced to fight my way past a bunch of Exterminator robots and Foundation agents was Ultragod's protection. Well, that and the President following Omega in the old timeline had been scared shitless of me.

That had been when I'd had a Primal Orb, though, and I didn't even have my Dungeon magic anymore. If the government did ever decide to turn against me, I wasn't prepared and that wasn't even considering the fact ninety percent of other superheroes did want to take me down. They'd offered me the chance to join their side and I'd briefly taken them up on the offer but, well, that was before I'd rebooted the universe and helped Cindy rob the world's richest dragon.

"Even though he won't get the credit," Mimi said.

"I don't do this for the credit," I replied to Mimi, really wishing she would dial down the hostility.

"What do you do it for, then?" Cindy asked, looking bored. "Because if there's a cash windfall, I deserve it for child support."

I avoided the obvious joke. "I do it because I, too, live on the planet. It's where I keep my stuff. Hence, saving the world is only pragmatic for a fiendish villain who fiends."

Gabrielle's expression was tired, and I'd learned to be able to read it like a map. She really wasn't in the mood for my cheerful insistence on being the bad guy. "My mother died right before the Nanoplague was cured."

Gabrielle was referring to Polly Perkins, intrepid reporter and Ultragod's wife. She was pretty badass in the 1930s and 1940s, but Ultra-Hypnotism had made her obsessed with uncovering Ultragod's secret identity for decades. Which would result in him marrying her or something. Apparently, he'd had to erase her memory of his secret identity to placate the Cosmic Editors. How the couple had managed to get past that and become the loving couple they'd been was anyone's guess.

Merciful, bastard that he was, had speculated that she had been Ultragod's primary reason for living as many years as he had. That without her, he lost that drive to survive. It was why Merciful had been able to kill Ultragod, combined with the fact he'd been wearing my face and carrying an ultranium pistol. By the way, I wasn't quite sure what the difference between ultranium and ultranite was. I'd have to ask Leia.

I stared. "I see. That sucks, I really liked her."

Mimi looked down, ashamed. "Yeah, you probably should have led with Grandma was dead."

Unlike Gabrielle, Moses and Polly had made a decent amount of time for their grandchild. They'd even treated Leia as one of their own, which just went to show what class acts they were. My failure to save the latter was something that induced a rare sensation within me: guilt. Hell, even regret.

"It'd be good for you to speak with your grandfather after this," Gabrielle said. "But right now, Gary, he wants to speak with you."

I was uncomfortable speaking with Moses Anders, knowing I'd failed to save his wife and wondered if this was the best time or the worst to give him the Crown of the Gods. I wasn't sure this was the right thing, but I was also certain that there was nothing worse than not using power when you had the ability to make it right.

Right?

"I'd like to take Larry," I said.

"Wait, why?" Larry asked, confused.

Mimi looked up at me, offended. "Really, Dad?"

"I need you to make sure that Cindy doesn't kill and eat any reporters," I replied.

"Pfft!" Cindy said, putting a hand on her hip. "Like she could stop me."

Mimi looked up. "Is this because you have an omnipotence-granting artifact you're going to give to Grandpa and don't want me to see it because you worry it'll be used to overwrite reality again, screwing up my already retconned and time-compressed life more?"

I stared at her. "No."

"Oh good," Mimi said. "Because my older self says you do that and it's bad."

"Tell yourself no one likes a snitch," I replied.

"It's not child abuse to say snitches get stitches," Cindy added. "We'd pay to have someone else do it. Then it doesn't count."

"No, Cindy," I replied.

"Oh," Cindy said, pausing. "I'll write that down. But seriously, if any of your family talks to the Feds then you're obligated to kill them."

"Which doesn't include Ultragod," I replied. "Who I am going to meet right now."

"Right," Cindy said, winking.

"I am leaving right now," I replied.

"It's okay, Dad," Mimi said, staring thoughtfully. "We'll avenge you."

"I keep a pre-loaded rifle with silver tipped cartridges for just the occasion," Leia said.

"Hey!" Cindy said.

"Children shouldn't use guns," I said, shaking my head. "Turn that over to Case and get yourself a magic crossbow instead."

"Right," Leia said, making a salute.

"Hey!" Cindy said.

Larry reluctantly accompanied me as I walked off with Gabrielle and Sam.

"Was any of that true?" Larry asked. "Or was it your family just messing with you?"

"I have no idea," I replied.

Chapter Twenty-Five

The End of the Age of Superheroes

There was a festive and optimistic mood to the gathering, which really shouldn't have been the case given so many people had died in the Nanoplague. It might have been cured, but there should at least have been some more masks on just in case. Of course, humanity had adjusted to being the ants at the picnic of the gods.

If not for the Nanoplague, there would have been an alien invasion or a portal to Hell or Pyronnus showing up to eat Earth again despite all his previous failures. I'd grown as numb to it as anyone else by the time I'd become a supervillain. My time in New Angeles and Falconcrest City had dozens of apocalyptic threats to the point they all sort of ran together. I remembered one specific incident had been the Nefarious Nine summoning dinosaurs for Big Game Hunter, only for my father to be annoyed they were going to make him late for work. Everyone assumed the heroes would always save the day and when they didn't, they just sort of shrugged it off.

Now? Now I was feeling extra nervous and not just because my family was present. I'd screwed up when I rebooted the world and there were now consequences that couldn't be avoided. Ones I couldn't see the end results of. My go-to move would have been discussing the issue with Mandy but she was gone, and I still wasn't comfortable with resuming my friendship with Diabloman. Hopefully, Moses could spare a few minutes.

"You know you're still a wanted terrorist, right, Merciless?" Sam the Eagle said, walking with me through the crowd of retired heroes, diplomats, and reporters. Gabrielle was ignoring everyone else trying to talk to her—some to offer their sympathies for losing her powers while others were hoping to get the inside track to her father's announcement.

None of them knew about the death of the First Lady yet and I wondered how Moses was holding it together. I would have cancelled if not trying to zip around the world so fast that I went back in time to bring her back to life. Larry seemed overwhelmed by all of it, and I didn't blame him. I'd spent the time walking with him on my phone, checking his backstory. He was green with even the Neo-Heroes rejecting him—and the Neo-Heroes were presently under indictment for that whole blown up school thing in Connecticut.

"I feel like the label of terrorist is thrown about too willy-nilly," I replied, remembering Sam had spoken to me. "It's like everyone who is a non-state actor attempting to effect political change through violence is called one."

"That would be literally the dictionary definition," Sam the Eagle replied.

"Yeah, but I'm not engaged in indiscriminate slaughter of civilians either," I replied, putting on "We're Not Gonna Take It" by Twisted Sister to cover up our conversations. My boombox was magical and provided numerous boosts to heroes around it but trying to explain that to other heroes was often a lost cause. It seemed I could still use Dungeon magic items even if I was now stripped from it as a power source.

Personally, I suspected this was Death's not-so-subtle way of making it clear she wanted me dependent on her and no other deities. That was fine, I was more comfortable using the Reaper's Cloak anyway. I was just glad she left the magic for the rest of the world.

"I'm serious, Merciless," Sam the Eagle responded. "Ultragod is always there to watch your back but there're plenty of people who want to see you dead or locked away in the deepest hole imaginable. They may not remember you killing the President of the United States—the bad one—but that doesn't mean you're not a threat."

Gabrielle was noticeably silent during all of this.

"Most governments believe that they maintain their power purely through the monopolization of violence," I replied, entering Doctor Merciless Mode. "This is a short-sighted and dangerous viewpoint as they should be focused primarily on their monopolization of the masses' consent instead. But it's the reason why governments and Supers are inherently antagonistic. The government will never trust a person that cannot be intimidated into obedience or is capable of rivalling the state for protection."

"Where did you come up with that, Anarchists R Us?" Sam the Eagle asked.

Gabrielle had told me it during our college years. It had been the subject of her grad school thesis before she'd been forced to drop out after being outed as Ultragoddess. My own plans to become a Doctor of Criminology had been scuttled by the more mundane fact I'd run out of money to pursue my education further and wasn't going to risk any more crushing debt.

"Just something I picked up along the way," I said, feeling the silence between Gabrielle and me. "You know, I kind of picked up a magical artifact along the way that could help you with your issue."

Larry looked at me. "Do you really think you should be—"

"Shh," I said, not wanting to hear any of this, "Don't use the evil artifact for good" nonsense that would have precluded all the present disasters I was dealing with.

Gabrielle didn't respond, continuing to walk with her armor making Robocop-esque whooshing noises with every step.

"Merciless, don't," Sam the Eagle said. There was an edge to his tone that told me I was treading on thin ice.

"It's either Gary or Eighties Man, Sam the Eagle," I replied, annoyed. "Some of us are maintaining a secret identity here, pal."

Sam did a double take, perhaps rightly noting how utterly ridiculous it was that I was maintaining a secret identity while living in the Nightwalker's old mansion with such a bizarre collection of weirdos as inhabited it. The thing that he didn't realize was that it being such a bizarre collection of weirdos was its own form of camouflage.

One of the things I'd learned was there was a reason that so many supervillains hid in incredibly obvious places like abandoned amusements parks, factories, and old castles. There was a filter in the minds of people that was instinctual as well as primal. A sort of, "Here be Monsters. Don't go in." Stately Warren Manor was hardly that sort of place but had a reputation like the spooky old house kids dare people to visit. The Foundation might know where I live, but the few times they'd tried to come and visit hadn't gone over well. I had to even pick up my mail at the post office. Well, except the stuff from Brazil.com as nothing on Earth could dissuade their deliverymen.

"Sure, Eighties Man," Sam the Eagle responded, sounding like he was having difficulty with the words.

"I don't need you to restore my powers, Gary," Gabrielle responded after the mother of all pauses. "I also don't blame you for causing me to lose them in the first place?"

"Really?" I asked, skeptical. "Because I'm prepared to accept responsibility there. Which is about a rare a sentence as 'I did have sexual relations with that woman', 'No, I don't need your money', and 'Mother Church admits that it was totally wrong about this issue.'"

Sam the Eagle struggled not to smile at that one. I got the impression he was determined not to like me but having difficulty with the decision. Then again, I couldn't imagine why he wouldn't want to like me, what with my being the international terrorist and him dating my ex-double fiancé. By the way, if you have a relationship that can be called "ex-double fiancé" then you can safely list that as a red flag.

"You were protecting the mother of your child," Gabrielle said, referring to Cindy.

"Yeah, by shooting the other one," I replied. "Even if she was temporarily evil. I feel like that was a situation where I should have come up with a third option."

Larry grimaced, clearly agreeing with me. Mind you, I had to wonder about how smart a person had to be to name themselves after someone like me. Larry really seemed like he should have thought better than that.

Gabrielle sighed. "I went to Ultraworld to undergo the Tests of Worthiness in order to get my powers back."

"Ah," I said, pausing. "I take it that it didn't go well."

"I failed," Gabrielle muttered. "They determined my soul was split between too many paths."

I felt immense guilt, which was the emotion I'd been feeling earlier, and it sucked. "Let me guess, being friends with a recidivist ne'er do well like me didn't help."

"No," Gabrielle said, surprising me. "I was thinking that might be the case, but the Ultra-Force said it had scanned your soul and determined that you were one man's terrorist but many other men's freedom fighter. That you were, ultimately, a good and worthy man."

"Well, clearly, it doesn't know what the fuck it's talking about," I said, offended on her behalf.

Gabrielle smiled, clearly still having affection for my quirky sense of humor. Which showed even the best of us still had weaknesses. "The Ultra-Force has already chosen a new champion even if she doesn't realize it yet. It's my place to mentor her."

"You're meant to be more than just Mimi's stage mom, Gabby," I said.

"We're here," Gabrielle said, arriving at the stage where Moses Anders was supposed to give his speech. The Secret Service was, unsurprisingly, less than pleased about my presence but not about to argue with the First Daughter or the First Agent of the Foundation. That, and I was apparently on the list. They also held Larry on the other side of the flap, which was a shame.

I was ushered away from the others into a private room that was just four curtains surrounding the President of the United States. He wasn't in costume, just a suit, and looked a great deal healthier than he'd looked before. Still, there was a sadness to him that made perfect sense knowing his wife had died—probably as soon as I'd gone off to space.

"I'm sorry about Polly," I said.

Okay, great opening, Gary.

"Thank you," Moses said, softly. "It seems you succeeded in your quest."

"Yes," I said, nodding. "The Trench Coat Magician was killed by a guy impersonating me, though. It's terrible. He's better now, though. Shame about that evil me."

Moses stared. "You know, Gary, that's actually the third time I've heard that excuse."

"Given that it's actually the second time I've used it, and the first time was when my evil doppelganger killed you, I'd say you have ample reason to believe it," I said, pausing. "So, anyway, I have the Crown of the Gods! You should use it to make everything awesome. Like the song in the Lego movie."

Moses stared at me. "The song in the Lego movie is an indictment of artificially imposed happiness by corporate overlords."

I paused. "In ten years, no one is going to believe I had a conversation with the superhero President of the United States about the political satire of a giant toy commercial."

"Given you'd be telling it to your family, they might well believe you," Moses said. "I don't need the Crown of the Gods, Gary. It was a last-ditch attempt to stop the Nanoplague and now that it is done, I don't need it. No one should have that power."

I paused. "You don't need it to fix everything, Moses, but it might be useful to fix some things. Your wife for instance."

Moses narrowed his eyes. "Don't tempt me with that, Gary. We're in a One Ring situation. I'm old enough to get that reference."

I blinked. "The Lord of the Rings movies are pretty recent, Moses. I mean, older than my kids but not old-old. Like you. Err, no offense."

"There're movies?" Moses asked. "Dammit, I knew I should have updated my Observatory view list. It's just been a really busy, oh, well, past century."

"You can't dodge the question, Mister President," I said, pulling out the crown. "With great power comes…something, I forget. But isn't it irresponsible not to use it? Hell, it's not selfish to use it for something for you and you alone."

"That's the very definition of selfish," Moses said, perhaps suggesting I needed that dictionary that Leia had mentioned buying me for my birthday. "But even if I wanted to use it to bring back Polly, it wouldn't work."

"I'm pretty sure it would," I said, pausing. "I mean, I don't know how much juice is in this thing, but there's probably enough to once more violate the laws of Death. You know, the Primal that I'm supposedly working for."

Moses' expression was empty. "You should know, Gary, it is impossible to violate the laws of the Primals unless they will it."

"She's pretty pissed at me," I said. "Resurrection was supposed to be stopped and here you are."

Moses looked down. "I didn't come back, Gary."

"I'm sorry, what?" I asked. It was a rare occasion that anything genuinely surprised me, but I had to say that Moses had succeeded with that statement.

"When I came back, I felt hollow and cold," Moses said, pausing. "Everything I experienced was a dim echo of what it was before even though I still felt my desire to help others. My memories and personality were intact as well."

I didn't like there was going. "Go on."

"I consulted with Isis the Invincible and the Trench Coat Magician among others," Moses said. "They determined my soul hadn't come back."

I stared. "Like a vampire."

"Not even the portion of the soul that becomes a demon," Moses explained. "Moses Anders, the real Moses Anders, moved on. So did Polly, my wife, and Lancel. I suspect many of the other people you resurrected as well. What you conjured in their stead was a simulacrum. People designed to fill their role."

"Shit," I muttered. "Are you sure?"

Which was a stupid question. You don't go around admitting you're a soulless NPC in a video game created by me unless you're sure.

Moses nodded. "I'm afraid so."

"Damn," I muttered. "Does Gabrielle know?"

"No," Moses replied. "But she will after this speech. Once the Superhuman Equality Act takes place, I'll be stepping down as President. The country deserves to be led by someone they actually elected and who is a true living being."

"Souls are overrated," I said, saying the stupidest thing I could have in this moment.

"Mandy might disagree," Moses said, commenting more on my love life than the apocalyptic series of revelations that had just occurred.

"Mandy left me," I said, pausing. "I guess she couldn't deal with the fact she was unliving in a house of the living."

"Could it possibly be living with Cindy?" Ultragod asked. "Your on-again-off-again relationship with my daughter, Splotch Woman, the Tsavong Princess that impersonated Splotch Woman, Julie d'Aubigny, Nightshade, Colonel—"

"That didn't bother her," I interrupted, perhaps too quickly. It was possible I'd gotten a little "walking hormone" during my grief over Mandy's multiple deaths. Okay, yes, there may have been a problem, but I decided to deflect in this conversation. "I think the only time she ever raised an objection was when she thought I was being fed on by Carmilla."

"The famously lesbian vampire," Moses replied, skeptical.

"Yes," I said. "But I get the impression all vampires are fundamentally blood sexual. Yeah, screw everyone else in the world but don't let anyone else drink from you."

"Wait, when did you meet Carmilla?" Moses asked.

"*Merciless: Master of the Universe* number fourteen," I replied, conjuring a copy of the comic with what little true magic I had. It had a hulking version of me with a bare chest and a sword raised in my hands over my head. I was standing on top of a mountain of skulls. "It's my third series after *Merciless: The Supervillain Without Mercy* and *Merciless and His Awesome Buddies.*"

"Whoever came up with Awesome Buddies as your team of criminals' name should be fired," Moses replied.

"Yes, they absolutely should," I said, pretending it wasn't me. "Anyway, I haven't been a good husband to her."

"Perhaps you should try being one," Moses said. "Sometimes, it really is that simple."

I put away the Crown of the Gods. "Listen, Moses, there's a possible attack—"

That was when the explosions and screaming started.

Chapter Twenty-Six

Why Couldn't It Have Been Communists?

"Dammit," I muttered hearing the attack. "I was just about to achieve a breakthrough with Mandy."

"PHANTOM," Moses muttered, growling. "There were rumors the Interdimensional Council of Terrors had planned to wage an attack on us."

The Interdimensional Council of Terrors was a collection of alternate dimensional and parallel universe versions of Tom Terror. It turned out that even if you killed the original one in a reality and prevented his resurrection, that didn't mean there wasn't potentially an endless number of other variants elsewhere. Which just went to show that if you tried to improve the world, you would inevitably fail, and it was best not to try.

Unless you liked killing fascists.

Which I did.

"Yeah, I hate those guys," I replied. "By the way, I was here to warn you that PHANTOM has rebuilt itself, is brainwashing superheroes, and planning an attack today."

Ultragod gave me a withering glare.

"What?" I asked, guessing that Gabrielle and Sam the Eagle hadn't clued Moses in on this due to his recent bereavement. Joke was on them, the best therapy for grief was finding

C. T. Phipps

someone evil to beat the crap out of. It wasn't for everyone, but for those that it was, it was remarkably cathartic.

"You should have opened with that," Ultragod said, waving his hand over his costume and causing his business suit to disintegrate before reassembling itself into his iconic superhero costume. Which, yes, meant that I briefly saw the President naked for a second like those Nineties *Sailor Moon* cartoons always implied but never showed. Dude was jacked for a century old astronomer turned superhero turned politician. "Gary, I'm going to give you a piece of advice before I go out and punch things. The only thing you need to make a marriage work is to make sure you put your spouse first. They need to know you always have their back and you can count on them to have yours. No matter what."

"Even when there's kind of a second and third going on," I asked. "I know you know this because of that mermaid you used to date."

Moses rolled his eyes. "Always with the damned mermaid. Now get your family to safety, Gary."

With that, Moses Anders disappeared out the tent flaps to do battle with whatever horror was going on outside.

I called after him. "You forgot to say, 'This looks like a job for Ultragod!' Branding is very important even at your age!"

That was when a female Secret Service agent ran in and stared at me. "Tell me the President didn't just rush into a massive fight with PHANTOM outside?"

I put "The Warrior" by Patty Smyth on cassette into my boom box before pushing play. "Listen, you elect a warrior for President, don't be surprised when he wars."

"If he dies, I'm blaming you, Merciless," the female Secret Service agent said.

260

"Eighties Man," I corrected, clearly having gotten a bum deal on my disguise magic. "Also, if you do, I'm going to reveal you're secretly my long-lost sister."

"You wouldn't dare," the agent said, horrified.

"Try me!" I snapped, walking through the tent flaps to see what was going on. I wasn't worried.

I should have been.

What was going on outside was no mere supervillain attack but a full-on insurrection. The skies were full of PHANTOM Death Troopers, Deathbubbles, SKULL robo-troopers, and all the other stuff I'd had toys of in the Eighties. That wasn't the worst part, though, as I saw a huge number of villains who should have been dead like Count Reich, the Übermensch, White Knight—a Klansman-themed *air quotes* superhero if you didn't get it from context—and several Nineties antiheroes including guys dressed up like Shoot-Em-Up that I was instantly prepared to murder.

That wasn't the only badness, though, as the place was under assault by a group of the various hate group militias that had been under heavy prosecution by the FBI since Moses had been sworn in: SKULL, The Knights for a Pure Mankind, the Friends of Normality, and some honest to god assholes cosplaying as the Brotherhood of Infamy with hoodies instead of robes. They were not going to ruin the hoodie for America! They'd been hiding among the protestors outside the park— there were always protestors with everything Moses did—and were now pulling out laser rifles and exo-suits.

This was an all-hands-on-deck situation where the entirety of the world's heroes was needed. The Society of Superheroes, Tomorrow Society, Texas Guardians, Canada Force One, Climate Commandos, the Aeon Society, Shadow Seven, and even the Neo-Heroes—if they could ever get out of legal trouble—should be fighting the threat.

Except almost all of them had retired.

Shit.

"I SUDDENLY HATE DEMOCRACY!" Sam the Eagle shouted, punching Gabrielle and growling as he activated the rockets on the back of his jetpack.

"Yeah, Sam, I'm sorry but you're brainwashed," I replied, waving my hand and causing the rockets to explode.

"You!" Sam shouted, turning his hands to me. Embedded in the palms of his armor were energy blasters. "You get everything, and everyone overlooks how undeserving of it you are!"

Sam unleashed two blinding beams of energy that would have incinerated most human beings outright.

"Yep!" I said, conjuring intense flames that served as a counterbalance to the immense amount of energy being projected at me. It had been a long time since I'd used the Reaper's Cloak and conjuring the level of power to hold the horror at bay was taxing. Not so much that I couldn't do it, but it felt like I was getting back on the treadmill after getting out of the habit. It was a lot more taxing than I remembered it being.

"Sorry, Sam," Gabrielle responded before clocking him across the face. She then pulled some sort of grenade or mine from her belt before slamming it onto his chest. A blue-white electrical field exploded from it and caused his armor to fall over.

"What's that?" I asked, confused.

"EMP," Gabrielle replied,

I blinked. "Surely, it's EMP shielded."

"Improved EMP!" Gabrielle said, as if a writer had been caught with bad science in a movie.

I shook my head. "Right. Well, everything has gone to shit. Where's Larry?"

That was when a male Secret Service agent was hurled past us and landed with a thud on top of Sam the Eagle's disabled form. Larry stumbled over with a broken sword and some cuts on his face. Newcomer or not, Larry was apparently tough enough to take on some of the President's bodyguards.

"Some of the Secret Service are on the side of the terrorists," Larry said, spitting blood to one side. "The cops too. Most of the DC police are fighting against the attackers. They're being overwhelmed and mostly trying to get the civilians to safety."

This was literally the one time in history I was grateful the police were around. I felt unclean. Up was down and right was left. Reaching into my cloak, I pulled out the Sword of Samael in its dagger form and handed it hilt-first to Larry. "Here, take this."

Larry looked uncomfortable. "I'm not sure I want your demon—"

"Samael's an angel," I replied. "We need every hero we can get, Ultra-Paladin."

"Good name," Gabrielle said.

It was Gabrielle's blessing for him using the name that caused him to break, I'm sure. The moment Larry's fingers gripped the sword, the blackened metal glowed and became brilliant white gold. A glowing white aura appeared around Larry and turned his homemade armor into something out of an MMORPG with huge shoulder pauldrons, a sculpted chest piece, and a pair of white wings sticking out of his back.

"Woah," Larry said, staring at what he could see of his newly empowered superhero form.

"I have no idea what just happened," I replied, honestly. I made a papal blessing gesture with my fingers toward him. "However, by the power of the Society of Superheroes, I deputize you as a member."

"You're not a member of the Society of Superheroes," Gabrielle muttered.

In fact, I was the only person ever offered membership and turned it down. "I'm not Catholic either."

Gabrielle sighed and did the same gesture, even though she was Baptist. "Save as many civilians as you can. Don't kill anyone unless they're undead, robots, or Nazis."

"They're all—" Larry started to protest.

"Go!" Gabrielle shouted.

Larry didn't need any more encouragement and flew into the air where he began engaging jet pack troopers led by the Extreme's Iron Cross. I'd never liked that guy. Well, this was probably a new one since I'd killed the first one.

"We need to hold off this mob until reinforcements arrive," I said, freezing guys in the air and hurling bolts of lightning at members of the mob trying to go for the journalists. This was designed to be a massacre and to create as big a set of casualties among Ultragod's supporters gathered here as possible. It was meant to make a statement which, unfortunately, was being heard loud and clear.

"Do you happen to know any armies?" Gabrielle asked, showing just how bad our situation was. "Right now, my father is holding the line, but he's not been the same man since the Presidency. I don't think he'll be able to hold them all off before the massacre is completed or he goes down."

I looked up and saw Ultragod streaking back and forth across the sky as he battled a half-dozen of his foes simultaneously. He was also blasting at the attackers below or trying to zip down to scoop people out of the way. It was an incredible display but one that became slower and slower with each second. Only slightly, a half-second or so each time, but it was a death of a thousand cuts with the villains hitting him three or four times for each blow he delivered.

"Well, crap," I said, turning insubstantial as Ultranium Man charged through me. The glowing rock man couldn't fly up to fight his traditional foe but was attempting to make an assault on the President's daughter.

"DEATH TO THE HOUSE OF ANDERS! PRAISE OMEGA!" Ultranium Man shouted, blasting out ultranium radiation in every direction. Unfortunately, for him, Gabrielle was in a suit of radiation proof armor. Also, as stated, I was insubstantial.

Gabrielle lifted her palm blasters and blew off his head, causing his corpse to fall to the ground.

"Which was he? Robot, undead, or Nazi?" I asked, dryly.

"Merciless killed him," Gabrielle muttered. "I officially condemn his actions while noting the guy has been trying to kill me since my fourteenth birthday."

Yeah, there was a reason Gabrielle and I had always liked one another. Still, I didn't like being her scapegoat. "Eighties Man doesn't kill, though."

"Then maybe you should change," Gabrielle said, activating her rocket boots. "And get your family involved! Mimi's powers may be our only hope!"

Watching her fly off into the sky to do battle with more of the terrorists, I debated my next move. I'd made a lot of progress trying to make the world a better place, but I'd also seen how horrifically that could go wrong. My family could contribute a lot to getting this bloody riot—insurrection even— under control but it would possibly kill them too. My daughters were not adults, and I wasn't going to sacrifice them on the altar of high ideals like Abraham and Isaac. On the other hand, I couldn't exactly stop them if they did want to throw down for democracy either.

So, I took a third option.

C. T. Phipps

Pulling out my cellphone, I let my Reaper's Cloak cover me and removed my Ray-Bans. I put down the boom box and put on "Holding out for a Hero" by Bonnie Tyler. Then I addressed the Dungeon Magic Discordium, my supervillainy fan club, my cult, the kobolds, and every villain I knew that wasn't complete scum.

"Hey folks, Merciless here," I said, guessing my picture wasn't going to be movie quality and not caring. "As you may have heard from the news networks, except Omega news I'm guessing, that the capital is under attack and PHANTOM is back. Yeah, I know, crush one and ten more rise in their place. Like cockroaches. Well, this battle isn't going well and I'm going to be honest that I think the Old Guard isn't going to be able to stop them this time. I know a lot of the problems are from these guys and not all of you are happy with Ultragod's Presidency. Too many compromises and not enough real progress. Don't worry, I'm not going to get too political here. The other guys are dicks, though, and even those of you who aren't aligned with Moses Anders know what a bunch of lunatic assholes these guys are. So, I'm asking you all, the ones who can teleport or know someone who can, to get your asses down here and join the Resistance. Oh God, I'm going to have to hashtag that aren't I? Fine. Hashtag Resistance. Whether you're a redneck who likes beer and country music like my cousins or a snooty limousine liberal jerkass like myself, let us all join together and punch some Nazis! Like, comment, share, and subscribe!"

Okay, if this didn't work and I died here today then I would have easily ended my life on its single most embarrassing moment. To quote Spike from *Buffy: The Vampire Slayer*, that hadn't exactly been the Saint Crispin's Day speech. Which was a reference to *Henry V* for those of you, like me, who were uncultured heathens when they first heard that reference.

266

I was about to head back into the fray that already had dozens of casualties when there was a brilliant light that flashed beside me. It also accompanied a crack boom sort of noise, akin to a jet breaking the sound barrier. Turning to look, I was prepared for the arrival of more PHANTOM reinforcements. It seemed like the initial assault that was totally overwhelming was just the beginning and it was about to get worse. That wasn't what the light had foretold, though, Instead, it was something distinctly different.

"No way," I said, doing my best *Bill and Ted* impression.

It was everyone.

And then some.

Standing in the middle of the crowd were the adult Time Cop versions of Gizmo and Ms. Teri. They'd presumably brought everyone else with their portable time/space machine wrist bands. There was Diabloman, Lisa, Kerri with about two dozen ghosts, Selena Darkchylde AKA The Black Witch, Clarissa Montehaven AKA The Human Tank, the rest of the Shadow Seven, Jane Doe AKA Weredeer, Cassius Mass AKA Star Count, Case Gordon AKA Agent G, William England AKA The Accountant, Nancy Loomis-England AKA Final Girl, John Henry Booth AKA Shoggoth, Mercury Takahashi AKA Chaos Witch, Reyan Masteron AKA Valkyrie, Ken Masterson AKA Viking, Amanda Douglas AKA Nightwalker II, two Galahad Warrens AKA Mister Inventor (no, I didn't know what that was about), Dana Vandergast AKA Damselfly, Nikki Tesla AKA Doctor Scientist, Ketra in full dragon form, and Lisa Karkofsky wearing a pair of shades to disguise her identity despite otherwise being in her one-piece swimsuit Fireworks costume. It was virtually every person I'd helped in my career as a supervillain.

That wasn't the end of it either. Two portals opened and a horde of LARPer-dressed fantasy and sci-fi heroes poured out.

The second and third generations of heroes had joined with virtually every serious Dungeon magic user to fight the fight. There was Prism Girl, the new Splotch my daughter was dating, his cousin White Out in her sleek hooded costume, both their parents, the teenage clone of Steve Soldiers, and a lot of other teenage heroes I did not recognize. Even if the government hadn't been particularly kind to them, I also saw a bunch of Tomorrow Society students among the crowd. It was a real Gondor calls for aid and Rohan answers moment.

"Everyone here is over twenty-one, right? That is the legal age to fight crime," I muttered, not exactly happy about employing Generation I Don't Even Know What Letter We're On, but knowing it was their future too that they were fighting for.

"As long as you don't card anyone," Adult Mimi replied. "A lot of these guys and gals are actually Cindy as well as Mandy's students. They're here for them not you. Everyone else? Well, you're everyone's favorite criminal."

I nodded as I saw Adult Mimi wave her hands up and down her costume, transforming it from her Ms. Teri costume to an identical version of her mother's. Gizmo, instead, generated a suit of Ultranian alloy before a bunch of extra-limbs like Nikki Tesla's popped out of her back. Both were ready to kick ass.

So was I. "Let's get 'em!"

"All Fired Up" by Pat Benatar started playing on my boom box.

Chapter Twenty-Seven

The Battle of Soldiers Park

The next time I went to the future, roughly 2098 or so, I went to a museum and checked on how the Battle of Soldiers Park was remembered. It was no surprise that it was considered one of the seminal events of superhero history, along with the first alien invasion of the nineteenth century, Hitler's and Stalin's capture by Ultragod, Scaremonger's attempt to take over the country with a fake alien invasion, Vietnam II where superheroes were banned in normal military conflicts, and the election of Android John before Ultragod.

These events ignored a vast swath of strange and unusual stories that, for whatever reason, didn't capture the public eye. The hordes of Hell turning New Amsterdam into New Dis for a few days, the flooding of Los Angeles by Atlantis, that time the sun went out, when Count Reich brainwashed much of America into being fascist for an hour, and when France was briefly turned into a nation of highly evolved dinosaurs. There were countless amazing events that just sort of faded into the background of history or were only even remembered by those who had extra-temporal perceptions.

But I understood why the Battle of Soldiers Park stood the test of time.

Everyone did.

The exact number of casualties would never be known, though it was far less than such a seminal event probably should have had. Despite the fact they were facing terrorists and alien invaders, the young heroes did their best to disable rather than kill. The LARPers had brought the White Mage Brigade and the Cleric Commandos who'd also saved hundreds of lives that might have otherwise been lost. Apparently, the "No resurrection" rule I'd established had a 7-12-minute rule before brain death.

There were also a lot more deaths in orbit above the park with Colonel Prism, the Prismatic Commandos, the Foundation for Solar Harmony Navy, and Venusian Allied Force working against an attack by PHANTOM moon saucers working with Thran invaders. The multidimensional baddies had thrown everything and the kitchen sink at Earth but forgotten that humanity had made a few allies in its efforts to help their fellow sapients. The Galactic Community would eventually arrive but that was long after the battle had been won, the deciding factor being the arrival of the League of Superheroes from Earth-B. Their versions of Nightwalker, Ultragod, and Guinevere were joined by their children. At the end of the day, five worlds of PHANTOM soldiers ended up exhausted in the battle and never really had a chance.

None of that was visible on the ground, though.

No, that was a brutal slugfest where it was every man, woman, and Super for themselves. The tide had turned from heroes struggling to survive and protect civilians, though, to a more or less evenly matched battle. I focused on blasting my way to my family, which proved remarkably easier once Ketra scorched a pathway for me through a bunch of undead Italian troopers that Mussolini had never deployed. Apparently, some militia had bought the zombie platoon off the Dark Web.

"I'm going to have to let her stay as long as she wants," I muttered, walking across the hot melted glass that was formerly the dirt and making little "ow" noises with every step. I regretted not having a *Protection from Fire* spell anymore.

I could see my family on the other side of the burning path. Cindy—as a giant wolf—was eating a few PHANTOM troopers while Gizmo used her ray gun as well as jetpack. Probably from her *Bag of Holding*. I didn't see any sign of Mimi and that turned out to be because her powers had finally kicked in and she was floating a hundred feet in the air and pounding the crap out of Ms. Totenkopf, Count Reich's witch granddaughter.

I continued hurling fireballs, ice, and lighting to provide support wherever I could. Weirdly, no one had moved to engage me and that was just bizarre since the heavy hitters had all moved to engage fellow Supers rather than do the grunt work of the mooks on the ground by massacring guests for the speech. Someone should have come to attack me by now, even if only because I was attacking them.

It was like that scene in the original *Highlander*—you know, the good one—where Connor MacLeod is having his first battle only to have the other Scots refuse to fight him. That was because the Kurgan, the bad guy, wanted Conner for himself. Anyone remember *Highlander*? Had a TV show in the Nineties with Adrian Paul? Lots of really shitty sequels? Queen did the soundtrack? Just me? Okay.

"Hey Gary, long time no see!" A man dressed in black and white spandex called, waving over to me from nearby. He was carrying a psychic boomerang in his hand and was covered in blood that wasn't his own.

"Mother pus bucket," I muttered, staring at the sight.

It was Psychoslinger.

Psychoslinger was someone I hadn't seen in years, and I meant real years, not whatever had happened to the timeline due to all the shenanigans from President Omega and Merciful. He was a serial killer, mass murderer, and war criminal who was not so much pure evil as incapable of seeing what he did was wrong. Now, this is going to surprise you, but despite the fact I'd faced Zul-Barbas and Entropicus, Psychoslinger was one of two supervillains who scared the shit out of me. The other was Sheriff Injustice for the record. Seriously, I hated that guy. But why did I fear Psychoslinger above so many others? A brief digression to explain.

Upon becoming a supervillain, I'd gradually learned that we generally came in three different forms. The first were the criminals of means and these were the guys, put simply, doing it for the money. They may like the fame and connections that come with wearing a costume of a purple hippo but weren't motivated by anything larger than their next paycheck. It's why so many bank robberies occur as it's the easiest way to get 20K in beer money. That didn't necessarily mean that these supervillains weren't hardened killers, but it didn't mean they were either. Murder and mayhem were a means to an end.

The second group of supervillains were the ideologues. People like Helios the Sun King, General Venom, or Sovi-Ape. These were the guys who were insufferably evil because it was all for a cause that somehow would lead to a utopia for all mankind once the bodies were finished dropping. Tom Terror might not care about racial supremacy or peace through power, but he certainly was willing to take advantage of all the goons under him who did. Technically, I qualified as one of these dipshits since I was a supervillain less for money and more about it as a lifestyle choice.

The third guys were like Psychoslinger, Mr. Chaos, Shoot-Em-Up, and the Radioactive Spine-Eater Man. They killed people because they liked it. These guys were not so uncommon that a percentage of Supers weren't bound to be them. Except, unfortunately, it seemed we had more than our fair share. Something about being a supervillain appealed to these jackasses and they were always first to volunteer for whatever deranged experiment or occult ritual that could grant them powers. Usually, it just gave them cancer, but there was always a replacement psycho for when it did work. Psychoslinger was their apotheosis. What I might become if I just stopped caring. You couldn't predict them, you couldn't control them, and they wouldn't stop until they were put down. Which I tried and failed to do with Psychoslinger.

"Wassup!" Psychoslinger said, jogging down my way. "Gimme five!"

I reluctantly did so. There was also the fact that Psychoslinger either thought we were best friends or was trying to kill me. That was another reason he freaked me out.

Psychoslinger pointed finger guns at me. "I know we didn't part on the best of terms, but I've been regenerating my psychic energy in space and that gave me a whole new perspective. I've decided to get political. Have you heard the Gospel of R?"

"Oh, Merciful Moses," I muttered.

"R is a secret agent working for the Department of Transportation who posted the secrets of the Illuminati, the real one, not the one Guinevere shut down on 10chan and—" Psychoslinger started to say.

I cleared my throat. "Okay, never in my wildest dreams did I think I would say this, but this is a little too political even for me. Superheroes should just be fun entertainment. Can we just get back to the punching of Nazis?"

"Yes, the real Nazis! Ultragod and his supporters!" Psychoslinger said, punching the air.

I stared at him. "Is this what other people experience when talking to me? Something so ridiculous your brain shuts down and leaves you open to attack? Because if it is, then I owe an apology to everyone I've ever fought because that sort of attack needs to be banned by the Geneva Convention."

"We're striking back, today! Taking back our country, even though I'm Canadian," Psychoslinger said. "For centuries, dark wizards and black magicians have been hated by the masses for the color of our magic!"

"You're a psychic manifestation not a wizard," I pointed out. Actually, he was a psychopath psychic manifestation, but I doubt he'd get the joke.

"Not true!" Psychoslinger said. "I took a correspondence course last week in Dungeon magic so I could easily escape all imprisonment to kill people! I used it to kill people for fun but now I do it for reasons!"

Okay, maybe releasing Dungeon magic in the world with no regulation wasn't the brightest of all ideas. "Psychoslinger—"

"Ted, please," Psychoslinger said. "Ted Bundy."

I stared at him. "Really?"

"Really," Psychoslinger said. "My parents were big *Married with Children* fans."

My brain short circuited again. "That doesn't make any sense—"

"Think fast!" Psychoslinger said, throwing a pair of psychic knives into me.

I got a full dose of Psychoslinger's powers in that moment, and they lit every pain center in my body on fire, all at once. It was a particularly horrifying way to die and were it not for the fact I'd suffered unimaginable agony several times in my life already, I probably would have immediately joined the ranks of the many killed by Ted. Who wasn't the actual Ted Bundy, I should clarify. The actual Ted Bundy had died in the moon riot alongside Charles Manson and Doctor Satano.

Despite surviving the psychic knives, I felt my heart start beating at a horrifying pace. A heart attack had started this whole ordeal and it was quite possible that one would end it. It was an undignified way for a superhero or villain to die, but one had claimed the original Nightwalker. Still, Jacob had put me through enough conditioning that I forced myself through the pain.

"Why, Psychoslinger?"

"Why? Why?" Psychoslinger laughed. "Oh, you sound like a victim, Merciless! The why is—"

"Psyche," I muttered, conjuring lightning from my fingertips and blasting him full force.

Psychoslinger howled as he was sent flying backward, twirling in the air before landing with a thud. Unfortunately, he was a construct of pure energy and had no organs or neurology to disrupt. He was someone who had to be destroyed utterly to deal with. Even then, he'd showed a remarkable ability to come back from the dead. He was the kind of person who the rules about preventing resurrection were meant to end for good.

"Nice one!" Psychoslinger said, giving me a thumbs up as he got off the ground. "It's why the Boss wanted to keep you for himself! However, I'm not very good at following orders! BOOMERANG ASSAULT MODE!"

Psychoslinger launched a dozen psychic boomerangs at me that I struggled to blast out of the air with my fire powers. I strained to control my breathing and slow down my heart, but it took everything in my power to keep up with Psychoslinger's attacks. It didn't help that I was in the middle of a blasted-out fire pit and the air was full of smoke. I tried to turn insubstantial, but not trusting myself, I moved to the side and felt one of his psychic boomerangs cut my shoulder. He was using telekinesis instead of psychic assault for these and the wound bled despite my intangibility. Because the attack was mental, I was vulnerable to it. The same way intangibility didn't protect against light beams, gas, or extra-dimensional blasts.

"Two points!" Psychoslinger said, holding out his hand to catch the boomerang.

Realizing what that signified, I made like Indiana Jones in *The Last Crusade* and kneeled! The boomerang that had cut my shoulder came back and I blasted the side of it as it returned to Psychoslinger's hand. That knocked it off course and it buried itself in Psychoslinger's chest.

Psychoslinger looked down at the psychic boomerang buried there. He didn't bleed but looked a bit wobbly. "Huh, I didn't see that coming."

I was about to blast him again with lightning, only for a shadow to appear around Psychoslinger like he was a coyote about to be hit by an anvil. Instead, a two-ton black metal figure shaped like a particularly tall and wide Medieval knight landed on top of him. It looked like a Dark Souls boss and topped in about twelve feet tall.

The metal figure had a long cape made from strips of plastic complete with a collar that stretched up the full side of his helmet. Both his hands were covered in glowing yellow energy with black dots bouncing around inside. If there was ever a guy who looked like he'd been designed by the Nineties, it was the Extreme!'s Major Disaster and Ninjess. However, this guy was their runner up.

"Medic," Psychoslinger said, crushed underneath its feet.

The figure blasted him with his energy fists and caused Psychoslinger to disintegrate back into his component particles.

"Idiot," the metal figure spoke, sounding vaguely familiar but not so much I recognized him on sight. It wasn't helped by the fact he had the full-on Darth Vader reverb going on and his suit was clearly equipped with a set of speakers. While grateful he'd killed Psychoslinger, I was guessing this newcomer wasn't on the side of angels or even the slightly less bad devils.

"And you are?" I asked.

"Oh no, it's Armageddon!" a helpful unnamed bystander proclaimed, pointing at the giant robot.

"Thanks," I said, offhandedly, doubting the guy could hear me through the horrifying battle going on.

I *had* heard of Armageddon before. He was a Tomorrow Society and occasionally Society of Superheroes bad guy who believed in the whole "survival of the fittest" nonsense. He believed war between regular humans and Supers was inevitable, so he was always there pushing one side or the other into it. He was also immortal and claimed to be ninety different leaders of history despite all those guys having extremely well-documented histories. Armageddon was, indeed, old as dirt but somehow, I think we would have noticed a twelve-foot-tall robot at Caesar's assassination or Waterloo if you get what I mean.

"I have walked through the annals of history, leaving millions dead at my hands and building thrones of skulls where I rested waiting for this day," Armageddon said, adopting a faux posh accent while balling his fists. "I have visited distant galaxies and crossed oceans of time preparing for our encounter! The Blood Gods of Old and Chaos Lords have blessed me while the technology of long dead species empowers my suit! Look upon me, Merciless, and know the face of your tormentor!"

I stared at him. "Dude, I have no idea what you're talking about. Also, why are you talking like the back of a *Warhammer 40K* miniatures box? I mean, I'm a *Dungeons & Dragons* guy. I'm not into grimdark. I don't even like *Ravenloft*."

Armageddon raised his shoulders and shook with fury before slumping them down. "Goddammit, Gary, you're ruining this."

"Sorry!" I said, having taken the time to calm my heart a bit. "It's been a really trying couple of relative months. Who are you?"

"You would not recognize my face," Armageddon said. "It has changed since we last fought."

The robot tapped the side of his helmet and opened it to reveal a transparent cannister containing a pair of eyes and a brain swirling with more of the strange energy coming from his fists.

I stared at him. "You're right, I don't recognize you."

Armageddon's eyes in the brain case lowered down to look at me. "I.AM.OMEGA."

Chapter Twenty-Eight

The End of an Age

Okay, you guys may not remember *Highlander* but most of you probably remember *Star Trek*. So, I'm going to take a brief digression to talk about Khan Noonien Singh. Yes, the villain from *Star Trek II: The Wrath of Khan*. Now, well before he was whitewashed to be played by Benedict Cumberbatch, it was damned *weird* for him to be the villain of that movie.

Seriously, he wasn't Kirk's archenemy. He was just one of the many villains of the week left behind at the end of the episode. But, you see, that was the point. For the original movie-going audience, Captain Kirk was dealing with a guy he hadn't thought about in decades. I thought about Omega on occasion, but I'd put him behind me. Mostly. He was a relic of another time.

Sort of like PHANTOM.

Which, now that I thought about it, was *probably* related.

The same with the Nanoplague.

Which, in fact, had been explicitly said to have been created by President Omega.

Crap. I was an idiot.

"Where the hell have you been?" I asked, confused but also aware that I had his attention.

I could tell the question was causing Omega considerable distress and it seemed he wanted to incinerate me right then and there, but something was holding him back. "When you damaged my time machine, I was sent spiraling back sixty-five million years in the past to the time when the Ultranians destroyed the dinosaurs to make way for humanity."

"Took them long enough," I said. "Humans are like only a million years old and that's stretching the definition of hominid. Did they get caught up in bureaucracy?"

"Silence!" Omega shouted. "You have no idea the eternal loneliness, misery, and despair. Hatred and sorrow gave birth to insanity until I grew so mad that I went sane again. Over and over again as the ages passed. Finally, I could see the beginning echoes of mankind and struggled not to exterminate them solely so I could catch my timeline up to you before stripping—"

"Did you fuck animals?" I asked, interrupting the speech he'd clearly rehearsed.

"What?" Omega asked.

"I mean sixty-five million years is a long time. I mean, no one is going to blame you if you had to seek companionship in whatever form you needed to—" I said, knowing absolutely that everyone would blame him and hoping to get him to admit it.

"I did not fuck animals!" Omega shouted.

"Sure, sure," I said, totally believing he did. "I believe you were one-handing it the entire time."

"Even my immortal shadow power-infused body began to collapse, and I slowly warped into a decaying living brain propelled by the pure hatred in my consciousness!" Omega said, ignoring my masturbation joke. "Armed with technology I found in the frozen reaches of the Arctic."

"Could we move this along?" I asked, knowing that I was massively outgunned here.

I'd been able to take President Omega with Diabloman's help, but Charles hadn't been taking me nearly as seriously as he was now. Also, Armageddon was a whole different league with him having taken on whole armies in the past. The Tomorrow Society had like a hundred members, and they'd barely won in some of the battles they'd had, often winning only because of other time travelers or cosmic forces. He was a guy who could throw down with Ultragod and the Society of Superheroes' heavy hitters by himself.

Omega's stare was full of madness and hatred. Well, I think. I mean, it was hard to tell from just a pair of bloodshot eyeballs floating in radioactive fluid. "The only reason you are still alive, Merciless, is because I wanted to let you know that I was the architect of all your pain. That your miserable tormented life was my master work."

I stared at him. "My life is actually pretty sweet, actually."

"What?"

"I mean, seriously, being Merciless is awesome," I said, shrugging. "Eighties Man is pretty sweet as a gig, too, even if I'm guessing it's only a stunt for my writers in Jane's world. You know villain-to-hero, hero-to-villain. It happens to all of us. I mean it never takes, but I love my life. It's like being Steven Tyler where the worst thing I must worry about is most of the world's male population and some of the female lusting after my daughter. Which, honestly, I still have a few years left on, and those that are already making websites are on my murder-list. Speaking of which, can you kill the Backwoodsman? I don't think he did the leak but I'm pretty sure as a century-old Canadian, his cellphone must be easy to hack. His password is probably 1-2-3-4 like mine."

"You have no idea what horrors I have unleashed on you over the years," Omega said, as if the irony of the situation wasn't perversely funny.

"Did you?" I asked. "Shoot-Em-Up killed my brother. A dragon killed Mandy. *I* was the one who fucked up and turned her into a vampire. Spellbinder is the one who screwed with me in Mandy's body and that was Merciful's doing. I mean, did you give my father cancer? Wait, don't answer that because I know that was because he had a bum ticker as well as smoked three packs a day."

I was deliberately baiting him at this point as every second that Armageddon wasn't engaged in battle against the other heroes was another second for the tide to be turned. It was also a lot easier for me to annoy the piss out of someone than engage them in epic hand-to-hand combat. I wasn't scared, like I said, it was only Psychoslinger and Sheriff Injustice who ever instilled that feeling into me.

Maybe Tom Terror once.

I don't know why, but I think that's because death doesn't hold any particular fear for me. Never has. Maybe it's the way I'm wired or perhaps it was simply because seeing my brother gunned down the way he was instilled a subconscious wish to join him—okay, enough Freud. No, what I feared instead was failure and if I didn't keep this guy occupied then I was pretty sure he could single handedly turn the tide I'd just turned back.

"I am the architect of all your woes," Omega said, whispering. Which was weird because he was on speakers. It was actually ASMR-like and kind of relaxing, or would be if it wasn't being delivered by a giant fascist robot from the future. "Since before the beginning of your life until now. Every step you took to this moment was by my design."

This reminded me of the only crappy Daniel Craig movie. And no, I don't mean *Quantum of Solace*—Olga Kurylenko and

Gemma Arterton forgive much. No, I mean *Spectre* where Blofeld is suddenly Bond's brother and claiming to have orchestrated all of the previous movies despite none of that making any goddamn sense.

"Uh no, you didn't," I said, knowing it was going to set him off. "I can also prove it because all of this would have had to have happened before you got sent back in time in the first place. I mean, you could argue it's a predestination paradox but those are stupid. I mean, don't get me wrong, causing World War Two to continue and locking down Falconcrest City are bad things. I also note this is awful with the Nanoplague and riot here, but you're really not even approaching archnemesis status. Sorry, you're kind of lame."

A long moment passed between us. Omega's rage reached a breaking point, and I knew I'd driven him insane again. "I will end you, Karkofsky. Then I will kill your daughters, girlfriends, ex-wife, mother, sister, niece, and the bitch you took to the prom."

"Nina Pavarti?" I asked, confused as to why she was on the list. "I think she's a dentist now."

"Ahhhh!" Omega screamed at the top of his nonexistent lungs before raising his glowing gauntlets in the air to smash me.

Omega didn't get to hit me because he was immediately punched at flying speed by both the Mimis present. One was dressed in full Ultragoddess regalia at the height of her powers while the second was my daughter showing just how much she'd been holding back.

That might have been enough, but dogpiling isn't limited to villains. The Mimis knocked Omega right into Gabrielle, who was carrying a Horus the Eagle's giant god mace. The mace crackled as it smashed Omega backward into Ultragod himself, who delivered a brutal series of Ultra-Force enhanced punches before tossing him back to my daughters. What followed was a pinball game of the Ultra-Family that was only occasionally interrupted by Omega blasting out with his suit's weird dot-filled energy beams.

None of which seemed to do anything to the four Ultranians beating the living snot out of him. If the brain in a jar had nostrils, which he didn't. What did robots have that would make a good metaphor? Hydraulic fluid? Brain juice? Eh, whatever it was, it sure as hell wasn't good him for him to be leaking it.

"Impossible! I have built this suit to be powered by ultranium radioactive ore!" Omega shouted, sounding more cliche and stereotypical as a villain than he'd ever sounded when he was the President of the United States. Then again, according to him, he was probably the origin of every single supervillain cliche there was. He probably had run out of new material during the last Ice Age.

Leia—the younger version—jetpacked over to my side as I started charging a mega-blast of my powers. "Should I tell him that I created a formula that made the Anders family immune to ultranium?"

"No dear," I said, patting my little super-scientist daughter on the back. "That might remind him that he almost killed Ultragod with his stupid disease."

I grimaced.

"Dad, don't say things like that aloud," Leia said, glaring at me. "That's like me mentioning the ultranium protection has an upper limit."

Leia covered her mouth in horror.

I looked both ways as if looking for some narrative cosmic force of destiny to screw with our lives. "You didn't do it, nobody saw you do it, they can't prove anything."

Leia nodded vigorously, taking entirely seriously the idea that some *deus ex machina* might make this a horrifying tragedy. Instead, she just jumped up and down for her sister. "Uh, go team!"

Omega was taking a beating worse than a first-year Jewish transfer student at Falconcrest City High School (yes, I'm referring to myself). His indestructible armor was proving pretty destructible, and a black smoky miasma was pouring out of several holes in his body work.

In my hands, a glowing ball of raw magical force was gathering as I poured all of my power to create fire, lightning, and ice into it. I hadn't learned much from Jacob during my time training in magic, but I'd learned at least a few raw essentials of Magic 101. Like the form it took was less important than the force behind it. The power in my hands was now stronger than anything I'd hurled at Magog, Entropicus, or Beelzebub.

But I kept gathering more.

"Surrender, Omega!" Moses said, hovering in the air. "Your followers are already scattering to the wind and the American people have shown that they want no more of your hate-filled nonsense. A new dawn rises on the world and—"

"Oh, do shut up!" Omega said, standing up with one of his arms falling off. "Do you think I care about what some pathetic comic book tulpa says? A soulless construct conjured from the depraved imagination of a self-styled villain who could have changed the world to whatever his darkest desires were but instead made this mediocre abomination of a world? You are nothing more than an ex-bank teller's imaginary friend!"

Omega leapt twenty feet at me, fist raised and aimed at both Leia and me.

I pulled all the energy I'd been channeling into a fist then pushed all of my meager levitation ability into my feet. Then jumped. "SHORYUKEN!"

I was about fifty percent sure this was going to kill me. Jacob had tried to beat out all of my suicidal flashy moves and force me to learn some practical fighting techniques. Well, this was about as impractical as it got, and I was jumping right into the mouth of the beast. But it would get my daughter out of danger, and really wasn't that the important thing?

So, imagine my surprise when all that magical energy in my punch connected with Omega's suit and proceeded to knock him out of the sky. Omega's armor detonated in a dozen directions, the pieces that would have struck me being disintegrated by an aura of energy gathered around me like I'd gone Super Saiyan. Both his eyes exploded in his brain case as Omega's brain was thrown across the ground, rolling into a tuft of grass below.

I levitated back down beside Leia. "Fatality."

"He's still alive, Dad," Leia said.

"He is?" I asked, doing a double take between her and the brain on the ground.

"Yes," Leia said, sounding scared. Which, given she'd discovered time travel and made a gateway to the Annihilation Zone by the time she was thirteen, was not a good sign.

"Uck it!" Omega said via telepathic signal, not quite able to swear as his brain had been pretty battered. "Uck all of ya! I am sick of how this universe coddles you all! Venerates the pedestrian morality of a hypocritical Western hegemony. If I can't have this nation, I will burn it to the ground!"

Most of the Ultra-Family gathered around the brain but started backing away as the glowing energy from his gauntlets appeared around Omega. It lifted him up off the ground before starting to expand around him as a shield. Lightning crackled inside the bubble and those damn dots multiplied a dozen times over.

"Dad, he's going to release all of his accumulated time energy!" Leia said, looking horrified.

"English!" I said to my daughter.

"He's going to blow up Earth!" Leia said in laymen's terms.

"Not good!" I said, struggling to think of another cunning plan to save us all. Maybe if I got Larry here to stab it with the Sword of Samael, or we could teleport it into a black hole. The Crown of the Gods was also an option.

Then Moses Anders took the decision away from me.

From all.

Moses encased President Omega's brain in a glowing ball of Ultra-Force that he seemed to struggle to contain against the ever-widening power inside. He took a moment to look at us all then spoke words that would stick with me for the rest of my semi-immortal life. "Thank you, my children. It was an honor to be part of your family. Even for a little while."

"Dad!" Gabrielle shouted, realizing what he was going to do.

Ultragod was gone, though. He had pushed his powers to the limit and launched himself skyward. It was only a few seconds later that we saw the shockwave. He'd managed to get as far as Jupiter before the detonation. The explosion, indeed, would have blown up the Earth, and then some. Instead, it had just killed the President.

Ultragod.

My friend.

Gabrielle fell to her knees.

Mimi—both—went to her side.

So did I.

Leia held my hand as we just stood there, the last minutes of the battle around us passing without comment.

The battle was won.

At the mere cost of everything.

And the question I asked at the end of it wasn't whether to use the Crown of the Gods to fix everything.

But why I didn't?

Chapter Twenty-Nine
Walking the Graveyard

I ended up walking in the Steven Soldiers Memorial Park several days after the disaster. It was going to be remembered as the place for the assassination of two United States Presidents, though I wasn't sure if one counted since I'd already killed him before. It was already a place for pilgrimage for Ultragod fans with thousands of flowers, pictures, and candles spread about the grounds. There was a day of national mourning that had turned into a week and would probably last until a month had passed. The rest of the world was also taking its time sharing in our grief. There was even talk of converting the park into a graveyard for superheroes.

Moses and Steven would have approved.

It was here that I decided to meet with Death and found one of the spots that was less inhabited than others before lifting the Crown of the Gods above my head and saying, "Hey, Death, could we have a moment to speak? I know you said we weren't going to talk again but I figure we could table that for now."

Much to my amusement, the Primal appeared beside me wearing leather pants and a Sisters of Mercy shirt with a silver star around her neck. She looked like Mandy once more and I was filled with regret. Regret that I hadn't been a better husband to her, that I hadn't tried harder to make it work, and that I had ended up giving her the space she'd asked for, but which hadn't been crossed. Whether being an enormous horndog was a feature or flaw was still up for debate.

"Here, you should take this," I said, handing over the crown.

"Sure," Death said, taking it. "You sure you don't want it?"

"It's no fun playing on god mode," I replied, hiding that I just didn't feel worthy of it. "I'm still half tempted to start fixing things again and that would just make things so much worse."

"Probably. How are things?" Death asked, adopting the casual tone you would not expect from the embodiment of entropy.

"Don't you know?" I asked, raising an eyebrow.

"I only see the last page," Death said. "Never the earlier chapters."

I shrugged. "Everyone rallied together after the death of Ultragod and has agreed that we should live up to his legacy by cooperating as well as continuing his good works."

"Really?" Death asked, knowing I was feeding her a line of bullshit.

"Hell no," I said, disgusted. "The government passed every single stupid law President Omega did in the old world and appointed the Extreme! as federal marshals. The Superhuman Equality Act is not only dead in the water, but they've also renamed the old Superhuman Control Act as the Ultragod Memorial Act. The Vice President—sorry new President— has vetoed a lot of it but the Superhuman Equality Act is finished. People took the exact wrong lesson from the attack. Jane says we've exited the Justice League portion of our history and gone on to the Civil War as well as Identity Crisis period."

"Which means what, exactly?" Death asked. Clearly, she wasn't a big comic book fan.

"I'm still catching up via trades," I said, shrugging. "However, it seems that the Age of Superheroes ended with a bang not a whimper. Things will never be the same without Ultragod."

It wasn't quite as bad as it sounded. President Omega had started World War 3 because he hadn't been able to get an actual organized legal genocide started. There was a lot more pushback this time around as well. The war was now less about punching Nazis and more about interpreting the law as well as winning elections. I wasn't nearly as useful in that fight.

"Yes," Death said. "It is now the Twilight of the Age of Superheroes. Not quite its end."

"Moses said I brought about the end of the Wild West," I muttered.

"The West never went away, Gary," Death said. "But it did become less wild. The same will be the case for superheroes, but death is also a word for change. The time of untouchable gods dictating to mortal governments will pass to demigods struggling against them. Bringing back Ultragod helped you stave off the change for a time but not forever. The time it was is gone and you'll have to deal with the broken pieces being scattered about the way they are."

I could already see how things would be going for the next few decades. Superheroes would now have bad reputations with the public yet still rally to the occasion. The government would be extra harsh on Supers, and this would inspire a new wave of supervillains to replace the old ones. Lines of morality would get grayer and darker. Cops and the military would start carrying more super-tech with things like the Exterminator robots being painted in pretty colors to make them less threatening. The moon base would be less and less relevant for street level heroics.

"Maybe there's another universe I could go to. Like, a Merciless Cinematic Universe where the archetypes still live on," I muttered, reaching outward. "Could I borrow back the Crown of the Gods to make it?"

"No, Gary," Death said.

"Fine," I muttered. "Even though I had Chris Pine, Deborah Ann Woll, Tessa Thompson, and Olivia Munn set up to play the big four in my biopic."

"Really, Chris Pine?" Death asked.

"Chris Pratt cost too much and Ryan Reynolds said I was ripping him off," I muttered. "You know what's funny?"

"Politicians choking and dying?" Death asked. "Because I can arrange that."

"Not today," I replied, noting that Death and I shared a sense of humor. "No, the fact that most of the retired superheroes have remained retired. It's their children and grandchildren plus a bunch of people inspired by their deeds that have stepped up. The Leias, Larrys, Mimis, and Lisas of the world rather than the Guineveres or Mercilesses."

"You're not the last of the old generation," Death said. "You're the first of the new."

"About a generation or two late for that," I replied, feeling old for the first time in my life. Okay, maybe fifteenth. "But no, I'm not feeling particularly retirement happy yet."

"Nor will you," Death said. "That's a benefit of godhood. You'll be my Chosen as long as you wish. It has always been your destiny to usher in great change. It was your fate to stagnate this world."

Fate and Destiny seemed to always be at odds in my life. Then again, that was life in general. Will you be your best self or your worst?

"And which did I achieve?" I asked.

"We'll see," Death replied, enigmatically. "But yes, it is the natural order of things for children to replace their parents. For stories to end. For new ones to be told. Speaking of which, how is Mimi adjusting to being Ultragoddess?"

"Badly. She whines about it every five seconds," I said, pausing. "So, typical teenager."

"I'm surprised that Gabrielle hasn't gotten her to Ultraworld," Death said. "Either that or trained her, herself."

I shrugged. "The only person in the world more stubborn than Gabrielle is her daughter. She's getting training for use of her powers but mostly from Behemoth and Viking. The former knows what it's like to be considered a hero and a villain while the latter doesn't respect the laws of mortal men. Also, Ken is sweet on Mimi despite her heart belonging to New Splotch."

"I also heard she's running into some legal trouble," Death said, striking a surprisingly conversational tone.

I nodded. "She has no interest in joining the Society of Superheroes—I can't imagine why—or bowing down to the United States' new officially sanctioned super teams. I don't think she's as dedicated as Moses or even Gabrielle to full-time superheroing either. Still, Gizmo is helping her properly plan her rescue work and she's stopped a few earthquakes as well as plugged a volcano. Really, the biggest fallout was from the media."

"Yes," Death said. "I read the fact the media is stunned you really were with Gabrielle, let alone fathered a child with her. That must be an embarrassment for the Ultragod Family PR Firm."

It had come out during Gabrielle's mourning period for her father and that was probably the best time it could have, all things considered. Even Omega News had given her a couple of days before starting the usual misogynist bullshit about her betraying her younger fans by hooking up with a—GASP—criminal.

"One reactionary talking head speculated on-air that I must have mind-controlled Gabrielle into it," I said, pausing. "He's lucky that Mimi got to him first. She left him in the middle of the Amazon. They found him three days later drinking his own urine. It was a real 'that's my girl' moment for me."

Death grinned. "She'll grow into the role. Or she won't. Mimi and Leia never would have been able to achieve their destinies, though, if not for the fact that there was no longer anyone holding a safety net under them. Yourself included."

"Which is why the sequel trilogy sucked. They needed Luke, Han, and Leia to be dead for a few centuries," I muttered. "That was what this was all about, wasn't it? To undo all of the good I tried to do and put the world back on the road to whatever oblivion it was set for."

Death shook her head. "Not oblivion. Change. Ultragod was never meant to come back, nor were the others. But not all of the people you restored to life have been returned to the grave. There's a bit of wiggle room I'm prepared to allow. Consider it a gift."

"A gift?" I asked, staring at her. "Are you insane—"

I cut myself off before I shouted obscenities at the being second only to God. Even *I* was not that stupid.

Death just gave a half-smile. "A little girl who died in Falconcrest City's zombie uprising will grow up to cure blood fever. A man saved by Ultragod after his death from suicide after he was sworn in as President will eventually raise the woman who signs a peace treaty with the Galactic Community, inducting Earth into its ranks. The Tsavong would have gone extinct in three generations before but will now limp along and become slightly less awful people as they search for a new homeworld. Most of the people you saved will simply live out their normal lives, like motes of dust, but infinitely important to themselves."

I understood then what Death was getting at. At least, I thought, I did. "It was never about banning resurrection, was it?"

"I get everyone eventually, Gary," Death said, sympathetically. "A few more years, even generations, did not bother me. But clinging to life forever does not help, it only hurts. You, I know, struggle with that."

"Who doesn't?" I asked, softly.

Death acknowledged that fact. "I hate being hated, Gary. It is the closest thing I have to a human emotion. I would love to be welcomed as an old friend or lover. However, almost everyone I know curses and hates me when we speak. Even you, the person dearest to my heart."

"Why me?" I asked a stupid question.

"Love makes us do the wacky," Death said, giving no explanation and all the explanation I needed at once. "The Balance has been restored in your universe for the time being. That balance remains fragile and will continually have beings seek to disrupt it: the Great Beasts, the Brotherhood of Infamy, Dracula once he crawls out of Hell, and Other Gary that will insist that he is the good guy until you end him."

"Sounds like the same old shit," I muttered, imagining the fact that I'd be up against these guys forever. "It never is going to end, will it?"

"The story ends where you stop reading," Death replied. "The cast of characters change, though, and consequences matter. You just must be willing to let go. In fact, if you want to give up the mantle of my Chosen now, I make the offer. I will find another one to carry the burden, difficult as that may be. Perhaps your daughters, though Fate and Destiny have their eyes on them, or complete strangers."

Death mentioned my children to make sure I knew exactly how much of a choice I really had. "I'm good. What do you need, oh mighty Primal Boss Lady?"

Death closed her eyes and the Crown of the Gods transformed in her hands. It became two separate books, one that I was familiar with and the other I wasn't. The first book was the dull, leathery, human-skin bound *Book of Midnight* with its tongue and puppy-like mannerisms. The other was an ivory bound volume that I was pretty sure was made of bone as well as decorated with teeth. That book was *The Book of Dawn*. It started barking as well, the two of them flapping their pages up and down before she tossed them on the ground, dancing around me like hyperactive dogs waiting to be fed.

"Guard these, Gary," Death replied. "You are Earth's Supreme Archmage and the God of Sex, Drugs, and Gaming. The Master of the Universe. The Pink Wizard. The Fool on the Tarot cards of the Primals. Lord of Kobolds, Outcasts, and Villains who are not Evil. You have proclaimed it to the multiverse, so it is so."

"I'm a terrible wizard and don't want to be a god," I replied, honestly. "Not even Jacob could shape me up."

Death's smile remained enigmatic, but I got the impression she thought Jacob had accomplished exactly what he had set out to do. "Remain an idiot hero, Gary. Repeatedly, those who know what they're doing end up becoming consumed by their power and ambition. They become Entropicus, Omega, and, yes, Merciful."

"And if I end up dying because I have no idea what I'm doing?" I asked.

Death shrugged. "I will be waiting there for you at the end. Your universe is probably screwed, though. The safety rails are off and everything that happens now is in the hands of its peoples. Congratulations, Gary, you have given them freedom of choice."

I made a wavey gesture with my fingers. "Wee."

"Such enthusiasm," Death said, chuckling. "You screwed up, Gary. Several times. You left Zul-Barbas some trace of his essence in the universe when you read from the *Book of Midnight* to resurrect your wife. You tried to use the Primal Orbs to subvert your own master's desire that death be permanent. You rebooted reality and interfered with countless timelines for fun."

"I'm getting called out for killing a hundred Hitlers?" I asked.

"No, fuck that guy," Death said, waving her hand dismissively. "No matter what reality you kill him in, reality is improved by killing him."

"Really? Because there was the one where he stayed as a painter in Paris and I almost feel bad for drowning him in his toilet," I replied. "Almost."

"His art was atrocious," Death said. "Seriously, science fiction is completely wrong about going back in time to take him out. It always works out. Eventually."

"Well, if I'm going to be Earth's Supreme Archmage, can we at least talk about changing my name?" I asked. "I mean my wizarding title, at least? I get all my correspondence from the Council of Archmages by raven and it always has the same damn title. Worse, I swear the birds are laughing at me."

"That's just how ravens act. You don't like being the Pink Wizard?" Death asked.

"No!" I snapped.

"Pink used to be considered a very masculine color," Death said, "Baby blue was once considered feminine."

"Well, it's not now," I said, dryly.

"Would you prefer to be known as Gary the Blood Red? Because that's the same color," Death said, pausing. "Depending on the oxygenation levels."

"Yes!" I replied, crossing my arms.

"Sorry, no," Death said. "As to why? Because it amuses me. Like the *Final Destination* movies or the Black Death."

I looked down at the two books of magic beneath me. They looked hungry. "Not to be ungrateful but I'm pretty sure there're a lot of people more qualified than me to be Supreme Archmage. Starting with all the other Archmages and working the way to the guy who does card tricks outside the bank. Like, I'm ninety-nine percent sure that Amanda Douglas would be pissed as Hell about this and mutter things about how it's a man's magical world over this."

"Amanda the Gray is currently on probation," Death said. "Cosmically speaking."

"She gets Gandalf's title?" I asked, annoyed. "Does everyone get a cool color except for me? Leia was Gizmo the Neon last time I checked. Also, another person I'd charge with being the Supreme Archmage over me."

Actually, no, speaking as her father, we'd all be her slaves within a week.

Death raised an eyebrow. "Are you advocating for her or complaining about her?"

"Both!" I said. "Why is Amanda on probation? Is that even a thing among wizards? I thought they were pretty much above good and evil."

Death shrugged. "It is when killing a wizard for their crimes isn't possible or good for the universe as a whole. In Amanda's case, she briefly went insane after finding out her children were illusions created by the Great Beasts. Also, her husband, Mr. Inventor II, was an android created by the original Mr. Inventor when he found out he was dying of cancer but was turned into an indestructible stunt driver. Oh, and Helios the Sun King was her real father, and she had a long-lost brother in Lightbeam. From there she destroyed Super Castle in Atlas City, killed a bunch of D-Listers, and then made a utopian paradise for all Supers but erased that as well as eighty percent of the Super population. Thankfully, it turned out it was all manipulation by the Brotherhood of Infamy's Inner Circle and the evil acts were undone by the living spirit of the Sphinx. A planet got destroyed in the process, so the Galactic Community may be putting her on trial soon."

I stared at her. "When the fuck did this all happen?"

"While you were off training with Jacob," Death replied. "A lot of people were unhappy with her at the battle."

"That was like two days!" I said, confused as hell.

"What, Gary, you thought you were the center of the universe?" Death asked.

"Yes!" I snapped.

"Honestly, it is pretty sexist," Death said. "You destroyed the Earth twice as Merciful, and no one cares about that."

"That's an alternate me, it doesn't count," I said, making a mental note to check up on Amanda after this. Superheroes sometimes went crazy. It was just a thing you accepted and went on with. Blame it on the massive undiagnosed PTSD most of us were suffering. — Not that I admit to being a superhero, no sir. Still in denial after all my back-and-forthing. — Either way, it was that or a supervillain was behind it somehow. Or both. Hell, Splotch used to eat people while he had his alien parasite.

"You have done me a great service, Gary," Death said, sighing. "You have given up ultimate power multiple times and done the far better thing of failing then getting up to make amends. So, I will grant you a boon. Not the kind you got for winning the Eternity Tournament, but a boon nonetheless."

"Could you show me where Mandy is?" I asked, not hesitating.

"Of course," Death muttered, annoyed. "It was never going to be anything else, was it?"

"Nope!" I said, cheerfully. "I am a one-track mind!"

Death gestured to a bit of empty space beside us. A portal opened, very similar to the ones generated by the Sword of Samael.

"I should probably learn how to do that," I said.

"Make another Reaper's scythe," Death replied, referring to the weapon I'd conjured. "Either that or stop giving away your godlike tools."

I smirked. "It's a matter of keeping the right balance of power. If you get too strong, it's not fun anymore. It's why I'm glad I gave away the sword to Larry. He's gotten himself on the Texas Guardians. Already, the Governor of said state and he have had a fistfight. Guess who won?"

"Be seeing you, Gary," Death said, smirking. "Either next week or the end of the universe or somewhere in-between."

The two magical books transformed into a pair of black and white bull terriers, which was a peculiar bit of magic, but one I suspected would make them easier to move around.

"Sure," I said to Death before addressing the two books/poochies. "Come on, girls."

"Bark!"

"Bark!"

I turned around and walked through the portal.

Epilogue

I walked through the portal and found myself on a rooftop in Falconcrest City with night having fallen. That was strange given it had still been daytime in Washington D.C. Then again, daytime in Falconcrest City was usually about 7:30 in the morning to 8:30 in the morning given the way our cloud cover and smog functioned. That and the fact the city existed on what amounted to a literal hellmouth.

I saw Mandy swinging around a silver plated Korean *ssangsudo*, which was a curved sword that you should *never* call a katana because my wife will take it personally. She was doing battle with a half-dozen feral dragur, which were what happened when vampires degenerated to the point that they were closer to zombies than your typical Edward Cullen or Louis de Lioncourt type. I felt bad for making fun of Larry being a half-vampire who hunted other vampires thing since Cindy was apparently correct: it *was* Mandy's thing.

Bloodscream the Retributive was lying on the ground, trapped in a silver net, and hissing at the sky. Apparently, I'd missed a throwdown between him and Calico AKA Nighthuntress AKA Mandy the Vampire-Vampire Hunter™. Not wanting to interrupt her fight, I stepped back and leaned up against the side of some air conditioning units.

"I'll just stand over here until you're done," I said, sticking my hands in my pockets. I then started humming "Cry Little Sister" from *The Lost Boys*.

I'd found out from a de-programmed Sam the Eagle that Mandy had missed the Battle of Soldiers Park. It had been for good reason, though, because she'd discovered the Brotherhood of Infamy had started converting the richest and most powerful in America into vampires as part of their plan to take over with President Omega. While a vampire who hunts other vampires was a bit cliche and I felt she should have stuck with being a cat burglar, I was glad she'd found her niche in the superhero world.

"God dammit, Gary! Help me!" Mandy shouted, clearly struggling with these undead more than she should have. She managed to swing her sword around two-handedly and decapitate one of the six vampires attacking her.

"Okey-dokey," I said, lifting my hand. "Back to the old ways. *FIREBALL!*"

The first of the vampires struck by my flames exploded into a pile of ashes before two more broke away from battling Mandy to go for my throat. I turned insubstantial and he smashed into the air conditioner behind me as I froze the next one, then blasted him with a fireball as well, showering me with painful steam. Yeah, that wasn't my smartest move. When the other dragur got up, still going for my throat, I pulled out Jacob's *Magic for Dummies* and smashed it across the vampire's head. It seemed whatever sorcery within it was strong because the vampire exploded as a result. Not into dust, either, but nasty gory bits that meant I'd have to get my cloak drycleaned after this.

The two Book Terriers—as I nicknamed them—had followed me through the portal and each went for one of the vampires, their teeth and claws penetrating the creatures' flesh, causing the dragur to fall to the ground as their throats were torn out. That didn't kill them automatically and I'll spare you the gory details, but apparently magical book/demon dogs loved the taste of feral vampire. That left Mandy, thankfully, free of her attackers.

"New pets?" Mandy asked, looking down at Bloodscream and starting to bind his arms and legs with blessed silver wire. I could feel the holiness from here. Also, just to satisfy you lore nerds, Mandy was using gloves to hold the wire. It wasn't really a secret technique or immunity.

"Old ones actually," I said, pausing. "Possibly Great Old Ones. What are you up to?"

"Dracula has sent a bunch of his new breed of Super Vamp after me," Mandy said. "Bloodscream becoming the first living whampyre means that Dracula's blood is a necessary part of the process of creating them."

I stared at her. "So typical superhero stuff. Wait, isn't Dracula dead-dead? I killed him."

Death had said otherwise, but I wanted to get confirmation because I was the kind of guy who questioned anthropomorphic principles of reality.

"He's cursed by God with immortality," Mandy said, looking up. "He can't be killed forever."

I nodded. "Ah, we're following *The Mummy* rules. You know, 'I hate you so much that I will curse you with godlike power.'"

"What do you want, Gary?" Mandy asked, sharper than I suspected even she intended.

My heart broke. "To talk."

Mandy sat on Bloodscream the Retributive who was growling and cursing. "Shouldn't you be off killing Nazis?"

"As much as I love that, I have more important things to do," I said, honestly.

"More important than thwarting PHANTOM's attempted coup?" Mandy asked, reminding me she'd grown up in a house of secret agents.

"Yeah, the whole come-back-tour for PHANTOM is more like the MMA than your typical rock band," I said, honestly glad they were all talk. Even I'd had my fill of killing recently. For once, the cops could do their job.

"What?" Mandy asked, confused.

"Well, whenever an MMA fighter is about to come back to show how awesome they are, they're usually out of practice and five years older so they get their asses kicked. All their fans are disappointed, and the hype ends up going nowhere. This is in contrast to most musicians who do a comeback tour can still do the songs," I explained.

Mandy stood up, walked over to a few inches from my face, and gave me a dope slap to the back of the head. "Not what I meant."

"Oh," I said, knowing that. "Well, PHANTOM got their leader killed and they're nothing without their Fuhrer. They're already fighting over who should be the next ruler: Tom Terrors from other universes, other General Omegas, and Lady Phantom who is basically the Baroness from *G.I. Joe*. I met her robot once. Very hot."

"PHANTOM is bad wrong fun, Gary," Mandy said. "You can't put them on t-shirts and sell toys of them. No matter how much Omega Corp tries."

"Don't worry, fascism is a major wood killer," I said, dryly. "Also, Omega Corporation has been suffering massive losses due to the whole being named for a terrorist thing. Leia has bought their entertainment division with her new company and is suing them to oblivion after acquiring a voting machine company. Or something, I wasn't paying attention. Leia thinks there is a better way to oppose PHANTOM than just punching them. I agree. Except my solution is killing them."

"Good for her," Mandy said, pausing. "I think."

"Leia gave me ownership of the *Miami Vice* and *Murder She Wrote* IPs for my birthday," I said, glad to be making small talk. "I prefer them to owning Raven's Roost. I think owning that city makes my net worth go down. Anyway, I'm thinking reboot with Ryan Gosling. He could really bring Jessica Fletcher to life."

"What did Mimi get you?" Mandy asked, not missing a beat. It was hard to make the undead laugh.

"The Eiffel Tower," I replied. "Shrunken to paperweight size. She borrowed some of Damselfly's particles for stealing it as a father-daughter bonding trip. I think we may have to return it, though. We forgot to clean out the tourists first."

Mandy stared, expressionless.

"I'm kidding," I replied. "We absolutely cleaned out the tourists first. It was a nice send-off to her supervillain ambitions, though. She left a clue that says that the authorities can find it if they look in their Seoul."

"South Korea," Mandy said.

"Got it in one!" I said, pointing at Mandy with two finger guns. "Personally, I would have made it harder, but the tower will unshrink in twenty-four hours, and you don't want it crushing the local esports league."

Mandy looked down at the rooftop floor. "You know why we can't work, Gary."

"I really don't," I said, sighing. "I'd also be betraying everything I believe if I didn't try to make this work."

"I know why you became a wannabe James Bond after I died, Gary," Mandy said.

"Tortured antihero or womanizing prick?" I asked, knowing she meant ridiculous horndog. "Are we talking Sean

Connery, Roger Moore, Dalton, or Brosnan here? I think we all agree I'm not pulling off Craig."

"George Lazenby," Mandy said, suppressing a smile.

"I'd argue, but Diana Rigg," I replied.

Mandy smiled. "You became a sex-starved college kid again because you wanted to try to recapture what had been lost between us, the love we shared when I was alive. You latched onto getting it anywhere you could, including Cindy who is your best friend but also kind of a psychopath."

"Kind of a psychopath would imply she's not clinically diagnosed," I said. "Mind you, that's from her own, *What's My Pathology?* app that she's charging fifty dollars for the use of."

"She's not a psychologist," Mandy pointed out.

"I believe that is just one of the problems there," I said, knowing Cindy's apo had already given about a million inaccurate diagnoses. "You were saying."

"And you tried to get back together with Gabrielle despite the fact you are manifestly a trash fire together," Mandy said, using my exact same description of our relationship.

"Not...necessarily," I replied. "I mean, yes, she tried to kill me, and I did kill one of her but that was ultranium at work."

Mandy looked down. "It all boiled down to the fact that I couldn't give you the stable monogamous relationship you wanted."

Mandy and I had agreed to try the open relationship thing because, well, vampires couldn't be monogamous since blood was sex and no single person could satisfy their need. Also, Cindy was emotionally dependent on me. But I admitted I'd wanted to have the kind of intimacy I'd had with Mandy while she was alive, and she'd always pulled back whenever I'd tried. I never understood why, and she seemed determined to push me to someone else even as she never left my life completely. At least until now, it seemed.

I took her hand. "It wasn't because of that. Really, I really did want to sleep with some of them!"

Mandy faked seriousness. "I don't believe you."

"No, no, honest!" I said, pausing. "I mean, yes, I may have made the mistake of being friends with the two superheroines I slept with—okay five—but time travel and video game sexcapades are just for fun!"

"Fun but not love," Mandy said.

That struck me to the bone. "Yeah, no, I've only ever loved you."

Okay, it was out there. I loved Cindy but as my bestie and Gabrielle was an established trash fire relationship. One that would never work, no matter how hard we tried. Anyone else? Well, fun was different. Jealousy over sex wasn't an issue when you were a supervillain. Jealousy over emotional intimacy? Very much so.

"Do you love me or the woman I was made from?" Mandy asked.

"Yes," I said, knowing my own heart, and kissing her. She kissed back, first hesitantly, and then deeper as well as more passionately.

"But I'm not her," Mandy said.

"I don't know how this vampirism stuff works," I said, sighing.

"Aren't you like, literally, the one person on Earth who should?" Mandy asked. "You know, Chosen of Death and all that?"

I paused. "I think we've established I'm objectively terrible at my job."

Mandy gave a half smile. "I can tell you, but it'll probably kill everything you still feel for me."

"I'm a big boy," I said, softly. "I can take it."

I mean, I was lying, I was as emotionally fragile as a bunch of champagne glasses at the Behemoth's wedding to Atomic Bombshell. At least where Mandy was concerned. Which is why I had plastic champagne glasses during my wedding and totally not because we were poor.

Mandy looked up. "When you're raised as a vampire, Gary, your soul splits in two. All the good parts of your soul ascend to whatever afterlife you're destined for. The bad parts of your soul are used to construct a new spirit."

"Yeah, Death told me something like that," I muttered. "I still don't get it. I mean, does the good part of your soul go to Heaven regardless of whether you were an asshole? Is there a tiny fragment of Hitler in Heaven that is his loving dogs?"

"You know, Hitler killed his dogs in the end," Mandy said.

"Okay, good, then I acknowledge he had absolutely no good qualities whatsoever as a dog man," I said.

"He was vegetarian too," Mandy pointed out.

"All vegetarians are evil. They're secretly plotting against us carnivores. Jane explained the conspiracy while we had deer burgers. You know how I know they're all secretly evil? Hitler was vegetarian. Boom! Mic drop." I made a mic drop gesture with one hand.

"Gary—" Mandy said.

"You can't argue," I said. "I dropped the mic."

Mandy stared, her eyes now a shade of red and tears of blood were coming out the sides. "There's a word for a spirit animating the body of a human being that has nothing but the dark side of a person. A malevolent entity that only has what you wish you could leave behind. It's demon."

"So, we're using *Buffy* rules," I said, distilling it down to pop culture basics. "Human dies. Demon inhabits body. Demon has all the memories and a twisted version of their personality. Got it."

"Gary—" Mandy said, tears now trailing down.

"That's my name, don't wear it out," I said, remembering what Death had also said. That the Mandy walking around the world after I used the *Book of Midnight* to resurrect her was also carrying around Mandy's love for me. That said, to me at least, that someone considered Mandy's love for me a toxic and evil part of her personality.

Thanks, God.

Mandy continued. "I was so full of anger when I rose up from the dead. Anger at the supervillains who'd ruined Falconcrest City. Anger at dying in the first place. At the years I wasted feeling sorry for myself rather than pursuing my dream of making the world a better place. Of being a hero."

"Those years spent with me," I said, taking on all the guilt that I felt I deserved.

"No, Gary," Mandy said. "Both I and the Mandy-Who-Was remember that very differently. Our regret isn't being with you. It's our regret that we didn't realize you'd support us in going out there to fight the darkness."

"Even though you got killed?" I asked.

"Heroes die, Gary," Mandy said, sadly. "It's the villains that live who get to live with the guilt. I'm not sure what that says about me because my return has only caused you nothing but misery."

"Anything but," I said, taking your hand.

"Merciful tortured me, Gary," Mandy letting go of my hand. "When he inserted the soul of Spellbinder to distract you by using my body. I was there in the back of her mind the entire time she possessed my body. The torture wasn't physical pain, though. It was mental. I could feel all the emotions that had previously been denied me: love, friendship, and her sheer joy at life. Most of all, I felt her regret at deceiving you."

"I feel *terrible* she regretted the whole sexual assault by deception thing," I said, sarcastically. "I let her around *my kids*. How the Hell did Leia not pick up on that?"

"Magic," Mandy said, as if that cheap answer explained everything. Which, honestly, it did. "Merciful has ways of getting around anything. He was a great wizard, unlike, well—"

"Me, yeah," I said. "I keep expecting them to revoke my Color Wizard status, but it's apparently like Discworld's Rincewind. If you can cast one spell, even one you really don't want to cast, you qualify as a mage and can keep your title."

I made a little rainbow cantrip like *Shang Tsung's Friendship*. After a few weeks I'd mastered this and a few other completely useless spells. Maybe in a few dozen years I might be able to call myself a proper wizard. Either that, or I would peak at the equivalent of t-ball for a baseball player.

"Awww," Mandy said, looking down. "That's so cute."

"I learned it for Pride month," I said, thinking about Larry. That was a bombshell I was going to have to drop in the most intense conversation I'd had with Mandy since, well, she died.

"Well, you are Gary the Pink," Mandy muttered, unwittingly causing my eye to twitch. "Either way, I did countless missions for Merciful in the future and past as well as alternate realities. I saw many variations of you, us, you and Gabrielle, you and Cindy, me and Selena, me and Splotch."

"Really, Splotch?" I asked, more interested than I should have. "Which one?"

"Not important, Gary," Mandy said. "I'm saying the vampire part of me learned to experience the emotions she'd been denied."

"That was Spellbinder, not you," I said.

"It was both of us," Mandy admitted. "When I was freed from our merger, I found I still craved the feelings I'd experienced as part of her. Love between two humans. The Hunger still dominated me, though. I didn't care that I had to share you because the blood was what really mattered."

"A part of you is better than all of someone else," I said, pausing. "I love you. Demon or not."

Mandy began to weep heavier, the blood flowing faster. "You deserve someone who can love you as a living woman can. Not this endless merry-go-round of misery, joy, and misery again."

"Honey, that's just being a superhero...or villain," I said, grasping her tight. "The merry-go-round never ends. Even when you die."

"You think?" Mandy asked.

"Mandy, I can only promise that my fragile male ego and insane devotion to being a professional criminal will lead to a life of endless drama. It will be full hedonistic excess compensating for the misery in our lives. Violence, angst, and soap opera levels of drama."

"You're really selling this relationship," Mandy said.

"But it will be *our* violent angsty hedonistic soap opera," I said. "One that you will always be at the center of despite weird cosmic attempts to break us up or get me to sell our relationship to the Devil like Stanley Oktid AKA The Super-Duper Splotch Man did for reasons still unclear to me."

"Splotch sold our relationship to the Devil?" Mandy asked, confused.

"No, he sold his relationship with his supermodel wife to the Devil," I replied. "For some reason that doesn't involve making a middle-aged superhero look utterly pathetic. It's a long story and we're working on undoing it. Either way, let no one from the Cosmic Editors to other eldritch horrors tear us apart."

"Even if the only way I can feed without killing someone is sex?" Mandy asked.

"I rode a dragon, Mandy," I muttered. "Both ways."

Mandy stared with her big red eyes then grinned. "I need details."

I coughed. "Yeah, there's also another thing I need to bring up."

"I know about my son, Gary," Mandy said, pausing.

"How?" I asked.

"I'm a superhero," Mandy said, frowning. "Also, Mimi told me about him. I was running away from him as well as you."

"You should talk to him," I said, pausing.

"I'll try," Mandy whispered.

"This is all very touching," Bloodscream said, looking up. He now had his erudite Londonium accent back, which contrasted to his wild Nineties mullet. "But I'm out of my blood rage. Can I be let out now?"

"No!" Mandy said, turning around and kicking him. "You bit me."

"I bite everyone during team ups!" Bloodscream said.

"Not without my permission," Mandy said, crossing her arms and growling.

"You want to go have a bite to eat and, try something?" I asked. "I mean, I'll eat and then you bite me?"

"Sure," Mandy said, sighing. "Just no garlic."

"I thought that was a legend."

"Yeah, I just hate it."

There had been the Golden Age of Superheroes, the Silver Age, The Bronze Age, The Iron Age, and then the Modern Age.

Who knew what the New Age would bring.

Bloodscream called out to us as we walked to the stairs. "No, seriously, guys, could you let me go? GUYS!"

MERCILESS WILL RETURN IN
THE RISE OF SUPERVILLAINY
Book Ten of The Supervillainy Saga

Bonus Short Story: "Dungeons and Garys"

A Supervillainy Saga Side Story

By C. T. Phipps

I first became aware of the kobold when I was lying on the couch, and it walked up to stare at me like a small dog. I was re-reading *Villain's Rule* by MK Gibson on my Kindle when I noticed it.

It was, undeniably, a kobold with its little reptilian-canine features and a leather suit of armor with horned Viking helmet that no true Northman had ever worn. It was about one foot tall and didn't have shoes but scaly paws with curled claws.

Now, I'm quite used to strange things happening in my house. I lived with a teenage inventor, a vampire, a werewolf, a robot butler, a weredeer, and the granddaughter of the world's greatest hero on most days. Still, it was surprise to see something straight out of my tabletop games and I wondered if my past use of recreational drugs was kicking in.

"Can I help you?" I asked.

"Are you a god?" the tiny kobold Viking asked me.

I knew the answer to this one ever since the original *Ghostbusters*. "Yes, yes I am."

It also helped that, yes, technically I was. God was not actually a title or really an exalted state so much as an actual race. They came in gods of pocket lint, Odin, *Star Trek* advanced alien, and omnipotent deity formats. Technically, all angels and demons were gods, but they just so happened to be working for someone else. Sir Terry Pratchett had defined the difference between gods and demons as the "terrorists versus freedom fighters" and that was literally true from my brief exposure to the cosmic truths of the universe.

"Praise be!" the kobold Viking shouted. "We have found our new lord! Lord, uh, sorry, what is your name, Your Gloriousness?"

"Gary," I said, looking over the side of the couch to see if I was being punked. It wouldn't be beyond my daughters to create animatronic kobolds to screw with me.

"Praise be to the Great God Gary!" the kobold said. "Come out, everyone!"

As if the situation couldn't get more surreal, a dozen more kobolds popped out from behind the furniture and started waving their hands back and forth like they were at a ball game. There were male, female, and indeterminate kobolds that were all dressed up like Vikings. Seeing the female ones with long braids like Brunhilda and exaggerated lipstick just continued the strangeness of it all.

"Listen guys," I started to say, "I don't really have time to. GURK—"

That's when it hit me. A sudden rushing sensation that was like someone had sent a jolt of electricity straight to my brain. It wasn't sexual, but more like someone had managed to distill the ridiculous rush of adrenaline Mountain Dew and energy drink commercials promise into physical form. My hands shook with power and my eyes briefly glowed with electricity as I experienced *worship* for the first time.

"Are you okay, master?" The lead kobold Viking said.

I blinked rapidly. "Yeah, just never expected to feel that rush."

I'd won the Eternity Tournament and that had apparently come with elevation to deity status, but a deity without worshipers was a king without subjects, a car without an engine, or a bowling ball without a liquid center (first-season *Simpsons* reference! Can't believe that show is still on!). Given I was technically, in the loosest sense possible—and I do mean loosest—observant of my Judaism, I wasn't looking for worshipers either.

"We pledge our lives and souls to you, Great Gary!" the lead Viking kobold said. "The prophecy shall be fulfilled."

Okay, that got my attention, so I swung my legs off the coach and sat up. "Ah, prophecies. The poor man's way of manipulating people into doing the stuff you need them to do. If you want the local dictator or wizard king killed, you say he's been prophesized to be killed. If someone does it, they fulfilled it. If they don't, I guess they weren't the chosen one. Am I right?"

The lead Viking kobold looked over its shoulder before coughing into his fist. "Uh, no, nothing like that is happening. Ahem."

"Okay, who are you guys and what the hell is this all about?" I asked, not saying no just yet.

"I am Potluck, one hundred and twelfth son of the Kobold King!" Potluck said. "Now I am the Kobold King because all of my brothers and sisters have been killed."

I blinked. "Yeah, that's rotten luck there."

"It wasn't luck," Potluck said.

Meanwhile, I heard noises from my kitchen and looked over to see some of the kobolds had gotten into the garbage and were eating the remains of last night's pizza.

"Praise be to the Great Gary!" one of the kobolds said. "We shall not have to kill one of the children tonight!"

Okay, that got dark quickly. Turning back to Potluck, I crossed my arms. "Okay, keep going, pal. You had my curiosity but now you have my attention."

Potluck sighed. "My people and I are from Dungeonpunk World, World of Numerical Progression Based Fantasy!"

I blinked. "Well, that's a bit on the nose."

Potluck nodded. "Many sages and clerics have debated the exact meaning of this description, but we were created by the Dark Undermaster. He was a terrifying wizard who wielded the power of the Primal Orb of Creation."

Wait, a second. "Is the Dark Undermaster about thirty-eight years old, brunette, a bit on the pudgy side, wears a bathrobe because he won't shell out for an actual wizard robe, and is usually eating out of a bag of Cheetos? Goes by Dave?"

"You know his secret name!" Potluck said, shocked.

"Oh, for fucks sake," I muttered, facepalming. "The plot thins."

Falconcrest City University has the dubious distinction of producing more supervillains than any other institution of higher learning in the world and that included PHANTOM Academy. Part of this was due to the twenty-year tenure of Doctor Thaddeus Thule AKA the Supervillain Maker. Notably, also my psychotherapist for my tenure there.

Dave Diceman was one of those supervillains, being part of me and Cindy's gaming club alongside Jerry Dabrowski AKA Cthulhuoid. Dave had gone on to be a semi-successful indie fantasy author with twenty novels in his Dark Undermaster series. I'd tried reading them, but they were too horny, violent, and meme-filled even for me.

Think on that.

"You know him?" Potluck asked.

"Yeah," I said. "Somehow, he ended up having a nervous breakdown after a Twitter feud with a twelve-year-old girl and got himself banned from multiple social media platforms. There's a yada-yada period where he ends up as an international assassin who built fantasy-themed death traps to kill superheroes. Traps which, as far as I know, have never killed any superheroes."

"I don't know what a lot of those words mean, but he is the terrifying overlord of our planet," Potluck said.

"Which he created," I said, thinking about whether that was possible with the Primal Orb of Creation.

"Or so he claims," Potluck admitted. "Among the eldest of our race, there is a memory of a time before when we were a peaceful race who were very different before he came. He reshaped the land, the skies, and seas, and turned us into many other species. Even our memories changed so that most of us only recall the history he gave our world."

I thought about that. The Primal Orb could theoretically do that but in no way, shape, or form was Dave Diceman strong enough to do it even with the Orb. It was a bit like the One Ring of Sauron to stay in genre: a hobbit got invisibility out of it while someone like Saruman or Sauron got godlike supernatural power. If he had somehow managed to get himself the juice to transform an entire alien planet into a replica of his shitty homebrew D&D setting, then he was an actual threat.

"Okay, I'll help you defeat him," I said.

"Oh, that's not what we want from you," Potluck said.

"What, really?" I asked, surprised.

"No, we're just hoping to flee through the dimensional gate to find a place where we're not enslaved or exterminated for being vermin," Potluck said. "I don't suppose you have a large amount of soft ground in which mines can be dug."

I blinked. "Yeah, I've got a pretty extensive backyard."

319

"Excellent!" Potluck replied. "Also, we're going to require provisions before we can begin growing the mushrooms and raising the giant moles that we feed on."

"That may be—" I started to say.

"By the Gary, what is this glorious substance!" one of the female kobolds said. "I have never tasted its like!"

I looked over to see she'd gotten into the dog kibble for our rescues. "Uh huh."

"Truly you are the Great Provider!" Potluck said. "Huzzah!"

———

So, about a week later, my live-in girlfriend and mother of my children walked up to me as I was playing the Remastered Director's Cut Enhanced Version of *Baldur's Gate* on my PSX210 Pro. Rather than simply interrupt me, she went directly to the console and turned it off, which was just not cool.

Cindy Wakowski AKA Red Riding Hood was a beautiful, scarlet-haired woman with pale skin and a button nose who was presently dressed in a red track suit while carrying a two-handed sword over her shoulder. There was a splotch of blood on her face and the sword was equally bloodied.

"Gary, we need to talk."

"Can it wait for after game?" I asked.

"No," Cindy said. "When were you going to tell me that you invited a bunch of reptile dogs to live with us?"

"I was hoping you wouldn't notice," I said, as a couple of kobolds were swinging from the chandelier above my head. Beside me, a kobold named Gary XII was wearing a tiny baseball cap and t-shirt to go with his miniature jeans. I would have asked where they'd gotten those, but I'd had to order a whole new wardrobe since massive amounts of our clothes had disappeared. I was starting to wonder if this was the answer to the eternal question of where missing socks went.

"You don't say," Cindy said. "You didn't think I would notice our house has become filled with Rizzo the Rat's family from *The Muppets Take Manhattan*."

"They do have a rather Muppet-like quality to them, don't they?" I said, staring at her. "Just out of curiosity, you didn't kill any of them, did you?"

"No, Gary, I had to kill the minotaur," Cindy said.

"We have a minotaur?" I asked.

"Not anymore," Cindy said. "Because in addition to letting in a bunch of fast-breeding hyperactive iguana puppies, the giant magical portal in our basement also is letting in monsters that feed on kobolds."

"Oh, shit, really?" I asked. "I hadn't thought of that."

"Praise be to the Wolf Queen!" Gary XII said. "She has slain the great persecutor of our kind! When we feast on the bull monster, we shall toast the consort of the Great Provider!"

"They're just so damned cute," I said, admitting to myself that I probably should have cleared this with my family.

"No, they're not," Cindy said. "They're annoying and flee whenever I turn on the lights. I'm constantly hearing them moving around at night and that's doubly irritating because I have werewolf superhearing. Not to mention the goddamn traps."

"Leia loves the traps," I said.

"Leia loves finding and disabling the traps," Cindy said. "I feel like she's developing levels in Rogue, and she's meant for better things than that. Mimi just walks through them and since she's immortal, she doesn't care. But I was almost crushed by a falling spike ceiling. I don't even know how they set that up."

"I'll ask them to keep the traps restricted to the basement," I replied.

"You better not!" a voice shouted from beneath the floorboards, which I presumed to be my vampire wife, Mandy. She, too, had superhearing.

"Well, Case has quit being our butler until they get some sensitivity training," Cindy said. "Apparently, being called the Master's Flesh Golem is a racial slur to him."

"Would he prefer Iron Golem?" I asked.

"The complex in the back is almost done," I said, defensively. "You really can't treat these guys as pests. They've got nowhere else to go."

Cindy stared. "We're going to Dungeonpunk World."

"We are?" I asked.

"Yes, we are," Cindy replied. "We're going to find Dave Diceman AKA the Dark Undermaster and kick his ass. Then his playground will become magically freed from tyranny, and they won't have to come here anymore."

I stared at her. "Somehow I don't think you have a future in international politics, Cindy. I also don't think I'd want you deciding when to stage a military intervention or not."

"Do it or I'll never get you off again," Cindy said, crossing her arms.

"You wouldn't survive without my technique either," I said.

"You'd break first," Cindy said, staring.

"Fair point," I said, standing up. "Let's get going."

"We'll bring Mandy along," Cindy replied. "If there's any place that needs an overpowered undead abomination to plow through it, it's Dungeonpunk World."

"I heard that!" Mandy shouted up from the basement. "Also, please tell me they're not emptying their chamber pots down here."

"No, they recycle all their own shit," I shouted down. "It's probably a mushroom farm."

"Get them out of here!" Mandy shouted back.

"Is that castle made to look like a giant skull?" Mandy asked.

"It's a replica of Castle Grayskull from *Masters of the Universe*," I said, staring at what stood atop the storm-ridden mountain before us. "And I thought *I* was a nerd."

"You are," Cindy said. "But it's very possible Dave Diceman is worse."

Mandy was wearing a hooded cloak that protected her from sunlight, which couldn't kill her but was certainly annoying, and she was riding on the back of a nightmare beside me. For those unfamiliar with nightmares, their names were puns, and they were redheaded, black-furred demon horses. I probably should have just led with that. Cindy was on the other side of me, having changed into her Barbarian Princess gear with leather armor and face paint. Her armor had a big cleavage window, but it was enchanted and made Cindy feel sexy so who was I to complain?

The journey from the portal in our basement to Dungeonpunk World's evil center turned out to be about an hour's ride and I was under the distinct impression that Dave's kingdom wasn't nearly as big as it had been made out to be. I lifted my cellphone and took a few pictures of the castle just to make sure.

"You have cellphone service here?" Cindy asked.

"I think this is the Hollow Earth," I replied. "I don't think Dave actually went to another planet. He just took the Orb of Creation down to the center of the Earth and turned one of the smaller kingdoms down here into a replica of his shitty fantasy novels."

"I can't believe he made a castle based on a Dolph Lundgren movie," Mandy said.

Both Cindy and I looked at Mandy strangely.

"What?" Mandy asked.

"Well, it's too bad none of us have read his books," Cindy said, sounding suspiciously specific in her denial. "Then we'd have advantage over him. We'd know that was the Castle Undermaster and it's inhabited by an army of deathless skeletons and Lich-Wight witches."

I stared at her.

Cindy quickly looked over her shoulder.

"Cindy," I said. "What are you hiding?"

"He sent us the full twenty book set!" Cindy said. "They were autographed! Was I not supposed to read them?"

"No!" I said. "I couldn't get through the first thirty pages! They had *Wheel of Fortune* jokes! *Wheel of Fortune!*"

"I thought they were funny," Cindy said, shrugging. "Anyway, that at least explains why you didn't sue him."

I paused. "Wait, why would I sue him?"

Cindy didn't respond, looking preoccupied with the landscape around the mountain.

"Cindy," I said. "Please."

"I mean, I finished the entire series and it kind of bears more than a passing resemblance to our home game at college," Cindy said, looking guilty. "I mean I thought it was obvious given you had kobolds as one of the main player character races. But yes, the Kingdom of the Hot Wood Elves is over there. The badass Jewish warrior kingdom and the fake Romans are over there. He really just added his shitty player character as the ruler of the place from here."

I stared at her. "That plagiarist son of a bitch."

"Please tell me you didn't actually name it the Kingdom of the Hot Wood Elves," Mandy said.

Before I could answer, I heard a throat clearing beside my horse. Looking down, I saw Potluck and Gary XII riding on the backs of a pair of pit bulls. The Kobolds were doing their best to domesticate riding mounts from the local rescue population.

Potluck, who was now sporting a suit of chainmail and helmet, said, "Forgive me, Great Gary but the Dark Champion of the Dark Undermaster is riding up on his Dark Steed."

"And I thought I was redundant," I muttered.

"You are," Cindy said.

The kobolds weren't lying, though, as a stereotypical black knight rode up on the back of his own demonic horse. The knight was radiating supernatural power and lifted his helmet to reveal the glowing skeleton inside.

"I am Lord Doth, Death Knight champion of the Dark Undermaster! You have come a long way to die, Gary Karkofsky."

I'd encountered a lot of undead in my time, but this guy wasn't giving off any death-related vibes. He was about as undead as a plastic skeleton on Halloween. However, there was a *lot* of magic radiating off him. He was composed almost purely of that energy and that was rare even on high magic worlds.

"Why do they always address you and not me?" Cindy asked me. "Is this a guy thing? This is a guy thing."

"He's not undead," Mandy said, staring at him. "There's no necromantic energy about him. He's some sort of magical construct."

"Yes, Mandy," I replied, ignoring the knight. "I kind of picked that up with the fact Death Knights don't exist."

"You don't know that," Cindy said. "It's a big multiverse. Hell, we've been to Krynn."

"Only for sex tourism!" I pointed out. "Mind you, Toril is much, much better for that sort of thing. It's a very, very churchy-churchy sort of place, Krynn. Paladine this, Takhisis that."

"Ahem," Lord Doth said. "I'm sorry, but you're about to die."

"Yeah, that's not happening," I said. "I've faced Great Beasts, gods, archdemons, and two dragons."

"Ix-nay on the dragons-ay," Mandy interrupted. "I'm really not comfortable with that topic given how those battles usually end for me."

Lord Doth lifted a single bony finger inside a gauntlet and pointed it at me. "Die!"

Nothing happened.

Lord Doth paused then stared at his finger. "That usually works."

I stared at him. "Yeah, because normally someone hasn't prepared with spells of protection against magical assaults. Too many D&D wizards don't prepare defensively."

"Huh," Lord Doth said.

"Cindy, sic 'em," I said.

Cindy pulled her sword and leapt off her nightmare. "Berserker rage!"

The actual invasion of Castle Undermaster was a bit anticlimactic. Bluntly, it illustrated a huge amount of the problems with dungeon design since almost the entirety of the map assumed you would go through the front doors and proceed to fight your way through the skeletons, animated suits of armor, and dragon that he'd set up. I knew the castle contained all this because I could see most of the monsters standing there past the mouth-shaped portcullis. They didn't attack me or my companions but stood there, waiting for us to arrive.

"Do you think he's on the top floor?" I asked.

"Yep," Cindy said. "There're some pretty huge staircases down the hall from where I can see."

"Gotcha," I said, raising my hands. "*Mass Levitate!*"

All our steeds and personages lifted themselves up into the air onto the roof of the castle, neatly avoiding the massive army below.

"This feels like cheating," Cindy said.

"No kidding," I said. "However, we're not here for the experience."

"We're not?" Cindy asked. "But we could be under leveled when we face him!"

Mandy shook her head, embarrassed. Both Potluck and Gary XII looked more confused than anything.

I stared at her. "I'm sure the Dungeon Master will provide us a reward for creative problem solving."

"Like hell I will!" A voice spoke from nearby. "Why the hell did you even come here unless you wanted to game?"

Coming out from a doorway to the rooftop of the castle was, indeed, Dave Diceman. He was almost exactly as I remembered—okay twenty years older, but I didn't particularly want to think about that detail. To his credit, he'd traded in his cheap bathrobe for a proper LARP wizard's robe, but the Cheeto dust was still visible on his permanently orange-stained fingers and beard.

He also hadn't put on any real weight since college, which was more than many of my associates from those days could say. Around his neck was the Orb of Creation, the glowing object about the size of a pool ball and wrapped in a metal amulet that looked like it had been purchased on Etsy.

"We're here to kick ass and chew bubblegum and we're all out of bubblegum! I will avenge the evils you have committed against these people and strike you down!" Cindy said, getting into full role-player mode.

"I'm sorry, who are you?" Dave asked.

Cindy's eyes widened. "Cindy? Cindy Wakowski?"

Dave shook his head. "Are you someone?"

"I am Red Riding Hood!" Cindy said. "Barbarian hero! Slayer of dragons! I helped kill the Extreme! Twice! Fought in the resistance against President Omega and Merciful. Was there to fight the zombie apocalypse."

Dave stared. "Sorry, not ringing a bell. Wait, hold on, were you part of our group?"

"Yes!" Cindy snapped.

"The DM's girlfriend!" Dave said, pointing at me. "I remember you now."

Cindy narrowed her eyes. "Son of a bitch must pay."

"He's just trying to taunt you, Cindy," Mandy said.

"It's working!" Cindy said, simmering with barbarian and werewolf rage.

"What the hell is all this, Dave?" I asked.

"Wait, is that Mandy Colton?" Dave asked, pointing at Mandy. "Lead singer of the Black Furies?"

"We played for four hours every weekend for two years!" Cindy said.

"I'm Mandy Karkofsky now," Mandy said. "Also, a vampire."

"God, how disgusting," Dave said. "Please tell me you're brainwashed. I mean, I can understand how Cindy got with him. She's not exactly a classy babe—"

"Okay, now you're dead," Cindy said, charging at the Dark Undermaster. Unfortunately, she was almost immediately caught in a magical field as he waved his hand.

"*Hold Person*," Dave said, positively cackling with glee. "Oh, by the way, Cindy, I totally knew who you were. I follow your Instagram."

Inside the bubble, Cindy screamed a variety of obscenities, some of which were in elvish.

"So, you have Dungeon magic too," I replied, feeling a bit guilty. After all, I was the one who had created it.

"Yep," The Dark Undermaster said, chortling. "For years, I was stuck using Daddy's fortune to build death traps with a fantasy theme, putting PHANTOM kill bots in costumes and holographic illusions. Then you posted actual magic online. You gave magic to the people! Idiot!"

"I am attempting to level society," I replied, dryly.

"You totally missed the pun there, Gary," Mandy said. "Assuming you mean leveling in creating equality versus destroying it."

"Actually, I mean leveling as in leveling them up," I said. "Everyone should stop being first-level Commoners and start reaching their inner Epic Level."

"That's somehow worse," Mandy said.

"Why are you doing this, Dave?" I asked. "Also, how the hell did you get the Orb of Creation?"

"Not Dave, *The Dark Undermaster!*" Dave said, an actual thunderclap happening along with organ music from down below. "Master of the Underthings!"

"You rule underwear?" I asked.

"No! I rule the underground races and underworld, which is also underground. Pay attention!" Dave said, as if I was the stupid one.

I blinked. I didn't usually have a leg to stand on when calling other villains out on theatricality and geekery, but I felt a good case could be made that he was just embarrassing himself. Because even if he was LARPing as his own player character, the fact is he'd enslaved an entire country. After all, just because you were ridiculous didn't mean you weren't fucking dangerous—I'd made an entire career out of that after all.

"Sure, DU," I replied. "We'll go with that."

Cindy cursed and growled inside her glowing magical force field.

Dave stretched out his hands. "As for why I did this? Wouldn't you like to know!"

I blinked. "Yeah, that's why I asked."

Dave blinked. "Oh, well, yeah. I did it because I think it's cool and I have a bunch of slaves doing whatever I want. Plus, my girlfriend likes it."

"Good for you," I said, not surprised that Dave could get a girlfriend. He was still a supervillain after all. "Except I understand you've been murdering a lot of kobolds. Kobolds who used to be regular people."

"Yeah, but they're *kobolds*," Dave said, sneering. "I don't understand why you put so many in the campaign setting in the first place."

At the reminder of his ripping me off, I paused. "I really should have read the entirety of the books. But yeah, I'm here to get you to stop hurting the kobolds and recover the Orb of Creation. How the hell did you get that anyway?"

"Wouldn't you like to know?" Dave repeated. "And I'm not saying!"

I stared at him. "I'm sorry, Dave. Okay, sorry, not sorry. I'm going to have to kill you for all of this crap."

"Haha," Dave laughed at me. "Gary, for all your pretensions of godhood, you've lost all the magical artifacts that made you terrifying. Hell, you created Dungeon magic and aren't twentieth level! Why even play if you don't min/max?"

"If I had to explain it to you, Dave, you wouldn't get it," I said. "However, what makes me dangerous is not my toys but what I do with them."

Mandy giggled.

"Oh, grow up," I said to her, making a secret hand gesture to the kobolds.

Dave raised his hands. "Prepare for your doom, Merciless! I shall send you to the Nine Hells to be eternally poked by the tentacles of Asmodeus!"

That was when Potluck and Gary XII grabbed Dave from behind and shoved his hood down over his face. I walked over and grabbed the Orb of Creation from around his neck. Dave pulled back his hood and stared at me as I held the orb in my hands.

"Pick Pocket levels," I said.

"Ah dangit," Dave muttered.

"Praise be to the Great Gary!" Potluck said, lifting a tiny tankard that was full of light beer. Apparently, that was just the right amount of alcohol for kobolds.

"Praise be to the Wolf Queen and Vampire Queen!" the other kobolds added.

The kobolds held a festival in my backyard with roasted minotaur and large amounts of canned fruit on the buffet. The song "Brand New Day" from *The Wiz* was being played by Gary XII, who was serving as DJ. They were swimming around the pool and had already built a demon head-shaped entrance to their dungeon. It was, notably, very similar to an iconic statue from *The Tomb of Horrors*.

Standing next to the dungeon entrance was the stone form of the Dark Undermaster, having been turned into statuary by

331

the Orb of Creation. I'd used the object to transform him but hadn't been able to use it to affect any of the kobolds. Apparently, after a time, it became their true form and there were already plenty who'd been born like this. Dungeonpunk World was the true face of their homeland, for better or worse.

Cindy had a paper plate full of minotaur ribs and I tried not to look disgusted. "Okay, I'm starting to get used to these guys. As long as they don't mushroom farm in the house and stay out of sight, they can stay."

"That's very sweet," I said, making notes on a yellow pad about my religion. Banning human and kobold sacrifice were notes one and two. I added "Do not leave your crap in the house" as note three. I decided to underscore that I meant literal crap because I didn't want some kobold rabbis debating the metaphorical nature of the subject for future generations.

"I can't believe you're eating that," Mandy said, sighing, as a group of kobolds dressed as Goths followed her around. They'd covered themselves in flour, sharpened their canines, and wore lots of black leather. Apparently, Mandy had inspired a youth movement.

"Werewolf," Cindy said, shrugging. "Besides, I don't give you crap about your diet."

Mandy rolled her eyes. "So, I guess we're stuck with the cast of *Gremlins*."

I shrugged and smirked. "Who else would worship me?"

Bonus Short story: "Merciless Versus Hitler"

A Supervillainy Saga Side Story

By C. T. Phipps

Chapter One
Having Lunch While Discussing Paradoxes

So, I was sitting in a Super Pizza booth across from my two adult daughters from the future, Leia and Mindy "Mimi" Karkofsky, AKA Gizmo the Girl Genius and Ms. Terri, the Mystery Woman. Yeah, wow, that was an opening sentence. Kind of tells you everything you need to know about the kind of world I live in, doesn't it? Honestly, as a supervillain I was tame, but that didn't mean I didn't have the same level of crazy going on in my life that other Supers did.

Anyway, my adult daughters' adolescent selves were playing arcade games over to the side of the pizzeria. Also present were my vampire wife Mandy Karkofsky AKA Nighthuntress, and my werewolf girlfriend Cindy Wakowski AKA Red Riding Hood. If you're wondering about the relationship dynamics, understand that Supers tended to be slightly more open about these things than regular mortals. You learned to adapt after the fifth clone or resurrection.

Super Pizza was a franchise I owned thanks to careful investment and management of my ill-gotten gains. It was also the tackiest place on Earth, at least for a reasonable family night price range. The staff dressed in discount Halloween costumes, and memorabilia from superhero fights covered every available surface. The food was basically just Pizza Hut rip-offs and the music was perpetual Eighties hits. There were also seventeen thousand restaurants and growing.

"So," I said, sipping my drink while addressing the adult versions of my daughters. "Do you two have any plans for college?"

Leia looked a lot like her mother, Cindy, except with platinum blonde hair instead of red. She was wearing a leather tracksuit covered in Tron lines, with a glowing time cube hovering over her shoulder. "Gizmo" was written in stylized lettering on her costume's right side. It wasn't the laziest superheroine branding I'd ever seen, but that was because her sister was even worse at it.

Mimi, dressed in blue jeans and a hooded sports jersey with a big "U"—possibly the laziest superhero costume of all time— was sipping her fourteenth Mountain Drew through a straw. Which meant she had a super-metabolism or was deeply addicted to sugar.

Mimi was a brown-skinned girl who looked a lot like her mother, Gabrielle Anders AKA Ultragoddess, which meant she looked like an MMA fighter that somehow also modeled. It also meant, yes, I had another girlfriend. But, if it's any consolation, she had two space husbands as well a boyfriend in the future.

Sitting to my left was Cindy, a pale-skinned redhead who continued what was now turning into a family tradition of lazy costume design with her store-bought outfit and picnic basket.

To my right was Mandy. She was a Eurasian woman who dressed like she'd been cast in the Wakowski sisters' newest installment of *The Matrix*. Mandy wasn't eating since, well, vampire. The fact she'd showed up despite the preponderance of garlic was also a point in her favor. Still, I had to admit we looked more like employees than customers.

Perhaps I shouldn't have been one to condemn their costume choices because I had a hooded black robe like a Sith Lord and that was it. I had the excuse it was the source of my powers, though. For I was Merciless: The Supervillain Without Mercy™ and Master of the Redundant Codename (that I gave props to Ms. Teri the Mystery Woman for continuing the tradition of). I had no idea why my daughters had invited me to meet them here, but I suspected it was the usual cosmic threats that time travelers were always warning us of.

Wow, I'd become jaded.

"We don't have colleges in the future," Mimi said, scarfing down four slices of Meat Glutton w/Stuffed Crust pizza in rapid succession. "All data is downloaded directly to our brains through virtual reality interfaces."

"Really?" I asked, glad to see the future had gotten around the flaws of our present-day education system.

"Nope," Mimi said. "I have a three-point-five GPA and am heavily in student loan debt. My father apparently wanted me to work my way through college."

"What an asshole," I said, knowing I was insulting myself. "What's the point of being rich if you can't spoil your children rotten?"

Supervillains generally came in two varieties in terms of resources: poor guys who robbed banks whenever they had cash flow problems, and Bond villains. I had started as the former but now was closer to the latter. It turned out that once you gained access to a billion dollars in stolen Nazi gold or evil cult money you were pretty much immune to having it taken away.

You also couldn't stay in prison for more than a couple of days. Society was designed around protecting the rich. I condemned that inequity and used it to justify my crime sprees while shamelessly taking advantage of it. At least I hadn't started donating to politicians to avoid paying taxes. I had some standards.

"I like younger you," Mimi said, smiling.

"Dad, we need you to be serious," Leia said, blinking rapidly "This is important."

"Asking your father to be serious is a bit like asking the elephant in the corner to stay still," Mandy said, shrugging. "Not only will he not understand it, but it will almost certainly result in the opposite."

A waitress dressed like Guinevere, the Champion of Camelot, brought us our second round of pizzas. All Supers had huge appetites, don't ask me why. Maybe it was where the eye blast energy came from instead of an alternate dimension. Her costume was the gold armor version that, for whatever reason, looked like a one-piece swimsuit with a cape and crown. "Is there anything else I can get you?"

"Probably more unclean animal for my daughter," I replied. "Everything non-kosher and lots of it."

The waitress rolled her eyes.

"Gentile meat," Mimi said. "Mmm."

Yes, we were a family of Jewish superheroes and villains. What of it? "Oh, and could I have some more cheese sticks?"

"Sure!" the waitress said, cheerfully, before heading off.

Mandy followed her with her eyes, her fangs sticking out as she did so.

"No eating the staff at Super Pizza," I replied. "We own this franchise and have a policy of not terrorizing our employees."

"But her veins are so nice!" Mandy said.

"We'll pick up someone on the way back," Cindy said. "Promise."

Mandy pouted. "Fine. I'm just saying if I'd known you were going out to eat, I would have grabbed a mugger or rapist on my way over here."

"There's a shortage of those in town thanks to you," I replied. "We'll have to start importing them from other cities."

Mandy smiled at the prospect.

My daughters grimaced. They were closer to the superhero side of the spectrum than villain. Where did I go wrong raising them?

"So, now that I've horrified you," I said, nodding to them, "what is it you guys want?"

Mimi and Leia exchanged a guilty look.

"It's complicated," Mimi said.

"Well, I guessed that since normal people rarely have their children break the laws of causality in order to visit," I replied. "I get that time travel is a thing in the future, but I don't think people are supposed to use it as casually as you two."

"Agreed," Cindy said. "Whenever children come from the future to talk to their superhero parents in the past, it's always a sign a series is on its last legs. Let's be honest, *Sailor Moon* was never the same after it happened."

Everyone stared at her blankly. I was, of course, just pretending I didn't know what she was talking about. I mean, what sort of forty-year-old nerd admitted to still getting anime references? I mean, aside from half my audience.

"What? Am I the only classic anime fan here?" Cindy asked.

Everyone continued to look confused.

"Gary, I know you're lying," Cindy said, crossing her arms. "We watched the Anime Power Hour every weekend with Billy in high school. You know, before he was killed by Big Ben's giant condor. God, growing up in Falconcrest City sucked. It was the only town in America where the school paper had obituaries."

"What is this anime you speak of?" I asked, waving my hands around confusedly. "I have never heard of this thing."

Cindy shook her head. "You have betrayed your nerd brothers and sisters."

"Clearly, my asking you to be serious was a stupid idea," Leia replied, looking like she was getting a stress headache.

"That's what I said," Mandy replied.

I gave a dismissive wave. "Come on guys, out with it."

Mimi sucked in her breath. "We want you to break time."

I suspected this was going to be what this was all about. There was another thing I knew about my future daughters and that was they were both time cops. Having children in law enforcement was a source of great shame but I sucked it up for the unity of the family. Unfortunately, they were dirty time cops and that just made it worse. Basically, they constantly came to me to make little adjustments to the time stream to, I dunno, prevent the end of humanity or other silly things like that. Apparently, it wasn't breaking the rules when I did it instead of them. I was quite sick of being their deniable asset.

"Which sounds a lot more dramatic than it is," Leia said, faking a smile. "Really, time is a hardier thing than it sounds like because it's also space and—"

"Nope," I said, picking up a slice of pizza. "Not happening."

"What?" Mimi said, stunned.

I leaned back to talk to Mandy. "Hey, remember when we used to rob banks?"

"Not really," Mandy said, poking at her salad. "Your third outing as a supervillain was a jailbreak on a moon base. I ended up having to defend Falconcrest City from a zombie apocalypse since if everyone was dead then there'd be no one to rob."

Sadly, she wasn't even exaggerating. I looked over at my henchwench. "Hey, Cindy, you want to rob banks instead of dealing with time travel?"

"You know it," Cindy said, cheerfully. "I need to go down to some nice crime-ridden city with an overworked vigilante who I can make myself the archenemy of. I'll hire myself some new henchmen, rent out an abandoned amusement park, and build myself some death traps. Get back to some old school supervillainy."

"Gary, hear them out," Mandy said, staring at me with her cold, predatory eyes.

I stared at her. "Are you trying to do that vampire mind control gaze thing?"

Mandy looked away. "Uh, no I wasn't."

"You totally were!" I said, horrified. "What have we said about mind control in this house?"

"Only when it's funny!" Cindy said, defending me.

I crossed my arms and turned my attention back to my adult daughters. "Listen, I love you both and I'm anxiously looking forward to raising you. However, I just got finished fighting a martial arts tournament against an evil space wizard god. I saved the multiverse. The entire multiverse—"

"Seriously, Gary, how long are you going to milk that?" Mandy asked, leaning back in her chair.

"Awhile!" I snapped.

"Dad, this is something that I'm sure you will be okay with," Mimi said, looking at me. "You won't have any moral objections to it."

"If your primary concern is my moral objections then you already have seriously misread me," I replied. "Supervillain."

"Eh," Cindy said, waving her palm back and forth. "You're kind of the Diet Coke of evil to quote Doctor Evil. The Lite Beer of Murder."

"I am not the Lite Beer of Murder! I kill lots of people!" I said, horrified.

"Yeah, but bad people," Cindy said. "That's not even bad. You're like Mandy."

"Yes," Mandy said, once more eyeing the waitress. "I kill bad people and just feed on regular succulent mortals."

I snapped my fingers in front of Mandy. "Over here."

"Hmm?" Mandy asked.

"How about you feed on me and Cindy," I asked. "Guilt free eating."

"It's a weight loss plan I can get behind," Cindy said. "A liquid diet that actually works. You know, if it doesn't kill you."

"Fine," Mandy said. "I don't know why you won't let me eat the waitress, though."

"She's seventeen," I said. "I actually know her mom."

"Oh shit," Mandy said, horrified. "Never mind then."

"You're supposed to be eighteen or older for this place," I replied. "I am going to have to talk to Sal the Fish about his hiring practices."

"Sal the Fish?" Cindy asked.

"Yeah, he's the manager," I said.

"Why is he called Sal the Fish?" Cindy asked.

"Because he's a giant floating psychic fish," I replied.

Cindy stared. "Only in Falconcrest City. Well, Falconcrest City or Atlantis."

Leia's stress headache looked like it was getting worse listening to us. "I can literally feel myself getting stupider the more I'm around my parents when we were young."

"I wonder if this is how Marty McFly felt," Mimi said, patting her sister on the back.

"No, he found out his dad was a pervert," Cindy replied. "Also, is it weird that they hired Biff to work for them in the new timeline? I mean, Biff is an attempted rapist."

"You know, I never thought about that," I replied. "If they'd just gotten that jackass arrested then they'd never have to deal with Hell Valley in the second movie either."

"I wouldn't count on it," Cindy said. "It was the Fifties, and he was a white dude. Hell, even today—"

"Gary, we need you to kill Hitler," Mimi said.

There was silence at the table.

I blinked. "Well, why didn't you say so?"

Cindy breathed out a sigh of relief. "Man, I thought you were going to ask for something difficult. Hell, I want in on that action."

"Me too," Mandy said. "Nazis are guilt-free eating. World War Two is going to be like a Chinese buffet."

"Not what I would be worried about but yes, I imagine it would be," I replied, shaking my head. "Okay. This is entirely okay by me. I've killed dozens of Hitlers over the years. It's why I'm considered a time criminal and yet no one really blames me for it."

Once I acquired my time machine, I'd discovered it led to alternate realities whenever I attempted to change the past. I'd killed Hitler multiple times before figuring it out. Then I kept doing it because fuck Hitler. It had somewhat mixed results. You see, Hitler was a moron. Strategically so bad at winning the war—partially due to believing his own press and being high as a kite most of the time—that the British had avoided assassinating him because they wanted him driving the German war machine into the ground. In the universes I did kill Adolf, that led to people like Tom Terror and General Omega taking over in his place. People who, for example, knew to equip their armies invading Russia with winter coats. That had taken quite a bit of sorting out and dampened my enthusiasm for extrajudicial Fuhrer murder.

But not by much.

"It's a bit more complicated than that," Mimi said. "Otherwise, we would have handled it ourselves."

"I mean, who gives up a chance to kill Hitler?" Leia said. "It's the one time I would totally kill a baby."

Mimi elbowed her sister. "Not that we would."

"Except I totally would," Leia said.

Mimi facepalmed. "We just need to know we can count on you, Dad. The Time Police have failed in all our efforts with this mission, and they've issued a Wells directive. That means that we're authorized to do anything and everything to stop this time paradox from reaching fruition."

My daughters had my full attention. As much as I loved to goof off, ignore danger, and play down every possible issue I ran into, I did have a serious side. It was well hidden and often required vast amounts of effort to find, but it existed.

I blinked. "What's so bad about—okay that was not the right way to begin this sentence—this Hitler?"

Mimi sucked in her breath. "In short?"

"He's a god," Leia said. "We need you to kill the God of Earth-Nazi."

Chapter Two
Where I Go to Earth-Nazi to Kick Its Ass

"Earth-Nazi?" I asked, looking at my daughters. "You must have spent a lot of time on that name, huh?"

Mimi stared at me. "It's succinct and to the point."

"It does give an impression of an Earth ruled by Nazis," Cindy said. "I'm not gonna lie."

"More than that," Leia said, a disgusted look on her face. "Once its version of Hitler acquires the Omegaforce, he proceeds to launch a war of conquest not only on Earth but on all the inhabited planets of the galaxy. It becomes a fascist-run universe which exterminates all life that doesn't come from their clone vats and brainwashing centers."

"So, they become Daleks," I replied.

"Shhh," Cindy said, leaning in. "You don't want to get the BBC's copyright lawyers on our ass. I don't mind fighting Nazis, but those guys are scary."

"Yes, like Daleks and *Warhammer 40K* plus all the other horrible fascist dystopias combined into one horrifying super one," Mimi replied.

"Not good," I said. "Mind you, I find it difficult to believe the Nazis could last more than a couple of decades. They're good at smashing shit but crap at running things. It's like all those realities where the Confederacy wins. The place falls apart before 1870."

"This reality only succeeds where the others fail due to the fact its Fuhrer manages to steal the Crown of the Gods," Mimi explained.

"What's that do?" Cindy asked.

"Makes him king of the gods," I said. "There's not really a story there."

"Except for Hitler becoming ruler of the gods," I replied. "Which is bad."

"You don't say!" Cindy said, sarcastically. "I never would have guessed!"

I knew this story. "Way back in 1945, Hitler escaped the prison Ultragod put him and Stalin in. Hitler joined up with General Omega and a bunch of aliens to rebuild the Third Reich for another round of genocide. They journeyed to Castle Lupindorf—"

"Legally distinct from Castle Wolfenstein," Cindy quickly interjected.

"—and attempted to harness the power of the Crown of the Gods. It was there because Odin persuaded the gods of Earth to all give their power over to him to stop the Great Beasts."

"Except Loki stole it," Mandy said, knowing the classic story. "Only to be killed by the Fuhrer. In our world, the Society of Superheroes of that time managed to steal the Crown of the Gods back, then banish the Great Beasts from this dimension. Ultragod proceeded to destroy the crown in the end because no one should have that kind of power."

"Amazing! Comics number fifteen," I replied. "An issue costs two hundred thousand dollars at auction. I have three copies."

"What a wonderful use of our money," Cindy said, rolling her eyes.

"They're collectibles!" I raised my hand. "They'll be worth even more in the future!"

"On Earth-Nazi," Leia said, sucking in her breath, "Ultragod and the other Golden Age heroes failed to get the Crown of the Gods from Adolf. So, he merged with the Great Beasts and rewrote reality so that his followers always won. No one could overthrow them or cause their insane system to collapse. It was genocide on an unparalleled scale."

"Why not just go back in time and stop him?" Cindy asked. "Which I know is what you're advocating for Gary to do, I just don't know why it isn't simple. Even if you're not in the baby-killing business—"

"Which I totally am," Leia interjected. "Nazi babies."

Cindy looked a little disturbed by her daughter but shook her head. "You could just shoot him on the crapper, to quote Scott Evil." Cindy paused, something obviously dawning on her. "Huh, the Evils are a fountain of useful supervillain advice."

"It's not that simple," Mimi replied. "Demon King Hitler—"

"Are we really calling him that?" I asked.

"If the shoe fits," Mimi said. "Demon King Hitler controls the timeline of that reality so all attempts to stop him fail retroactively. The gods and cosmic beings of other timelines thought the situation to be so bad that they quarantined the timeline. Except the hatred and evil eventually grow so powerful that they will break forth and spill into other realities."

"Which is bad," I said.

"I mean, Space Nazis invading other realities is bad, yes," Mimi said. "There'll be Death Stars, Daleks, Space Marines, and zombie cyborgs."

"That would be awesome if it wasn't fascist," Cindy said. "You're telling me they'll take over everything in the Multiverse."

"Not even close," Mimi said. "The fascists will get crushed until eventually all the forces of the surrounding timelines obliterate that reality. That's going to be a huge multiversal time war, though, and I'd like to prevent that. There's one possible way according to my superiors."

"Prayer?" Mandy asked.

"Doctor Who?" Cindy asked. "No wait, he refused to wipe out the Daleks in 'Genesis of the Daleks.' Dumbass."

"His name is the Doctor not Doctor Who," I replied. "Fandom point!"

"This is why I only sleep with you every other night," Cindy said. "Think on that."

Both our adult children looked disgusted.

Mimi was the first to shake her mind clean of the idea of her father having sex. "Dad is the Champion of Death and technically a divinity according to the cosmic laws of reality."

"Like on a scale of one to one hundred million, he's a one, maybe a two," Leia said. "But he is a death god. A really, really tiny, miniscule death—"

"They get the idea," I interrupted.

Cindy and Mandy both grinned.

"Well, as I was saying, there's an equally tiny and miniscule chance that Gary can kill Demon King Hitler," Leia said. "As Death's Champion, he is theoretically able to kill anything. Perhaps even things that think themselves immortal."

"Theoretically," I said.

Leia grimaced. "Yeah. Plus, as a god, Dad can kill other gods. Theoretically."

"I'm loving this plan," I said, sarcastically. "So, what happens if I can't do exactly what you think I can do?"

"You'll die horribly and be unable to be resurrected because your soul will be trapped in the reality that gets wiped out of existence," Mimi explained. "Oh, and Nazis will pour forth over this reality and others until enough die that Demon King Hitler—"

"Can we call him Ted instead?" I interrupted.

"Until Ted is weakened enough to be unmade," Mimi said. "That'll probably be trillions of people on both sides."

"Do we get a do-over if I fail?" I asked.

Mimi shook her head. "The time police only have enough cosmic energy for one try."

"Super!" I said, lifting my Mountain Dew. "I'm going to need a personal concert from Patty Smyth, a guest starring role in *Star Trek: The Original Series*, and for Billy Idol's *Cyberpunk* album to be remade not to suck."

"Done, done, and done," Leia said. "Thanks, Dad."

"You're bargaining to kill Hitler?" Mandy asked, stunned.

"If you're good at something, never do it for free," I replied. "I heard that from another reality's movie about superheroes. It's good advice, either way. I'm also very good at killing Nazis."

"I'll get the time portal ready," Mimi said, standing up and exiting the room.

"I'm coming with you," Cindy said.

"You won't be able to kill Ted," I replied. "Apparently, I'm the only super-special Rand al'Thor pony who can kill the Dark One."

"No *Wheel of Time* references," Cindy replied. "We agreed on that. If you're putting down *Sailor Moon*, I'm putting down that series. Besides, you're not going to be facing just Nazis at Castle Lupindorf. They have aliens, werewolves, vampires, robots, and zombies. There's going to be crap ton of regular soldiers and if you get shot, you die."

"I'm able to survive a couple of bullets," I replied. "Usually, I just turn insubstantial."

I had the powers of a ghost with my magic cloak, also the power to throw fire, lightning, and ice like a *Final Fantasy* wizard.

"Yes, which won't help against poison gas," Cindy said.

"Or magic," Mandy said. "I'm with you too, Gary."

"Alright," I said, cheerfully. "Then we'll all die horribly together!"

That should have been the end of it, but life didn't function like a movie, and it ended up being about half an hour until the time portal was set up in the back of the pizzeria. The waitress got a little annoyed at our continued presence until Sal the Fish floated over to point out that I owned the restaurant. Well, I owned the restaurant as well as the Super Pizza franchise along with Super Cola and a bunch of other businesses that were mainstays of the American exploited working-class diet. I left a tip of paying off her college fund and headed out back when Mimi finally called us to go.

"So, we're going now?" Cindy asked, walking behind me through the kitchen.

"No time like the present," I said. "To go to the past. Well, an alternate past that led to a dystopian hellscape parallel universe."

"It bothers me I understood every word of that," Cindy replied.

"Too much *Star Trek*," Mandy replied, accompanying us. "I much prefer *The Lord of the Rings*."

"It's apples and orange juice," I replied. "Also, I'm not interested in fandom wars."

"Pfft!" Mandy and Cindy said simultaneously before we reached the back of the restaurant and headed into the alleyway beyond.

"Are you really discussing fandom when the fate of millions is at stake?" Leia said, standing in front of a glowing purple doorway that crackled with strange energies. Mimi was beside her, holding a small calculator-sized device that I swear was a prop from Quantum Leap.

"Yes," I said, staring at them. "Yes, we are."

"We're about to fight in the last battle of World War Two," Cindy said. "Probably going to die horribly trying to do something good. All for no payment other than Gary's inane requests."

"I'm inviting you to see Patty Smyth with me," I replied.

"We're billionaires! We can just hire her!" Cindy snapped. "Or kidnap her!"

"You can drop out, Cindy," I replied. "Someone will have to raise our kids if Mandy and I are dead."

"I'll go then," Cindy said. "Not that I don't love them, but the prospect of being a single mother is horrifying."

Both the younger versions of Mimi and Leia came out behind us, having been listening to the whole business of our insane plan to kill Ted while playing their arcade games. Neither of them said anything as I gave them both a hug. This was far from the only suicide mission I'd been on in my strange career and yet I'd always returned alive. They had faith in me even if I was secretly terrified every time.

"Don't get killed, Dad," Adult Leia said. "You too, Moms."

"I hate when you call me that," Mandy said.

"Ditto," Cindy said.

"You *are* my mom!" Leia said.

"Oh right!" Cindy said. "Sorry."

Leia rolled her eyes. "The portal won't stay stable much longer."

"How do we get back?" I asked.

"If Demon King...Ted," Mimi corrected herself, "is killed then nothing will stop us from being able to retrieve you. If not, you're probably dead."

I nodded. I expected nothing less. "Then I guess it's time to fight."

I made a running charge into the portal and emerged to a sight that defied description. What followed was something that threatened to drive me to my knees in the first few moments of adjustment. I had seen some wild things in my time and more than my fair share of death. However, being dumped into the Battle of Castle Lupindorf was something that still resulted in me being momentarily stunned.

Caste Lupindorf was an enormous, towering creation that resembled a Dark Lord's castle from fantasy art versus anything I'd seen constructed by medieval artisans. The towers were like skyscrapers, the walls covered in anti-aircraft guns and enormous banners showing the Nazi war flag with the swastika replaced by an Omega symbol.

Castle Lupindorf had been constructed by General Omega, a time-travelling jackass from the future who thought that his present was so boring that going back to help the Nazis win the war was a valid use of his time. He'd pretty much kept the Nazis chugging along when America had Ultragod able to leap tall buildings with a running start or the Nightwalker's dark wizard detective schtick.

Either way, my surroundings were like a reproduction of the opening scene of Saving Private Ryan except they involved Nazi robots, zombies, gasmask-wearing mooks, and demon hordes summoned from portals all around me. The SS's Occult and Eldritch Science Division were throwing everything they had left to delay the Allies from reaching their masters before they'd successfully absorbed the power of Earth's gods.

Standing against this living *Call of Duty* level was a collection of America, Britain, France, and the Soviet Union's finest, plus resistance forces collected from just about everywhere. Most of them were normal folk—among them my grandfather according to family legend—who were fully committed to seeing if the weaknesses of demons included bullets. Given they seemed to be tearing apart the monsters, it looked like it was so. Many superheroes of the time were among the people there, but it was the muggles carrying the day, if you don't mind a gratuitous Harry Potter reference.

Historically, this had been one of the most famous battles of WW2's final days. The Nazis had pulled back every single weird invention, insane idea, and superhuman they'd created with their foul experiments to prepare to murder everyone in Europe. When the forces of Good had finally killed the last of the insane fanatics defending this place, they'd found enough poison gas and prototype planes to murder everyone from Berlin to Paris. Mind you, they hadn't had enough to get the very vengeance-minded Russians too, but, again, the Nazis sucked in their planning.

Seeing the sheer amount of carnage and murder going on, I wondered perhaps for the first time whether I was up to the task. Killing was nothing that bothered me, I was the Champion of Death and probably possessed of numerous issues a psychologist might call "insane". But this was one conflict I felt unworthy of joining. Parallel universe or not, these were the people who had originally defeated fascism.

Then one of the Nazi officer's shot me in the shoulder. It stung. Glaring, I snapped my fingers and incinerated him before starting to fry more Nazis. That hopefully told the Allies I was on their side. Which was good because I'd hate to accidentally kill my granddad here.

Cindy and Mandy arrived soon behind me, Cindy turning into a werewolf and tearing through a Nazi in power armor like it was made of tissue paper.

"You think we should have covered ourselves in flags or something?" Cindy asked, covered in gore.

Mandy chowed down on a German private as he screamed, tearing his throat out. Gulping down the blood, she looked up. "It occurs to me that vampires, werewolves, and evil wizards may be viewed as the bad guys in this time."

"Ridiculous!" I said, melting a Nazi mecha that looked like someone had fused a Gundam with a tank.

351

That was when the glowing form of Ultragod jumped down in front of me before delivering a glowing punch to my face.

Chapter Three
Fighting with Golden Age of Superheroes

"Take that, evil doer!" Moses Anders, aka Ultragod, shouted in a deep heroic Keith David-esque voice.

If you're a criminal on my Earth then—provided you stay free long enough—you're likely to have been punched in the face by Ultragod. He is the greatest of all superheroes, empowered by the Ultra-Force, solver of racism, and possessed of one hundred years of ass-kicking behind him. Sure, he was presently dead, but I was hoping that would be solved in the not-so-distant future.

I had nothing but respect for Ultragod despite being a supervillain. Part of that was due to having a kid with his daughter and him not tossing me into the sun. Here, now, he was still in the early years of his career with that horrible gold and white leotard and wearing a headband. He also looked angry all the time, which given the conditions for even a superpowered black man in the 1940s, I didn't blame him one bit. He was a monument of muscle, though, and surrounded in a crackling ball of otherworldly energy with truth and right on his side.

Thus, it confused me that with actual Nazis nearby, he chose to come down and punch me of all people. It was doubly problematic because my whole plan, if you could call it that, was to carve a swath through the Third Reich's soldiers here to make a path for Ultragod. If he was stopping to fight me then that just bought more time for Hitler—hereafter referred to as Lord Dumbass—to claim the Crown of the Gods. Hell, if it was a stable time loop then any delay here could be what caused the end of this reality in the first place. Wow, if that was the case then my family would never let me hear the end of it.

"I'm on your side, goddammit!" I snapped as I rolled around on the ground past a bunch of dead Nazis. Normally a good thing.

Ultragod posed dramatically, which made me think he wasn't quite the paragon of virtue he would later become. After all, his fellow Americans were dying around him. "Don't lie to me, Ratzi, you're wearing black and traveling with a werewolf and a vampire! Those are marks of pure evil!"

I almost shouted, "You're black!" But instead, I contemplated that I was dealing with the Golden Age of Superheroes where things were, for lack of a better term, blacker and whiter than they would be in other times. This was a time when heroes killed gangsters and fascists both with impunity. There was no room for supernatural heroes like Mandy, Cindy, and me. We were the guys the heroes destroyed.

Unfortunately, before I could figure out what to say to Ultragod, Cindy jumped on his back in her "war form" that was halfway between a wolf and man. I didn't exactly know what she intended to accomplish since even if Ultragod was only a fraction of his future strength, he was still a guy who could leap large structures with a running jump and well as stop speeding vehicles. Wow, there had to be an easier way of saying that.

"I've got him, Gary!" Cindy said, attempting to tear into his invincible flesh with her teeth. The problem with that is, being close to Ultragod's family, I knew the whole "vulnerable to magic" lesson about them was complete crap.

Ultragod responded by flicking her, literally, away with two fingers. "All I know is that I know every mystery man in the Squadron of Superheroes and you're not among them. So, you have to be a bad guy."

"I've been killing Nazis!" I snapped, trying to figure out a way to talk him down. I'd defeated Ultragoddess once when she was mind controlled, so it was within my power, but the problem was I didn't want to do that.

"So have plenty of those vile bastards," Ultragod said, advancing on me. "The Third Reich's supervillains are full of insane berserkers who can barely be controlled. Products of mad science and dark occultism that violate the natural order."

It took every ounce of my willpower to keep from saying something about the natural order not including a guy who could leap large construction in a squatting jump (there had to be a better way of saying that). Ultragod was, after all, a guy who had taken down the KKK and American Bund. He was, in general, not the sort of guy who had much in the way of a sense of humor about his powers.

"Listen, I came back in time from the twenty-first century, well an alternate twenty-first century, to stop Lord Dumbass from getting the Crown of the Gods," I replied. "It allows him to take over this reality and launch an invasion of other ones. We need to stop fighting immediately to get it away from him so we can save uncounted trillions from following the world's stupidest ideology."

Okay, that sounded ridiculous even to me. Ultragod also wasn't paying attention either as he reached me, grabbed me by the throat with one hand, and lifted me in the air. I'd survived his first punch because I had some pretty effective resistance to being pummeled as part of my powers but a full strike with all of Ultragod's powers would take my head clean off.

"Prepare to die, fiend!" Ultragod said dramatically.

"Wait, I know how to prove myself!" I said, holding up my hands then making the Vulcan salute. "Shalom."

Ultragod blinked then dropped me. "Okay then."

I landed on the ground on top of an SS officer's corpse. "Really? That's all it took?"

"No Nazi super soldier would admit to being Jewish," Ultragod said. "Now let's kick some Nazi ass, fellow Ally!"

I was more confused than enlightened by his reaction but decided not to look a gift horse in the mouth, particularly when he was the most powerful superhero in the world. As a result, I proceeded to look over at Cindy who was making a tasty meal out of a corrupted Valkyrie, then turned on the remaining Nazi horde.

"Excelsior!" I shouted, before throwing lighting, fire, and ice at the hordes of the undead. They were the three basic black magic types according to Dungeons and Dragons. I wasn't sure how much good I was doing compared to all the other people giving their lives to fight the Huns, but I hoped I would be able to save some of the lives of the brave men fighting here today. Assuming I didn't fail and get this entire universe killed with the few minutes of Ultragod's time that I'd wasted.

I didn't see any sign of Mandy, but Ultragod punched out the carnivorous plesiosaurus in the castle moat and I headed into the castle. I found a large number of undead Nazi troopers torn to shreds in a fashion similar to Mandy's claws. What followed was the biggest monster bash I'd ever seen since the time I went through *Castlevania* in Video Game World with Lara Croft. Long story, but the gal is a helluva kisser.

If what I'd seen outside was gonzo, it was harder to describe the running fight that met me on the inside of Castle Lupindorf. Just a short summary of the things I encountered would fill multiple books with Frankenstein's monsters, mummies, dark elves, alien lizard people, spider-tanks, and various costumed saboteurs that had menaced the Allies for the past decade. There were even a few Japanese villains joining the fray. I barely recognized them because, no shit, they didn't look anything the caricatures of them I'd read about in my grandfather's historical comics.

I probably killed more people in the next fifteen to twenty minutes than I had in my entire career thus far as Merciless: The Supervillain without Mercy™. I didn't regret it; they were fascists, and we were on a literal save the universe countdown. Still, it was something to see Ultragod brutally blast, crush, kill, and destroy everything in his path. I knew the Golden Age heroes had very different attitudes towards killing but it was still something to see the world's most beloved hero tearing his way through what technically qualified as human beings the way he was.

"I'm with the Wehrmacht!" one guy said, throwing down his machine gun when he realized that it wasn't working on Ultragod.

Ultragod incinerated him with one blast of Ultra-Force. "Still, a Nazi."

"Not that I disagree with the sentiment," I said, looking at him. "Not a fan of Wehrmacht apologia in the slightest. But killing a surrendering soldier doesn't seem like you."

Ultragod stared at me, his face barely containing his fury. "And how do I seem, stranger?"

"Like me, Gary Karkofsky, aka Merciless," I said, looking for someone to interrogate about Lord Dumbass' location. The problem was that we hadn't left many people alive to do so. Which was the only time I'd ever mourn the death of a Ratzi, as Ultragod had so succinctly put it.

"Not a very superhero-esque name," Ultragod said.

"Yes, well, Gary is what my parents named me so what can you do?" I said, dodging his question. I wasn't about to try to explain to him that in the future I was a supervillain that wasn't so bad. Sort of like an anti-villain. I felt that was a bit more nuance than this time was ready for.

"I get it, you're Russian," Ultragod said, finally calming down. "They hate the Nazis too."

"Polish American, actually," I said, trying to figure out how to reassure him. "Listen, I don't have a right to lecture you on how the world is or isn't going to change."

"You're right, you don't," Ultragod said. "I had to fight to get on this mission. The Army hates using me. If not for Roosevelt, I would have been left providing support back in the United States. I could have ended this war—almost did—if they'd just let me."

I didn't bother asking why that was. It was obvious. "Well, you're here now."

"I just don't know if anything is ever going to get better," Ultragod said, muttering under his breath. If it was directed at me, he gave no sign of it.

I paused. "Listen, I'm not the kind of guy who can give you advice on your situation. My experiences are completely different."

"No shit," Ultragod said.

"Ultragod swears!" I said, putting my hand over my heart in mock outrage. "I am stunned."

"I take it my reputation is not as a scary radical?" Ultragod asked, sounding almost disappointed.

"No," I said. "But you do make things better. You, personally."

"For whom?" Ultragod asked.

"Everybody," I said. "Including, admittedly, a lot of jerks who don't deserve it."

Ultragod gave a half-smile. "Let's go find, what did you call him, Lord Dumbass?"

I nodded. "It seems a more accurate title to what the idjit accomplished."

"Well at least he'll be forgotten and no one flying the swastika in the twenty-first century."

"Only a bunch of basement-dwelling cosplayers and terminally out of touch terrorists," I said.

Much to my surprise, Mandy and a human-form Cindy arrived seconds later, both positively bathed in gore like they'd just escaped a Quentin Tarantino movie. Well, given this was close to the plot of *Inglorious Bastards 2*, it might actually be an accurate description.

"Where the hell have you guys been?" Cindy said, pulling an ear out of her hair. "We've been looking everywhere for you."

"Looking for Lord Dumbass!" I said, pausing. "I swear, you'd think a giant castle full of monsters would be easier to navigate. He could be anywhere."

"Did you consider the bunker in the basement?" Cindy asked. "You know, where he died in real life?"

I stared at her then grimaced. "Mother pus bucket."

Ultragod looked at me and shook his head. "You're not very good at this, are you?"

"I'm very good at killing Hitlers!" I said, throwing my hands in the air. "I'm just not doing very well this one time."

"When it matters most," Cindy muttered, rolling her eyes. "So disappointing."

"I don't suppose you can get us to the basement quickly?" Mandy asked Ultragod.

"I don't need your help," Ultragod said, looking between the three of us. "I'll take care of this."

With that, Ultragod grabbed his cape and wrapped it around himself before spinning around like a top. He drilled through the floor and the floor beneath that until there was a series of holes leading down into the castle depths.

"Huh," Cindy said, looking down. "I thought that was just something Ultragod could do in the old Hannah Barbara cartoons."

"Do you think he can handle it?" Mandy asked.

"I think it's not something we should leave to chance," I replied, looking down. "What with this entire universe depending on us."

I didn't want to admit that I was worried that I'd slowed down Ultragod with my attempts to help. I could feel the rage bubbling within him and could only imagine what had triggered him. Not just the racism and xenophobia he'd experienced in America but the kind of horrors he'd likely seen in the European and Pacific theaters. If I'd stumbled upon what the Nazis did without foreknowledge, I probably would want to burn all of Germany down.

"Well, we better get down there," Cindy said, preparing to descend into the hole.

"Take my hands," I said to both.

They did so with only the slightest bit of reluctance. It was rare that my plans ended in complete disaster, but they tended to be "bumpy" to say the least. This was something I'd done before, though, and didn't foresee it causing any problems. Well, beyond the fact I was going to be leading the charge—or following it up technically—into the heart of the lair of history's biggest jerk.

Either way, the three of us began levitating down through the floor of Castle Lupindorf. We kept going for what felt like a mile into the dark corners of the Earth. I would have questioned how the Nazis built it so deep, but I figured the answer was probably borrowed alien technology. It said something about the Third Reich that even armed with advanced technology from the Tsavong Empire they'd still managed to botch conquering the world.

Either way, the three of us arrived in the middle of the bunker where Lord Dumbass and the remainder of his cronies were holed up. The place had been a concrete maze of cubicles, maps, flags, and pneumatic tubes to continue the defeated Fuhrer's micromanaging of the war to the bitter end. It was a grand guignol of carnage as every single person huddled down here with him was dead. Hitler's remaining bodyguards had opened with Tsavong energy cannons on Ultragod the moment he'd arrived. Being as he was invulnerable, those had ricocheted and tore through the secretaries and support personnel surrounding them.

"I hope they didn't hurt his doggies," Cindy muttered, looking at the corpse of Hitler's mistress.

"You're worried about them?" Mandy asked as we landed and turned solid.

"It's not their fault that their owner is an ass," Cindy said.

"Hush!" I said, looking around for some sign of Ultragod. It wasn't like he was hard to spot. That was when I heard a crashing noise past a wall with an enormous hole in it. That should have been my first clue that Ultragod had gone that way. Classic Ultragod had never used a door when a more dramatic entrance was available.

Rushing through the man-shaped hole he'd created, I saw the ritual chamber that General Omega and Tom Terror had set up with the remaining members of the Brotherhood of Infamy. It was stock Hollywood Satanism with the pentagram on the floor, robed cultists, and big banners on the wall, with a stone statue dedicated to the Devil.

That was shattered and with good reason since Lord Dumbass had never intended to share power with Lord Scratch. In the original timeline, Ultragod had punched everyone out and shattered the Crown of the Gods. This timeline? Well, this timeline had gone a little differently.

I didn't have to worry about Hitler taking over this reality because Ultragod had blasted everyone with the Ultra-Force until there was nothing but a fine powder where the Inner

C. T. Phipps

Circle of Nazi High Command had once rested, supervillain or normal asshole. If Lord Dumbass was among them, I couldn't tell from all the other shadows burned into the ground accompanied by fine white powders.

No, slightly more concerning was the fact Ultragod was holding the Crown of the Gods over his head with both hands. His eyes were staring into the glowing entwined snakes linked at their base and the awesome power that rested within. It was not the face of a man who planned to forsake ultimate power for the good of all.

"Well, at least he's not Lord Dumbass," I muttered, unsure of what to do. "I call that a win."

That was when Ultragod crowned himself God.

Capital G.

Chapter Four
Ultimate Power vs. Ultimate Freedom

There's a thriving subgenre of fiction on my world called "Super Tyrant Fiction." Written mostly by anti-Super bigots or people with a strong sense of distrust toward superheroes, it was a literary market based around the idea of superheroes taking over the world. Ultragod—or some version of him with the serial numbers filed off—would get sick of the existing governments and then use his powers to take over. He'd proceed to run the world into the ground or otherwise behave as a monster with the idea that "absolute power corrupts absolutely."

While attending college, I'd had to listen to my fair share of professors suggesting that superheroes were an inherently fascist concept. I'd always thought this was complete horseshit. Fascism depended on a collectivist surrender to a leader figure, worship of authority, as well as hatred of minorities that superhero fiction almost universally rejected.

Superheroes were sometimes allies of existing authorities, but they were just as often opposed to them in the name of personal ideology. There was a reason that minorities tended to trust people like Moses Anders over the police or government. Superheroes might sometimes defend the status quo, but they were always pushing it to be better. They might not be as radical as some misunderstood supervillains—I mean me specifically—but they were never tools of The Man either.

The thing that few people admitted, at least publicly, wasn't that Ultragod or the other heroes would never be willing to seize power. That they couldn't if they combined their powers and promptly tore the world's militaries a new one. No, it was a much more insidious but wildly held view: that most of us thought a world run by superheroes would be better than the one we currently had. Democracy was all fine and dandy but there was a primal savage part of us that believed a benevolent dictator would do things better. There was just one problem with that: there's no such thing.

Power didn't corrupt, it attracted the corrupt, if you believed the Bene Gesserit. However, you couldn't enforce your will on everyone and not have that be an inherently violent act. You couldn't take away a man or woman's freedom for their own good. Even if it would be to give them a paradise that they would love. Humanity would rather die than live that way. That was basic *Star Trek*. It was the plot of "The Cage", the original pilot before the executives forced Gene Roddenberry to make a new one.

"Gary, what the hell are you thinking about?" Ultragod asked, staring at me as the crown glowed with tremendous energy. I assumed he could read my mind now since telepathy wasn't one of Ultragod's powers but was likely an ability the crown bestowed. After all, what was the point of omnipotence without omniscience to go with it?

"Sorry, I was trying to think of a speech that would convince you to give up your magic crown," I replied. "Obviously, my mind went to *Star Trek* but strangely I wasn't thinking of Picard. Kirk did speeches too, but they weren't as good."

Ultragod stared at me.

"You probably aren't familiar with those shows yet," I replied.

"Gary, we can jump him," Cindy said.

I stared at her. "No, we're not doing that thing where all the heroes gang up on the villain or misguided hero only to be beaten up. That's just a thing to fill page time in comic books and is always contrived."

Mandy covered her face, backing away from the holy power of all the gods that was now concentrated on Ultragod's head.

"He hasn't reached his full potential. Once that happens, there will be no stopping him."

"I know, like Gary Mitchell in 'Where No Man Has Gone Before'," I said. "Kirk had to kill him with a rock due to his becoming a god."

"This is not *Star Trek!*" Mandy snapped.

"I write science fiction," Ultragod said, surprising me. "For the pulp magazines. My night job is an astronomer, so my days are open. Obviously, I don't get invited for the writers' photos. Neither does my girlfriend. I can fix all that, though."

Yeah, I was uncomfortable with the fact I was going to have to argue that Ultragod shouldn't fix racism. I was a supervillain precisely because with great power comes great irresponsibility. Ultragod wanted to use it to make the world a better place and that wasn't something that I liked being on the other side of. This was the Forties after all, and the Forties sucked for the vast majority of people. Ultragod could change all that. Be a one-man Marshall Plan. Yes, omnipotence was different from the power he wielded before, but was it really?

"I can hear your thoughts, Gary," Ultragod said, approaching me. "My consciousness is expanding, and I am learning how to use these powers. Just like your wife and mistress said, though I'm not sure which is which by the way you feel about them. How they feel about each other. That's another thing that I can fix in this time. Humanity can love each other unconditionally. I've already eliminated all the Nazis outside. No one else has to die."

"You can probably bring back the dead too," Cindy pointed out.

"Cindy!" I snapped.

"What?" Cindy asked.

"Resurrection of non-superheroes never works out!" I said. "Do you want a *Pet Sematary* thing happening?"

365

"Can we use references he understands?" Cindy asked. "I mean, there's *The Wizard of Oz, Gone with the Wind*—"

"Let's not use that one," Ultragod said.

"Ooo, yeah, right," Cindy said, embarrassed. "Shirley Temple. Okay, yeah, maybe this isn't the best time for pop culture references."

Ultragod pointed at me. "I can see your future in your head, Gary. It's still a terrible place despite almost a century of difference. You're still struggling to make the world a better place. There're new evils, too, like environmental collapse and wars between Supers that don't even bother serving nation states. We can fix all that. Now. We can protect the Earth. I don't have to lose any more friends to crooked cops, a bum system, and wars like this one. There will be no Cold War, Vietnam, or War on Terror. No world hunger or global warming. No PHANTOM or Fraternity of Supervillains. Can you really say it won't be better?"

I stared at him. "Nope, you've got me."

"Gary!" Mandy snapped.

"I mean, he's right," I said, looking between them. "I know plenty of world leaders in my time who, if they got this power, would blast away half the planet or mind-control the other half into obeying them. Lord knows we're running it into the ground, and this is an actual chance to stop everything. I would make Ultragod President of the United States if I could."

Ultragod nodded. "Thank you. I'm glad you didn't try to do anything stupid."

"Oh, I am," I pointed out. "It's just not going to be arguing that it isn't going to be better."

"Then what?" Ultragod asked, looking like he was about to will me out of existence.

"I'll just point out that if you have to mind control or threaten humanity into having paradise then is it really worth anything?" I asked. "How would you react to someone like you assuming this crown? Are you a god, really, or are you a man?"

Ultragod stared at me. "I took that title because I wanted to scare people into not attacking me. When I stopped my first bank robbery, they thought I was one of the thieves. It worked. People looked at me, heard I was a god, and stopped trying to hurt me. I never wanted to be a god, though. Just a man."

Ultragod removed the Crown of the Gods then crushed it between his hands, turning it into dust.

"Holy shit, I can't believe that worked," Gary said.

"Because it was dumb!" Cindy said. "Uh, no offense, Ultragod."

"Moses," Moses replied, dusting off his hands. "I saw how you viewed me in your mind, Gary. If you can look at me as a hero, then maybe I should live up to the standards that you expect from me."

Mandy hissed and lowered her gaze. "I'm just glad we were able to fulfill the mission that we were given."

"Assuming we have," I replied.

"What?" Cindy asked. "We convinced Ultragod not to become an all-powerful deity and make a paradise! Something that stupid has to be enough to satisfy our daughters from the future!"

"Be that as it may, my Merciless-sense is tingling," I said. "Albeit, that might be a concussion from where Moses punched me."

"Sorry," Moses said, looking sheepish. "Have you considered not dressing like a villain?"

"No," I said, frowning. "Black is the new black."

That was when I felt a chilling energy start to fill the chamber and swirled inside the pentagram. Turning around, I saw the ashes turn into a miniature tornado before a pair of glowing red eyes filled them. That was when a demonic voice filled the chamber, shouting, "FOOLS! You have given up unlimited power! The magic released is something that I shall feast upon, though, and—"

I proceeded to conjure a scythe and sliced the spinning tornado in half, causing it to dissipate. The spirit animating it let out an ear-piercing scream before the sounds of distant thunder and explosions of hellfire volcanos were heard. The demonic presence inside the room was gone.

"Well, that was easy," I said.

"Was that Hitler?" Cindy asked.

"I think so," I said. "At least it was his ghost, probably reanimated by all the black magic around here."

"It was a bit of an anticlimax," Mandy said. "I was expecting more."

I shrugged. "I'm the Chosen of Death, Mandy. It's like Fire Man attempting to fight Water Man. The latter has a distinct advantage over the former."

"There's a Fire Man and Water Man in the future?" Moses asked.

"No, that's just a metaphor," I replied. "I don't think you would get a reference to Pokemon."

"Probably not," Moses said, shaking his head. "If you'll excuse me, I need to go rejoin the troops. They need to know that we've won."

"I'm sure they figured that out by all the Nazis dying," I replied, pointing a pair of finger guns. "You're going to be the biggest hero in America when you get back. Savor that."

Moses looked at me sideways. "Were you kidding when you suggested I should run for President?"

"Not in the slightest," I said. "Go for it."

Moses chuckled. "Yeah, a Black President. That will be the day."

He then walked off, jumping through the hole in the ceiling in the next room and vanishing from our lives. The three of us stood there for a moment, soaking in the atmosphere of this hard-won triumph. Moses would have a long road ahead of him, but if we'd done our parts right then we'd just set this timeline back on the right path.

Not only would this timeline not evolve into a Nazi hellhole that eventually invaded other realities, but it would become something more akin to my timeline. Ultragod would team up with Guinevere and the Nightwalker to form the Society of Superheroes, independent of the world's governments, and try to inspire humanity to do better. There would be countless fights against supervillains, terrorist organizations, tyrannies, and alien invasions. It would all ultimately end in a triumph of the good guys, though. People would get better because there were heroes to remind them that being good was possible. I mean, I wasn't one of them, but I wasn't not one of them, if you get me. No? Okay then.

"Hey, Gary," Cindy said, not bothering to turn to me.

"Yeah?" I asked.

"Do you have any idea how we're going to get home?" Cindy asked an obvious question.

"Actually no," I said, pausing. "I think I accidentally blew up General Omega's time machine when I was fighting alongside Ultragod. At least, that's what it looked like in the seconds before his laboratory went boom."

Cindy sighed. "Well, that's just great."

"Eh, don't worry," I said, putting my arm around her shoulders. "There's plenty of ways to get back to the future if our daughters don't come and pick us up. We can cryogenically freeze ourselves, contact a god to take us through a time portal, get a spaceship to do a slingshot around the sun, or visit

Fairyland. One year there is a hundred years outside so we can just take a six-month vacay."

"I'm not hanging around with hobbits," Cindy said.

"Me either," Mandy said, walking forward into Hitler's bunker. "I mean, they're just not a meal."

That was when we both heard dogs barking.

"Ooo, doggies!" Cindy cried out. "We can rescue Hitler's doggies and reeducate them to be good puppies!"

I laughed and followed her. "Sure, why not."

Epilogue
Time Is on My Side (Yes, It Is)

Ultragoddess stared at me from across the table, slurping the last of her drink through her straw. The two of us were sitting in Super Pizza, at the exact same table from earlier no less, waiting for our meal.

"Bullshit," Gabrielle said. "That did not happen."

I lifted my hands up in surrender. "It absolutely happened and that is why I am late for our shared custody day. You have no idea the difficulties inherent to getting the legally distinct guy who resembles a certain British Time Lord to send me not just through time but realities. I mean the guy acted like I was some sort of criminal."

"I think my father would have mentioned you killing Hitler with him," Gabrielle said.

"Alternate timeline," I defended myself. "Besides, I bet he came up with some sort of ridiculous story to look better rather than give me credit. Oh, Lord Dumbass committed suicide rather than face defeat. Pfft."

Gabrielle rolled her eyes. "Whatever Gary."

"I'm owed at least a slice of Freedom Pizza for this," I said. "I'm a veteran after all."

Gabrielle's mouth fell open in shock. "You own the restaurant chain!"

In the corner of the restaurant were my two adult daughters. They were sniggering about some private joke.

I personally didn't see what was so funny.

Bonus Content: Supervillain Playlists

By C. T. Phipps

As a bonus for my adoring readers, I've decided to add a playlist set for my heroes and antiheroes! Basically, music is one of the ways we define ourselves and I thought it would provide some insight into how they view the world. Also, it would be nice to share some great tunes as well! Feel free to leave a comment in your review about what you think would be a song a character would listen to.

Gary's Supervillainous Playlist

Gary's favorite songs are a collection of Eighties pop rock, novelty songs, and a few Death-themed musical numbers that reminds people he's actually quite a bit dangerous. Perhaps the most meaningful of the songs to him is No. #7 as it is his and Mandy's song. No. #10 is also the closest to defining him as a hero. He's really not as stupid as he appears to be.

1. "Holding Out for a Hero" by Bonnie Tyler
2. "Everybody Wants to Rule the World" by Tears for Fears
3. "I Want It All" by Queen
4. "When You're Evil" by Voltaire

5. "Super Villain" by Powerman 5000
6. "Villain Song" by Kirby Krackle
7. "I'd Do Anything for Love (But I Won't Do That)" by Meatloaf
8. "I Fought the Law (and the Law Won)" by The Clash
9. "Dare to Be Stupid" by "Weird Al" Yankovic
10. "Nobody's Fool" by Kenny Loggins
11. "(Don't Fear) The Reaper" by Blue Oyster Cult
12. "No One Lives Forever" by Oingo Boingo

Cindy's Supervillainous Playlist

Cindy shares some of Gary's taste for Eighties pop rock but is a bit more modern, with a fondness for artists from the Nineties and today. There's a lot of self-awareness that she's a terrible person but she owns that.

1. "Hungry Like the Wolf" by Duran Duran
2. "Werewolves of London" by Warren Zevon
3. "Material Girl" by Madonna
4. "Bitch" by Meredith Brooks
5. "Blow Me (One Last Kiss)" by Pink
6. "Bad Reputation" by Joan Jett & The Blackhearts
7. "Sweet but Psycho" by Ava Max
8. "Toxic" by Britney Spears
9. "Crazy on You" by Heart
10. "Love Is a Battlefield" by Pat Benatar

Mandy's Supervillainous Playlist

Mandy is a fan of Goth rock, hard rock, metal, and symphonic metal. In a better world, she would have been able to make a career in it herself, but life got in the way. The one exception is No. #1 that represents Gary's influence on her. Also, No. #10 is how she views her relationship with the Karkofsky household.

1. "The Warrior" by Patty Smyth
2. "Bela Lugosi's Dead" by Bauhaus
3. "Daughters of Darkness" by Halestorm
4. "Lucretia My Reflection" by The Sisters of Mercy
5. "The Phantom of the Opera" by Nightwish
6. "Swamped" by Lacuna Coil
7. "If You Want Blood (You've Got It)" by AC/DC
8. "Poison" by Alice Cooper
9. "Pet Semetary" by the Ramones
10. "Dance Macabre" by Ghost

Gabrielle Anders AKA Ultragoddess' Playlist

Gabrielle has an eclectic taste of Spanish and Caribbean music mixed with singers that look like her. She prefers uplifting, powerful, and enjoyable music. No. #1 makes her feel like her invulnerability is at immense cost, though. No. #9 lives rent free in her head due to the questions she has whether she's really making a difference.

1. "Titanium" by David Guetta
2. "Conga" by Gloria Estefan and Miami Sound Machine
3. "La Rubia" by Charity Daw
4. "What's Love Got to Do with It?" by Tina Turner
5. "Just a Girl" by No Doubt
6. "Stronger" by Britney Spears
7. "Girl on Fire" by Alicia Keys
8. "Criminal" by Britney Spears
9. "We Don't Need Another Hero" by Tina Turner
10. "Invincible" by Pat Benatar

C. T. Phipps

Diabloman's Playlist

I was wondering whether or not Diabloman would be listening to primarily Spanish language music, but it occurred to me that he would probably be an Eighties hard rock and metal fan. There's a distinctly infernal theme to his music but that's to be expected. No. #1 is also what I consider to be the theme song for Falconcrest City.

1. "Short Change Hero" by The Heavy
2. "Ain't No Rest for the Wicked" by Cage the Elephant
3. "Sympathy for the Devil" by The Rolling Stones
4. "Highway to Hell" by AC/DC
5. "Runnin' with the Devil" by Van Halen
6. "Shout at the Devil" by Mötley Crüe
7. "The Number of the Beast" by Iron Maiden
8. "Devil's Child" by Judas Priest
9. "Crazy Train" by Ozzy Osbourne
10. "Devil's Dance" by Metallica

Author's Note

I'd like to thank you for reading this book. The publishing industry is changing dramatically since the advent of eBooks. It is now very difficult to get any book noticed, regardless of quality. If you enjoyed this book, you could do some very simple things to help me attract attention. Word of mouth is the number one source of success for novels, so simply telling family and friends about the book is a great start.

Here are a few other ways of helping out, if you are so inclined:

* Post a rating or review where you purchased the eBook
* Post a rating or review on Goodreads
* Talk about the book or write a review on Facebook
* Tell folks about the book in a blog post

Readers interested in Jacob Riverson AKA Wraith Knight and Ketra AKA Dragon Girl should check out the *Wraith Knight* series. While not as wacky as Gary's adventures, they show what life is like on the Three Worlds and how a formerly good man deals with waking up as a ~~Ringwraith~~. Err, Wraith Knight.

About the Author

C. T. Phipps is a lifelong student of horror, science fiction, and fantasy. An avid tabletop gamer, he discovered this passion led him to write and turned him into a lifelong geek. He is a regular blogger and also a reviewer for The Bookie Monster.

Bibliography

<u>Novels</u>
The Rules of Supervillainy (Supervillainy Saga #1)
The Games of Supervillainy (Supervillainy Saga #2)
The Secrets of Supervillainy (Supervillainy Saga #3)
The Kingdom of Supervillainy (Supervillainy Saga #4)
The Tournament of Supervillainy (Supervillainy Saga #5)
The Future of Supervillainy (Supervillainy Saga #6)
The Horror of Supervillainy (Supervillainy Saga #7)

Tales of Supervillainy: Cindy's Seven (Supervillainy Saga #8)
The Fall of Supervillainy (Supervillainy Saga #9)

I Was a Teenage Weredeer (The Bright Falls Mysteries, Book 1)
An American Weredeer in Michigan (The Bright Falls Mysteries, Book 2)
A Nightmare on Elk Street (The Bright Falls Mysteries, Book 3)

Esoterrorism (Red Room, Vol. 1)
Eldritch Ops (Red Room, Vol. 2)
The Fall of the House (Red Room, Vol. 3)

Agent G: Infiltrator (Agent G, Vol. 1)
Agent G: Saboteur (Agent G, Vol. 2)
Agent G: Assassin (Agent G, Vol. 3)

Cthulhu Armageddon (Cthulhu Armageddon, Vol. 1)
The Tower of Zhaal (Cthulhu Armageddon, Vol. 2)

Lucifer's Star (Lucifer's Star, Vol. 1)
Lucifer's Nebula (Lucifer's Star, Vol. 2)

Straight Outta Fangton (Straight Outta Fangton, Vol. 1)
100 Miles and Vampin' (Straight Outta Fangton, Vol. 2)
Vampiraz4Life (Straight Outta Fangton, Vol. 3)

Wraith Knight (Wraith Knight, Vol. 1)
Wraith Lord (Wraith Knight, Vol. 2)
Wraith King (Wraith Knight, Vol. 3)

Predestiny (Predestiny, Vol. 1)
Lost Future (Predestiny, Vol. 2)

Brightblade (The Morgan Detective Agency, Book 1)

Space Academy Dropouts (The Space Academy Series, Book 1)
Space Academy Rejects (The Space Academy Series, Book 2)
Space Academy Washouts (The Space Academy Series, Book 3)

Psycho Killers in Love

Anthologies (as editor)
Blackest Knights
Blackest Spells
Tales of Capes and Cowls
Tales of the Al-Azif
Tales of Yog-Sothoth

Curious about other Crossroad Press books? Stop by our website: http://crossroadpress.com
We offer quality writing
in digital, audio, and print formats.

Subscribe to our newsletter on the website homepage and receive a free eBook.